The Hidden Chamber

Book II of the Skyroar Trilogy

Balthazar Dusk

The Hidden Chamber: Book II of the Skyroar Trilogy

FROGASUS PRESS

Copyright © 2024 Balthazar Dusk

All rights reserved.

ISBN: 979-8-9888256-3-0

DEDICATION

To my brothers in the Valley.

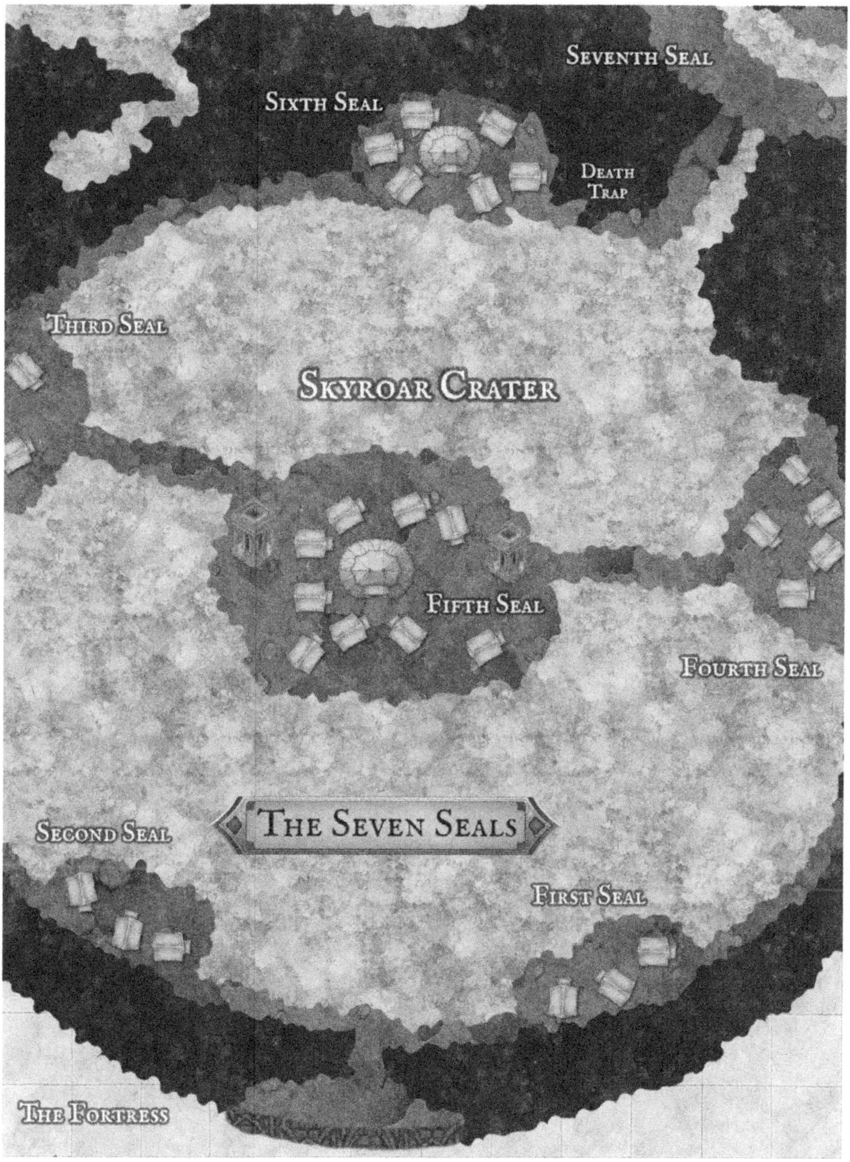
Seventh Seal
Sixth Seal
Death
Trap
Third Seal
Skyroar Crater
Fifth Seal
Fourth Seal
The Seven Seals
Second Seal
First Seal
The Fortress

CHAPTER ONE

This is it, he thought. *If I go through this door, I'll never see Kaina again, or the twin suns... or Tabatha. My life will end here. In the heart of the Skyroar volcano. Defending the Prophecy and guarding the Passage to Hell. If this is Skyroar's highest honor, it sure doesn't feel like it.*

Not even Shiroan could turn away from the highest distinction in Skyroar, even if it felt like a burden. Especially given the risk that the Great Preceptor had taken by choosing him over Gildar. Everyone knew that Gildar had been groomed almost from birth to becoming the next Seven Warrior. Many, perhaps most, Conclave members couldn't have agreed with her decision.

Only a true survivor, like she is, would have had the courage to do what he did, he thought.

Even Tabatha, when given the choice, supported his nomination. The recklessness he showed when Ponthos died had damaged beyond repair his relationship with her, however. She may have forgiven him, but he certainly hasn't forgiven himself.

"Move it! I have places to be, you know," a raucous voice said from inside the Seventh Seal. "Scratch that, there's nowhere to go in here. I'm just impatient. Are you coming in or not?"

"Why should I enter a life prison sentence voluntarily? Moreover, why must I listen to you?" Shiroan said. He was in a bad mood and receiving orders from a stranger didn't help.

"You don't have to. If you want to go back to your old life, be my guest. This life is not for everyone and, to be honest, you don't look like you could handle it."

"Oh, I can handle this in my sleep, my friend. Whatever terrors await inside the Seventh Seal, they're nothing compared to what I've been through. After all, we in the Sixth Seal are the ones providing the Seven Warriors the safety they need so they can sit down and relax while we keep Skyroar safe," Shiroan said with anger in his voice. Or, more than anger, impotence. It was the frustration of the many opportunities he had lost forever talking, not him.

"Talking is easy. Courage is not something you tell, is something you show. But well, if you change your mind and decide to join the true protectors of Skyroar, give me a shout."

"True protectors? Come on, tell it to my face," Shiroan said stepping in. The cave door shut behind him. He was inside.

"Look how blue you are. Are you sick or something?" the massive Elgarian hybrid shouted from across the precipice.

A narrow stone bridge joined the ledge where he stood and the plateau where the colossus was smiling.

"I'm a Cloudhunter and I'd appreciate some respect!"

"I've never seen one like you before, I'll call you Blue."

"I'm the last one of my kind. My name is Shiroan."

"I'm Kishi, one of the Seven Warriors. We've been expecting you," he said waving the scroll with the Great Preceptor's stamp on it.

"I'm sure you have," Shiroan said crossing the bridge.

"Welcome to the party, Blue!" Kishi exclaimed hugging him.

"Let go of me!" Shiroan said pushing back. He was around the same height than Kishi, but not nearly as robust, so he was the one that was propelled back. The sudden bounce made him trip and almost fall to the sea of lava.

"Be careful, my friend. I hear is pretty hot down there."

"I'm not your friend," he said with the rougher tone he could produce.

"Oh, you will be, Blue. You have no choice. Now follow me," said Kishi without losing his smile.

Shiroan followed in silence. They walked in a circular plateau. A series of narrow bridges along its circumference joined it to the volcano sides. The large vault, as tall as the Wall, was inundated with the orange glow of the sea of magma running beneath. It felt hot and dry, even to him, coming from the intense temperatures of the Sixth Seal. Streams of perspiration traveled down his neck and back.

He stopped in awe when his eyes found what could only be the Hidden Chamber.

A sphere made of rock and roughly the size of a Village hut, was floating in the middle of the hollow center of the plateau. It shone green with an ethereal light. A multitude of runes and characters were sculpted on its surface. Most of them were Vespertian although, to his great surprise, some were Cloudhunter in origin. The symbols danced up and down, and back and forth, to the rhythm of an inaudible melody. Shiroan continued approaching it, bewitched by the irresistible spectacle. The biggest surprise came once he approached the edge.

It's just suspended in the air. No ropes, beams, or columns keeping it in place, he thought while taking determined steps to the abyss where the sphere was. *How something so beautiful can be the root of all evil?*

"It's not your fault. I hear you. I understand you. I'll keep you safe," he said as his left foot took a step into the void.

"Wake up!" Kishi shouted taking Shiroan by the shoulder. "You're just arriving, Blue, let's try to keep you alive a little bit longer."

"That's the Hidden Chamber, isn't it? It was calling me," he said as he forced his eyes away from the sphere.

"I don't think so. I've never heard it calling anyone," said Kishi.

"Maybe it was my imagination," Shiroan said attempting to drop the subject. He was not interested in having a conversation.

"Perhaps, perhaps not. Time will tell. For now, come with me, I'll show you around!" he said, grabbing his shoulder with his massive hand.

"Easy, mate, I don't like to be touched," he said jerking his shoulder back.

"Yes, you made that clear. You sure are a fountain of joy, Blue," he said taking his hand back. "Don't worry, here we'll cheer you up."

"You're certainly welcome to try."

"Jesting aside, your people put up one Hell of a fight against the demons, from what I've heard. It's an honor to have you around," Kishi added using a serious tone for the first time. "Let's go now, Blue. There're some other people you need to meet."

"Where are they?" Shiroan asked looking left and right without seeing anybody.

"They're around, of course!" Kishi said laughing at his own joke. "Follow me."

The circular basalt plateau surrounding the Hidden Chamber was tall as a mountain pine at its widest. The hollow center made it look like a crater within a crater.

"You'll outgrow the sweating, eventually," Kishi said as

Shiroan dried streams of sweat from with his shirt. "I used to perspire like a pig. I mean, at the beginning, I had to walk naked most of the time. One cycle, it just stopped. I can tell you; the other six warriors were grateful when I started wearing clothes again!" Kishi said laughing.

Since they first met, he had always been either smiling or laughing. He wasn't sure what to make of his behavior, but it certainly didn't bring Shiroan any closer to trusting him.

"No nude walking for me, mate. I can tell you that."

"We'll see, Blue. Give it time," Kishi replied with a wink. He patted Shiroan's back and walked to the edge to pee. Shiroan looked away.

"What do you do for water?" he asked when Kishi finished.

"Funny you should mention that. We drink each other's pee. You should've asked me before I relieved myself!" Kishi answered.

"What?" Shiroan said as he made a grimace.

"I'm jesting, Blue!" Kishi said with his loudest burst of laughter yet. "You should've seen your face! You sure believe anything, don't you!" he said as he walked in the direction of the nearest bridge. "Follow me."

Shiroan's doubts around Kishi grew stronger after every exchange. In his mind, a Seven Warrior must set an example of earnestness, wisdom, and courage. So far, Kishi had come across simply as an oversized jester.

"This is our water room," he said crossing one of the basalt bridges and passing through a narrow crevice on the crater. Shiroan followed.

Inside the small cave, it was pouring. Soaking wet, with droplets clouding his vision, Shiroan took one step forward and tripped, almost falling to the ground. Squinting his eyes to see through the water and the orange twilight, he noticed a myriad of objects lying on the floor: pig skulls, concave stone plates, metal glasses and all sorts of improvised containers. He crouched and lifted a very old Vespertian wooden helmet, filled to the rim with water. He drank until it was empty.

"The subterranean river that feeds Skyroar is above us. The porous ceiling of this cave filters the water down," Kishi said pointing up. "We can only drink a little bit at a time, though. When it mixes with the volcano minerals, it becomes poisonous. You'll be dead soon, but don't worry it'll be painless. We don't really like new faces."

"What the Hell!" Shiroan shouted, spitting the liquid he still had in his mouth and quickly drawing his sword.

"Calm down, calm down!" Kishi said laughing. "I'm jesting! You're so easy, Blue."

"What's wrong with you? I can't believe this! Are these the warriors responsible of protecting the Prophecy and guarding the Hidden Chamber?" Shiroan yelled. His face had turned dark blue, and his hands were shaking.

"Oh, c'mon! Have a sense of humor," Kishi said between giggles.

"Go to Hell!" Shiroan exclaimed, storming out of the cave, and crashing into another Seven Warrior, a Solis.

"Watch out, mate!" she said pushing him aside hard enough to almost make him fall down the precipice.

"Great, now I'm pushed to the lava!"

"Is this the scroll holder?" she said to Kishi, ignoring Shiroan's complaint.

"He's indeed. A fragile one, or so it seems."

"Fragile! You –"

"Calm down, Blue, you'll have to adapt to how things are here. Stop being so serious," Kishi said interrupting him. "You are part of our family now. We don't have anyone but ourselves."

"I had a family once. They are dead," Shiroan said.

"You're a dark one, aren't you? Our job is bleak enough without us adding to it, you better learn it fast. Gregoria, this is Blue. Blue, this is Gregoria. You don't want to mess with her, she doesn't have any of my natural charm."

"Or your patience, so listen to Kishi and we'll get along just fine," Gregoria said going into the cave and drinking from a quartz bottle she carried in her belt. Shiroan looked at the athletic Solis woman walking down the path. Her dark brown skin contrasted with her white, sleeveless sheepskin shirt and pants. She held a long spear with twin blades in her left hand and a shield was attached to her back. A pigskin strip kept the long curls of her black hair off her face.

"My name is Shiroan!" he exclaimed, but Gregoria didn't seem to hear him.

"Let's go. There're still more of us to win over with your

incredible people skills," Kishi said with a playful tone.

"I'm looking forward to meeting them," Shiroan said with a sigh.

They walked around the plateau until they reached the next bridge. At the end of the pass, they found eight steps leading to the round entrance of a cave. A soothing chant surrounded him the moment he stepped in, the words were foreign, but the rhythm was spellbinding.

"This is Lethos," Kishi said.

"Where is he?" Shiroan asked looking at the seemingly empty room but hearing words coming from somewhere in the cave. Kishi pointed his finger to a small ledge close to the ceiling. An elderly Vespertian was sitting with his back straight and his legs crossed. His leathery wings —grey with ashes and dust— covered most of his body, except for the top of his head. A green glow surrounded him. "What's he doing?" Shiroan asked in a low voice, afraid of disturbing him.

"No need to whisper!" Kishi exclaimed laughing. "Lethos is in trance, nothing can bring him back unless he chooses to."

"Trance?" Shiroan said surprised.

"Or meditating, if you want to use fancy words."

"Yantil tar pariliius, Lartico dirium faris morter… Yantil tar pariliius, Lartico dirium faris morter –" Lethos kept singing the same words from his place of rest, high in the cave.

"What's the meaning of his chant?" Shiroan asked.

"Nobody knows. It's a very old Vespertian dialect. We can't understand it. What we know is that his incantation is linked to the Magia scaling the Hidden Chamber and keeping it floating in the air. Without him, it'd have fallen in the lava a long time ago."

"And why would that be a bad thing?" Shiroan asked.

"They really don't teach well in the outside, Blue. If the Hidden Chamber is destroyed in the lava, the Gateway to Hell would open and new hordes of demonphantoms will enter the Known Territories. In other words, we'd be doomed. We don't have many ways to kill demonphantoms, blue, so we need to keep the Passage to Hell closed until we are ready to send the demonphantoms back. Then we'll destroy it forever. That's what the Prophecy is all about, and that's why keeping the Hidden Chamber safe is so important, because Hell is inside it, waiting for a mistake."

"Do you mean there are at least some ways to kill a demonphantom?" Shiroan said as he followed Kishi out of the cave and back to the path.

"You should ask Gregoria about it," Kishi said with a smile. "For somebody so full of pride, you know very little about what really matters."

Shiroan was about to erupt with anger when they stumbled upon the three remainder warriors sitting on a pile of dirty sheepskin while eating wormbread.

"Parktikos! Botharhi! Rexora!" Kishi exclaimed. "Wake up! We've gotten ourselves a new Seven Warrior!"

The trio looked at him and, without hurry, stood up to greet him. "He's blue," Parktikos said.

"Your eyes work. What a relief," Shiroan said with a grin.

"Blue, is that so?" Rexora said. "Interesting."

"You probably can see it yourself if you take your headpiece off your eyes," Shiroan said with an attitude that worsened by the moment.

"Trust me. It wouldn't make a difference," Botharhi replied.

"An Oceaner as a Seven Warrior? That's just ridiculous!" Shiroan said looking down at Botharhi, who standing up barely reached Shiroan's chest.

"It is, isn't it," Botharhi said with a wide smile. "And I don't even have a seahawk to help me out. Life is full of surprises."

"I'm sorry," Shiroan said. "I'm just… I shouldn't be here. I'm exhausted, angry, and frustrated. I'm not a Seven Warrior. I don't belong here."

Botharhi's friendly response was what he needed to help him realize how unfair he had been. Nobody but himself was to blame for his situation. He accepted this role, and he pushed away Tabatha, more than a few times.

"Let me feel your face," Rexora said taking a couple of steps towards him. "Ah! A Cloudhunter, how peculiar," she said as she let her fingers discover his features. "Shiroan, we are all exhausted, angry, and frustrated, believe me. It's impossible to feel any other way here. We just learned how to hide it, and how to use that energy to fulfill our mission. You'll learn it as well, give it time."

"Thank you. You can't see, can you?" Shiroan said as he felt the callous fingertips investigating his straight nose, narrow eyes, small round ears, and bald skull.

"Not like you can, no," Rexora answered.

"The Conclave and the Great Preceptor must know secrets that are hidden from me. I apologize, Rexora, I never thought that one of the Seven Warriors would be blind," Shiroan said with a calmer tone.

"This one is really raw, Kishi," Parktikos said. "Let's wait and see what he thinks of us after his first raid, if he survives it, of course."

"If you have survived until now, I will as well, I assure you," Shiroan said as he walked away. He needed some time alone before he did something foolish.

"Welcome to the Seventh Seal!" Botharhi said at Shiroan as he went away. "And remember, if you are here, is because you deserve it!"

Walking without a specific destination in mind, Shiroan crossed one of the bridges that joined the plateau with the side of the mountain. This one led to a cavern he hadn't seen before. He went in. Three hallways, equidistant from each other, stood in front of him. Shiroan chose the one on his left and, after a short while, he entered a tall dome-like vault.

The walls and the ceiling had been polished to the point that they were as smooth as the marble of the Fortress. Rectangular altars were built against the wall, all around the circular chamber. Roughly half of them were empty and surrounded by twilight, the other half was illuminated by several torches. A collection of objects was placed on top of each one.

Walking left from the closest lit altar Shiroan absorbed every detail. All sorts of weapons, fragments of armor, clothes, and helmets rested on the altars dressed in mooseskin. A Hellblood vial — necklace and name tag included— hung from the wall by each one of them. The armors and weapons were Elgarian, Oceaner, Vespertian and even Icedorfer. The very last altar looked almost as empty as the ones sitting in darkness. Only a chainmail, some clothes shredded to pieces and a small dagger rested on top of the flat rock.

Shiroan lifted the dagger, the yellow bone handle was stained with blood and a canyon rammer skull was sculpted on its hilt. The trailing point blade was spotless, shining under the light of the torch above.

"You discovered the Mausoleum, I see," Kishi said entering the cavern. "These are the belongings of each fallen Seven Warrior since we were first appointed as protectors of the Hidden Chamber. This is how we honor our heroes."

"What happened to this one? Where are the armor and the Hellblood?"

"That's Ulrik, the Seven Warrior that came before you. He fell in the volcano wearing his armor. His Hellblood is lost. This is all that he left behind."

"Fell? How?"

"He jumped. Nobody knows why. Ulrik was the strongest amongst us. His mind was a fortress and his essence as strong as duranese. One cycle he leaped to the lava without saying a word."

"I don't get it," Shiroan replied looking at him. "If he was so strong, why would he do something so reckless?"

"We don't know. He attacked Gregoria out of the blue a couple of cycles before jumping. I found them battling and had to intervene. Since we can't leave the Seventh Seal, we can't talk to the Conclave about what happened here. I trust the Great Preceptor, however. She will find a way to the truth."

"How?"

"I sent a message with a deliverer."

"Mehrik," Shiroan whispered.

"What?"

"Doesn't matter, I'm exhausted, all I want now is to get to sleep," Shiroan said between yawns. He wasn't lying, but he also needed time to be alone and think.

"Follow me, the barracks are not far from here," Kishi said leaving the room.

Shiroan followed him in silence to a nearby cave with seven low-ceiling holes at ground level.

"That one there, the empty one, is your new home," Kishi said.

"Perfect," Shiroan said dropping his rucksack inside the hole. "Now, if you don't mind, I'd like to rest," he added crawling inside.

"Sure thing, regain your energies. You'll need them. Nice to meet you, Blue."

Shiroan heard the words but was too tired to answer. Closing his eyes, he allowed himself to be carried to a much better place, one of peace and tranquility where the City in the Sky still existed and he was a child again.

CHAPTER TWO

Mehrik had been raised to be loyal to Skyroar and follow the Conclave blindly, just like everyone else. He was taught that the demonic hordes wanted to reach the Hidden Chamber to forever open the Gateway to Hell. He witnessed hundreds dying at the hands of Icedorf, The Hundred Kingdoms, and Oceano's soldiers attempting to steal the secret of the Hellblood. Everyone at the other side of the Wall was the enemy. If they ever conquered Skyroar, Hishiro's Prophecy would never come to be, and Hell would be unleashed upon them.

He was part of something bigger than himself. His city was the last bastion of hope for the Known Territories. And that made him proud.

His devotion was tested when he was marked as a traitor, sent to the dungeons, and sentenced to death. Not even then his loyalty waivered.

Until he met Paumeron, an enemy of Skyroar – his enemy – that treated him not only with compassion, but also with the respect reserved only for warriors. They escaped together, fought together, and traveled to Icedorf together. Paumeron opened the doors of his home to him and accepted him as one of them. He changed him and, perhaps, if Sehrsil wouldn't have kicked him out of the City of the Thousand Lights after finding out the truth about his past, he would have stayed there forever.

But she did and, in doing so, triggered a series of events ending with him saving her life and discovering Mortagong was a traitor. A traitor working in conjunction with Belgoriel, their greatest enemy.

Mehrik did the only thing he could do. He came back to Skyroar to warn Galanta, the Great Preceptor, about what he had witnessed. She would have the power to take Mortagong down and dismantle whatever plans he was devising.

But he was too late.

Mortagong had taken over as Great Preceptor and Momo, the only person he could trust, was unreachable.

And Galanta was most likely in the dungeons, or worse.

"I should leave, Lork, go back to Icedorf and let the Conclave deal with this," Mehrik telepathized. "I'm completely overwhelmed. This is much bigger than me."

Galanta friend, Mehrik helps, Lork telepathized from the sky.

"Somebody else will have to help her. There isn't anything I can do about it."

Mortagong bad. Galanta in danger.

"And what do you want me to do? Go fight the Conclave and the Skyroar army? How could I ever win?"

Mehrik can help. Mehrik more strong. Mehrik more brave. Mehrik has good blood.

"What do you mean with that, Lork? You're making no sense. The reality is that I'll be killed on the spot, and how does that help anyone?"

Mehrik good blood, Lork repeated as he perched in Mehrik's shoulder, grabbed the starfish amulet with his beak and showed it to him. *Good blood. Hero blood. Mehrik mother proud.*

"Are you saying that this would make my mother proud? You are probably right, but even then, I am sure that my mother would have preferred me alive. Don't you think?"

Lork trust Mehrik. Galanta in dungeon. Mehrik goes. Lork helps. Mehrik and Lork enough. Galanta in trouble. Mehrik trust Lork?

"Lork, I trust you. You are my best friend. You might be right. Galanta is probably in trouble, and I might be the only person in Skyroar that knows that Mortagong did a deal with Belgoriel. If we could free her, she could stop him. I know she could."

We go?

"Yes, my friend. We'll go, but I need your help. You need to show me the way you used to find me, the one that leads to the waterfall. This is the right thing to do but we can help more if we don't die. If our lives are in danger, you and I will get back and come up with a different plan. Deal?"

Deal! Lork messaged letting out a squeak of satisfaction.

"Let's go then. We still have a long road to go before reaching the dungeons."

CHAPTER THREE

Mehrik reached the vicinity of the small cave entrance after a few periods. He considered waiting until sunsdown to enter. He barely felt his legs. His throat was as dry as ashes, and his stomach had forgotten the sensation of having something inside. He decided against it. Blorg was gone, but someone as cruel as him might have taken his place. Galanta's life was in danger while she stayed in the dungeon. Chills ran down his spine thinking how close he had been to dying there.

"Lork, take a look at those turrets and let me know when the archers are distracted."

Lork didn't have to fly too close to the Fortress to complete his task, his powerful seahawk eyes were able to check on each one of them almost immediately.

Mehrik wait, the seahawk communicated as he flew in circles. *Mehrik wait. Now! Mehrik run.*

Mehrik didn't hesitate. He crossed the distance separating him from the entrance and jumped inside, sliding down a polished ramp of basalt rocks ending in a shallow underground stream. He fell inside it with a splash.

Mehrik well? Lork messaged.

"I'm well," he said as the bird perched in his shoulder. "This will hurt later, but nothing is broken. On the bright side, I'll be thirsty no more."

A soft squawk showed Lork's agreement.

They were in a narrow corridor, barely high enough for Mehrik to walk upright at some points. *How did Paumeron carry me through this? He's much taller than me, I don't understand. Why didn't he just leave me here?* He thought. He had admired the tough, yet gentle Icedorfer since he first met him but realizing the true extent of Paumeron heroism awoke in him an extraordinary sense of awe.

Paumeron loyal. Paumeron friend, Lork communicated, catching Mehrik off-guard. The mental link they shared had always been strong, but it felt stronger, livelier, after they reunited in that very same cave and he was able to see through the seahawk's eyes, or at least dreamt that he was doing it. His memories of that cycle were covered by a thin layer of fog.

The corridor expanded as the stream widened, fed by six brooks flowing into it. Mehrik looked at the imposing river and wondered about the reasons behind rationing the precious liquid for the Village. It looked like there was enough for everyone.

The sound of the waterfall started as a shy buzzing in the distance and soon became a deafening roar. The mist generated by the water breaking at the bottom of the fall filled the passage, dampening his clothes and giving the surroundings a ghostly feel. He had entered an aquatic world.

"I can't believe our luck!" Mehrik said. "The rope we used to escape is still here! I assumed Goldenmane would have removed it. Go check if it's safe to climb down," Lork flew into the cave and then down to the tunnel that led to the prison.

Safe. Go, he messaged back.

Mehrik inspected the cogs anchored to the rocks, then grabbed the rope with both hands and pulled as hard as he could. *It should hold*, he thought as he stepped on a small prominence just below the edge before jumping into the void. The water had made the rope heavy and slippery. Mold had grown in some sections, making the descent more complex. Minuscule splinters pierced his fingers, painting his wrists and sleeves red.

"Hell!" Mehrik exclaimed as his right foot lost its balance halfway down. The overhang of the wall kept him suspended in the void. He kicked, turned, and twisted, in a futile effort to get closer to the rock, but all he achieved was burning his hands as he slipped down the rope. He was too far from the ground to let himself go. Even if he didn't die from the fall, it wasn't a good time to break an arm or a leg.

Lork helps, said the black seahawk clawing Mehrik's sheepskin vest and pulling up. Mehrik felt the air from Lork's frantic flapping on his face. He wasn't strong or big enough to lift him, but his remarkable effort was enough for Mehrik to regain control and continue his descent. Once the overhang ended, he was able to hold onto the wall and rest for a moment before completing the last stretch.

Thank you, buddy, you saved me, Mehrik communicated when he reached the safety of the basalt ground. His hands were bleeding, and a large cut on his right biceps had stained his shirt red. He felt currents of pain traveling through his body as he pulled out the largest rope splinters from his palms. *This was the easy part. Now, let's go to the dungeons and hope that Goldenmane was relocated to the West Wall,* Mehrik messaged as he ripped a piece of his shirt to wrap around his arm.

Soaking wet from the waterfall descent, he ran down the path hoping it would be enough to warm him up. It wasn't, as his continued shivering demonstrated. He needed to raise his body temperature fast, and he knew exactly where to go.

Mehrik went down the spiral stairs. As he did, he started breathing fast and feeling a hole in his stomach. An irrational fear spread through his body biting his bones and taking control of his muscles. *Blorg really scarred me for life,* Mehrik thought as he tried to keep his anxiety in check. It wasn't only the agonizing torture he suffered at his hands, but also the fact that he had taken a life for the first time in that place. It mattered little if he was evil and Mehrik was defending himself. Even in a world at war, he didn't take any joy in what he did and pledged to himself to do whatever he could to avoid killing again.

"What an example for a warrior I am, Lork. The only one in Skyroar that doesn't want to kill."

Killing bad. Mehrik good warrior.

"Thank you, buddy, I know you truly think that. Regardless, warrior or not, I'll have to get closer to the lava to warm up just enough to continue."

Mehrik was half down the spiral staircase when the sound of voices made him stop.

"You ceased being my sister the same cycle you stopped being my empress!"

Goldenmane! And could it be... Mehrik thought as he tiptoed down the stairs.

"It was an eternity ago, Golden, you can't hold onto that grudge forever," said the other voice. As Mehrik suspected, it was Galanta.

"I can do whatever I please, this is my realm. You forfeited yours," Goldenmane retorted.

"I did it to save our people! If I didn't lead the survivors to Skyroar we would be extinct, just like the Cloudhunters," Galanta said, her tone was firm but soothing, full of empathy.

"I saw them all die. Soldiers, friends, our brothers, our parents, our people. One by one, killed in cold blood by the demonic hordes while you ran away. You should have stayed to fight with us. We may have had a chance if you did."

"You can't be serious, Golden. A handful of us, our young, our elderly, wouldn't have made any difference where the elite troops of the Sandlands failed. You were the only survivor, and not by much. What else could we have done?"

"We'll never know, won't we?" Goldenmane's words ended in a deep growl.

"My duty as the Empress of the Sandlands was to save our people. I suffer every single cycle with my choice, but it was the right choice."

Goldenmane let out a roar that resonated in the cave like a thunderstorm.

"Didn't our soldiers deserve to be saved? Wasn't I worthy of your rescue mission?"

Galanta didn't answer.

"You left us to die, sister," Goldenmane said with a breaking voice, almost whispering.

"Doing the right thing doesn't have to be easy, it only has to be right. I love you, Goldenmane, you're my brother. Leaving you behind killed me inside as your sister, but it was my duty as your empress. I don't regret it, Goldenmane. It haunts my dreams, it consumes my essence, but there was no better alternative. My suffering, our suffering, ensured the survival of the Lionkin. What will it take for you to accept it?"

"I don't want to accept it. I want every demon dead, every dragon, every single one of them. I want revenge."

"Revenge won't bring back our dead, dear brother. It'll only multiply the corpses and cause even more desolation. I want to defeat Belgoriel and the demonic hordes as much as you do, but blind rage is not the way."

"You don't know the first thing about real battle. You can't win a war without rage," Goldenmane roared.

"That might be the case, but all the rage in the Known

Territories won't be enough to succeed against the demonic hordes in a frontal attack. Not without a strategy."

"Well, it looks like you missed the opportunity to strategize, dear sister, after all, you aren't the Great Preceptor any longer."

"And that's why I need your help, Mortagong is plotting against Skyroar, I... We must stop him."

"Those sound like the words of a traitor," Goldenmane said with a touch of irony.

"Don't be ridiculous, Goldenmane, nobody hates me more than you in all the Known Territories, but you're also the one that knows me the best. You know I'm no traitor. Mortagong set me up."

"It's not only Mortagong, but also every Conclave member supporting him. Are you saying all of them are lying?"

"He manipulated the evidence and fabricated a story based on a lie. Those that followed him, that follow him, are hostages to his deceptions."

"Hostages? How dare you use that word! Didn't you kill a Conclave member with your own claws?"

"I did, after being drugged and threatened."

Mehrik couldn't believe his ears. *Galanta killed a Conclave member, how bad things have gotten while we were away, Lork?*

"Why would Mortagong drug you? You may not be a traitor, perhaps the Elgarian you killed deserved it, but that doesn't mean Mortagong is a usurper. I'm still loyal to Skyroar, and to the Great Preceptor, whoever that might be."

"She's telling the truth," Mehrik said stepping out of the shadows. "Mortagong is involved with the demonic hordes. He and Belgoriel have some sort of understanding. I saw them talking in Tenebris with my very own eyes."

"You!" Goldenmane roared. "Coming here was your last mistake!" The imposing Lionkin leaned forward, put his hands in the ground and pounced towards Mehrik, arms extended, claws ready to draw blood. Before he could react, Mehrik found himself laying down on the floor. Goldenmane's claws were piercing his shoulders.

"Golden, stop! You'll kill him!" Galanta shouted.

"Good!" He said looking at Galanta with his good eye full of rage. "He killed Blorg!"

"He didn't belong in the dungeon. It was a mistake sending him here. My mistake," Galanta said.

"He helped escape the enemies of Skyroar. Do you need more proof?"

"I had no choice, at first, but then I —" Mehrik whispered, his lungs crushed under Goldenmane's weight.

"I'm not talking to you, traitor."

"Mehrik chose to risk it all. He knew the consequences of bringing Ulrik's Hellblood to the Conclave and confessing to entering the Seventh Seal. He didn't have to do it and yet he did what was right. Will you follow his lead, or will you continue to be Mortagong's watchdog?"

Mehrik gasped for air as Goldenmane released the pressure on his chest. The Lionkin claws still had him pinned to the basalt floor.

"Mehrik, I'm so glad to see you alive. Please accept my deepest apologies, you risked your life trying to warn me of, what I'm sure now, was an incident related to Mortagong's plan. Perhaps if I had listened to you all of this could have been prevented. This is the price we are paying and, unless we can leave this place, all Skyroar will fall with us."

"That may have been true before, sister," Goldenmane said turning to Galanta. "But can you be certain he still can be trusted after he spent cycles doing who knows what with our enemies?"

"Those enemies you talk about are my friends," Mehrik said trying to free himself from the heavy pressure of Goldenmane's paws. "Every one of them is as valuable as any Skyroar citizen. I didn't see it then, but now I do. Not everyone beyond the Wall is our enemy and not everyone in Skyroar is our ally. I learned how to recognize them. "You, Goldenmane, aren't the enemy," Mehrik said looking at him in the eye. Goldenmane opened his mouth to speak but stopped at the last instant, his deep yellow eye going intermittently from Mehrik to Galanta then back to Mehrik until, without a word, he lifted his paws.

Mehrik stood up and walked past him to Galanta. "Great Preceptor. Skyroar is in danger. I need your help. I can't defeat Mortagong alone."

"I'm not the Great Preceptor any longer, my friend, only Galanta. You have my support, of course, and let's hope my brother's as well. Goldenmane, it's time to choose your place. Will you stand with us or against us?"

"I've let my rage grow inside me for too long. It's been an

uncontrollable fire devastating all that was once worthy within my essence. I don't know if I can come back from where I am, but I'll try. I'm with you. For now."

Galanta walked to his brother and hugged him. "I have wanted to do this for so long, Golden. Enough bickering. I love you," She whispered between tears.

Goldenmane accepted the hug but didn't hug her back.

"Great Pre… Galanta, do you have any insight into what Mortagong will do next?" Mehrik asked.

"No, I don't," she said. "And that's his advantage. Ours is the element of surprise. Let's make sure we use it wisely."

"Mortagong summoned the War Council to the Conclave Hall, according to the Fortress guard that brought us here. I'm unsure if they are still in session," said Goldenmane.

"We certainly can't just go and open the door," Galanta said stating the obvious. "Every soldier of Skyroar has sworn loyalty to the Great Preceptor. We'll be killed the moment we put a foot in the hall, and even if we are able to utter a word, it seems unlikely we'd get a confession. The members of the War Council are his allies."

"Let's find a way to bring him here, I can make him talk," Goldenmane said.

"Torture is the solution of the weak to break what can't be broken. We'll talk more about this when the time comes," Galanta said with a serene yet firm voice.

"Listen to your sister, Goldenmane, she's clearly the smart one in the family," Mehrik added with half a smile as he approached the stairs. "Now follow me. Time is not abundant, and I've got a plan."

Chapter Four

Shiroan was wide awake. He wondered if Audax and Ingens were high in the sky, or if it was night in Skyroar. Judging by the snores coming from the surrounding bed-caves, it was time to rest in the Seventh Seal, regardless of the time outside. Lying down on his back, staring at the low basalt ceiling, he struggled to find a comfortable position. Too proud to grant himself permission to grieve for the life he had left behind, he attempted to banish every memory from his mind. It was useless, the images of Kaina, the Winged Squadron and Torok haunted him every time he closed his eyes. And rising above them all, consuming him from the inside, there was Tabatha. Her voice like streams of fresh water, her laugh like bells, her unmatched courage, the way her fiery green eyes looked at him. The haunting rage she felt when Ponthos died. Like an inextinguishable fire, every memory burned a hole in his essence.

Tabatha was the first face he saw when he arrived at Skyroar, and the last one he saw when he entered the Seventh Seal. He would never see her again, so he tried his best to bury those thoughts where he couldn't find them, so deep that he would one cycle forget her name.

"This is useless!" Shiroan said getting up after spending a few periods trying to fall asleep. "I won't be able to rest."

Outside the cave, the Hidden Chamber shone green. Its ancient runes and symbols flickered and changed, performing its eternal dance. At times, he thought he recognized a symbol from the City in the Sky, but his early memories felt as slippery as freshly caught fish. Whenever he could grab one, it quickly slipped out of reach, back to the depths of his mind.

"It's fascinating, isn't it?" Gregoria asked. Shiroan, startled, almost fell off the edge.

"It really is. I thought you were sleeping," he said regaining balance.

"I was. A nightmare woke me up."

"What was it about?" Shiroan asked.

"It doesn't matter. We all have our past. We all have suffered. We're all damaged. Every single one of us. There's no happiness left in Skyroar, and beyond our city there's only death. My night terrors are, at least, harmless."

"That's a gloomy perspective."

"It's a gloomy world."

"Why do you fight, then? Why don't you go ahead and jump into the sea of magma?" Shiroan said waving his hand in front of the precipice.

"Revenge," she answered without hesitation.

Gregoria was shorter than him. Her hair looked almost like a demonphantom wrapped around her head. Her strong features were exacerbated by the fury conveyed by her black eyes. A thin scar ran across her neck from ear to ear.

"That's an interesting weapon," Shiroan said changing the subject. "I haven't seen it among Skyroar warriors before."

"Her name is Phantomslayer," Gregoria said taking the spear with both hands and presenting it to Shiroan. "Go ahead, hold it. It's perfectly balanced, but be careful, it cuts through most things, and the serrated edge makes a lot more damage coming out than going in."

"Extraordinary," he said holding the double-edged weapon, first with two hands and then with one. "What are the blades made of?" Shiroan said looking at the thin yellow-orange crystal on both edges.

"Hellium," she said.

"What's that? Never heard of it."

"I'm not surprised, as far as I know, the hellium from Phantomslayer is all there is left. If there was ever more, now is lost. Most likely when Solisium was invaded —"

"By the demonic hordes," Shiroan completed the sentence.

"That's what they want you to believe, but no, by the Hundred Kingdoms."

"The Hundred Kingdoms invaded Solisium?"

"They did. You see, my people had unlocked the power of the twin suns and, with it, the ability to harness energy. Everyone in the Known Territories wanted it, The Hundred Kingdoms just got there first. We were not ready for war, so we gave our secrets away to preserve the peace. Little did we know that we'd end up massacred by the demonic hordes seasons later anyway."

"How come I've never heard of this before?" Shiroan asked.

"Oh, Shiroan, you aren't the smartest one around, aren't you? Have you seen who rules Skyroar? Who do you think wrote our sacred books? There are more than a few passages left out from the scriptures and believe me, the events recounting how we arrived here are far from accurate."

"Why are you telling me this? Your words are dangerously close to treason."

"I trust your face. You're trapped here. You've probably said and done worse. Pick one, I don't care. It's not like you can go and betray me but, if you ever do, you'll live just enough to regret it, count on it," Gregoria said pointing Phantomslayer at his neck.

"I would like to see you try, I'm —"

"Shush! Get down. Now!" whispered Gregoria as she squatted.

"What?"

"Down!" She repeated as she grabbed him by the sleeve and pulled him to the ground.

"What's wrong with you?"

"Look," she said pointing towards the Hidden Chamber. The silhouette of a person could be seen against the bright green light of the sphere. The figure stood still, looked left and right, and crouched at the edge of the precipice. His face was in the shadows, but it was easy to guess who it was.

"It's only Parktikos," Shiroan said.

"I see him also. Now shut up and pay attention," Gregoria said with impatience in her voice. Shiroan was tempted to continue the argument but decided to give her a vote of confidence.

Parktikos sat down in front of the Hidden Chamber, his legs hanging on the edge of the plateau. He moved his hand as if searching for something in the precipice. A few moments later, he lifted a long and thin wooden pole with a bone hook attached to one end. Leaning forward, he guided it until the hook was underneath the sphere.

Parktikos moved it with the precision of who has done the same exercise a thousand times before. When he pulled it back a large container rocked back and forth, hanging from the hook by a thin pigskin strap. With the outmost care, Parktikos took it and placed it by his side before retrieving a bottle from his belt and filling it with the contents of the bowl. Once the operation was complete, he put the container and the pole back where he had found them.

"It's not the first time I've seen Parktikos doing this. It's time to find out why. Follow my lead," Gregoria said walking to Parktikos before Shiroan had time to agree. "Hey! Can't stay in bed either, huh?" she said casually. "Neither can we, right Shiroan?"

"Indeed, I haven't been able to sleep well since I came to this hole. Too much lava, too little suns. Terrible for my skin."

"I can imagine. So, what's in the bottle?" Gregoria asked with an indifferent tone.

"Nothing. Just water," Parktikos replied.

"Oh, can I have some? I'm thirsty as Hell," she said.

"I spat on it, sorry, it's an old habit of mine."

"That's fine, I don't mind. It's not like we can be picky in this dump," she said reaching for the bottle."

"I said no!" Parktikos exclaimed, moving back with such force that some of the content spilled to the ground.

"I knew it!" Gregoria said looking at the liquid in the floor. "It's Hellblood, isn't it? What are you going to do with it?"

Shiroan witnessed the events in silence. He wasn't sure what was happening or why Parktikos was in the wrong. But judging by his reaction, he was most definitely hiding something.

"Let's keep calm, I can explain," Parktikos said.

"Hold on, that's how Hellblood is produced? It's made with a substance leaking from inside the Hidden Chamber?" Shiroan asked.

"Why do you think is called Hellblood? Where else can it come from but Hell." Parktikos answered.

"Stay on subject, mate, and start explaining why you are stealing Hellblood, and you better hope I like your answer," Gregoria said standing so close to Parktikos that their noses almost touched.

The sound of the cogs and machinery distracted them.

"That's the tray at the entrance of the Seal, isn't it? Are you waiting for someone, Parktikos?" Gregoria asked. A drop of sweat climbed down Parktikos cheek and fell to the ground. Gregoria arched one eyebrow. Shiroan closed his hand around the hilt of his sword.

"Let me go. Trust me, it'll be the best for all of us if you do," Parktikos said.

"Let me decide what's best for me. Who is your contact?" she asked.

"The less you know, the better, getting yourself involved in this matter is a mistake. For your own good, you and Shiroan should go back to your cots," Parktikos said putting his hand on her shoulder.

"You're dreaming if you believe we'll let you go alone, let's go meet your friend," Shiroan said unsheathing his sword and grabbing the Hellblood container from Parktikos. He was muddled in some dark business, no doubt about it, and he was going to find what it was.

"Be my guest, hero," Parktikos said. "Going out is high treason. Put a foot outside the Seal and you're as good as dead."

"Perhaps, but I'll make sure your name is above mine in the executioner's list," he said crossing the bridge and looking for the concealed lever that opened the passage.

"About time. Why didn't you just use the tray? Doesn't matter, do you have the Hellblood?" said a familiar voice. A warrior in full Elgarian armor, including a closed helmet, waited in the cavern.

"I do," Shiroan answered lifting his left arm to show the container as he tried to match the distorted voice coming from inside the helmet to a face.

"Shiroan? Is it you?" the voice said with amazement.

"Gildar?" Shiroan said, finally recognizing the warrior under the armor.

"Where's Parktikos? What are you doing here?" Gildar said with a voice charged with suspicion.

"He and I reached an agreement, he collects the Hellblood, I deliver it," Shiroan lied, refraining from his initial impulse to jump into action.

"But you just got here. It took Mortagong, pardon me, the Great Preceptor, a long time to get Parktikos on board, he must have offered you a sweet deal, lucky you."

Mortagong is involved, that's not surprising, but Galanta is as well? Shiroan thought, trying to dissimulate his surprise.

"Oh! You didn't know Mortagong is now our Great Preceptor. Of course, he took over after you entered this prison," Gildar said reading the confusion on Shiroan's face. "Galanta is accused of treason and murder, she'll be judged soon, a short trial is expected, with only one possible outcome, from what I hear," Gildar said, without realizing the true reason of Shiroan's surprise.

"I'm glad all is going according to plan," Shiroan said almost in a whisper while looking down. He was doing his best to process the news without his body language betraying him.

"Aren't we all!" Gildar said letting out a laugh. "And to think that the Great Preceptor was furious when you were chosen as the next Seven Warrior instead of me! He was sure his strategy was doomed. He didn't believe you could be *convinced*, me neither, to be frank. Not so flawless after all, huh, hero," he added, taking his helmet off to reach for the Hellblood container. "Well, let's finish off here, I've got places to be."

"We never saw eye to eye, Gildar, but I always considered you a worthy rival. I'm not sure what dark scheme you are concocting alongside Mortagong, but it ends here," Shiroan said unsheathing his sword.

Gildar was livid, his face disfigured in a sinister grin. Without uttering a single word, he drew and charged in a single movement. His sword reached for Shiroan's stomach as he tried to grab the Hellblood with his free hand.

Shiroan dodged the attack. Then he turned, placed the container in the ground, and swung his sword in a wide semi-circle. Sparks flew as it scratched Gildar's armor plate. Maneuvering wasn't easy in the reduced space of the cave, especially given Shiroan's height. Gildar crouched and with a quick attack made a deep cut on his calf. Shiroan kicked him in the face with his other leg, sending him flying against the wall.

"What the Hell is going on?" Kishi exclaimed from the inside, his raucous voice echoed in the narrow passage.

"This isn't over, Shiroan. You picked the losing side this time," Gildar said running away.

Shiroan ran after him.

"No! Stop!" Gregoria yelled. "You're a Seven Warrior! You can't go after him!"

"But he'll alert Mortagong," Shiroan said. "We must stop him or, if we can't, go to the Fortress and alert the Conclave."

"There'll be a deliverer here tomorrow. We'll sort it out then," Kishi said. "Listen to Gregoria, the moment you set foot in the Fortress you'll be arrested... and executed."

Shiroan rolled his eyes as he turned around and went back. *I need to figure out what's going on and I got to do it fast. If Skyroar is in real danger, no stupid ancient law will keep me here,* Shiroan thought entering the Seventh Seal, the concealed stone gate closed behind him.

"What did he tell you, Blue?" Kishi asked once he rejoined the group.

"Mortagong. He's an errand boy for Mortagong," Shiroan said.

"I never liked that weasel. What do I always say, Botharhi, huh?" Kishi said.

"Mortagong is a weasel, I don't like him. That's what," Botharhi said with half a smile.

"Then you'll like this even less. He's the new Great Preceptor, Galanta is being accused of treason. I hope now is clear why we need to leave this place and fight this conspiracy," Shiroan said.

"That's not happening," Gregoria said with her spear still against Parktikos throat. "There are other ways to help. Parktikos, it's story time for you. You can start by telling us who's your contact."

"I don't know much about him," Parktikos said.

"I do. His name is Gildar. An official of the Sixth Seal, commander of one of our squadrons. A remarkable warrior, skilled and lethal, full of pride and ambition. Come to think of it, Mortagong did come looking for him on more than one occasion. I never pegged him for a traitor," Shiroan said.

"Life's full of surprises," Gregoria said. "How long have you been doing this, Parktikos?"

"Collecting Hellblood? That's what we all do, it's part of our duties, what right do you have to question my loyalty?" Parktikos said with a breaking voice.

"I wouldn't test Gregoria if I were you. I may be blind, but I can feel she is this close from slicing your throat," Rexora said bringing her thumb and index fingers together until just the smallest of gaps was left between them.

"She's got a point, you better cut the crap. We've been collecting Hellblood for many seasons, this isn't how we do it," Kishi added.

"They took Agatha and Stella, they'll kill them," Parktikos said with a low tone, almost whispering. The streams of sweat running down his neck mixed with the blood drawn by the tip of Gregoria's spear. Tears rolled down his eyes.

"Your wife and daughter?" Kishi said.

"We'll find a way to protect them, Parktikos, but you need to tell us what's happening," Gregoria said lowering Phantomslayer and taking a couple of steps back.

"I don't know much, I swear by Hishiro. Cycles ago, Ulrik took me aside and, out of nowhere, he showed me a lock of hair from Agatha... and the index finger of my wife. I couldn't believe it. We had fought together for so many seasons. He was the best of us. Then I saw his eyes, full of evil, staring at me in a way I can't explain, as if he wasn't himself. 'Mortagong will send you instructions. You must follow them blindly if you want to keep your family alive,' he told me. Look at what happened tonight! I killed them. I killed my family."

"Mortagong is clever, he won't make good on his threat without ensuring he can't get anything else out of you. I'm the one that Gildar faced, not you. If anything, he'll come after me," Shiroan said.

"You can't be sure! Nobody can! This is all your fault!" Parktikos yelled.

"You're right, we don't," said Kishi. "But it does sounds logical, and it's also your only hope, so cling to it and let's work through this together."

"Why would Ulrik act like that? I still don't buy it. He was the most honorable warrior I ever met. This is all a lie. He's trying to save his neck," Botharhi said.

"It isn't. I know why Ulrik did what he did," Rexora said. "What a fool! I should have paid more attention! I was the only one that could have prevented this."

"What are you talking about?" Gregoria asked.

"Ulrik was possessed," Rexora sentenced.

"That's not possible. He never transmuted, not even at the end. I was there," Kishi said.

"It's true. My eyes live in Hell. Demonphantoms is the only thing I see. Demonphantoms and blackness. Ulrik started to avoid me cycles ago. He stopped eating with me, left when he saw me coming, and went to sleep at a different time. I didn't make much of it, we all get sick of each other from time to time, it's just the nature of this place," Rexora said.

"That doesn't mean anything," Kishi said.

"Not yet. Three times I saw something near me. It wasn't a demonphantom, at least not like I've seen them before. It was more like a washed-out stain of evil, a layer of decay wrapped around a cloud of purity. Every time I tried to focus on it. The thing hid, distorted itself, dissolved inside the essence it was covering. The essence of Ulrik. I didn't quite understand it until now. Every time I encountered it, Ulrik was there. The thing was inside him. It was a different type of demonphantom, stuck to his essence like a leech. Possessing him. Controlling him like a puppet. Forcing him to threaten Parktikos. Ordering to kill himself. It's all clear now, and it's all on my shoulders."

"Don't blame yourself, Rexora, it's not your fault," Botharhi said.

"But why did he jump? Why don't do what Parktikos was doing instead?" Gregoria asked.

"Because that was Mortagong's plan all along!" Shiroan exclaimed. "Kill a Seven Warrior so Gildar could take his place. Galanta thwarted his plan by choosing me instead. That's probably why she was overthrown. Parktikos was the perfect backup in the event Gildar wasn't selected. Mortagong knew it was not his decision to make, so he had to be prepared."

"But, to do that Mortagong needed to control the demonphantom. Does it mean he's working alongside Belgoriel and the demonic hordes?" Gregoria asked.

"That's exactly what it means," Shiroan said.

"But how could he be possessed in the first place? He was wearing his Hellblood necklace, wasn't he, Kishi?" Botharhi said, still unconvinced.

"I don't know," Rexora said. "But the demonphantom is real. I'm sure of it now."

"He was carrying it," Kishi confirmed. "But he was also fighting inside. A struggle I couldn't explain until now. Ulrik was battling the thing as his essence was consumed, and he lost. It was Ulrik, not the demon, who gave me the Hellblood that I passed onto the deliverer. True to his character, his last action before jumping to his death wasn't for him, it was to help us stop what Mortagong had started. I misread that message, thinking it was meant as proof of his decease to deliver to the Conclave, when it may have been a clue to the true danger we are facing," said Kishi.

"The key was inside his flask, something in it allowed the demonphantom to possess him," Gregoria said.

"I hope so, because the alternative is that there are demons able to possess us regardless of our Hellblood. If so, it would mean the end of Skyroar," Shiroan said.

"I don't think that's the case, otherwise the demonphantom could have possessed any of us after he killed Kishi, even Parktikos," Gregoria said.

"And it didn't, I can confirm it," said Rexora.

"If all this is true, and that's a big if: what could we do against the Great Preceptor himself?" Botharhi said.

"Not only that, what will he do with all the Hellblood he collected?" said Gregoria looking at Parktikos for an answer.

"I don't know, but I have extracted enough of it to equip an army," Parktikos said.

"And that's without considering the Hellblood that Ulrik might have sneaked out," Kishi said.

"We need a strategy. Gildar will talk. Mortagong may already have enough Hellblood to complete his plan. Galanta's life is in jeopardy, and Parktikos' family might be used as bargaining chips. Are we really going to stay here and do nothing?" Shiroan asked.

"Skyroar law is clear, Blue, we're here to protect the Hidden Chamber, once we enter the Seventh Seal, only death free us from duty. You committed High Treason just by stepping out to confront Gildar. You're new to the job, so I'll give you a free pass this time, but don't think you have any right to judge us. We were protecting the Prophecy and the very existence of Skyroar when you were still wetting your trousers," Kishi said with a serious tone that felt out of character.

Shiroan remained in silence. Not only he didn't trust them, he was underwhelmed by the legendary Seven Warriors so far. Kishi was jesting most of the time. Rexora conveniently ignored a detail that could have changed the outcome of the latest events. And Parktikos chose the path of deception over seeking the advice from his peers. *I wonder how long it'd be before I find out what Gregoria or Lethos are hiding*, Shiroan thought as he shared a poorly disguised look of suspicion to the group standing in front of him.

"He may have a point," Parktikos dared to say aloud.

"Of course you'd say that, Parktikos. You want your family to be safe. That's understandable but is still putting the wellbeing of two people over the entirety of the Known Territories," Gregoria said. If she felt empathy, she didn't let it show.

"Besides, I guarantee you'll be dead or otherwise silenced before you can utter a word. Do you think Mortagong will allow any of us the opportunity to address the Conclave? Hell! He got rid of Galanta, that's how astute he is. The sentence for leaving the Seventh Seal is death, plain and simple. Do you want to make Mortagong's job easier? Then be my guest, leave, but don't do it thinking it'll make any difference, because it won't," Botharhi said. His passion turned his bronze face dark orange.

"I don't care. We can't stay here," Shiroan said taking a step forward. "At least not all of us. Somebody needs to tell the truth to the Conclave."

"That's not your decision to make, Blue. Parktikos is not thinking clearly. We're the Seven Warriors and we all must remain here. including you," Kishi said.

"And who is going to stop me?" Shiroan said as he looked at each warrior in the eye.

"You're acting out of rage and frustration. No good will come out of it. Hundreds will die if you leave. You'll have to kill our brothers and sisters to reach the Conclave. Are you ready to pay the price?" Kishi said. "Your life is not the only one at risk, but also that of all the troops Mortagong will send to hunt you."

"And to be clear, the Conclave may not even believe you," Botharhi said.

"Then I'll find Galanta," Shiroan added confidently.

"And what if you go and somehow can meet with Galanta while keeping collateral damage to a minimum, but the Seventh Seal is attacked in the meantime. There're traitors amongst us, don't you think they'll try to get to the Hidden Chamber if they know we are weaker?" Kishi said. "It's a big bet, Blue, are you willing to make it?"

"Listen to them, Shiroan. We can plan together and agree on the safest way to reach the Great Preceptor and unmask Mortagong. We want justice as much as you do, but what you're about to do can only end up in bloodshed," Botharhi said in a conciliatory tone.

"It's clear we stand on opposite ends on this matter. Stay here and see if I care. I'll deal with this my way, as I always do," Shiroan said walking away.

"What part of 'we're a team' didn't you understand? We need you. Who knows what Mortagong will do? The Seven Warriors must stay together, now more than ever," Botharhi said.

"I'll be back. I won't let you down," said Shiroan pulling the lever that opened the Seventh Seal entrance.

"You already did, 'hero'," Gregoria said walking away.

CHAPTER FIVE

Audax and Ingens hid behind the horizon periods ago, almost as if the tragedy that had befallen upon The City of the Thousand Lights was too much to bear. The cries of children merged with the grunts of soldiers spilling their blood and sweat in a desperate effort to collapse the tunnel. The muffled squeals of desperation coming from hundreds of demons resonated in their ears and filled them with fear.

"It took us all night, but it's done, my queen," Arisko said. "It's shut at both ends. Nobody can enter. Nothing can leave."

"Thank you, my friend, there's no point in staying here. It's almost dawn. The faster we leave this Hell, the better. Gather everyone. Don't forget the demonium."

"How can I help, my queen," Marko said approaching.

"How is Mereia?" Sehrsil asked.

"She's holding up. Not many Icedorfers are stronger than her. She's helping the children, not only hers, but every kid that survived the… catastrophe. Paumeron would have been proud."

"I'm sure he's proud, wherever his essence lies."

"I thought you didn't believe in the eternal essence," Marko said.

"I didn't, but looking at all that's happened, perhaps I am starting to. But this is a conversation for a different time, we need to go."

"Agreed, consider it done, my queen," Marko said walking over towards a group of guards.

Once the proud inhabitants of a country untouched by the demonic hordes, the incredulous convoy of refugees shared tears as they walked alongside the west bank of the lake trying to internalize what happened. Arisko was leading, Sehrsil was last. She had lost their king, their home, and their families, but she would not lose them. Or so she thought.

She heard the demons before she saw their greyish bodies

shining under the timid rays of the incipient morning. They were attacking the vanguard of the convoy.

"We are under attack!" she shouted as she ran to the front of the line. "Where are they coming from?" Nobody answered.

Nobody but Faranides, who signaled her to stop for a moment.

"I'm afraid they've outsmarted us, my queen," he said pointing at the ruins of the city. "Listen how the tone of their squealing has changed. It's not desperation anymore. It's something else."

"I hear it," Marko said joining them. "Looks like they're in agonizing pain, as if they were –"

"Dying!" Sehrsil exclaimed.

"Correct, the creatures realized there was no way out of their prison, and therefore, opted to kill each other, thus freeing the demonphantoms within them. Those are the sounds of hundreds of demons committing mass murder. We must move faster," Faranides said.

"Mereia, go to the front of the line, find Arisko and tell her to take the glacier route. Her sole mission is to keep us alive."

"Yes, my queen," said Mereia.

"Also, make sure she uses the demonium to kill any demons that attack you. That's the only way," Sehrsil said chopping a big piece off the door. "Be well and be safe, my friend."

"Be safe and be well, my Queen," Mereia said as she rode away with the black crystal.

"You!" she said pointing to a group of guards. "Make weapons out of the rest of this door and kill any demons that spawn among us."

"What about me, my queen?" Marko said.

"Do you have to ask?" Sehrsil said with a smile. "You're the decoy."

"Do you mean—"

"Yes, I do. Faranides you're with us. Both of you, take a piece of demonium and follow me. We need to lead the demonphantoms away. Let's go Ursa!" Sehrsil said riding close to the shore while waving her arms to make herself as visible as possible.

"But my queen. What good will the demonium be against a demonphantom?" Marko asked as he pointed at the immense dark swarm floating in the morning sky.

"Who said anything about demonphantoms? The demonium is to kill each other if we are possessed. As for the demonphantoms, be quick and be alert. The demonic look wouldn't suit you," Sehrsil said.

Arisko was already guiding the rest of the Icedorfers up the snowy glacier. If her plan worked, they should be able to escape untouched.

"Do you want the Queen of Icedorf? Then come get me!" Sehrsil yelled off the top of her lungs as she turned her head towards the lake.

She almost regretted her words.

The swarm of demonphantoms seemed to freeze in the sky. Then, slowly but deliberately, it turned to her. Her challenge had been heeded.

"Go!" she ordered Ursa. "Stay ahead of them but don't lose them. We want them to follow us and us alone," she told Faranides and Marko.

"I believe you may be underestimating the velocity demonphantoms can achieve, my queen. It won't be a question of not losing them but rather of not letting them catch up with us. Judging by how fast they move, how far they are, and the strength of the wind, we would need the power of three bears each to stay ahead."

"It's not the time for numbers, Faranides, just ride and shut up," Sehrsil said with a meaner voice than intended. She knew he was right. The demonphantoms were closing on them. They were moments away from being possessed but she wasn't afraid for herself. She was terrified of what would happen if she failed.

If I hadn't searched for my father in Tenebris none of this would have happened, the City of the Thousand Lights would still be standing, our king would be alive, and my people wouldn't be about to disappear forever. Not now, there will be time later to count your sorrows, now is the time to fight, Sehrsil argued with herself.

"They're almost here!" Marko shouted, looking over his shoulder.

"Ride faster! We can make it, I know we can," Sehrsil said even if she couldn't back up her words.

The demonphantoms were above them, one by one, they rained from the sky. The dark cloud of Hell made everything black.

"Watch out, Faranides!" she yelled as a demonphantom

reached his back and got lost inside his body. "Go back Ursa, we got to help him!" Sehrsil shouted full of despair as she pulled the reins as hard as she could. Ursa, unable to brake on the snowy path, slid a few palms before she was able to turn. Sehrsil was ejected from her mount and flew through the air until she hit the side of the glacier, headfirst. The impact broke her helmet in two and made her dizzy. As she tried to stand up, she stumbled and tripped but, before touching the ground, Marko had grabbed her by the waist and lifted her to the back of his saddle.

"He's gone, my queen, we need to keep moving," Marko said looking at the creature that once had been Faranides.

The thick cloud of demonphantoms floated above their heads, almost as if they were savoring the moment. They had no escape, and the monsters knew it.

"I'm sorry, Marko," Sehrsil said. "I'm sorry for your brother, I'm sorry for pulling you to this terrible fate."

"Nonsense, my queen. We're warriors, not puppets. We won't be bought, and we won't bow down. We'll fight to the death, and we'll make our ancestors proud. I would rather die a thousand times fighting alongside you than live one more instant as Belgoriel's servant. You've set us free, my queen."

Sehrsil put her hands around Marko's shoulders and gave him the tightest of hugs. "You'll die as a hero one cycle, I'm sure of it. But this cycle, this cycle it's my turn. You're worth dying for, never forget it. Now go, go, save our people, and bring Icedorf back to life," Sehrsil said standing in the saddle and jumping back to Ursa, who was riding alongside them. Pulling the reins hard, but not as hard as before, she signaled Ursa to stop. Her paws sank in the snow, her claws screeched against the frozen ground as the momentum dragged her forward. As Ursa halted, she turned around and galloped straight to the demonphantoms, ready to meet her fate.

The black, soundless swarm elongated its shape as it sped up.

"I love you, girl," Sehrsil whispered to Ursa as the first demonphantom passed rubbing her hair before regaining altitude. An endless string of creatures followed it, passing her by as they picked up speed. Sehrsil panicked for a moment, fearing the cloud of Hell would chase the Icedorfers escaping through the glacier. It didn't. Every one of them flew south, away from them, merging with the horizon as they got lost in the distance. They were safe.

"What the Hell?" she said.

"Watch out!" Marko, who had come back for her, yelled as he threw the improvised demonium sword forward. Sehrsil heard it whistling as it passed by her left ear.

A despaired squeal came from her back. Turning her head, she saw how the demon that Faranides once was fell to the ground. There, it expanded into a blistered, deformed mass before exploding.

"Thank you," Sehrsil said, wiping her face from the rests of the creature.

"Don't mention it. Where do you think the demons are going?"

"Only one way to find out," she said.

"I'm right behind you, my queen," said Marko.

"No, not behind, never behind," she said. "Always by my side."

CHAPTER SIX

"Do you understand, Frothos?" Goldenmane asked the prison guard for a third time. Frothos looked at him with undecipherable green eyes. Mehrik first, then Goldenmane, twice, had explained to him the plan. It had been an impossible task to grasp if he had fully gotten it, judging by his shrugged shoulders and vacant stare, it didn't really seem so.

"I think I do, sir," Frothos said with a low tone, almost a murmur. "Stay here. Feed the prisoners. Guard the prison."

"And if somebody comes asking for Goldenmane or the Great Pr... Galanta, last you saw them he was interrogating her," Mehrik said talking faster than usual. He was getting impatient. "That's the key part. You never saw them leaving. You never saw me."

"Frothos," Galanta said smiling. "I need you. Skyroar counts on you. The city is in grave danger and only we can help. You must protect us so we can protect the citadel. Will you assist me?" She said resting both her hands in the Vespertian's shoulders.

"I will. I'll protect Skyroar," he answered with the most confident tone he had voiced so far.

"Thank you, my friend." Galanta said.

"Now that this is settled, can we go?" Mehrik said with a tad of anxiety in his voice. Every moment spent in the dungeon stirred memories he would prefer to keep deep inside. *This is where I killed for the first time,* he thought. *I wonder if I would need to kill again.*

Mehrik Warrior. Mehrik brave, Lork telepathized.

Thank you, buddy, but I rather don't take any other lives, although judging by how things are going, I think it'll be all but inevitable that I do.

"Yes, let's go." Goldenmane said picking up a pair of shackles from a corner. "Your wrists," he asked. Mehrik and Galanta extended their arms. "I need to tie you up. It needs to look real."

"Do what you must," Galanta said.

Goldenmane locked them up as he had done to so many prisoners so many times before. Mehrik got goosebumps when he heard the lock clicking in place.

"What about Lork?" Mehrik said looking at the seahawk perched in one of the wooden chairs.

"We can carry him in my rucksack," Goldenmane said taking a pigskin bag and passing it around his shoulders. "He'll need to be still, please make sure that's the case."

"No problem. Go, Lork, it's fine, we trust him."

but be alert just in case, Mehrik added without speaking.

The bird disappeared inside the bag.

"Take care of our home, Frothos," Goldenmane said. "We don't know if we're coming back." The Lionkin took a long look at the room. He touched the table, rubbed the sheepskin chairs, and extended his palm against the wall. Then he walked out.

"This wasn't your home, brother, this was your burden," Galanta whispered in his ear. "All the home you have left is me, your family."

"It might not look like much to you, but this is my refuge. Here, I was never betrayed," Goldenmane answered while taking a large bone key from his pocket and inserting it in the lock of the main prison door. The hall was empty, as expected. Goldenmane walked in front, pulling a chain attached to the shackles. Mehrik had trouble keeping up the pace, one stride from Goldenmane was equivalent to two steps for him. The group moved in silence until they reached the door at the end of the narrow passage.

"A guard will be waiting behind this one. Let me do the talking," Goldenmane said as he knocked two times, waited a moment, and did a final knock. A round face appeared on the barred small square opening in the door.

"What a privilege! What could I do for the great Goldenmane, Emperor of the Dungeon," the guard said with a mocking smile full of yellow teeth.

"I'm bringing these prisoners back to the Conclave to be interrogated," Goldenmane said.

"Oh, I see," he said looking at Galanta intently. "Of course, I'll call an escort."

"No time for that," Goldenmane said with a commanding voice filled with confidence. "We need to get there right away. The Great Preceptor himself called for them."

"That's not protocol," The guard replied lifting his left

eyebrow. "Also, how do you know the Conclave needs to see them? I haven't let anyone through."

Goldenmane fell silent, Mehrik read in his eye that he didn't have an answer.

We're done for. Be ready, he communicated to Lork.

"Do you understand why I'm in chains?" Galanta asked with a gentle yet firm tone.

"You've been accused of high treason, I think, your Eminence."

"Correct. Tell me something, do you believe in those charges?"

"I have clear orders, I –"

"I'm sure you do, but I didn't ask about your orders. I asked you if you believed the accusation brought upon me."

"I... no," the guard said with a trembling voice through the little opening in the door.

"You're correct. The Conclave didn't call for me. The Conclave must see me, nonetheless. The information I possess can change the course of the war and save many lives. You have the fate of the entire city on your shoulders. The question is, will you let Skyroar down?" Galanta asked with a tone so soothing that sounded like a purr.

The guard closed the lid without saying a word. For a few moments, nothing happened. "He could be calling for reinforcements right now, sister," Goldenmane said.

"Be patient," she asked.

The sound of the door unlocking startled them.

"You can go. I never saw you."

"Thanks, you've made a difference today. A meaningful one," said Galanta placing her hand-paw on his shoulder.

"We still need to find a way to reach Mortagong in his apartment. You two aren't exactly easy to miss. We may fool some of the guards, but as we get nearer the Conclave Hall, we're bound to catch the attention of the wrong people," Mehrik said.

"You're right, Mehrik. What do you propose?"

"Let's go to the kitchen. I have friends there."

The group shifted positions. Mehrik and Galanta walked in the vanguard while Goldenmane, sword in hand, pushed them forward every now and then to keep the charade going. The couple of guards they encountered didn't ask any questions. Goldenmane's intimidating attitude took care of that.

"I never thought I'd see the cycle when you'd stood up against the Conclave, sister. I guess it's true what they say, if you live long enough, the impossible will come to happen."

"You can't be serious, Golden. You know perfectly well the reasons behind me joining the Conclave and accepting the position of Great Preceptor. There are more ways to fight than using claws and teeth and, as I hope you realize by now, those are much more powerful than a sword will ever be."

"Yes, yes, you wanted to 'change things from the inside' or something equally pointless. Look where your good intentions brought you. They've always hated us, Galanta, and their hatred is born from fear. Your battle was lost before it started. You played right into their game. You helped them wash out the blood off their hands with your tears. While you were playing Empress, oblivious to the treason happening in front of you, the demonic hordes grew stronger, Skyroar grew weaker, and the Known Territories got closer to Hell. Was this also part of your master plan?"

"Don't patronize me, little brother!" Galanta roared. Then added with a more serene voice, "you can't generalize. Not every Elgarian is the same, and not everyone in the Hundred Kingdoms is Elgarian. Don't be fooled by a loud minority into thinking that the majority follows them blindly."

"Yes, you keep fooling yourself, but remember, the minority is loud because they shout with the voice of their weapons."

"What should I do then, brother? Do tell me. Must I strive to end up like you, locked down in a hole, cleaning up the bodily fluids of prisoners and serving a master you hate?"

"How dare you!" Goldenmane said showing his canines and protracting his claws. "You know why I ended up there. How can you bring that up?"

"Hey! Will you control yourselves?" Mehrik said looking at both. "Keep it up and we'll end up in the same hole you're talking about."

"Yes, Mehrik, we can. Brother, you're correct. I shouldn't have mentioned it. And we shouldn't be fighting. I've made mistakes and I take responsibility for them. Letting you rot in the dungeons was one of them and I'm sorry for it."

"It's too late to be sorry, Galanta. We can't change the past.

But you can be sure as Hell that I'm going to change the future."

"We're here," Mehrik said turning right into a narrow side corridor. At the end, a wide arch marked the entrance to the kitchen. "Follow me, don't talk, don't look around."

A world of chaos met them the moment they crossed the door. It was almost supper time and a battalion of chefs and assistants moved at a frantic pace. A multitude of aides went from station to station collecting soup, meat, and fruit. Feeding all Conclave members at the same time was quite the challenge, so a predefined menu was prepared for all. Customizations were only taken for the Great Preceptor and the Ministers.

Mehrik guided the Lionkins through a maze of cabinets, shelves, aisles, and stoves. Everybody around them was so busy that Belgoriel itself could be dancing in the middle of the kitchen and nobody would care. Mehrik went through the larder door and closed it shut once Goldenmane and Galanta were through.

"How's the prettiest lady in Skyroar?" Mehrik said to Larin, who was on a wheeled ladder retrieving some spices from the top shelf.

"For all the demons in Hell! What in the Prophecy's name are you doing here? Have you lost your head? The whole citadel is looking for you," Larin said as she went down the ladder. Her wooden leg made a hollow thump with each step.

"It's no time for hiding. There are things we need to do. I had nowhere else to go. I need your help," Mehrik said as he rushed to the ladder to help Larin down. He extended his hand, but she didn't take it.

"Don't get me wrong, I'm more than happy to see you, especially alive, but Mortagong has made you his number one priority, kid," Larin said. "And I presume, you are priorities two and three," she said pointing her cane at Galanta and Goldenmane.

"Indeed," Galanta said.

"I am not sure how can I help you, my friend. I am just a kitchen clerk. But anything that I have, you can take," Larin said.

"General, you might be a kitchen clerk now, and only by choice, but I know who you really are. Without you leading our troops all those seasons ago, Skyroar would be no more," Galanta said placing her hand-paw on her shoulder.

"Well, Great Preceptor, I'm at your disposal to do what must be done," Larin said shaking the wormflour off her clothes and wiping it from her face. If she had any on the top of her head, it was well concealed by her short grey hair.

"General, I'm not the Great Preceptor any longer."

"You are to me. I'll be sent to Hell before recognizing that scoundrel of Mortagong. And Mehrik, you came to the right place, you're my friend and friends don't betray each other, no matter what."

"Thank you," Mehrik muttered with a smile of appreciation.

"So, what do you have in mind?" Larin asked.

"I'm actually not completely sure myself. Mehrik, do you care to share your plan?" Galanta asked.

"Larin, what do you say, is this a good cycle to become a traitor?" Mehrik asked with a casual tone.

"Well," Larin started to answer, then stopped for a moment rubbing her wooden leg with the tip of her cane. "If that's what it takes to join such a distinguished group, count me in."

"I don't understand." Goldenmane said. "Why are you so quick into helping us over your own Elgarian kin?"

"Because Mehrik and the Great Preceptor have won my trust and my loyalty. I couldn't care less about your appearance or origin, Goldenmane. It's what's inside that define us, and what's inside Mehrik is more than enough for me."

Goldenmane didn't say anything. He just nodded his head and looked at Mehrik.

"This is what we need from you, once Mortagong's aide comes to the kitchen to pick up the dinner cart, can you find a way to lure him here and then keep him for, let's say, a couple of periods?" Mehrik asked.

"I probably can. What's your plan?" Larin asked, resting both her hands on the top of her bone cane.

"I'll put on an aide uniform and bring the dinner cart to Mortagong's room with Goldenmane riding inside it, hidden by the tablecloth. It's a silly trick but it might work. Once in there, Goldenmane will force Mortagong to reveal his true intentions, including the details of the deal he made with Belgoriel," Mehrik said looking at Goldenmane, knowing it was the first time he heard about what he had in mind.

"You're not only asking me to betray Skyroar, but you're also sending me, us, to our deaths. What makes you think we'll be able to elude the guards or make Mortagong talk? This is the Great Preceptor we're talking about," Goldenmane said unconvinced.

"What do you suggest then? We can't stop Mortagong unless we know what he is planning. We're all fugitives. Going to the Conclave with only our suspicions is crazy. We need a confession, or at least evidence," Mehrik said. "I'm more afraid than you are, believe me, but I don't see any other way."

"I'll do it, Mehrik, but I promise you this, this is a point of no return. If we survive this little game, we better finish what we're starting," Goldenmane said.

"You've got my word," Mehrik said.

"What about me? Where will I be?" Galanta asked.

"You'll wait for us here, your Eminence, Goldenmane is right, we're risking our lives, if we die, so be it, but you're our leader and our inspiration. Skyroar can't afford to lose you," Mehrik said.

"Like Hell! I won't let you two take all the risks while I stay here. Larin, please look for Louriel's aide and bring her here. She's a friend, she'll help."

"As you wish, your Eminence. You already know this, but talking won't be enough for someone like Mortagong. You'll need to be ready to go as far as necessary."

"We are," Goldenmane said dryly.

"In that case, wait for me here," Larin said leaving the larder.

"Are these carts big enough for us?" Goldenmane asked as he inspected the medium sized wheel cart. "It looks like we should be doing this the other way around."

"Seriously? how many scarred, one-eyed Lionkin have you seen in the Fortress? People may be looking for me, but dressed as an aide, I am unremarkable. You are, on the other hand, quite the sight with or without a white gown," replied Mehrik.

"I agree with Mehrik. We would be spotted immediately. We can't expect to be left alone either, the Conclave guards will be much more alert and inquisitive than the ones we encountered so far."

"This way, I've got Lord Mortagong and Lady Louriel's special requests right here," Said Larin entering the room. One Elgarian man and one Solis woman wearing white gowns followed her.

"What's going on here?" the Elgarian man said realizing who was in front of him. That's all he could say before Larin's cane hit him in the head. A soft thump echoed in the room when the unconscious body landed on a pile of wormflour sacks, creating a large cloud that painted their faces white.

"Great Preceptor?" said the Solis aide.

"Hello, Marta. We need a favor from you."

"Anything," she said without hesitation.

Chapter Seven

"What do you think, Larin. Can it be done?" Mehrik asked pointing at the two carts in front of them. Goldenmane and Galanta had been able to somehow curl and twist their massive bodies in the empty space between the top and the bottom. The red tablecloth bent ever so slightly along the sides, but the plates, food and bottles on top contributed to the illusion, making it almost perfect.

"It may very well be, my friend, if we just adjust one or two small details," Larin said as she walked to one of the carts and pushed the golden tip of a tail under the cloth. "Dinner service is crazy around here. Nobody will give you a second look. This setup wouldn't survive a close inspection though, so make sure to go straight to the apartment, and please do not trip anyone!"

"Listen to me, my dearest friend," Larin said grabbing Mehrik's head with both hands. "You may think it odd that, in our darkest time, we put our fate on your shoulders. But trust me, a stronger will than yours I have yet to encounter. I have no doubt in my essence; you can carry us all to a better place. But it isn't me the one needing to believe. Look me in the eye, Mehrik, do you have what it takes?"

"Not really, Larin. I may be more than a deliverer, a warrior even, but the future of Skyroar rests on Galanta's shoulders, not mine. I'm here to help her save us, and that's enough for me."

"Maybe, little one, maybe not, only one way to find out. Good luck and let Hishiro give you the might."

"To send the demons back to Hell!"

Mehrik and Marta pushed the carts. Drops of sweat rolled down their necks and got lost inside of their white robes. The Lionkins, several times heavier than them, forced them to move at a pace so slow that made it impossible to go unnoticed. Heads turned every time the bone wheels screeched against the basalt floor of the larder. Mehrik felt his muscles tense with each step. Once they reached the corridor, pushing was a whole lot easier over the polished marble surface. They quickly got lost between the many aides maneuvering similar carts.

Mortagong's door was visible not too far ahead. Four guards, two per side, were standing by the entrance.

"Dinner for the Great Preceptor," Mehrik said without looking up.

"Who are you?" asked one of the guards. "I haven't seen you around here before."

"He's new," Marta answered from behind. "Started today. A clumsy mess, as you can see," she added with a quick laugh. The soldiers smiled.

"I see, don't worry, kid, you'll learn, give it time. Anyone can be an aide, even you! Not everyone can be a soldier," said one of the guards. The other three laughed heartily.

"You can go ahead and enter. "Is that one also for the Great Preceptor?" He asked, lowering his spear in front of Marta as she followed Mehrik.

Marta's eyes opened wide.

She doesn't know what to say, Lork. This might be it, get ready.

"As a matter of fact, that's my dinner, and my aide. I'm joining Mortagong this evening," said Louriel, walking down the hallway.

"Of course, my lady," said the guard moving aside.

Marta let out an almost imperceptible sigh of relief.

We're good now, Mehrik telepathized to Lork. *But this is a weird coincidence. Larin probably let her know what we were doing in case we ran into trouble. Good call.*

"Don't let anyone interrupt us, we have matters of the outmost importance to discuss," Louriel said with a grave voice as she entered the apartment ahead of Mehrik and Marta.

"Consider it done," The guard said helping them to rush the carts in. "What do you carry in there, a whole moose?"

When he heard the question, Mehrik lost the strength of his legs, and he felt a layer of perspiration forming in his back.

"Skinny little me carried this cart all the way from the larder, don't tell me it feels heavy to a strong warrior such as yourself," Mehrik improvised with eyes glued to the floor.

"Of course not! I'm jesting, little friend," said the guard with a smile as he left the apartment, closing the door behind him.

A brown mooseskin sofa covered the far wall. In front of it, a solid block of polished marble served as a table. Above it, hanging from the ceiling, a chandelier with four lit torches illuminated the room. The mounted head of a canyon rammer decorated the wall to the left while its armored hide rested flat by the table.

Behind the long sofa, close to the ceiling, Mehrik saw something curious. A window, narrow as the palm of an Icedorfer hand, and wide as a mountain snake was carved high above the wall. Two blocks of rock, roughly half the width of the window, rested at both sides of the opening, presumably, Mehrik thought, to close it shut in case of need. A gentle, cold breeze coming from the slit freshened up the room.

Mehrik had never seen a window anywhere in the Fortress, outside of the archer posts in the battlements.

Three Elgarians were sitting on the sofa, drinking ale, and eating pigtails. Two of them wore black robes, Mortagong wore a red one.

"Well," Mortagong said with a smile that sent chills running down his spine. His tongue showed briefly through his thin, pale lips, savoring the moment. "You should have told me you were planning to visit. It'd have saved us both a whole lot of trouble. I have half of Skyroar looking for you, and here you are, in front of me. There was no need to setup this elaborate ruse, I was looking forward to speaking with you, Mehrik."

Mehrik fell silent. He was petrified in front of the tall, bony Great Preceptor. The plan he had carefully crafted, where he had the upper hand catching Mortagong off guard, had backfired. His calculated, cold reaction indicated he was expecting him, and in consequence, he most likely was ready for him.

"Did you come here solely to stare at me, dear?" Mortagong asked as he ran his fingers through the burn scars on the side of his face.

"I came here to unmask you as a traitor to Skyroar," Mehrik said, his hands —closed tightly around the cart's handle— were trembling. "I'm glad I'll have witnesses while I do so."

"That's a whole lot of bravado for a deliverer, isn't it? It'd make killing you much more rewarding, please, go on," said Mortagong with a smirk looking at the other two Conclave members in the room.

"He has more courage in the tip of one fingernail than you'll ever have in your entire life," Galanta roared amidst the sound of spilling trays and broken plates, as she came out of her hiding place, obliterating the cart in the process.

Goldenmane followed her lead, to similar results of shattered bottles and the deafening rumble of kitchen utensils flying across the room.

"Great Preceptor, is everything well?" Asked a Fortress guard cracking the door open.

"Yes, indeed," Mortagong answered as he removed some berry jam from his lap. "But we do have some unexpected guests, could you please be a dear and enter? Bring the rest of your squadron with you."

"Guards! With me!" He said as he came inside the room. The other three guards followed.

"Things are more balanced now, aren't they? Marta, can you please clean up this mess? I'd hate to see my canyon rammer hide ruined. Ale stains are impossible to remove," Mortagong said with the gentlest of tones as he finished tidying up his robe.

Marta looked at Louriel. She nodded at her. "Yes, Great Preceptor," she said getting to work.

"Louriel, my dear friend, you shouldn't have come. You're risking your life for me, escape if you can. And please seek help," Galanta pleaded.

"Louriel isn't going anywhere," Mortagong said, wiggling his body on the couch with snake-like movements. "How pleasant it is to see the siblings back together. It's certainly grand of you to have forgiven your sister, Goldenmane. To be frank, if she would have betrayed me not once, but twice, I'd have killed her with my own hands," Mortagong said. Goldenmane's yellow eye opened wide.

"Oh, yes, I've heard the story," he said. "I know every little dirty detail of it. Skyroar holds no secrets for me."

"Well, you couldn't find me, so there are at least some secrets, I would say," Mehrik remarked with defiance in his voice. Lork flew out of the bag and perched on his shoulder.

"True. And allow me to add, neither could anyone else in Skyroar. You came alone, nobody knows you're here. Forgive me for stating the obvious, but you aren't leaving this room alive. I'd be a fool to waste the priceless opportunity you've put in front of me."

"Whatever it is you're trying to do, Mortagong, it'll fail. The

Prophecy will come to happen, the Passage to Hell will be forever destroyed and, I swear on the essence of Hishiro, Skyroar will be stronger than it ever was," Galanta said protracting the claws from her hand-paws. "Go ahead, kill us, even if you do, someone else will take our place. I guarantee it."

"As amusing as your spirited words are, they are as meaningless as the Prophecy. You think you can stop me? Don't fool yourself, beast, you were the Great Preceptor only because I allowed it. You think the citizens of Skyroar will rebel against me? Most of them are Elgarians with Hundred Kingdoms ancestors. I assure you; every Elgarian will support me when the time comes, and everyone else will be dead."

"You underestimate us, Mortagong, you underestimate our strength," said Galanta.

"Strength? You must mean luck, my dear. The only reason you're here is because, by sheer chance, Louriel realized something was wrong with Ulrik's Hellblood flask," Mortagong said, still sitting in the sofa. "If not for that, you would still be in the dark and, who knows, perhaps Gildar would have been chosen the new Seven Warrior, as I'd planned."

"I knew it! That's why you pushed so hard to get me to choose him. I should have known you were plotting something."

"Plotting is such a demeaning term. This is not some petty plan or common conspiracy, this is my life's mission, and not you, nor your lackeys, will be allowed to get on my way."

"Did your life's mission include making deals with Belgoriel? Selling us to the demonic hordes? How many of us have died because of your dealings with the demons?" Mehrik said.

"You never cease to amaze me, deliverer, as if your poor attempt at sneaking into my chamber wasn't pathetic enough, you felt the need to open your mouth and show us once again how naïve you are. Please, be quiet, the adults are talking," Mortagong said looking back at Galanta.

"Don't change the subject," Mehrik said with a poorly disguised breaking voice, Mortagong's words had gotten to him. "You sold Skyroar to Belgoriel, I'm sure of it. I just don't know why."

"Don't be stupid! Do you really think I'd side with the demons? What benefit could I get from giving Belgoriel the means to destroy us? Those creatures are more disgusting than your kin or your half-animal friends here. Belgoriel is but a tool the same way Galanta was, or Ulrik. You are all pieces on my board, I control every one of your actions," Mortagong said with a smirk.

"I've heard enough, Mortagong, you're coming with me, there's a cell in my dungeon ready for you," Goldenmane said taking a step towards him. Before he could take another, a sword whistled through the air and stopped against his throat.

"You don't want to do this," the guard holding the blade said in Goldenmane's ear.

"As you can see, you're in no position to threaten anyone, Goldenmane," Mortagong said, adding a dry, short cackle, like an old raven. "Thanks to your sister's killer instincts, I'm the Great Preceptor now. I would have preferred to stay in the shadows and control her like a puppet, but this also works. It could work better, actually."

"And how long do you think you'll stay Great Preceptor? You may have fooled us before, but you'll be unmasked sooner rather than later. I'd even say that your minister friends over there could be considering it right now," Galanta said.

"Oh, don't be so small minded," Mortagong said standing up. "Do you believe I lust the Great Preceptor seat? To rule over this empty hole full of refugees and despair? For simpler creatures, like you, sure, ruling over Skyroar would be a dream come true. Me? I'm going to claim the Known Territories for the Hundred Kingdoms, and then I'll rule them all."

"What are you babbling about? You've clearly lost the little sanity you had left," Goldenmane interrupted.

"I'm talking about returning the Elgarians at its rightful place as the masters of this world, and me as the ruler of them all."

"The Elgarians have a king already, in the Hundred Kingdoms, fighting alongside them. I don't think they are looking for a new one," Galanta said.

"Garkun is a weakling! Don't make me laugh. A sheep would be better suited for the throne. He'll kneel in front of me, just like everyone else."

"The Conclave will stop you. You can't kill us all," Galanta said showing her canines.

"Oh, but I can. The Wall will collapse this cycle. As we speak, the demonic hordes are making their way to the West Wall. As per my unquestioned command, they'll find it unguarded. Without resistance, they'll have no problem breaking through. Once inside, they'll march to the Seventh Seal, killing everything and everyone on their path. When the Hidden Chamber falls, and it will fall, a fresh army of demonphantoms will infect the Known Territories and only those wearing Hellblood will survive."

"The Seven Warriors will stop them," Galanta said.

"That's something I would have expected to hear from a simpleton like Mehrik, Galanta, not from you. The Seven Warriors are in the place where they can do the least damage to my plans. Why do you think we have imprisoned the most skilled warriors in that Hell hole?"

"To save the Prophecy, everyone knows it. If the Hidden Chamber falls, the Known Territories will be doomed. So said Hishiro," Mehrik said.

"The Prophecy?" Mortagong said letting out a cackle. "The Prophecy is but a well-crafted story to instill obedience in simpler people, like yourself. A means to an end, that's all. And the Seven Warriors? We put them away for good because they are too dangerous to keep outside. They are too powerful, too loyal, too popular, or too impulsive to have around, so we invented a prison for them and took advantage of their sizeable ego to accept life sentences willingly. A stroke of genius, if I may say so myself, and yes, Galanta, something only the key people at Skyroar knows about, and that doesn't include you."

"I forfeit my life so Skyroar can live. Let the core of the mountain be the keeper of the Passage to Hell and let us all be the guardians of the mountain. And forget not that, if we fail and Skyroar falls, Hell will rise and we will be no more," Mehrik closed his eyes as he recited the Prophecy with outmost conviction, modulating each word with respect and tenderness, like a powerful spell. When he opened them, he was half expecting to see the essence of Hishiro appear in front of them, ready to bring justice to Skyroar.

He couldn't hide his disappointment.

"You're back with us, little friend? Those are just words, like I told you, there's no power in them. The power is in how they're used and, as you can see, the Conclave has been using them for a long time. The scriptures were written hundreds of seasons ago by many people. The books may be loosely based in reality, I grant you that. Hishiro probably died to protect us, and the Hidden Chamber hides the Gateway to Hell. But do you actually believe somebody was taking notes in the heat of the battle?" Mortagong said.

"Mehrik is right. The Prophecy is clear. You will pay for your deal with Belgoriel in blood and suffering. We will stop you and then we will destroy the demonic hordes. We have the courage, the warriors, and the Hellblood. You can't win," Galanta said.

"You might be overflowing with courage, but believe me, you don't have the people. I do. And, you certainly don't have the Hellblood, not anymore."

"What do you mean?" Galanta said with a tone that showed a growing concern.

"Do you think I would invite the demonic hordes to Skyroar without having a plan to protect the Hundred Kingdoms, my dear subjects? For some time now, I've been collecting Hellblood outside of its normal cropping cycle and, our excellent Minister of Science," Mortagong put his hand on the shoulder of the Elgarian to his right, "has been hard at work for several seasons. We have been stealing and storing away thousands of flasks. They are now ready to be distributed among the people of the Hundred Kingdoms. The Skyroar chancellor, newly appointed by me, is negotiating terms on site as we speak."

"The citizens of Skyroar will stop you. The Hellblood will never leave the citadel," Galanta said walking towards Mortagong, three swords reached her neck from different directions. She growled at the guards but stopped moving.

"I see you're losing your composure, Galanta. Perhaps you're realizing at last the inevitability of my victory. Most of us are Elgarians, and loyal to the Great Preceptor. Who do you think they'll follow? And as for the rest, the Oceaners, the Solis, the Lionkin, the hybrids, they'll die a terrible death, I'm afraid, now that their Hellblood is tainted," he said.

"What did you do, monster?" Galanta said taking half a step forward before two blades caressed her neck.

"Me? Not much, our minister friend, on the other hand, was busy. Weren't you, dear friend?" Mortagong said looking at the Minister of Science with a smile.

"Great Preceptor, as you commanded, we have been

contaminating the Hellblood of Skyroar's non-Elgarian population, just like we did with Ulrik."

"I'll kill you with my own hands," Goldenmane roared.

"Don't you mean your paws?" Mortagong said looking at Goldenmane with repulsion. "Do you see the beauty of it all, Galanta? The fools will see the demonphantoms come and won't bother running thinking they're safe. It'll be a most astonishing sight," Mortagong said looking through the narrow window, as if his twisted mind was picturing the suffering and the impotence he would soon inflict upon thousands.

"You've condemned us all!" Galanta shouted as she pushed herself against the swords of the guards until blood drops ran down her neck.

"No. Not all. Not my people. I'm finishing what they started. The Known Territories will be a better place after this is over," Mortagong answered with the same affable tone he had been using.

"Louriel," Galanta called without being able to look back to find her. "If you're still here, now it's the time! The guards are on me and Goldenmane, run! Go to the Conclave and tell them what you heard from Mortagong's own mouth. They'll stop him. They must."

"They'll never believe me, Galanta," Louriel said, walking towards her, away from the door. "The Conclave has been mesmerized by Mortagong. You're asking the impossible,"

Something isn't right Lork, Louriel looks so serene, no, not serene, emotionless, I don't like it, Mehrik telepathized.

She smells like dead, Lork messaged.

"You need to try, Louriel, they'll know you are telling the truth, the Conclave respects you," Galanta insisted.

"No, they won't," she said with a low voice as she approached with slow steps and the beginning of a smile in her mouth. Mehrik looked at the scene without knowing how to react. *I hope you're sure of what you're doing, Galanta,* he thought.

"They'll trust you, just as I do," Galanta said, forcing her head to turn, the drops of blood became streams as the swords sank further in her flesh. Once her eyes found those of Louriel, her expression transformed into one of sheer horror.

"You see it now, don't you," Louriel whispered in her ear as she caressed her cheek with the back of her left hand, Mehrik could barely hear the words. "Your friend is dead, and so are you."

"Louriel, what do you mean?"

"No, not Louriel, Melgorth. Remember me? I tried to possess you before and that didn't work. I'm almost happy it didn't, so I can do this instead," the demon inside Louriel whispered.

"This thing isn't Louriel! Golden!" Galanta shouted before letting out a deep moan and bringing both hand-paws to her abdomen.

Blood poured from the open wound, covering the blade that Louriel had pushed inside Galanta and dripping to the floor. Galanta scanned the room searching for Louriel.

"Louriel, fight it, kick the thing out!" She pleaded.

"She's long gone, Lionkin, as dead as you'll be very soon."

"Sister!" Goldenmane shouted as Galanta fell to the floor. His remarkable dexterity allowed him to catch her before her knees hit the ground.

As carefully as if she was made of crystal, Goldenmane cradled her in his arms and sat down on the canyon rammer carpet.

Mehrik unsheathed his sword and stood between the Lionkins and the guards. Lork was perching on his shoulder. *Well, Lork, this is it. We can't let them get through to her.*

A loud cackle filled the room. It was Mortagong's laughter.

"Oh, how I will miss you, deliverer. Finish them, including the new traitor," Mortagong said pointing toward Marta. "Come with me, Louriel, no need to further spoil our appetite."

Louriel and Mortagong walked out of the room and a guard closed the door behind them. *Coward,* Mehri thought. *He's just scared of Goldenmane. And with good reason.*

"Are you sure you want to do this?" Mehrik bluffed as the guards approached.

"Louriel is –" Galanta began saying behind him but couldn't finish.

"No need to speak now, Galanta, just stay here and rest while I help Mehrik out," Goldenmane said.

"Wait," Galanta said before vomiting blood all over the carpet. Her eyes looked for his brother's gaze. "You were always right, Goldenmane. You didn't betray your principles... not when we were invaded... nor when you were sent to the dungeons... I see it now... you were the stronger one out of both of us... help Mehrik help us all. I love you, Goldenmane, make me proud," Galanta murmured before collapsing in Goldenmane arms, lifeless.

The whole chamber fell silent with Galanta's dead. Even the guards stopped moving. Only their breathing could be heard, and over it, another sound started to grow. It was a deep growl, like the sound of a distant waterfall. It increased in intensity until it drowned every other sound.

"Attack!" Shouted one of the guards, pointing his blade forward.

Mehrik moved his sword to block the first blow. Lork jumped to the face of a nearby guard. A third attacker took Mehrik by surprise. In order to avoid the blade swung at him at full force, he moved back, tripping with Goldenmane and falling to the ground.

"No!" Goldenmane roared as, still kneeling on the canyon rammer's hide, he pushed the guard so hard that he crashed against the wall. He placed her sister's body on the carpet with heartbreaking tenderness. Tears ran down his golden cheeks. "I love you too, my empress," he whispered in her ear.

Wiping away his tears, he looked at the other guards and roared with the force of a thousand thunders. Everyone in the room turned their heads towards him. Mehrik held his breath. The guards' eyes showed the purest kind of fear. Nobody attacked until the last echo of the roar had faded away.

Then the massacre started.

Goldenmane pounced. Before landing, he had ripped the throats of three guards. The other five, swords readied, didn't dare to advance. A deep, guttural snarl filled the room. A thin thread of drool dripped down from Goldenmane's large canines. He was ready to attack.

"Stop!" Mehrik exclaimed, surprising himself with the firmness of his voice. "Don't kill them. They aren't the enemy."

Goldenmane ignored Mehrik's words and leaped forward, arms extended, claws protracted.

"Spare their lives, Goldenmane, do it for Galanta!" Mehrik shouted, placing himself between the Lionkin and the guards. "Let's just go, more troops are coming. Lork can hear them."

Goldenmane let out a warning roar as he pushed Mehrik away, then, with two strokes, he sent the five guards flying against the marble wall. All of them fell to the ground and stayed there.

"What's your plan?" he said, turning to Mehrik.

Mehrik cracked the door open and looked at the hallway. "Not through here. It's full of soldiers," he said closing the door.

"That slit is the only other way out, you'll have to make it work," Marta said.

"What do you mean 'you'? You're coming with us," Mehrik said.

"No, I'm not and we don't have the time to argue about it. I'll play dumb, the guards won't know better, I'll be fine."

"Are you sure?"

"Yes, go save us all, Mehrik."

"I'm not going anywhere without Mortagong," Goldenmane said.

"Then you'll die, just like your sister. You want to make her proud? Help me find others to fight with us. Let's save Skyroar together," Mehrik said.

Goldenmane nodded and retracted his claws at once.

"Lork, go out the window and tell me if it's safe," Mehrik asked.

The seahawk rushed to the narrow window at the top of the wall.

Empty. Good, Lork telepathized.

"I'm small enough to go through, Goldenmane, but there is no way you can fit," Mehrik said looking at the massive size of the Lionkin.

"Not yet." Goldenmane said, grabbing a battleax from the floor and standing on the sofa. He hit the wall with such power that the room trembled. Debris flew in all directions as the narrow opening widened. Without notice, the battleax broke in half. Pausing only for a moment, Goldenmane proceeded to claw the sides of the opening to finish the job.

"They're here!" Marta yelled, pushing a large sideboard against the door.

"What you did so far will have to do. No time for more," Mehrik said. The Lionkin jumped through the hole. His chest got stuck in the opening. The soldiers broke into the room.

"Go!" Mehrik exclaimed pushing Goldenmane forward. It was like a fly pushing a moose.

The five guards in the corner of the room, with renewed courage thanks to the incoming reinforcements, and Goldenmane's vulnerable position, ran to the window.

One of them grabbed Mehrik's waist and pulled him back. Goldenmane was through. Mehrik grabbed the edge of the window and struggled to break free. An arrow flew by his left ear and lodged in the wall. Fast as lightning, Lork attacked the guards trying to capture Mehrik. The one grabbing his waist let go to defend himself. Two hand-paws grabbed Mehrik by the shoulders and pulled him through the opening like he was weightless. Lork followed. The faces of the guards showed through the hole.

"Move!" Goldenmane yelled as he threw a boulder five times Mehrik's size against the opening, sealing it. "This should buy us enough time to escape."

"We can't go down. They'll be searching for us. We have no choice but to climb up the mountain, most of the defense turrets point to the other side, it'll be safer," Mehrik said.

"You're the leader," Goldenmane said. "Show me the way."

CHAPTER EIGHT

Standing with one foot placed outside the Seventh Seal, Shiroan hesitated.

It was an unusual feeling for the Cloudhunter. He hated it.

What a band of demon-kissers. The Seven Warriors are supposed to be the ultimate protectors of Skyroar. These jesters, strong as they may be, are nothing but a disappointment. I should have gone after Gildar when I had the chance, Shiroan thought. *What's more important, to stay here, like cowards, protecting what needs no protection or go unmask whatever conspiracy is happening at the heart of the Conclave? The answer, to me at least, is more than clear.*

Too proud and too confident to change his mind or to ask for help, Shiroan, for the second time that cycle, stepped out of the Seventh Seal.

"It's a Raid!" Rexora shouted at the top of her lungs. "The demonphantoms are coming!"

Shiroan turned his head. Rexora was pointing to an empty space, just above the Hidden Chamber.

"These people are crazy," Shiroan said taking one more step away from the Seventh Seal.

"Shiroan, come join us!" Gregoria yelled before unsheathing Phantomslayer and running toward the sphere.

The memory of Tabatha blaming him for the death of her brother hit him like a boulder. There was no way around it, Ponthos' dead was on him, even if Tabatha had forgiven him. *I did what I had to do then, and I'm doing what I got to do now. If I stay here, who knows what Mortagong will do,* Shiroan thought. *They're all courageous warriors, they'll do well without me.*

Gregoria swung her spear against an ethereal black cloud with uncanny precision, but she was clearly surpassed by the sheer number of demonphantoms.

"I'll regret this!" Shiroan exclaimed running to her help.

"Back so soon, Blue? I'm charming, sure, but didn't think I had such a strong hold on you," Kishi said.

"It's your sense of humor," Shiroan said looking for Gregoria. "Where are the demonphantoms coming from? Isn't the Passage to Hell shut?" He said when he caught up to her.

"It is. Most of the time. Every now and then the Hidden Chamber color shifts to purple and the demons pour out."

"But that's impossible," Shiroan said.

"Impossible is not a word that has meaning around here, now prepare to fight. And, by the way, thank you for showing up."

"Is Lethos well? His chant is much louder," Shiroan said looking to the cave where the old Seven Warrior lived.

"He's protecting us," Botharhi said. "Trying to seal the passage."

"C'mon, Lethos! What are you waiting for, old fool?" Gregoria shouted as she cut a demonphantom in two. "Do your thing!"

"I didn't know of any weapon that could do that," Shiroan said.

"No other can, Phantomslayer it's the only one of its kind, a relic of my people's past. The twin suns power is trapped in its blades. It slices through demonphantoms as if they were flesh and blood," Gregoria said.

The Hidden Chamber's green glow had changed to deep purple, and the characters engraved in it were bleeding a viscose, yellowish secretion. A cold wave, so strong that froze Shiroan's breath and made him shiver, emanated from the sphere.

"Watch out, Gregoria! Incoming! From the left, at shoulder level," Rexora said.

"I thought you couldn't see," Shiroan said.

"That's my curse, Cloudhunter. I'm blind but I can see the demonphantoms," Rexora said.

"Watch out!" Gregoria yelled jumping in front of Shiroan and cutting through the air with Phantomslayer. A demonphantom squealed as Gregoria's double-edged spear cut it in half. He was looking at the two parts vanishing on the basalt floor when the rests of the other fell at his feet.

"*Morter lanius dirium. Cartinomicon tar marcaris glorium. Morter ramilium morter. Portilus lau portialis. Glomius!*" Lethos' voice filled the cave with increased intensity.

"Why is it so loud now?" Shiroan said, turning his head. His jaw dropped. Lethos was out of his refuge and approaching through the air, but he was not flying — his wings were wrapped against his body — he was levitating. Legs crossed, on a sitting position, he floated on a straight line towards them. His hands moved at the rhythm of his chant and were surrounded by small bursts of green sparks.

The Hidden Chamber seemed to be reacting to Lethos' presence. The deep purple changed to green tones, and the yellowish secretion that oozed from the runes was boiling.

"He's trying to heal it. Hell is fighting back," Kishi said.

"This will get worse before it gets better," added Botharhi.

"Heal it, what do you mean? What the Hell!" Shiroan exclaimed, bringing his hand to the hilt of his sword. It was vibrating and hot to the touch. Unsheathing it for a closer inspection, he threw it away as the blade started to glow green.

"What's the matter, Blue? Are you scared?" Kishi asked holding up high his battleax, also glowing green. "Only Gregoria has a weapon that can kill demonphantoms. This is Lethos helping us change that."

"Eleven more coming from the east!" Rexora yelled pointing in the direction of the attack. Shiroan turned his head and squinted his eyes but was unable to see the demonphantoms.

"Cloudhunter, get ready and help, we can't let any of them escape!" Gregoria shouted as she rushed to the attack. "And be careful, they can't possess you, but they can go through you. If they do, the pain will be unbearable and will stay with you forever."

Shiroan picked up his glowing sword and, ignoring the burning sensation in his hand, rushed to help. A few dark shadows were now distinguishable against the wall of the crater. He ran to the one closest to him. The deafening noise made by the moving sphere disrupted his thoughts. Every time the sphere hit the edge of the plateau, the ground shook and made him stumble.

The demonphantom was in a collision course with him. Shiroan swung his blade in a wide arc. A mix of surprise and disgust invaded him when it sliced through a slimy substance, like rotten meat at the bottom of a lake. When the sword came out the other side, two halves of the demonphantom fell to the ground before evaporating into the thin air.

"Wake up, Shiroan!" Parktikos shouted. "That's the first one. Plenty more are coming."

Shiroan looked in the direction that Rexora was pointing in and rushed to battle.

The Seven Warriors were fighting alongside the circular path. Kishi was slicing demonphantoms two at a time with his battleax. Gregoria swung Phantomslayer left to right, slicing through her fair share with the grace of a dancer. Botharhi had found a ridge in a wall nearby and was shooting a continuous stream of green arrows. All their efforts were futile, the seal was getting darker, covered with an ever-expanding cloud from Hell. For each demonphantom they killed, three seemed to take their place. If Lethos didn't succeed at what he was trying, Belgoriel would have hundreds of new recruits for his demonic hordes.

"How much longer, Lethos? We don't have all night. Fix it!" Gregoria yelled as her spear passed through five demonphantoms. Everyone was moving as fast as they could, but it was Rexora who moved the fastest. She had stopped pointing and was fighting, one sword per hand, slicing everything on her path, pausing only to find the next place to attack.

"Where did you learn to do that?" Shiroan asked approaching Rexora.

"What do you mean?" Rexora said.

"You clearly can see the demonphantoms, even through your blindfold. How?"

"Behind you!" Rexora warned before throwing one of her swords, pinning a demonphantom against the rock wall before it dissolved in smoke.

"See what I mean," Shiroan said as Rexora rushed to pick her sword up.

"There's more than one way to see, my friend. It cost me my eyes to learn that secret. I'm giving it to you for free. Don't let it go to waste. Look out!"

Without looking back, Shiroan nailed the demonphantom behind him. "What does that mean?" he asked after rechecking his surroundings.

"I don't use my eyes to see but my essence. Through it I see the demonphantoms as if they were made of flesh. I also see your essence, Shiroan, and what I see answers a question I had had since I arrived at the Seventh Seal."

"Shiroan, Rexora, come help! Lethos, it's now or never!" Gregoria shouted.

Shiroan turned his head and saw a swarm of demonphantoms above Gregoria's head. They were getting out of reach. Botharhi was bringing down as many as he could but there were more of them than arrows in his quiver. Each demonphantom that left the Seventh Seal would become a new demon. They needed to take them all down.

"You'll have to tell me about it some other time," Shiroan said before joining Kishi.

"Get ready!" Shiroan yelled as he ran. "Extend your arms and throw me up!"

It took Kishi a moment to understand Shiroan's request. By the time he did, the Cloudhunter was running towards him at full speed. By crouching and holding his battleax horizontally in front of him, he created a narrow platform for Shiroan to use as a step. When he placed both feet, Kishi stood up and lifted his arms, throwing Shiroan at the group of demonphantoms that were escaping.

Shiroan maneuvered his blade as skillfully as he did on the ground. Turning over himself, he sliced one demonphantom after another. As he landed on the basalt path, he saw a few dark shadows disappearing through the solid rock wall.

The one he didn't see was the one that entered his body.

The agonizing pain he experienced wasn't comparable to anything he had felt before. It was as if thousands of blades were slicing him from the inside. His mind had shut down to the world. All he could see was Ponthos' flesh being consumed by the magma, Tabatha's tears transforming in minuscule arrows that lodged in every pore of his skin, and his parents being mauled by demons.

When the darkness came, he almost welcomed it. For a moment, he looked around and all he could see was red shapes flying around him. The shapes were blurry but resembled people. And every one of them had their mouths open wide in a silent scream.

When the pain was at its highest, an ethereal force knocked the wind out of him. Then everything came back to normal.

Shiroan was kneeling in the ground struggling to catch his breath. The Hidden Chamber was at peace. The final vestiges of the yellowish ooze dripped down to the sea of lava, and the purple glow had been replaced by the usual green. Feeling the heat on his hand recede, he looked down to find his sword losing its glow.

"You can't say I didn't warn you. I am glad you are well," Gregoria said helping him up.

"I saw things that couldn't be real, and others that I wish weren't. Rexora, is this how you lost your sight?" Shiroan said.

"It is how it started. In my case, it wasn't only one inside me but many. Tens of demonphantoms fighting for my essence just to be defeated by my Hellblood. They left me blind, leaving in the same darkness you just experienced firsthand."

"I'm sorry. I can't fathom how hard it must be for you," Shiroan said looking down.

"The important thing is that we stopped most of them," Rexora said with a smile.

"And that's really all we can do. Some of them will always find their way into the Known Territories, no matter how much we try to get them all. Each of them will possess an innocent person and may one cycle be back in Skyroar, ready to take us down. One life lost for every failure, that's the price we pay."

"Stop it with the dark comments. Parktikos, we saved as many as we could. That's all we can do," Kishi said tapping his shoulder.

"Without mentioning this Raid was probably triggered by you stealing our Hellblood. So, measure your words, or even better, stay quiet," Gregoria muttered with a clenched jaw.

"Now, can anyone explain to me what just happened? Since when are the demonphantoms entering the Known Territories? The Conclave has assured us the Passage to Hell was forever close. They promised that, as long as the Hidden Chamber was protected, it would stay shut. That's not at all what I witnessed. We're not really winning this war. We are only losing more slowly."

"It started, perhaps, two seasons ago. The first Raid wasn't large, less than ten demonphantoms, Gregoria was able to take them all down," Kishi said.

"It got worse every time, but never like this, never this bad," Botharhi added. "Without Lethos, this battle would have been lost already."

"Have you ever wondered why this happened all of the sudden?" Shiroan said.

"Very ancient essence inside it," Lethos explained as he

descended to stand by their side. "Very ancient. Hellblood disturbs essence. Then essence weakens. If essence dies, we die. Magia inside me helps heal essence. Magia makes essence strong to keep gateway closed."

"You're the one keeping the Passage to Hell closed?" Shiroan asked with eyes wide open. "What will happen when you die which, judging by how you look, may not be that far ahead."

"Hey!" Botarhi exclaimed. "Show some respect! Lethos has done more for Skyroar than any other warrior since Hishiro."

"So, what's the plan when he's gone?"

"I don't keep the gateway closed. I heal the essence that keeps it closed. When I'm gone, Magia remains. Magia will find a way."

"What if it doesn't?" asked Shiroan.

"The essence inside it can't heal. When it dies, we die. When the gateway opens, we become Hell."

"But you won't die, and the Hidden Chamber will continue to be closed!" Kishi said. "We won yet another battle. Stop the grim talk and enjoy the victory. I say we celebrate!"

"I say we don't. I've been fighting for as long as I can remember. Skyroar has lost thousands upon thousands of its citizens and what do we have to show for it? Every demon we kill comes back stronger. Entire lands have been decimated by creatures that never get tired, never back down, never have mercy. What's your plan, Kishi? Stay here until everyone else is dead?" Shiroan said with passion in his voice and trembling hands.

"I thought you were leaving, Shiroan, don't let us stop you," Rexora said.

"No. Let's hear him out. What's your suggestion Cloudhunter? I hope is a better one than the one your kin had, or we'll end as dead as them," Gregoria said with an incensed tone.

"That's uncalled for!" Kishi exclaimed.

"I apologize, Shiroan," Gregoria said. "We do what we can to protect the Hidden Chamber and the Passage to Hell. Our duty also includes ensuring a healthy supply of Hellblood for Skyroar. I don't appreciate you coming here and suggesting we are cowards, or worse."

"It is, you must all agree, suspicious to keep the best warriors of Skyroar away from battle. Including a warrior whose spear slays demonphantoms and another one able to transform anyone's weapon into a demonphantom killer. That's all I'm saying. We could attack Tenebris and finish this war. Kill the demons first and then the demonphantoms until all of them are gone. That's my plan. Let the deliverers take care of collecting the Hellblood and let the warriors win this war."

"It'd never work, if Lethos leaves the seal, it wouldn't be long before the Passage to Hell opens, or he dies," Rexora said.

"Then we bring some other Vespertian capable of reciting the spells," Shiroan rebuked.

"Only I can do the spell. Magia resides in me and not in others. I am the Nexus," Lethos said. "I can't leave. Too old. Too weak."

"There's nobody else that can do what he can do, Shiroan, we had the same questions you had, and he gave us the same answers," Kishi said.

"Then we need to find another way! Aren't we the seven strongest warriors of Skyroar? I can't believe your plan is to sit here and wait for the city to fall," Shiroan said.

"We're soldiers, Shiroan. We follow orders from our superiors. We obey the Conclave. We trust the Prophecy. That's our role and yours as well. You better accept it," Botharhi said.

"Are you all as blind as Rexora? Can't you see the signs? I witnessed myself how Fortress guards created the dragon attack that almost killed us all. Mortagong is clearly stealing Hellblood for purposes unknown. Ulrik was somehow possessed to the point of suicide, am I the only one seeing a pattern here?" Shiroan's brought his hands to his head. If he didn't let it out, he'd just explode.

"Botharhi is right," Kishi said with a voice so low it was hard to hear. "It's our duty and our honor to defend the Hidden Chamber. That's what we ought to do. If you want to go, you'll have to go alone, Blue."

"No. Not alone," Gregoria said taking a step forward. "Every word out of Shiroan's mouth is the truth. We are not warriors. We're prisoners. Perhaps the battle will reach us, but if it does, it'll be after it has reduced Skyroar to cinders. Do you really want to sit here and wait until then?"

"You must be jesting," Botharhi said.

"No, she isn't, neither am I. I don't need eyes to see the righteousness in Shiroan's words. I also think we must act before is too late," Rexora said.

"I thought that I could protect my family by betraying my people. I was wrong. If you can forgive me, I'll make Mortagong pay with blood what he made me do. I want to help," Parktikos said.

"Thank you, Parktikos. Even our combined might be insufficient to stop Mortagong. Without you, our chances will decrease. We'll give you a vote of confidence," Shiroan said.

"Not so fast. What if he betrays us again? What if he's betraying us right now?" Gregoria asked.

"What's the option? Should we go ahead and throw him to the sea of lava? We'll need all the help we can muster. I also support giving Parktikos a chance," Rexora said.

"Fair enough. But if you betray us, I'll kill you with my bare hands and feed you to the demons," Gregoria said.

"What do you have in mind, Blue? It's your time to shine," Kishi said.

"Does that mean you are with us?" Shiroan asked.

"Indeed. Considering your people skills and your fighting ability, you clearly need us," said Kishi with a smile while rubbing Shiroan's bald head.

"Well, there isn't much for me to decide, if you're all in, I won't be the only one out. You can count me in," Botharhi said.

"I don't have a firm plan yet, but I do know we must find out why Mortagong needs the Hellblood, so let's start with that," said Shiroan.

"I don't think he'll come to confront us, even after Gildar tells him what happened. He believes we are too loyal to leave the seal and he probably has more pressing matters to attend to," Botharhi said.

"How about the deliverers, can we try to get information from them?" Kishi said.

"No, we shouldn't. Mortagong is nothing if not clever, he'll send only deliverers he trusts from now on, you can count on it," Rexora said.

"It's all the same, we can't talk to any of them anyway or they'll share their fate with the Oceaner I met a few cycles ago. We don't want to be the cause of more innocent people going to the dungeon," Shiroan said.

"What? Was he sent to the dungeon? But it was I pulling him inside and talking to him! Poor kid. I should have realized he was too noble to lie," Kishi said.

"What if he just stops sending people altogether?" Botharhi said.

"He can't. Skyroar needs to replenish the Hellblood reserves. He knows we'll give it to him, not doing it would condemn innocent lives to demonic possession," Parktikos said.

"So, what do we do, Shiroan?" Gregoria asked.

"We break the law," Shiroan said. "And we bring Mortagong down."

"Tell me more." Gregoria said with interest.

"We'll use the rules to our advantage. Since nobody can enter the Seventh Seal, they can't know how many of us are inside at any given time, correct?" Shiroan said.

"Not on the outside. We would still know," Rexora said.

"Exactly. Only us. And how many of us are absolutely needed here?"

"Well, we need Lethos to protect the Hidden Chamber," Botharhi said.

"And Rexora to alert us if demonphantoms are coming through the gateway," Gregoria said.

"Also, we can assume that Gildar has talked to Mortagong already, so Parktikos should stay here in case Mortagong, or one of his lackeys, comes asking for him," Botharhi added.

"So, Gregoria, Botharhi, Kishi and I, are free to leave the seal and unmask Mortagong."

"Gregoria, Kishi and you," Botharhi said. "Rexora or Lethos can't really keep an eye on Parktikos. As much as I want to believe his words, we can't risk him sneaking unseen and backstabbing us, again."

"I concur," Gregoria said.

"It's settled then. You cowards stay behind, and we go save the Known Territories," Kishi said with a dead serious face. When Botharhi opened his mouth to retort, he added: "I'm jesting, we're the Seven Warriors, there're no cowards among us, only greatness," he said laughing heartily and the rest of the group laughed with him.

"Well, Shiroan, what would you have us do," Gregoria asked.

"I don't know yet. I'm more of a do first think later type of person."

"You don't say. Well, now it's the time to make a change. You stayed. You stirred the waters You got your crew. Now you'll have to lead us forward," Gregoria said.

"Trust me on this one, Gregoria, I'm no leader, my squadron in the Sixth Seal can confirm that," Shiroan said.

"Well, you either take control or not," Gregoria said taking a step towards him. "But if you choose not to, then we'll just stick to our duties and consider this matter finished. You can go save the Known Territories by yourself."

Shiroan closed his fists tightly and grinded his teeth. Every fiber of his being wanted to reply something nasty, turn back, and abandon the warriors to their luck. Then he took a deep breath and looked at them. Their eyes were filled with expectation. Kishi was smiling. Gregoria had her black eyes fixed on him.

"I make no promises," Shiroan said. "If we end up dead or, worse, bring harm and danger to our people, I won't be responsible. If you want to take the risk, I'll guide us."

"Thank you, Shiroan. If you could find the time to check on Agatha and Stella I would be forever in your debt," Parktikos said.

"I'll see what I can do," Shiroan said.

"We'll take the risk and join you," Gregoria said.

"That's right, it'd make it a lot easier to blame it on you when everything goes to Hell, Blue," Kishi added before laughing heartily.

"It's settled then. Come closer. I have an idea."

Chapter Nine

Ursa's paws barely grazed the ground. Each stride was so powerful that Sehrsil felt like they were flying. The bear was as determined as Sehrsil to avenge the City of the Thousand Lights. Behind them, the eternal white prairies of Icedorf were forever stained with the blood of their people. Ahead of them, the opportunity to atone for the massacre she had brought upon her kingdom. She might die searching redemption, but not without killing Belgoriel first.

The twin suns were close to completing their cycle across the sky. As the twilight settled around them, Sehrsil heard Marko's bear, Lorion, puffing and panting. He was struggling to keep the pace. They had been traveling for endless periods, even though they left the demonphantom swarm behind a long time ago, she knew where to go. Belgoriel was the only being able to summon demonphantoms at will; and there was only one place to find it. Sehrsil was experiencing, not for the first time, how difficult it was to come up with a plan without Faranides. And they needed one, a good one, more than anything else. Hordes of demonphantoms were at Belgoriel´s disposal and ready to launch their final strike Unless she devised the right strategy, thousands, including Marko and herself, were as good as death.

"We're entering Tenebris!" she announced looking at Marko. "The Dark Castle is but a period from here."

"Where is all the fog coming from?" Marko said, looking around.

"I don't think is fog but smoke and ashes from the burned trees. Belgoriel killed this land before inhabiting it, nothing but demons are left."

"What's the plan, my queen? You and I can't take the entire demonic hordes alone, and I couldn't let you try."

"You can't stop me, Marko. You know that. But I concur, a frontal attack is doomed. If only Faranides was here! He'd close his eyes and ideate something like that," Sehrsil said snapping her fingers.

"It's true. What bothers me the most is how he died. A warrior shouldn't have to die a monster," Marko said.

"He may have looked like a monster, but he had the essence of a hero. That's one more life Belgoriel will need to answer for and, make no mistake, I'll be the one settling the debt."

A green flame lit the dark sky in front of them. The swooshing sound of heavy, leathery wings followed it. The unmistakable shape of a dragon showed above the charred trees and flew away.

That was the first one.

One after the other, a caravan of dragons covered the night with horror.

"How many are there? Where are they coming from? My queen, we need to go back, is too dangerous to continue."

"Let's go to the woods. We'll be safer," Sehrsil said pulling the reins to indicate Ursa the path to follow.

As they approached the Dark Castle, screams of pain reached their ears. Sehrsil didn't recognize the language, but the words were filled with anguish and desperation. She lifted her right arm to signal Marko to stop.

"Let's leave the bears here, it's better to continue on foot," Sehrsil said hopping off.

The last time she had been in the Dark Castle, she precipitated the events leading to his father's assassination. If not for Mehrik's fortuitous intervention, she would be dead. Now she had Marko by her side but, if something went wrong, they didn't have a backup plan, nobody even knew they were there.

She still didn't hesitate. This wouldn't be a bad way to die, on the contrary, dying in battle was the greatest possible honor.

"My queen? Are you seeing what I'm seeing?" Marko said placing his hand around Sehrsil's forearm and pulling her behind a scorched trunk.

"I am, how the Hell are they doing it?" Sehrsil said.

From the nearest tower, dragons could be seen taking off, one after the other, in a macabre procession.

"Where are they coming from, there isn't enough space on the top to keep more than a handful of dragons," Marko said. "And they obviously wouldn't fit in the tower's stairs."

"You are right, no dragon would fit, but Vespertians would. Dragons must be created on the spot by possessing them," Sehrsil said.

"How? As far as we know all the Vespertians that survived the massacre of their home country are in Skyroar."

"For all the demons in Hell! Imagine for a moment that Belgoriel, instead of killing them all when the demonic hordes invaded Vespertia, decided to make them prisoners. It is known that the Vespertians are the only people that transform into dragons when possessed, and dragons are immensely more powerful than demons. Belgoriel must have been holding them in Tenebris all this time, waiting for the precise moment to attack."

"That's why the demonphantoms left us alone. They were summoned here to possess these Vespertians. This can only mean that Belgoriel is preparing for the final battle. There's no other reason to create this many dragons at the same time," Marko said.

"It makes sense to attack Skyroar when Icedorf is at its weakest," Sehrsil said. "We need to find a way to stop this. Otherwise, the battle will be lost before it starts."

"I wish we could do something; I really do. If we move closer, we'll just join the demon ranks. Our demonium weapons aren't good against demonphantoms. And even if they were, there are just too many of them. We wouldn't stand a chance."

"What option do we have, Marko? Leave? I'm not letting the demons win without a fight. And I am not dying before killing Belgoriel first," Sehrsil said.

"It makes no sense arguing with you, I learned that a long time ago. Show me the way, my queen."

"Sehrsil, Marko, call me Sehrsil. We'll probably be dead in a couple of periods, nobody will ever know you did," Sehrsil said with a wink as she analyzed the Dark Castle.

The tower being used by the dragons was right to the castle where Sehrsil met Belgoriel, and it was surrounded by a wide moat.

"Last time I was here I used that slit in the main in the main building to go in, but I'm not sure that it connects with the tower. Even if it does, walking that much distance inside the castle is too risky."

"Not to mention the group of demons guarding it. They probably learned their lesson from your last 'visit'. We might be able to kill them, but not without them raising the alarm," Marko added.

"You're right, we need another way in. The tower gate bridge us up, but I think we can do something else. Follow me. And be ready to get wet." Sehrsil said.

The Icedorfers sneaked their way to the border of the moat that surrounded the tower. They were far from the gate to avoid being seen.

"If we can swim to the wall, we might be able to climb to the top of the gate, looks like the there's a large enough gap up there," Sehrsil said.

"You must be jesting, that water looks blacker than the rest of this forsaken place, who knows what lies beneath," Marko said looking at the immobile, dark mass of liquid surrounding the castle.

"Only one way to find out," Sehrsil said carefully sliding down the muddy edge and into the water.

Marko followed with a grunt.

"I'm freezing," Marko said with chattering teeth.

"Well, you better start swimming and stop whining then. The faster we get to the wall, the faster we'll be out of the water," Sehrsil said already halfway through the moat.

That's when the ripples appeared. First one, then another. In the space between Sehrsil and the wall.

The ripples gave way to the subtlest of waves moving straight towards the Icedorfers. Sehrsil continued to swim to the castle, oblivious to what was below her. The thing prowled closer.

"Careful!" Marko exclaimed. "There's something underneath!"

Sehrsil looked around. Water splashed all over her face as the creature jumped out of the water. When she opened her eyes, a mouth filled with fangs, large enough to swallow her whole, was all she could see. With no time to swim away or to unsheathe her sword, she opened her arms as wide as she could. Grabbing each corner of the pestilent mouth, she managed to keep it away from her head. The weight of the thing sank her deep in the muddy water. The palm of her left hand was impaled by one of the fangs. She didn't care. She was drowning.

Webbed, rough hands kept her down. The air from her lungs escaped quickly as she struggled to survive. She was close to fainting when the grip receded. The jaw softened up and the fang through her palm heated up before it dissolved. Sehrsil swam to the surface and took a mouthful of air. Around her, the water bubbled.

"Are you well, my queen?" Marko asked, sheathing the demonium shard he had used to stab the creature.

"Yes, I believe so. Thank you. Was that a water demon? I didn't know such a thing existed."

"Me neither. But judging by its reaction to the black crystal, it must've had a demonphantom inside," Marko said.

"How did you know the demonium would work?" Sehrsil asked.

"I tried my sword first. It barely did any damage. When I looked at the viscose blood and the grey hide, I took a chance. I thought it had to be a demon. I wasn't wrong."

"We've never seen a water demon before," Sehrsil said.

"No, we haven't. We also lived sheltered lives, as we have come to realize. We have almost no knowledge of what lies beyond Oceano and The Sea. We'll have time to ponder its origin later. Let's go before another one comes, my queen."

"You're right, Marko, let's go. And call me Sehrsil."

Sehrsil started to climb the stone wall of the tower. The gap left by the partially lift bridge was indeed large enough for them to squeeze through the main gate. The edges and holes were wet and slippery, but also large enough to allow for quick progress.

This creature caught me completely off-guard; I would have died if not for Marko. Will we even have the slightest chance to succeed or are we wasting our lives for nothing? In a few moments, we'll face demonphantoms and dragons. What will we do? Am I sacrificing yet another life for nothing? Sehrsil thought.

"Almost there, my q… Sehrsil. I'm with you until the end, but this is your last chance to reconsider this path. We will most likely die here," Marko said and his words, voicing her own thoughts, were enough to force a change of plans, small as it were.

"I've got you. We'll still go in, but we'll do it through the window rather than the main door. You are right, it is only logical that demons will be guarding the main entrance," Sehrsil said changing course and heading to a long and narrow side window higher up the tower. She slid through it, landing on the main spiral staircase.

Lined up in the stairs, covering every space up and down the steps, a gathering of thin, pale, hopeless Vespertians stared back at her.

"You could have told –" Marko didn't finish the sentence. "This is impossible. How many of them are here? How long have they been imprisoned by Belgoriel?"

"It doesn't matter how. Each one of them will be a dragon unless we do something,"

"Can they understand us?" Marko asked.

"I don't think they speak Icedorfer, perhaps Elgarian, let's try. You, sir, can you understand me?"

The Vespertian she was addressing didn't utter a word. He looked at her with wide eyes and an expressionless face, Sehrsil could tell he was afraid. He turned his head and moved up three steps, following the flow of the Vespertian crowd.

"How about you, milady?" She asked a woman looking at her with curiosity.

"I do," a skinny Vespertian boy —about half of Sehrsil's height— said running up the stairs to catch up to her.

"Good, tell me, how long have you been here? Do you know what's at the top of the tower?"

"I hope it's meat and water. We have only eaten roots and leaves for a long time. The demons came to the dungeon at sunszenith and told us that our imprisonment was about to end, and a feast awaited us to celebrate our release. I'm starving," the Vespertian kid said.

"Where did you learn Elgarian?" Sehrsil asked, looking at Marko with a concerned gaze that interpreted her thoughts exactly.

"My mother taught me."

"Where is she, can we talk to her?" Marko said.

"She disappeared. Every few cycles, they come and take several of us. They never come back. My mother –" the boy's voice broke, and he started a soft, shy sobbing. Sehrsil squatted and hugged him.

"Don't worry, you'll be safe, I promise. And if your mother is still alive, we'll find her. But we can't stay here. You can't stay here. There's no food for you above, trust me. It's true that you won't come back to the dungeon, but your impending fate is much worse than captivity," Sehrsil said, hesitant to disclose to a child the whole truth of what was at the end of the line.

"I knew it! I knew they had to be lying. I just didn't want to believe it. I'm so hungry and so tired… What are they doing then, are they killing us?" the boy said, raising his voice and clenching his fists. Even in a world at war, covered with the blood of the innocent, it was still shocking for Sehrsil to listen to children talking about death with such familiarity and passion. *Did you act well, father, by allowing our people to live happy lives at the expense of everyone else? Are we as responsible as Skyroar for this suffering and these deaths? It's not my place to judge you, but it's my duty to lead my people. And I'll guide them to victory, or we'll die trying,* Sehrsil thought while giving the Vespertian boy the tightest of hugs.

"In a way, but it's more sinister than that, my dear. They'll abduct your essence and rob you of your body. We need you to save you and your brothers and sisters. Will you help us?" Sehrsil said.

"Yes, I will, what should I do?"

"I don't speak Vespertian, so I want you to tell your people to let us through and to run downstairs the moment they hear a loud thump. Understood?" Sehrsil said.

"Yes," said the boy as he turned to pass the message to his people.

"Marko, I know where to take them, I'll go down and clear the way. You must go up and find a way to block the stairs. It needs to look like an accident. That'll buy us some time," Sehrsil said in Marko's ear.

"How can I do that? I have no clue where to start. If I get to the top, I'll be seen. I'll have to risk the Vespertians atop the stairs, and—" Marko didn't finish the sentence, one look at Sehrsil's purple eyes was enough to send him running upstairs.

Thank you, my dear friend. I'm certain that you'd have rebelled against these orders if they came from anyone else. All I know is that the trust you've placed in me carries me forward. If there was a way to save them all, I'd have chosen it instead. We had to decide between saving most or saving none, and that's exactly what we did, Sehrsil thought. The only way to stop the creation of the dragon army was to bring down the tower and sacrifice those that were on the highest levels. It was an imperfect plan, or perhaps a perfect plan for an imperfect world.

"This is the only way," Sehrsil whispered as she saw Marko turn a corner and disappear. "I'm sorry."

Sehrsil climbed down the steps. She stopped almost at the bottom of the stairs. Then she waited. It was unclear how Marko would collapse the tower, but she was positive that he would succeed, no matter the cost.

Vespertian eyes looked at her with a mix of confusion and fear. She wasn't sure if they had ever seen an Icedorfer before. Taller, paler, wingless, and with furry calves, white hair and purple eyes, the differences were plentiful. She smiled and nodded, always keeping a hand on the knob of her sword, just in case.

Suddenly, the ground shook under her feet and a sound louder than a glacier cracking filled the stairwell. *That's my signal,* Sehrsil thought as she found her way to the base of the stairs.

A cloud of dust and dirt came down fast, making breathing difficult and darkening everything around her. A voice arose over the echoes of the collapsing tower. It was the Vespertian boy shouting directions. Like a winged tide, the crowd turned and moved downstairs.

Sehrsil looked around to ensure that no demons were around. The road was clear, but she unsheathed Spero anyway. The explosion couldn't have gone unnoticed, and it was only a matter of time before the demons came to check the damage, and to look for survivors that could still be useful.

The distinct sound of claws scratching the cobblestone floor confirmed her fear.

"Halt! They're here!" Sehrsil yelled extending her arm with an open palm, trusting that they could see it through the dust, and understand its meaning even if they didn't understand her words. *The sounds are too close, I need to clear the path before we can go anywhere,* she thought without waiting on the Vespertians' reaction.

She turned around — and not a moment too soon. A demon jumped at her from the darkness. Sehrsil stabbed it deep in the abdomen. Big mistake, Spero got caught in the swelling body of the monster while three others were already pouncing on her.

She let herself fall flat in the floor. The movement unstuck Spero at the same time. With uncanny dexterity, she stood up and sliced through the throats of two of them, all in one swing. The fourth one turned around and tried to escape. Sehrsil threw the scepter like a spear and nailed it in the back. With all the demons on sight dead, she had the opportunity to rip a piece of her blouse and cover her face. Her mouth tasted of pulverized rock, and demonic ooze, and breathing had become a challenge. After coughing a few times in a futile effort to bring some relief to her throat, she signaled the Vespertians to follow her.

Sehrsil knew where she wanted to go but she had no idea how to get there. Lowering the bridge and using the main gate was not an option. The explosion must have attracted every demon in the vicinity. Her intuition told her that there should be a passage underneath the moat that connected the tower to the main castle. She just needed to find it. The squeals of incoming demons forced her to guess a path and hope for the best.

The long hall that she entered was dark and humid. She didn't care. The more she advanced, the wetter the floor. Her feet now splashed at every step. She took it as a good sign. The sound of Vespertians' wings brushing against the wall filled the passage. At the end of the path, a closed door brought doubts to Sehrsil's head. If she entered, and the room on the other side was crawling with creatures, everything would have been in vain. She stopped and the pressure of hundreds of bodies pushed her forward. Her chest and legs were compressed between the door and the Vespertians. The decision was made for her. She either opened the door or she would die crushed against it.

"I can't believe it!" Sehrsil exclaimed as she was forced into the room by the Vespertian wave. They had gotten to the exact place where she intended to go: the basement she had used as an entrance the first time she visited the Dark Castle. "Come inside!" she exclaimed as she pulled in every Vespertian she could grab.

The room was crammed with people when Marko arrived, closing the door behind him.

"I didn't doubt you for a second, my friend. Well done!" Sehrsil said to him with a smile as she was trying to maneuver between wings, arms, and bodies, looking for the boy that had helped her before. She needed to make sure he had also made it.

"Kid!" she called when she saw him climbing on top of a barrel. "Thanks for your help, well done." The boy smiled at her and, for the first time since she followed her father into Tenebris, Sehrsil felt she was doing the right thing. "Marko! Come!" She said with renewed energy waving her hand.

"I can't tell if the demons realized the tower collapsing wasn't fortuitous, but whether they did or not, it won't be long before they realize there aren't any bodies below the rubble," Marko said.

"I agree, we need to go, now. Kid, how many of you are strong enough to outfly the demonphantoms?" Sehrsil asked.

"Nobody can. Look," the Vespertian boy said turning around and pointing to his upper back. A metallic ring passed through both wings, joining them together and preventing them from opening.

"That's why you haven't escaped, of course, what a fool, I should have imagined something like this," Sehrsil said. "I just brought you into a dead end. A mortal trap."

"Not necessarily," said Marko. "There may be a way."

"I'm listening," said Sehrsil.

"I can break these rings, I believe. We have enough time to free twenty or thirty Vespertians, the strongest among them. They can escape with us. If we are lucky, the demons will follow us. I'll leave my sword and battleax here. Once the path is clear, the rest of the Vespertians can leave the Dark Castle on foot, walk until you can't see the castle anymore and then use my weapons to break the rest of the rings," Marko said.

"How about the ones that stay behind? Not every demon will chase you," the kid said with a hint of concern in his voice.

"No, Marko is right. Most are already gone. The dragons are flying towards Skyroar. This is Belgoriel's final battle. The Dark Castle will be empty within a couple of periods. Especially if they see a group of Vespertians flying away. There's no reason for the demonic hordes to suspect that some of you would be left behind. Trust me," Sehrsil said. Her tone and her words suggested more confidence than she really had.

"There! You're done, kid," Marko said holding the broken ring in his hand. "Take me to the next one."

One by one, Marko broke the rings of thirty-three Vespertians while the boy explained the plan. They exclaimed foreign phrases and gesticulated with their arms, Sehrsil was fairly sure those weren't words of support. The boy raised his voice and looked at the Vespertians with eyes full of determination and confidence. Sehrsil didn't understand one word he was saying but she got goose bumps from listening to him. After she finished, the Vespertians' look had changed, and their words took on a much gentler tone.

"They'll help, I'll stay here and make sure the rest of my people are safe," the boy said.

"Thank you. Marko, it's time. Let's go!" Sehrsil said walking to the small window that led outside.

"I'll go first, Sehrsil, to ensure you're safe," Marko said.

"That's not needed," Sehrsil answered putting her hand on the edge of the window.

"It is for me. You are still the Queen of Icedorf, and I am still your subject," Marko said.

Sehrsil nodded and moved away. She understood Marko and, although she didn't agree, she respected him enough to comply.

"It's clear, the demons we saw before must have run towards the tower or towards Skyroar," Marko said.

The thirty-three Vespertians passed through the window one by one. Sehrsil took a last look at the boy before climbing up. His eyes, full of strength and innocence, were looking back at her.

"What's your name, boy," she asked.

"Ladruc," he said.

"Ladruc. I'll remember that name. I'm sure I'll hear it again," Sehrsil said.

"Thank you. I won't forget you saved my people," the boy said.

"I didn't, you did," Sehrsil said before disappearing in the darkness outside.

Chapter Ten

Shiroan stood just outside the cave that connected the Sixth and the Seven Seals, at the edge of the narrow path ultimately leading to the Fortress. Even after all this time, he was amazed at the vastness of the world inside the mountain. The orange glow covered every wall and crevice and shared the warmness of the magma with the volcano-dwellers. The crater couldn't be seen from his location, it was most visible directly above the Fifth Seal. The narrow walkway, carved over hundreds of seasons by thousands of people, invited him to consummate the betrayal of the law ruling over his adopted home. As the heat of the moment faded out, the weight of reality settled in. So far, he had accomplished one thing and one thing only: sentencing Kishi, Gregoria and himself to death.

If we undo our steps and go back to the Seventh Seal nobody would find out we left, not even the Conclave, Shiroan thought. *Most importantly, when the Prophecy comes to happen, we'll be at the Seventh Seal, ready to destroy the demonic hordes and keep the Passage to Hell shut. If we take this path, my mistake will not only condemn Gregoria and Kishi, but it may also sentence the Known Territories to Hell. Isn't Ponthos enough of a burden on my shoulders?*

"So, did we come all the way here only to enjoy the view, Blue?" Kishi said from behind pushing him forward with his belly.

Kishi's gesture was all the help Shiroan needed to make up his mind. He couldn't go back, not only because he truly believed on his choice, but also because he was too stubborn to admit defeat. He didn't know how to win, but he knew that any real chance they got passed through getting to the Fortress and talking to the Conclave.

"We can't just take the pathway to the Sixth Seal; chances are the guards will shoot us in sight. I have an idea, wait here," Shiroan said looking up.

"We will, but you better do what you plan to do quickly. My trust is not a bottomless pit," Gregoria said.

Shiroan didn't answer. He was already finding holds for his hands and feet in the crater wall. The distance between him and the narrow ledge increased as he climbed up. A faux movement and he would fall to certain death in the sea of lava. He didn't make any. Testing every single hold before placing his full weight on it, he ascended to the terrace he had seen so many times from the air while riding Kaina. It was a much wider ledge than the one below and it went all the way to the Sixth Seal. He didn't have a plan for when he reached it, but at least he'd be able to assess the situation without being killed.

With his back against the wall, Shiroan walked sideways along the ledge. Sixth Seal guards rarely looked up, but he was not about to test his luck. As he approached the far edge of the path, he decided to crawl the last few steps of the way. The Sixth Seal sat on top of a plain, by the sea of lava. At its tallest, the ceiling was taller than the Fortress, but it steadily shrank as it went inside the mountain. At the lowest point, not even an Oceaner could stand without their head hitting rock. Some elders at the Village told stories about the vast number of architects that died carving it. As far as Shiroan was concerned, the Sixth Seal had been shaped by the magma itself. It was too wide, too deep, and too massive to have been built by people.

Sticking his head out, he observed each tent looking for anything out of the ordinary. Nothing. The ballistae were unattended, a sign that all was quiet. Groups of three or four warriors gathered around small fires, eating frogasus meat.

Think, Shiroan, you can't just show up like this. Everyone knows you are a Seven Warrior now. Best-case scenario they'll chain me to a rock and send a message to the Conclave. If Gildar is there, or talked to Torok before going to the Fortress, they may already think I'm a traitor. We could fight our way through the seal, but not without wounding, or perhaps killing, brave soldiers.

Four guards stood outside Torok's tent, protecting the entrance. It was the regular protocol when Torok held an important encounter, perhaps with Gildar.

I wish you were here, Tabatha, I could really use your eyes, Shiroan thought as he tried unsuccessfully to peek inside. *And your company*.

Realizing he would never be able to do it, he continued perusing the area. Shiroan didn't know what he was looking for, but he hoped to recognize it once he found it.

"Kaina," He murmured.

The drakovore was resting by a small fire. If he could only find a way to attract her attention, she could fly them all out of there without the Sixth Seal guards ever noticing it, but no ideas came to mind. His friend was too far and too asleep. To talk to her, he would have to risk being seen. He decided to wait at least until the meeting at Torok's tent finished, knowing who he was talking to would define what to do next.

"Anything to report?" Gregoria asked, startling Shiroan, who had to regain his balance to avoid falling off the edge.

"Are you insane?" He said, looking at her. She was smiling.

"I could've killed you if I wanted to, some warrior you are."

"You wish, I was focused on the Sixth Seal but would have stopped you at the right moment," Shiroan said realizing he had been so imbued in his machinations that forgot to come back and disclose to Kishi and Gregoria his findings.

"Sure, any sight of Gildar?" Gregoria said.

"Not yet, but Torok is holding an important meeting inside his tent and, knowing what we know, it's probably with Gildar. I'm waiting for the gathering to be over to confirm it," Shiroan said.

"Torok?"

"The commander of the Sixth Seal. I trust him, but he's loyal to Skyroar, and we are fugitives, so we need to assume he'll want us detained."

"I know who he is. I don't trust him, so I'll assume he wants us dead. Look! They're coming out," Gregoria said.

The Sixth Seal battalion commanders exited the tent one by one. Shiroan had trouble catching his breath when he saw Tabatha, almost as if an invisible fist had punched him in the stomach. He peered at Gregoria out of the corner of his eye as he regained his strength. The last thing he needed was being interrogated about a reaction that surprised even himself. The moment he had walked away from her and entered the Seventh Seal, he assumed he would never see her again. Having her so close and yet so far made him realize how much he missed her.

"No sign of Gildar," he said, making a conscious effort to focus on the matter at hand. "Torok is still inside, Gildar may be with him. It's impossible to tell."

"This ledge is getting quite crowded, I need to find another place to hang out," Mardack said.

"What the Hell?" Shiroan exclaimed standing up. "Mardack!

It's so good to see you!"

"Who is this one?" Gregoria said unsheathing Phantomslayer.

"This is Mardack, one of the best warriors you'll ever meet and star member of the Winged Squadron. My squadron. I trust her with my life."

"I also make an incredible wormbread. The secret is using sweaty hands," Mardack said showing her palms, both filthy and humid. "And, of course, picking the fattest worms only –"

"Mardack, we need you to tell us about Gildar. Is he with Torok?" Shiroan interrupted.

"Wait a moment. Shouldn't you be in the Seventh Seal. You're breaking Skyroar's law big time, aren't you? I'll have to place you under arrest," Mardack said with a serious face.

Shiroan didn't know how to react, Gregoria put forward her spear.

"I'm jesting! I'm with you to the end of the world, or to treason, in this case. You can go and come as you please for all I care," Mardack said letting out a hoarse laugh.

"Thank you, Mardack," said Shiroan placing his hand on her shoulder.

"We don't have time for craziness, lady. Is Gildar here or not?" Gregoria said.

"No, he isn't. He went to the Fortress for a special mission and hasn't come back," Mardack explained.

"Mardack, were you aware of Gildar's visits to the Seventh Seal? I never saw him leaving when I lived here," said Shiroan.

"Yes, a few of us had seen his little nocturnal escapades. At the beginning I thought it may be a romantic interest what drove him," Mardack said winking at Gregoria.

"Thread carefully now," Gregoria replied with a killing stare.

"But now I believe it was something else entirely as he used to come back with a package that he gave to a hooded deliverer who, I think, took it to the Fortress. Having you here asking for him confirms he was up to no good," said Mardack talking faster than usual.

"The Hellblood!" Gregoria said. "He was passing it on to someone, the question is who."

"And who would receive it in the Fortress. Mortagong was involved, that's certain, but I imagine he wouldn't risk receiving the delivery himself." said Shiroan.

"The package was Hellblood? So, all is well," Mardack said.

"No. Gildar was stealing Hellblood, we don't know why," said Gregoria.

"Looks like we'll need to get to the Fortress and find out. Let's go down and talk to Kishi," Shiroan said.

"Talk to me about what?" Kishi said showing his smiling face behind them.

"I should've done this alone," Shiroan said with a sigh.

"It's too late now, Blue, we're on this together," said Kishi.

"That's right," Mardack said. "We're a team," she confirmed as she pushed and pulled a few levers. "See you in the camp!" she shouted as she jumped off the cliff. The pigskin wings opened with a mechanical sound, and she glided down with so much grace that it was difficult to believe she wasn't a Vespertian.

"Are we really going down there? Gildar might be gone, but he could have talked with the warriors and alerted them we were coming. We may be forced to fight them. I am aware some of them are your friends, Shiroan, but if attacked, I will defend myself," Gregoria said.

"Without mentioning that we could lose the element of surprise if the news of our escape reaches the Fortress before we do," Kishi added.

"This is a risk, it's true, but a risk I'm willing to take. With Gildar away, we can undo whatever he might have done. We just need to get to Torok unnoticed," Shiroan said.

"I'll play along, but don't hold me responsible if something happens," Gregoria remarked.

"Are we going or what? I'm hungry," Kishi complained.

Going down the wall took them longer than it took Mardack, but even Kishi managed to move fast enough to arrive to the Sixth Seal undetected. Before going to the tent, Shiroan made a small detour to say hi to his best friend.

"Kaina," Shiroan whispered hidden inside an empty barrack.

The drakovore lifted her massive head, straightened her ears, and smelled the air. When she saw her friend, her tail started wagging so hard that she put out a nearby fire. She went to him and licked Shiroan's face with her long, purple tongue.

"Calm down, girl, calm down. I missed you too," Shiroan said hugging her.

"What the Hell is wrong with you, Shiroan? You could be killed for this!" Tabatha exclaimed walking from the side, startling him.

"Will you keep it down? I'm supposed to –" Shiroan stopped talking when his gaze locked with Tabatha's green, deep eyes. Her long brown hair was braided around her head like a crown, her wings, closed behind her back, accentuated the silhouette below her white blouse and pigskin pants. He couldn't look away. "I… you're –" Shiroan couldn't get himself to say what he truly wanted. He said something else instead: "We're on a mission, Skyroar is in danger. Gregoria, Kishi, come out," Shiroan said. The two Seven Warriors emerged from the tent.

"Skyroar is always in danger, what do you mean exactly?" Tabatha asked, looking at Kishi and Gregoria.

"We have evidence that a threat to our survival is growing from the inside, from our very core. Mortagong is up to something that, we suspect, may put an end to Skyroar. Gildar has been stealing Hellblood for him. We must uncover Mortagong's plan and halt it. If we die for this, it'll be a warrior's death," Gregoria said with her usual confidence.

"She's telling the truth," Shiroan said. "Mortagong was also likely behind Ulrik's assassination. We need to find a way to stop him."

"That would be ideal, but Mortagong is not only clever, but he's also the Great Preceptor of Skyroar now. He commands the entirety of the Skyroar army, including you… and me," Torok's voice reached him before he could see him.

"We know. That's why we took the risk of leaving the Seventh Seal. He's the most powerful person in Skyroar. If we don't succeed, all will be lost," Gregoria said.

"Gregoria?" Torok said.

"The one and the same," Gregoria answered.

"You also left the Seal. I can see it's a full-blown rebellion. I thought I'd never see you again. I'm –"

"Save it, Torok. The person I'm now is not the person that left this very seal so many seasons ago. Let the past stay in the past," Gregoria said.

"So, what now, Blue?" Kishi asked, breaking a suddenly

awkward silence.

"Now we talk," Torok said. "In my tent. In private. I need to understand what you have on Mortagong and why you think Skyroar is in peril. Tabatha, please join us. Mardack, keep guard. Nobody enters or sees who's with me. If the news spread, our hand may be forced."

"No one in. Not one word. Got it, chief," Mardack said.

"Shiroan, care to explain what's going on?" Torok asked once inside.

"Well, Kishi and Gregoria would probably do a better job than me at explaining, since they have witnessed how these events have unfolded from the beginning."

"But my enquiry was directed at you, wasn't it?" Torok said, keeping his eyes on him. "When I have a question for them, it'll be evident."

"Yes, sir, of course. We have reason to believe Ulrik was murdered and Mortagong was behind it. We know that Gildar has been stealing Hellblood and delivering it to Mortagong for some time, although we can't figure out why. We think Skyroar is in danger and Mortagong being elected Great Preceptor could precipitate the outcome.

"Going to the Fortress, finding out what's going on and stopping it felt like the right thing to do, regardless of the risk. Not only because we are the only people aware of the situation, but also because we are, after all, the Seven Warriors, or at least three of them," said Shiroan.

"Let's straighten things out first," Torok said. "I command the Sixth Seal. I owe allegiance to Skyroar, respect to the Conclave and loyalty to the Great Preceptor. Our opinions matter as long as they don't interfere with the sacred duty bestowed upon us. We're in charge of ensuring the safety of the Seventh Seal and the Hidden Chamber. That's our primary responsibility and our biggest burden," Torok said.

"I understand, sir, but –" Shiroan said.

"As of now, you are fugitives of Skyroar," Torok said interrupting him.

"Have you even heard what Shiroan said? Skyroar is in danger, it's –" Gregoria said with a mix of frustration and contained rage.

"I heard it. Let me finish," Torok said twisting his moustache as he locked his eyes on Gregoria.

"I'm listening," Gregoria said.

"Our sworn obligation is to detain or kill anybody or anything trying to reach the Seventh Seal uninvited. You three are going in the opposite direction. Why would we stop loyal Skyroar citizens traveling to the Fortress? Do you see any reason to do so, Tabatha?"

Tabatha didn't answer. She had her eyes on Shiroan and her mind somewhere else.

"Tabatha?" Torok asked again in a firmer voice.

"No, sir. Yes. What you said."

"Just know that going back to the Seventh Seal will be a different matter entirely. You'll have to go through Sixth Seal troops, my troops, to reach it. An experience that has been described, not without reason, as quite uncomfortable. I strongly recommend ensuring that the actions you undertake to change the direction of the unfolding events will yield the expected results. It's you who will define how we will proceed when we meet again, if we ever do."

"Thank you, sir. You're bending your responsibilities as much as you possibly can to assist us, I appreciate it. This isn't the first time you've come through for me," Shiroan said.

"Don't let it be the last. Now go. And be careful, there aren't a lot of Cloudhunters, Solisians, or Icedorf-Elgarian hybrids in Skyroar. You'll shine like our suns in a cloudless morning. Tabatha, get them some robes before they leave, preferably hooded. Those should help," Torok said.

"Thanks, Torok," Gregoria said hugging him tightly. "And I'm sorry."

"Looks like you have a story to tell, Gregoria, I've never seen you hugging anyone. I bet you and big moustache met before," said Kishi with a smile as they walked out of the tent.

"Wait!" Torok commanded. The trio stopped on their tracks. "It wouldn't be unreasonable to think that, if tribulation does find you, an honored and respected member of the Sixth Seal might be able to devise a suitable solution, either by the power of words or the force of the sword. Tabatha?"

"Yes, sir," Tabatha said.

"Would you be willing to accompany Shiroan and his fellow warriors in their quest?"

"I'll do what my commander tells me to do. I'm a soldier," she answered hiding her smile behind her wing.

"It's settled, then. Tabatha will join your group. Good luck in your quest." Torok said.

"Give me a moment to gather some robes. I'll catch up with you before long," Tabatha said.

"Be fast, Vespertian," said Gregoria as she walked to the road that led to the Fortress.

"Kaina!" he shouted to her friend, who was laying down on a flat basalt rock, looking at them with eyes full of curiosity. "It's time to go. We've got work to do."

The drakovore jumped to her paws and trotted to him wagging her tail.

"I hope you know what you're doing, Blue." Kishi said catching up with him. "If we fail, the Hidden Chamber falls, the Prophecy collapses and, with it, Skyroar."

"We won't fail, Kishi," Shiroan said with confidence in his voice. "I don't know how."

Chapter Eleven

The twin suns had long disappeared behind the horizon. Mehrik and Goldenmane walked in silence. The death of Galanta had left a profound void inside them. Not only they were deeply hurt, but also hopelessly lost. Mehrik's plans began and ended with Galanta. She would have known the precise way to defeat Mortagong. His own role was nothing more than communicating what he knew and following her commands. With her gone, somebody else would have to carry the burden of imagining a strategy and, judging by Goldenmane's attitude, it would not be her brother.

The night was beautiful, cloudless, clear, and warm. It reminded him of the many times he sat with Momo on the porch to sing old Oceano songs. Skyroar already had too few of these nights, if they failed, there may never be a peaceful night again. The responsibility was almost too much to bear. Almost.

"The summit is in sight," Mehrik said noticing the edge of the mountain not too far away.

"What do we do now?" Goldenmane asked.

"That's a good question. One that I can't answer yet. I wish the Seven Warriors were here. They'd come up with a plan in a heartbeat," Mehrik said climbing the last large obstacle before reaching the peak.

"What makes you think we'd know what to do?" Kishi said showing his round head and extending his hand to help Mehrik up.

"Mehrik, watch out!" Goldenmane said taking his battleax and jumping forward.

"Kishi!" Mehrik said with a smile.

"The Seven Warrior?" Asked Goldenmane, stopping on his tracks.

"The one and only," said Kishi.

"But wait, if you're here... Is the Hidden Chamber —" Mehrik said.

"Take it easy, buddy, the Hidden Chamber is in as good shape as ever," Kishi said.

"How is that possible? Leaving the Seventh Seal is punished by death," Goldenmane said.

"We had our reasons. I hope that's not going to be a problem, mate," Kishi said closing his hand around the handle of his battleax.

"Not yet," Goldenmane said under his breath.

"We?" Mehrik said.

"Yes, we," Gregoria answered stepping forward. Kaina and Tabatha landed behind her.

"I know you, deliverer," Shiroan said dismounting. "I thought you were imprisoned. Did you escape?"

"Mehrik is no deliverer, Cloudhunter. He's a true warrior," said Goldenmane.

"And this is Goldenmane, Galanta's brother. She was murdered. We watched her die," Mehrik said quickly and with a straightforward tone, holding back his tears.

"What? How?" Gregoria asked.

"Mortagong is a traitor. He has been stealing our Hellblood to give it to our enemies. He and his band of crooks want the downfall of Skyroar. We just don't know how they plan to achieve it. Even Louriel, supposedly a friend to my sister, is involved. Mortagong might have given the order, but Louriel held the blade that killed her. We would have been next if we didn't escape," said Goldenmane.

"So, you're aware of what we are facing," said Kishi.

"If you're talking about Mortagong's being a traitor, we know it all too well. I saw him myself in Tenebris making deals with Belgoriel," said Mehrik with a grim voice.

"You went to Tenebris and survived? I don't believe it. Something smells rotten here," Shiroan said, taking a step towards Mehrik.

"We have no time for this, Shiroan, we must trust them. They have no reason for lying to us," Gregoria said. "If we join forces, we still can stop Mortagong. Will you help us, Mehrik?"

"I will, but that may not be enough," Mehrik said pointing to the West Wall.

"The demonic hordes!" exclaimed Goldenmane.

"Is this what you were expecting, Mehrik?" asked Tabatha.

"I'm afraid it is," Mehrik said with his eyes glued in the scene in front of him.

Beyond the West Wall, still at a great distance, an army of hundreds upon hundreds of demons was illuminated by the green fire of the battalion of dragons traversing the night sky.

"This is the largest demonic attack ever, by a long shot," Tabatha said focusing on the horizon with her uncanny Vespertian eyes. "Including more dragons that I even thought possible. Where did they found the Vespertians to create them?" she added with a breaking voice.

"This must be Belgoriel's final strike. The battle for the Hidden Chamber," Shiroan said. "Leaving the Seventh Seal may have been a bad idea after all, we should come back."

"Too late for that, Shiroan. It's a long trip. Going back means we can't help here or there. I say we stay, and we fight," said Gregoria.

"It gets worse," Tabatha said. "The guards of the West Wall are deserting, all of them. The demonic hordes will find no resistance!"

"Mortagong is giving the orders. He's surrendering Skyroar to Belgoriel. That's their agreement," Mehrik said.

"No! It can't be! They are throwing ropes down the Wall for the demonic hordes to climb. The Villagers will be massacred! How could Mortagong do this to his own people?" Tabatha said with her uncanny eyes glued to the events unfolding in front of them.

"No. Not to his people. In Mortagong's eyes the Hundred Kingdoms are his people. He wants to destroy Skyroar and all it represents. I'm afraid he'll succeed," Goldenmane said looking down as he let out a deep growl. "We can't stop that. It's impossible. We are doomed."

The group fell silent after Goldenmane's gloomy prediction. They stared at the upcoming catastrophe as if they had been transformed into marble statues. Overwhelmed by the circumstances, they couldn't find the strength to respond, or the will to react. Despair had taken hold of their essence. Not even Hishiro would be able to save them now.

Mehrik couldn't help but contemplate the bizarre beauty of the spectacle unfolding in front of him. Audax and Ingens rose from the west, purple, red and orange joined the green fire palette, painting the sky like a canvas. The sea of grey demons expanded like a massive tablecloth, covering every available space. The tenuous echoes of claws against gravel reached his ears and the dragon wings whooshing in the air created a mesmerizing sound, almost like music. A song of death.

An Oceaner, a Vespertian, a Cloudhunter, a Solis, a Lionkin, an Elgarian-Icedorfer hybrid, and a drakovore stood at the summit of the Skyroar volcano. Exhausted, dirty, and hungry, they looked like warriors after a taxing battle; with the difference that their battle hadn't yet begun. The fate of the Known Territories rested upon their shoulders. And its weight was almost unbearable to carry.

Mehrik looked at each one of them. He admired the fire in their eyes, shared their determination, and revered their courage. With clarity he had never experienced before, a plan took form in his head.

"Lork and I must stop Mortagong. He's the key," Mehrik said breaking the silence. Lork nodded once.

"You can't go by yourself, you'll be killed," Shiroan said.

"I'll go with you, my friend," Goldenmane said. "I'll protect you."

"Protect Skyroar. Look at the hordes coming our way. Every warrior is important, but you are indispensable if we want even the slightest chance at winning," Mehrik said with a firm, confident voice.

Goldenmane nodded.

"When I pulled you in to give you Ulrik's Hellblood, all those cycles ago, I saw something in your eyes, something showing me not only that I could trust you, but also the great fortitude hiding within you. I wasn't wrong. Your strength is starting to show, Mehrik. Go, do what you must, my friend. We have your back," Kishi said giving Mehrik a tight hug.

"Thank you. Let Hishiro give you the might," Mehrik said lost inside the arms like tree trunks of the Seven Warrior.

"To send the demons back to Hell," Kishi replied.

"Let's go Lork. It's time."

Mehrik descended using the same path that had brought them there. His legs complained at each step. His lungs felt as if filled with lava. His mind assessed every possible way to accomplish what he had promised. Each one of them was a dead end.

"Perhaps I made a mistake, Lork, I have no idea how to get to Mortagong, let alone force him to reveal his plan. The moment I enter the Fortress, I'll be killed on sight. Without Goldenmane, I won't be able to put much of a fight. While I think of a solution, let's go to the Village. I want to check on the East Wall. If Mortagong went as far as cutting a deal with Belgoriel, he may have done the same with the King of the Hundred Kingdoms. Not that I can do anything about it, but it'll give me some more time to think," Mehrik said looking up to Lork.

As a deliverer, Mehrik had walked between the East and West Walls many times before. A feeling of despair and desperation possessed him every time he went West. That sensation accompanied him now, even if he was going in the opposite direction.

Most of the beliefs he had held sacred throughout his life had been pulverized in the past few cycles. From his unconditional loyalty to Skyroar, to the blind hatred against the enemies in the outside, everything was now upside down.

He had made friends from foes and foes from friends. He had gone to forbidden places and done unthinkable things. He had fought and he had killed. Yes, Mehrik, the humble deliverer, had come a long way.

The question he asked himself was: would it be enough to do what needed to be done? Did he have the strength? He didn't know, but he was surely about to find out.

Mehrik stopped and looked at the East Wall. A continuous line of archers stood on top, facing toward the Hundred Kingdoms, alert but immobile. A row of infantry soldiers was placed behind them, ready to recharge quivers or fight any invaders fool enough to attempt the deadly climb. At the bottom, a handful of deliverers run up the wooden stairs carrying weapons and water.

"What is happening beyond the East Wall?" Mehrik said squinting his eyes. On top of what looked like an improvised stage made with upside down carts covered with pigskin, two Elgarians wearing black robes seemed to be addressing a crowd of soldiers. "Are those... are those Conclave members?"

Lork thinks. Lork fly there.

"Good idea, go. Tell me what you see," The black bird squealed in agreement and flew closer to the gathering.

As Mehrik searched for a better vantage point to make sense of the strange occurrence, additional details became evident, including something that stole the blood from his face and sent shivers down his spine: not only the small metal door was open, probably to allow the Conclave members to come and go, but a few guards were rebuilding the mechanism to pull open the main gate. The levers, chains and cogs had been removed many seasons ago, after a group of Hundred Kingdoms soldiers entered the city and attempted to open the gate to let their army inside.

What are you doing, Mortagong? Are you offering Skyroar to the Hundred Kingdoms? If that's the case, you must be getting something big in return. What could it be? You may think you're playing them, but it could very well be the other way around, Mehrik thought.

Whatever the case might be Mortagong was well aware of the situation at the East Wall. So aware in fact, that he was at that very moment climbing the steps to the improvised stage to join the Conclave Members. His cane and red Great Preceptor robe were impossible to miss.

What could they be saying? he thought before noticing the moose galloping at them. The imposing Elgarian riding it was tall, and broad shouldered. He wore a golden chainmail, a crimson cape, and a silver helmet with a long purple plume. The soldiers surrounding the platform opened a corridor as he approached with a majestic pace. Mortagong and his companion extended their arms. The rider took off his helmet and dismounted. His full light brown beard and hair covered most of his face. Mehrik was sure it was Garkun, King of the Hundred Kingdoms.

Mehrik walked faster, then ran. He knew in his essence that he was in the presence of a pivotal moment. Something big was happening. The King of the Hundred Kingdoms waved to a cheering crowd. Lork circled the area a couple of times before deciding to perch on top of a nearby boulder. Regardless of how fast he moved, Mehrik wouldn't be able to make it down the crater, across the Village and through the Wall on time, or without been seen.

What can I do? I need to get closer. I must listen, Mehrik thought. *Lork won't be able to tell me every word, our link doesn't work like that.*

"That's it!" Mehrik exclaimed, remembering the odd, dreamlike experience he had back in the dungeons when he was escaping from prison through the waterfall. When lying on the ground, half unconscious, and with his head bleeding, he felt as if his essence left his body, flew through the air, and entered foreign eyes. Seahawk eyes. *It was Lork! It had to be. I somehow was able to see and hear from his perspective, I think. There won't be a better moment to try it than now! After all, Momo always told me black seahawks were the rarest of creatures. This may be one of the reasons why.*

Looking around, Mehrik saw a pile of medium size and large boulders. He squeezed in the narrow space between them until he was completely out of sight. With legs crossed, eyes closed, and hands against his knees, he called Lork with his mind. Nothing happened. The bird was too far to respond. *This can't be how. I'm not attempting to talk; I'm trying to reach into his essence.*

With a deep breath, he thought about his black, shiny feathers, sharp orange claws and fierce yellow eyes. He thought about his unmatched bravery, incontestable loyalty, and unreserved love. He thought about their tight bond, about their friendship. They were inseparable, and always have been, almost as if they were one, they were one. One.

"...roar is not the real enemy, at least not all of us. Tenebris is the enemy, Icedorf and Oceano are the enemy. Not us. We have the same goal. We want the Hundred Kingdoms to rule the Known Territories for a thousand times a thousand seasons. Even though most of the Skyroar citizens were once part of the Hundred Kingdoms, we have been condemned to forever see our own people die just outside our borders. Our old rulers, the ones that held the power, like that Lionkin, Galanta, made sure of that. I'm here to change that. Perhaps to do so this very cycle. Who's with me?" Mortagong shouted lifting his cane in the air.

The crowd returned his enthusiasm clashing their swords and spears and cheering loudly.

"I've fought for you, we've fought for you," he said holding the hands of the two Conclave Members that were by his side.

Louriel! Mehrik thought. *How low have you fallen? Wasn't enough to be the murderer of your best friend?*

"Risking our lives, we were able to regain control of Skyroar and unmask those wishing to see us fall. We painfully collected as much Hellblood as we could, and we are ready to distribute it to those willing to join us," he said taking the Hellblood flask that Louriel was giving him. The crowd went wild.

"Let the first Hellblood flask be for you, milord," Mortagong said handing the vial to Garkun. "Take it. All I ask in return is the right to lead the Hundred Kingdoms to victory against the demonic hordes. All I ask is for you to bow down to me. All I ask is your crown. A modest price to pay in exchange for a most rewarding victory and the lives of our people."

"Are you threatening me? Have you completely lost your mind, Mortagong? How could you believe for a second that I'll renounce my crown in favor of a madman? What makes you think you can lead my people when you were unable to lead Skyroar?" Garkun said taking one step towards the Conclave member.

"Don't make the mistake of confusing the puppets with the puppeteer, little man. If I had no control over Skyroar, how do you explain this Hellblood? You call me a madman, is it insane to have the courage to save one's ancestors? To bring us back to greatness? Isn't it perhaps crazier to barter the lives of your soldiers, of your children, in exchange of one more cycle in the throne?" Mortagong said with a smirk, looking at the crowd below. "Is this the king you want? A king that will sacrifice his own brother to keep a crown above his head. Oh, wait, you haven't told them."

"How dare you! Killfred, my beloved brother, died so we could live. He's our greatest hero. I would have taken his place gladly!" Garkun exclaimed.

"Really?"

"You heard me," Garkun said in a whisper. His face had lost all trace of color, his lips were trembling.

"Well, prove it then. This cycle you can redeem yourself, not by saving your brother, it's much too late for that, but by saving the kingdom you stole from him. Your subjects, after all, are the ones sacrificing their lives fighting without a plan, a path, or a worthy leader. They're nothing more than bargaining chips to allow their king to be king just a little longer. You can save them all, this cycle, this moment even, if you just comply with my very reasonable demand. What do you say, my friend?" Mortagong said with a wide smile.

"How dare you? You can't talk to me like this in front of my people! You're still an Elgarian and I'm still your king. Your insolence will not be tolerated any further," Garkun said unsheathing his sword and pressing it against Mortagong's chest.

"I would thread carefully, my king. There's no need of spilling blood among brothers," Said Louriel as she took out the dagger concealed in her robe and placed it on the King's throat. It was still tainted with Galanta's blood.

"Is this true?" Said one of the soldiers nearest to the stage. "I've got three children and a wife. When I left, I swore to them I was going to war to make them free. Isn't that what we're doing?"

"Well, Garkun," Mortagong said. "Are you going to grace us with a response? What's your big plan? What are you really fighting for?"

"I'm a king, Mortagong. I answer to no one."

"You'll answer to me," Mortagong replied pushing the sword to the side and taking a step forward.

"Is that what you think? You're here with four guards and two Conclave members. Your only leverage is the content of these carts. Only my kindness, no, my pity, is keeping you alive. I could as well save me some time, kill you all, and take the Hellblood."

"Be my guest, my liege, but you may have some trouble commanding the respect of your troops now," Mortagong said. "Without mentioning that the Hellblood is useless unless a very precise last step is performed."

"If that's the case, I'll torture you first, then kill you when you've spilled every secret kept inside your rotten essence. Detain them!" Garkun shouted looking towards his soldiers.

Nobody moved.

"I said detain them!" Garkun yelled louder.

"It looks like they have made their choice. Don't feel bad, Garkun, relieving you of the crown is nothing but a favor. You can stop trying to be something you are clearly not. You're less than the shadow of your brother. You are the worm he stepped on when he walked, the filth on his boot, the reason why we are no closer to ending this war than we were ten seasons ago. You've never been more than an embarrassment for your people," Mortagong said.

"Not to mention," said Aura, the Minister of War as she pointed to the East Wall, "that several companies of archers are waiting for my signal to shoot if we are betrayed."

"Not many options, aren't they?" Mortagong said pushing Garkun back and lowering his sword. "This is called strategy and is how a true king act. Not that you have ever acted like one."

"My loyal subjects! Don't listen to this traitor. Come forward and defend your king!" Garkun shouted just to be met with the silence of the crowd.

"Convinced?" Mortagong asked.

"I did it for you!" Garkun exclaimed with a breaking voice, as he pushed Louriel back and turned to his people. "Do I have to remind you where Tenebris stands? It's in the land of my family, of our ancestors. Belgoriel destroyed our towns and killed our people until it became evident that we were fighting a fight we couldn't win. I went to Tenebris. I risked my own life to talk to Belgoriel and save what I could of my Hundred Kingdoms. I had but one choice, I either paid tribute by sending soldiers to battle against Skyroar, or the demons would transform the Hundred Kingdoms into Hell. What would you have done in my place?" tears were streaming down the king's eyes.

"You lied to us! Coward! You sent us to die!" The recriminations and insults escalated and echoed across every row. Then, slowly but without pause, their words mutated, changed, until all that could be heard was one single word, more than a word, a clamor: "Mortagong! Mortagong!"

Mortagong smiled and looked at the king that had become a man in front of his eyes. The fallen monarch observed his people with his face purple with rage. He threw the Hellblood flask at Mortagong's feet and left the stage. With a quick nod of his head, Mortagong indicated to the crowd to let him go. Garkun untied his cape, which floated more than fell to the ground. He took out his helmet, smashed it against a pine and mounted his moose. The eyes of his people followed him as he was lost in the distance.

Unnoticed by everyone but the people closest to him, Mortagong made a subtle gesture to a high ranked officer standing by his side. With nothing but a slight nod, the officer left the stage, jumped on his moose, and rode after Garkun.

"My children," Mortagong said opening his arms. "Let the bygones be bygones. Without Hellblood, that excuse of a king won't last long, the demonic hordes have been unleashed upon us. He's already dead. But us, we are alive! And now it's our time, the time for freedom! Swear loyalty to me and receive the Hellblood you have always deserved. Serve me and we will together rise to the highest of places to rule this world forever!"

A soldier in the third row came forward. He walked with short steps to the stage. "I'm ready, my king," he said kneeling.

"Louriel, give him a flask of Hellblood," Mortagong

commanded.

Louriel signaled the soldier to approach her as she placed a shallow basin on the ground. "Open your hand," she said, proceeding to make a shallow cut in the middle of his palm with her dagger.

Thick drops of blood fell in the container. The soldier gasped but didn't resist. Louriel grabbed the sample and, with dexterous moves that concealed her hands from prying eyes, combined it with secret herbs before pouring the mix inside one of the Hellblood flasks.

"Come, take it, this Hellblood is yours. It will protect you against the demonphantoms and preserve your essence, but only yours, no one else's," Louriel said.

Mortagong looked at her and nodded. She raised her hand inviting the next person. A line formed in front of the stage. One by one, the soldiers gave blood and took away their Hellblood.

When the first non-Elgarian arrived, a Solis officer, Mortagong raised his hand, requesting her to stop. "Give me your blade." He asked. The Solis woman complied. "Now Kneel."

"Yes, milord," she said bringing her left knee to the ground and looking down. Mortagong held the sword high with both hands and let it fall on the back of her neck. The woman fell to the ground as a pool of blood formed on the stage. The crowd looked at each other confused, not knowing how to react.

"Only Elgarians are to receive this gift. Only Elgarians deserve it!" Mortagong said. He didn't have to say anything else.

The Elgarians, the vast majority of the Hundred Kingdoms people, looked around, zeroing on their preys, ready for the kill. Unsheathing their swords, they executed whoever wasn't one of them. Mortagong smiled. Aura, the Minister of War, cheered. The Hundred Kingdoms army cheered with her.

"Come here, my children. Come and receive this treasure. The protection only we deserve. The Hundred Kingdoms will now be the most powerful people in the Known Territories, and soon, we'll rule over every living thing. Let's prepare for war. We'll attack tomorrow when the twin suns are halfway up in the sky."

Mehrik came out of his trance screaming in horror. He struggled to understand what he just saw. If he didn't do something, Skyroar would fall under the Hundred Kingdoms forces and thousands would be killed or made prisoners, Solis, Vespertians, hybrids. The question was what he could do. He was a fugitive, a traitor. Nobody would believe him. There was only one person in the Village that could help him, but before getting to him, he needed to see someone else.

Chapter Twelve

Kaina rode the warm air currents around the Skyroar volcano with the majesty and the confidence of the only creature in the Known Territories strong enough to hunt dragons. The stamina of the drakovore knew no boundaries. She carried a heavy load. Transporting Shiroan, Kishi, Goldenmane and Gregoria on her back made her look small. Still, she flew with her usual grace and swiftness. Tabatha was right behind her, if she had trouble keeping the pace, it didn't show beyond the drops of sweat rolling in her forehead.

Shiroan had always wondered how the demonic hordes managed to kill so many drakovores, perhaps all of them but Kaina. His memories of the massacre of the City in the Sky were blurry patches in his mind. To him, life started with Kaina rescuing him from the flames of his home and flying him to Skyroar.

The additional hurdles she had to face, and the enemies she had to fight to save him were impossible for him to remember. Kaina's reasons were her own, Shiroan didn't care. He only wished that, one cycle, he could return the gesture. So far, it was Kaina the one saving him from certain death, again and again.

She was without a doubt the noblest, fiercest, and most reliable warrior in the Known Territories. He trusted her with his life. Having her around made him better. The drakovore represented all he aspired to be. As they faced the largest demonic attack Skyroar had ever seen, he just worried he had drawn her friend into a battle they could not hope to win.

The demons painted the ground grey as far as he could see. Hooked ropes and ladders hung every few steps, between battlements. No guards were in sight. Not a single arrow was shot. The gravity of the situation hit Shiroan right in the stomach as they got closer. It wasn't possible for a handful of exhausted warriors to stop what was coming. They were going to die.

"Let's look for an empty patch in the Wall and land there,"

Shiroan said pulling the reins to the left.

"Does it really matter what we do here?" Gregoria asked as she pointed to the Sky, covered with dragons, too many to count but more than enough to break into the crater and reach the Hidden Chamber.

"It sure does, my grumpy friend. We can't be everywhere at once. Let's worry about this first, then we'll take care of the dragons," Kishi said jumping to the Wall. He was smiling, as usual.

"I agree," Shiroan said. "Tabatha, it's time to show off those amazing archery skills you've got. Get to a battlement and take down as many demons as you can. Kishi, Goldenmane, go cut as many ropes and ladders as possible to minimize the entry points. Gregoria can deal with any demons that make it to the top. Her weapon can kill demonphantoms."

"Who made you the leader of this mission, Shiroan?" Gregoria said.

"Now it's not the time, Gregoria. It's a good plan. Let's go do it," Kishi said.

"I'll go hunt some dragons," Shiroan said jumping back to the saddle.

"What a surprise!" Tabatha said as she released the first arrow.

"What would you have me do?" He asked. "Those dragons will go straight to the Seven Seal if I don't stop them."

"Have you seen how many of them there are? Twenty drakovores and five hundred warriors, all as stubborn as you, wouldn't be able to halt the attack. But please, don't let us keep you, go away, Shiroan. That's what you do best. It's not that we need you here to face a thousand monsters. We'll be fine without you. We always are," Tabatha said turning to shoot another arrow.

Shiroan didn't move, his eyes were fixed on Tabatha. Her dexterity was uncanny. She shot arrow after arrow in what looked like a seamless stream, stopping only to take a new quiver from the ground.

Her comment had lodged deep in his essence. It angered him because it was true. He wished to ride to the sky and face unsurmountable odds in an unwinnable battle, so he didn't have to see any of his friends die. So, he didn't have to see Tabatha die. Her eyes showed him the same thing he saw in them when Ponthos was killed: disappointment. That couldn't be the last gaze he got from her.

With a quick movement of his hand, Shiroan unlocked the saddlebags and jumped to the ground. Reaching below Kaina's body, he untied the saddle and let it hit the floor. As he released the collar and the bearing rein, he looked at Kaina in the eyes. She couldn't speak, but it was clear to him that she knew exactly what was happening.

"You're my best friend and I'd like nothing more than battle with you, girl. But the people of Skyroar need me. Tabatha needs me. If I go with you, I'll just slow you down. Here I can make a difference, trust me. You're a drakovore, Kaina, the most fearsome beast in the Known Territories. I'd ask you to go away and hide until this is over, but I know you too well and respect you too much to even attempt it. Do what you must, Kaina. Go hunt some dragons!" He said patting the side of her neck. "But, please, be careful," he whispered as the majestic animal took flight.

Three demons approached them. Tabatha was cornered between them and the turret when Shiroan arrived. With her right hand, she tried to dislodge her sword out of the ribcage of one of them, her left hand brandished a small hunting dagger, slicing and cutting the pale skin of the creatures without inflicting meaningful damage. Shiroan adjusted his helmet, unsheathed his twin swords from the covers on his back and ran forward.

He cut clean the head of the nearest demon and put his back against the turret, by Tabatha's side.

"I hope you didn't stay for me," Tabatha said as she recovered her sword and stabbed another one in the stomach. "I can take care of myself."

"You don't have to tell me. But the real question is, how many more than me can you kill?" He said slicing the throat of another demon. "Three!"

"One!" Tabatha said. "For a total of seven! You better start catching up, loser," she said laughing as she cut down two ropes with one swing before grabbing her bow again.

"How are you doing back there, Gregoria?" Shiroan asked.

Gregoria was the most skilled warrior Shiroan had ever met, not counting himself, of course, and it showed on the field. Holding Phantomslayer with both hands, she sliced a demon's throat with a wide upper movement, and then twisted her wrist as she turned her spear to nail the demonphantom with the other end. Without blinking, she moved to the next target while cutting down yet another ladder. The squeals of the desperate demons falling to their deaths filled the air.

"Far better than you, I assure you. For starters, I was here early and I'm not wasting my time talking," she said as she cut the abdomen open of the demon behind her.

We may even win, Shiroan thought looking at Goldenmane in the distance lifting a demon above his head and throwing it down the Wall, *how can anyone be strong enough to do that?* he thought.

Then he heard the howling.

A deafening sound like the enraged lament of a thousand grieving mothers filled his eyes with tears and instilled fear in his essence. It entered his eardrums uninvited and brought him to his knees. Forced to let go of his swords to cover his ears, he squatted and waited for the unnatural screech to pass.

"You're welcome," Gregoria said removing her sword from the demon about to sink its claws on Shiroan's back.

"Did you hear it?" Shiroan asked.

"Yes, we all did, take this piece of cloth, put it in your ears. The situation just went from dreadful to hopeless."

"What do you mean?" Shiroan asked. A powerful thump that made the Wall tremble under their feet answered his question.

The four warriors ran to the edge of the Wall and looked down. Gregoria was right. They may not be able to win after all.

"Belgoriel," Goldenmane confirmed to the group. "I knew it was big, but never thought it was a giant."

"Look at the veins across his body, they are shining green, I've only seen that in dragons," Tabatha added.

"It's trying to break through," Kishi said.

"Trying? It's halfway there already!" Gregoria yelled from the edge of the Wall as she signaled the deep dent that Belgoriel's mace had created.

The demons were pouring in from everywhere now, many of them had made it to the ground and were running towards the Fortress and the Village. Shiroan felt as if he was battling against the roaring winds of a winter storm.

"This is the end, Skyroar! You hear me? This is the cycle the Gateway to Hell opens," Belgoriel roared as he hit the Wall with such force that the vibration took down every demon climbing it.

"What's happening? Why am I crying?" Kishi asked.

"I think it's Belgoriel's voice. It rips through our essences and fills them with angst." Gregoria said.

"The Wall won't resist many more of those, we must stop him," Tabatha said releasing the bow from her back and taking a handful of arrows from her quiver. She shot one, three, ten times. The arrows looked like pins in the creature's skin. Belgoriel didn't even bother looking up. Shiroan took a bow and quiver from the floor and joined Tabatha. The result was no different. Belgoriel was impervious to every attack.

"Tabatha, I need to go down and confront that monster face to face, there's no other way," said Shiroan.

"I'll go with you then," Tabatha said.

"No, please stay. You're needed this side of the Wall. You're the best archer amongst us. Goldenmane, Gregoria and Kishi will try to keep at bay the demons that avoid your arrows. You're also the only one able to fly. If a message needs to be delivered to Torok, you're the one that can get to him the fastest," Shiroan said.

"You are also needed, and you still are planning to go, just like you almost did before. Just go, Shiroan," Tabatha said looking away.

"I stayed before because you were right, Tabatha. Here I could do more. Kaina can kill the same number of dragons with or without me. This is different. When Belgoriel enters Skyroar, everything will be lost. I need to at least attempt to stop it."

"But… Belgoriel is down there Shiroan, Belgoriel! You may not come back to me."

"Great confidence you have in me, I see," Shiroan said forcing a smile.

"You know what I mean, Belgoriel is as strong as forty of us, perhaps more. This is a one-way mission, no question about it. Let us at least go with you."

"We've killed hundreds of demons already. If we were not here, those demons would be on their way to the Village, the Fortress, and the Hidden Chamber. Also, if I'm killed, you three will need to find a way to stop Belgoriel."

"I know when you are right because those are the moments when I hate you, Shiroan. This is one of those moments. I must stay. You must go. But you better don't die, or I'll find you, wherever you are, I promise!" she said.

"I've survived worse," Shiroan said with a smirk as he stepped on the edge of the Wall, looked down, winked at Tabatha, and jumped. As he fell, he maneuvered his body to land on Belgoriel's oozing shoulders. Before the demon could understand what had happened, Shiroan unsheathed his swords and sank them in the creature's wrinkled neck.

It wasn't his brightest moment.

Belgoriel grabbed Shiroan's right arm and sent him flying against the Wall as if he was weightless. When he hit the ground, five demons surrounded him. With his blades deep in Belgoriel's chest, he could only take the dagger attached to his boot.

"Ready when you are," he said with a smile.

"Halt!" Belgoriel roared as he broke the hilt of the swords, leaving the blades inside his colossal body. "A Cloudhunter, are you not?" he added bending forward and placing one of his thick, slimy fingers in Shiroan's face.

Shiroan looked at the monster in front of him with eyes full of tears. Every word uttered by Belgoriel pierced his ears and darkened his essence. Tall like a tree, and wider than six moose put together, Belgoriel was one of a kind. A creature able to consume a limitless number of essences and keep them all inside its massive body. The green flame spilled from his mouth, ears, and nose as it spoke.

According to the sacred scriptures, Belgoriel had never left the Dark Tower since the cycle he entered it. For countless seasons, it had commanded the demons from its throne made of bone and rotten flesh. Its mere presence, Shiroan was certain, meant that the demonic hordes were attempting their final attack. If he could stop Belgoriel, Skyroar and the Prophecy might stand a chance.

"Interesting, I thought we had killed you all. You seem unaware of the power your kin hold, otherwise you wouldn't be attempting something as stupid as this. It doesn't matter now, you're as good as dead," Belgoriel said with overlapping words that echoed forever inside Shiroan's head, as if hundreds of voices were talking at the same time.

"We'll see about that," Shiroan whispered with eyes full of tears.

"We shall, indeed," said Belgoriel unsheathing a sword two times Shiroan's height. "Kill him!" He ordered inflating his pale, varicose chest as he screamed.

Only his dagger separated Shiroan from the six demons charging him. There was no time to think, only to react. He went after the leftmost demon and, sliding on the gravel path, he sliced both its ankles. It squealed in pain and fell to the floor. He was able to use the same strategy one more time before the rest squatted and moved forward, taking any available space. So near were the greyish bony hides and yellow claws, that the ooze from their bodies was dripping in Shiroan's nose and mouth, making him gag.

Shiroan moaned when the vicious claws of another demon sank on his right thigh. *If I don't find a way out of this mess I'm done for,* Shiroan thought as he felt sharp teeth biting his shoulder.

All he could see were veiny legs, grayish torsos, and yellow paws. The only way out was up. Stabbing the chest of the demon in front of him, he stepped on its thigh and jumped up, keeping a firm hold on the grip of his dagger. His feet slipped on the ooze-covered skin, but he was able to gain enough momentum to jump over its head and land on the other side. The stratagem, however, had cost him his dagger, which remained deep inside the demon's rotten skin.

Weaponless and still in the middle of the demonic hordes, he looked around for abandoned swords. He didn't find any, but a large battleax was pinned to the Wall not far from him. Drawing a mental path across the battlefield, he zigzagged between demons and bodies and, holding the ax with both hands, pushed it out, and, with the same movement, sliced a demon in half.

"This isn't over, Belgoriel," Shiroan said sprinting forward.

"I hope not," said Belgoriel with the force of a thousand voices.

Shiroan lifted the heavy battleax above his shoulders and — boosted by lean and powerful leg muscles— performed a jump impossible for almost anyone else. Still in the air, he dealt a crippling blow to Belgoriel's pale, gelatinous chest. The weapon sank and, as it did, a black foul substance erupted from its entrails. Shiroan landed on the ground. The battleax fell by his feet. So loud was Belgoriel's shriek that Shiroan thought his eardrums would explode. When the scream stopped and he was able to pick up the ax again, a thin line of blood was coming down his earlobes.

Wiping his face of blood and tears, he leaped forward. Making a quick half-turn to gain momentum, he sank the battleax on the lower thigh of the creature. Belgoriel moved faster than Shiroan thought possible and swatted him like an annoying bug. Shiroan crashed against the Wall.

Stand up! You've got to stand up or you're done for, Shiroan thought but his body had stopped responding to his commands.

Rising above the sounds of the battle, a shy humming grew into a dark chuckle before transforming into the loudest of cackles. Jaws moving up and down, hundreds of fangs trembling, and a stream of drool that reached the ground accompanied the sinister laugh of Belgoriel.

"What makes you think I can be hurt by your metal weapons? I'm Belgoriel, I can't be killed by the likes of you! You've amused me enough, Cloudhunter. Now you die," it said lifting its foot high in the air, ready to crush Shiroan against the rocky ground.

Belgoriel's foot was frozen in the air. Its shade completely covered Shiroan's body, but it didn't fall. Belgoriel had turned its head and was looking at the distance. Squeals of agony grew in intensity and frequency until nothing could be heard but pain.

Shiroan seized the opportunity and rolled out of danger. Standing up, he prepared to resume fighting. When he looked at the battlefield, the same sense of awe that had paralyzed Belgoriel on its tracks took over him.

This can't be happening, it's impossible, he thought as two polar bears galloped towards him. The Icedorfers riding them sliced and cut every demon on their path, leaving a trail of bubbling innards, pestilent ooze, and rotten flesh. *Why are they not changing back? Why are they killed so easily? Where are the dead bodies?* Shiroan thought as he looked incredulous at the one-sided battle unfolding in front of him.

The Icedorfer lady in the vanguard carried a scepter made from a polished black crystal that Shiroan didn't recognize. The Icedorfer behind her had what looked like a badly crafted sword of the same material. *It's got to be that black crystal,* Shiroan thought.

Belgoriel laughed as he saw the Icedorfers approaching.

"I spared your life once, princess, that was a mistake. It won't happen again," Belgoriel said.

"It's not princess anymore, monster, it's queen. Queen Sehrsil of Icedorf!" she shouted between tears as she took her scepter with both hands and jumped off the bear, rolling in the ground before standing to face Belgoriel. "And I'm sure you'll recognize Spero," she added pointing the scepter at its head.

Sehrsil fought against the demons defending its master showing courage like Shiroan had never seen before. Dancing more than fighting, she sliced through rows of greyish monsters, leaving a trail or rotten puddles behind her.

Sehrsil's path to Belgoriel was clear, but not for long. By swinging its hand, Belgoriel summoned a fresh new wave of its minions to form a barrier between them.

There are too many of them, even for an Icedorfer warrior and her fantastic weapon, she can't kill them all, one of them will get her, Shiroan thought.

The second Icedorfer came from behind him, ramming every demon on his path until he joined his partner. Back against back, the unstoppable duo continued to advance until they couldn't move anymore. Each creature they killed was replaced with two more. They were bound to be overwhelmed by the sheer number of their attackers. From where he stood, Shiroan saw countless more running in their direction.

If the Icedorfers can't find a path to Belgoriel now, they'll never do it, Shiroan thought.

"I think I know what the problem is. You forgot your invitation, didn't you?" Shiroan said joining the Icedorfers.

"You're blue," Sehrsil said. "A Cloudhunter."

"Your weapon." Shiroan said pointing to the scepter. "Will it kill Belgoriel?"

"I don't know, but if it doesn't, I'll murder him with my bare hands," Sehrsil said.

"That's good enough for me. Go, I'll hold them off," Shiroan said.

"We'll be worse off with his help, Sehrsil. No Hellblood to protect us," Marko said.

"Does your weapon kill the demonphantoms inside?" Shiroan asked.

"Indeed, it does."

"Worry not then. I'm not killing them. I'm only maiming them, trust me," Shiroan said picking up his battleax.

"We need to take his offer, Marko, we have no choice. But I'll go alone. There are too many demons for one warrior. You must stay and fight with him," Sehrsil said.

"Whatever, just go!" Shiroan said while slicing a pair of wiry ankles.

"Thank you for this, stranger. Hit like an avalanche, be slippery like ice" Sehrsil said as she turned towards Marko. "Can you give me a lift?" she said with a wink.

"At your service, my queen," Marko said, squatting as he intertwined his fingers to create a step. Sehrsil held tightly to Spero and placed her right foot on Marko's hands. In a single movement, he stood up and raised his arms over his head, sending Sehrsil flying above the horde.

"The time of reckoning is here, monster. Come meet Spero and die!" She shouted at Belgoriel as she flew in the air.

The demon laughed.

Sehrsil stabbed him in the abdomen two times before landing at his feet. The pale skin around the wound swelled and blistered. Belgoriel squealed and shrieked. Purulent blisters invaded the immense gut of the monster. Shiroan couldn't believe his eyes. Belgoriel was hurt.

It can't be this easy, Shiroan thought.

It wasn't.

Without notice, the blistering stopped, and the inflammation receded. A green glow appeared around the wound and, as it shone brighter, the gangrene receded until all that remained from the attack was the scar where the scepter had entered.

"My turn," Belgoriel roared lifting his sword in the sky and bringing it down with fury. Sehrsil leaped out of reach just in time.

Belgoriel stomped his foot on the ground making her lose her balance and fall. Pulling a boulder from the Wall half his size, he threw it at Sehrsil. Shiroan couldn't check on her as Belgoriel, opening his jaws, let out a mouthful of green fire their way. Shiroan reacted quick as lightning and pushed Marko out of the way as he did the same. As he stood up, he looked for Sehrsil. She was well.

"He's mad! You hurt him. Do it again!" He shouted from a distance. Sehrsil looked at him and nodded. She used the boulder lying at his side as an improvised ramp and leapt at Belgoriel with Spero pointing forward. It sunk deep inside its chest. The demon slapped her like an annoying bug before covering the wound with his hands. Sehrsil was catapulted in the air like a broken ragdoll. Belgoriel squealed in agony. The mighty Queen of Icedorf landed unceremoniously on a pond of rotten entrails by Shiroan's feet.

Shiroan could tell from the deafening sound that Belgoriel was badly wounded.

"Are you okay?" Shiroan said helping Sehrsil to stand up. He needed to yell to make himself heard. "I believe it's working. Just hear how it screams!"

"How did you do it, Sehrsil?" Marko asked. The battle around them froze as hundreds of demons looked in awe at how the chest of their master was filled with blisters and pus.

"I left a gift inside his chest. A gift from my father," Sehrsil said.

Belgoriel reached inside his body with both hands, with frantic movements he moved them in circles, as if it was hollowed inside. Its chest, deformed before recognition, had expanded around its arms. Blisters exploded with pus almost as quickly as they appeared. A purple viscose matter secreted through every pore of the skin. As a melting snow figure, Belgoriel shrunk and flattened. Its face was nothing but red eyes and a gelatinous mouth full of fangs. Spero, victorious and proud, emerged from the chaos of rotten flesh and oozing bones.

"It killed Belgoriel from the inside. How did you know?" Shiroan asked.

"I didn't," was Sehrsil's candid response.

"The demons are coming back to their senses," Marko said looking at the creatures around them. "Here, take my black crystal weapon, Sehrsil,"

"Marko, I don't need to—"

"You don't, I do. You're still the Queen of Icedorf and it is my sworn duty to protect you. The black crystal will do just that."

"I understand," Sehrsil said picking up the shard.

"Stop the nonsense and be ready!" Shiroan said cutting through the ankles of a demon on the verge to attack Sehrsil. Shiroan took a sword from the ground and passed it on to Marko. "This fight isn't over."

"Good," Sehrsil said.

Then what was left of Belgoriel's mouth spoke in a language he had never heard before. Each word pierced like nails in his eyes and burned like lava in his ears. Every demon went to him. Some of them tried to take the scepter out, suffering a horrible death. A second group came with hands and arms covered in chainmail and pigskin.

Digging in the purulent chest, two of them grabbed the hilt and pulled.

"They're trying to remove Spero! I need to finish him. Now!" Sehrsil shouted while she ran to reach Belgoriel, lying on the ground, dying, and squealing.

"You will… not win… it's much too late," Belgoriel said with a thick voice, rolling every syllable.

Sehrsil grabbed Marko's demonium shard with both hands and went straight for Belgoriel's left eye. A good push shoved the shard deep in his rotten head. Belgoriel raised his putrid arm and tried to reach her, but it was over.

The creature laid down in the ground, twisting, bursting, melting. From its remains, silhouettes made of dead skin and pus started to form. The faces of the many that Belgoriel had consumed over the cycles opened their mouths to let out silent screams. Thin, hunched, and lost figures made of rotten flesh, waking up from the unimaginable torture they had suffered for so long. Sehrsil was entranced, looking how the amorphous yellowish mass of blisters, veins and flesh transformed in Vespertians, Solis, Elgarians, Oceaners and Icedorfers. Each one of them, with a green glow surrounding them like an emerald armor. Belgoriel's severed head rested on the ground. Its jaw gasping for air like a fish out of water, drooling a pestilent purple substance.

Sehrsil turned her face away to escape the smell when she saw a familiar shape with the corner of her eye.

"Father?" she whispered.

"What are you doing?" Shiroan exclaimed as Sehrsil walked to the figure she had recognized.

"Father!" Sehrsil said with breaking voice.

The decomposing matter in the shape of the King of Icedorf extended its ooze dripping arms towards Sehrsil. As it did, it shone brighter.

Shiroan, witnessing the events from afar, couldn't believe his eyes.

How is this possible? It must be a trick from Belgoriel, he thought looking at a face that, even if it was made of ripped flesh, conveyed indescribable suffering.

"Be careful, Sehrsil," Shiroan said. "This looks like a trap."

"It isn't," Sehrsil said taking the pestilent hand. "He's my father, the King of Icedorf. I recognize his essence. I'm sorry for everything, father. I love you." She said hugging him. "You taught me to be strong. You gave me the strength to rebel against injustice and to protect those that couldn't protect themselves. You made me brave. You did well as a father, and as our king," Sehrsil said.

With a trembling hand, the King of Icedorf caressed the face of her daughter. She put her hand on top and, at that precise moment, her father melted away with a smile. The green light covering him floated away, joined by the light covering all other hellish bodies, that, like her father, rejoined the pool of rotten remains.

The gelatinous mass that had been Belgoriel spilled flat in the ground as it inflated like a giant bubble. Sehrsil moved to the side as it expanded even more before exploding. Pus, skin, blood, and rotten flesh flew across the battlefield, spraying Marko, Sehrsil and Shiroan.

Belgoriel was dead.

"This was for my father, for my people and for all the people you killed, ugly piece of crap!" Sehrsil shouted. Residues of the demon dripped down her chin.

"I believe this belongs to you," Shiroan said handing her Spero.

"It does, and so does the honor of having liberated the Known Territories from Belgoriel," Marko said picking up his own demonium piece from the blistering rests of Belgoriel.

"From Belgoriel, sure, from the demonic hordes, not by a long shot," Shiroan said, pointing at the opening in the Wall.

There where Belgoriel had hammered the rock, the demonic hordes were traversing at such numbers that the hole was completely hidden by the sea of monsters.

"My name is Shiroan. I don't know why help us now, after your kin has been trying to bring us down for so many seasons, but you did, and that's what matters. Thank you. I must go now. My battle is just beginning, but I'll tell your story everywhere I go and will let everyone know of the hero that killed Belgoriel."

"I am Sehrsil, Queen of Icedorf. My people did what needed to be done to survive and I'm proud of them. Don't be so quick passing judgement. You try surviving outside this side of the Wall, without Hellblood around your neck. You can't understand what it is to see your loved ones become monsters. You can't imagine what it feels to kill them in cold blood. You think that you're guarding the Passage to Hell? Look around you, Hell is not what lies inside the volcano, it is what exists beyond the walls surrounding it."

"Outside only? That's what you think? We fight endless shifts. We die protecting the only thing worth saving in the Known Territories. We live in fear that, because of us, the Hidden Chamber will fall and the Passage to Hell will open again, creating fresh demonic hordes until none of us is left. We are the reason you're alive. We fight for you even if you battle against us, so spare your lectures for somebody that cares," Shiroan said reacting to Sehrsil's challenge the only way he knew, with harsher words.

"The Passage to Hell!" Marko said without giving Sehrsil the opportunity to rebuke. "The Cloudhunter is right, my queen. If it opens, all will be lost. We may live in Hell now but at least some of us can fight. If everyone is a demon, then who will be left to free us?"

"Marko is right, Shiroan, we might have fought against you in the past and, perhaps, we'll fight against you in the future. But this cycle, it seems that we'll battle together. How do we reach the Hidden Chamber?"

"You can't. If you beat impossible odds and survive the Fortress and the first Six Seals, the Seven Warriors will kill you on sight. You must go back, without Hellblood you'll only serve as demon fuel," Shiroan said pointing in the direction opposite to Skyroar.

"And without our demonium weapons, you'll get everyone possessed, including my people. We're staying, that's final!" Sehrsil said.

"Then give me one of your weapons, I'll do the killing for you," Shiroan said.

"We do our own bidding, Shiroan, make no mistakes," Sehrsil said looking him in the eye before turning her head to Marko. "We must find Mehrik. He'll know what to do, I'm sure."

"You can't possibly mean Mehrik the Oceaner?" Shiroan said.

"Mehrik, yes, the bravest of warriors. I owe him my life. He rescued me from the jaws of Belgoriel himself. Do you know him?" Sehrsil said.

"You must be jesting. I've met him. He's nothing more than a deliverer," he said, now with a less confident tone than before. It was the second time in less than a cycle that somebody praised Mehrik's courage.

"He's more of a warrior than you'll ever be, trust me. You know where to find him?" Sehrsil said.

"He's in Skyroar, traveling east. He's going to face Mortagong."

"Then that's where we'll go."

"I can't stop you from going after the deliverer. I will ask you to remember that there is just very little time between a demonphantom entering your essence and you losing control of your body. If one of you is possessed, the other must act without hesitation," Shiroan said.

"We are aware, Cloudhunter, we've never had the privilege of Hellblood to protect us. What will you do?" Marko said.

"I'll gather my companions and go to the Seventh Seal, that's where the hordes are heading."

"I thought you said that only the Seven Warriors could enter?" Sehrsil said.

"Exactly," Shiroan said standing tall, unable to hide how proud the comment made him feel.

"In that case, take this demonium with you." Marko said, splitting his shard into two dagger-sized pieces. "It'll serve you well."

The twin suns were well on their way to reaching their resting place. They had been fighting for most of the cycle. A period at most, was all they had before nightfall. "Marko. Let's set camp over that hill tonight," Sehrsil said pointing Northeast. "No fires. Catching the attention of demons in the dark will only get us killed. Cloudhunter, you're welcome to stay. Resting may serve you well."

"Thank you, but I need to go. I'll make sure your gift is put to good use."

"Attack like an avalanche, be slippery like ice, Cloudhunter."

"I will," Shiroan said as he walked away.

The opening in the Wall was deserted. Every single demon had already gone through and was heading to the Hidden Chamber. With Belgoriel dead, the demonic hordes could be either easier to beat or more savage than ever. Shiroan was leaning towards the second option.

He went through the rubble with uncanny dexterity. It didn't take him long to reach the other side. As he marched to share the fate of Skyroar, he couldn't help but think that leaving the Seventh Seal may have been a big mistake after all. Sehrsil would have killed Belgoriel whether he was there or not. Nothing he could do now other than going back, although, considering how many demons had entered Skyroar, he was bound to only find death and destruction.

Chapter Thirteen

As soon as Audax disappeared behind the horizon, Mehrik came out of his hiding place. Lork was asleep, nested between his crossed arms. When the seahawk returned from the incursion into the Hundred Kingdoms, exhausted beyond all measure, he collapsed in Mehrik's lap and hadn't moved much since. Lork denied it when Mehrik asked, but it was more than clear that the effort he made to channel Mehrik's essence had taken a substantial toll. He will need to be careful going forward and use their newfound ability only when absolutely necessary. Lork was more than a friend, he was an extension of his own self. Life without him was impossible to imagine.

The Village was perhaps one period away. As a deliverer, he had learned every trail and walked every path. He knew what road to use to go by undetected and how to read the dim light from the stars to find his way. He had complained hundreds of times of his fate, but without the knowledge he had gathered as a deliverer, he probably would be dead by now.

As he walked to the Village, he reflected on the events that had transpired since the moment he received the flask of Hellblood from Kishi. Not too many cycles ago his job was to deliver packages from one point to another. Even considering that his travels took him sometimes to the heart of a battle, to bring messages to officers and provisions to the troops, Mehrik had lived mostly a sheltered life. Reasonable cozy inside his bubble of hope and purpose.

A bubble that had exploded in a thousand pieces.

He regretted how naïve he had been. How he had blindly followed the Conclave, and how he never, not once, questioned the citadel laws. Even the ones he deemed unfair, such as forbidding the entrance of people in dire need of protection.

Mehrik was raised, like everybody else, in the irrefutable belief that Skyroar was a sacred place and everyone in it were the chosen saviors of the Known Territories. All his life he remained loyal to a

Prophecy and a prophet that might be as false as the idea that whoever dwells beyond the Wall is the enemy. What else will he uncover? Did the Hidden Chamber truly contain a gateway to Hell? Did Hishiro, the Elgarian hero, really exist? So many questions unanswered.

He wished Momo had helped him join the army. 'When you are ready, my dear. When you're ready I'll see to it personally,' Momo used to say. Well, he is ready now and even his grandfather would have to treat him as more than a simple deliverer.

The torches illuminating the streets and alleys of the Village could be seen at the end of the sinuous path. He was almost there.

"Lork, wake up," Mehrik said rocking his arms tenderly. "Let's go buddy, time to get to work. I need you to fly ahead of me and tell me if the streets are safe. We're going home," after listening to Mortagong, he wasn't sure what to expect, for all he knew, the Hundred Kingdoms army was already in the Village.

The black seahawk, invisible against the starry sky, flew ahead looking for guards, gatherings of people, or signs of trouble.

Take path of the old worm farm, square full, Lork telepathized.

Mehrik knew that road very well. It was south of Hishiro Square and didn't have kiosks or food establishments. The path was usually empty in the evening.

I hear them, Lork. Mehrik messaged stopping as he looked to his left where a group of guards drank ale and smoked herbaltum out of a hollowed branch. Mehrik recognized the smell but had never tasted it himself. Made with tender leaves of herbalium —a rare plant only found in Arboris— only Conclave members, Fortress officers, or very well-connected Villagers, had access to it.

"They probably stole it, Lork," Mehrik said. "I'd say that's why they are so far away from the Fortress. Judging by their laughing, they had too much to drink. I don't think they'll see me, but I'll take that alley just in case," he said pointing at an entrance on his right.

The chosen path smelled like rancid urine, dry blood, and rotten meat. He didn't care. Mehrik detailed the cobblestone roads and rubbed the basalt walls of the buildings as if they were the most beautiful piece of art in the Known Territories. Even the imponent majesty of The City of the Thousand Lights fell short when compared with the Village, at least in his eyes.

Until then, he hadn't realized how much he had missed it.

Some of the corners were lit by oil lamps that were replenished once per night at midnight. They were meant to show the way in case of an emergency. But most of the street length was a long patch of blackness. Mehrik summoned all his concentration to avoid tripping over a cart or a misplaced stool.

He had seen the dimly lit corner in front of him a thousand times. The light from the oil lamp reflected on the rainwater filling the large pothole in the otherwise perfect cobblestone path. Mehrik used to stomp on it and splash everyone nearby until somebody, usually lady Mereva, shouted at him. A block away lived Berthin, the bonecrafter. Growing up, every time he went to say hi, the old Elgarian would stop what he was doing, fetch a tiny canyon rammer or a cart made of bone and give it to him. Those were the only toys he ever had. Across the street, the grey walls he knew so well, the doorway he had crossed so many times. Momo's house. His home.

Mehrik didn't risk just going through the front door. The memories of what he witnessed last time were still fresh in his mind. He had to make sure it was safe before attempting to enter. Walking around the block, avoiding the yellow circle that the streetlamps drew in the cobblestone streets, he carefully inspected every rooftop and look over every wall before going in.

"Momo?" He called. "Momo, are you here? Grandfather?"

No answer. A cold current traversed his spine and made him shiver.

Mehrik looked behind the kitchen counter before going to the bedroom. A smile took over his face when he saw him sound asleep in his bed.

"I'm so happy to see you, Momo. I've missed you so much," Mehrik said bending over to kiss his grandfather's forehead.

His wide smile transformed into a grin of terror when he looked at his face.

Bandages drenched in blood covered his skull. A black patch hid his right eye. His arms were so bruised that Mehrik thought he was wearing a purple gown. At least three of his fingers seemed to be broken.

"Momo," Mehrik said with a voice filled with sadness and anguish. "What happened?"

"Are you here for more?" Mehrik's grandfather exclaimed lifting his fists. "Let's go! I'm ready. I'm not saying one word," he said trying to stand up.

"Take it easy, Momo, it's me, Mehrik. Stay down."

"Mehrik? Is it really you?"

"It's me, Momo," Mehrik said.

"You aren't safe here, Mehrik. They'll come back, the Fortress guards, and they'll kill you."

"They won't, Momo, don't worry. There's nobody outside, I checked. What happened to you? Was this done by our own people?"

"Don't be concerned about me, my dear, I've had it worst. I've —" Momo fell prey of a sudden burst of dry cough that echoed deep in his lungs. His pale face changed to red, Mehrik helped him sit on his bed and tapped with care his back. Once the fit was under control, he rushed to the kitchen and brought back a bowl of water.

"Here, Momo, drink up."

"Thank you, son," he said while reaching Mehrik's arm with his trembling hand. "All of Skyroar is looking for you. Where have you been?"

"It's not important, Momo, the important thing is to take care of you. You need a healer. I'll get one for you. I also need to check your Hellblood to make sure it's still good."

"There's no time, Mehrik. I thought I would die without seeing you again and all would be lost. Now that you are here, we need to talk," The old Oceaner said glancing at the window.

"We can talk later, Momo," Mehrik said.

"Listen to me, son. Skyroar was built countless seasons ago as the last stand of a tormented world. We all had the same wish: to save the Known Territories by protecting the Hidden Chamber from all those who wanted to destroy it. The Wall was built and the Fortress and each one of the Seven Seals.

"The early seasons were hard, we didn't have Hellblood, and the Wall was only a dream. Still, the original settlers persevered and, if not thrived, at least survived. As of late, a seed of corruption planted long ago germinated in the core of our beloved city, and it has spread and expanded and rotted everything it touched.

"Mortagong won't rest until Skyroar falls, Mehrik. I don't know what his plan is or why he's determined to accomplish what the demonic hordes couldn't. But he'll succeed, I am persuaded of it. Whatever his strategy is, he has planned it through tens of seasons with the help of hundreds."

"He won't win! We can still stop Mortagong. I'll make sure of it!"

"You can try, but Mortagong is a formidable enemy."

"I won't just hide and leave you or our home suffer a terrible fate, Momo. I'll fight and I'll make you proud. I've changed, I've grown. I'm a warrior now. I promise that I'll set things right," Mehrik said.

"I don't care about what you did or where you were in the last cycles, Mehrik, that's your business. I do see that something inside you has changed. I can hear it in your voice and see it in your eyes. Your tone is commanding. Your bravery is evident. But you are no warrior, Mehrik, you are something else. Something else entirely. And because of my own fears I almost robbed you of the gift that is your true heritage. I was not only overzealous but also a fool. Allow this old man to try to amend his mistake."

"You are making no sense, Momo, are you well?" Mehrik asked, placing his hand on the wrinkled forehead of his grandfather to check for a fever.

"An Oceaner will grow as big as their circumstances, Mehrik. Your circumstances have made you grow, but mark my words, you'll be the biggest among us. And only then you will be able to defeat Mortagong. Would you be a dear and help me get up?"

"No way. You're in no condition to go anywhere."

"Please, do it, yes?"

Mehrik put away the filthy and stiff sheet that covered him. He gasped when he saw Momo's legs, crossed with bumps, bruises, and burns. They were in even worse shape than his arms. Mehrik took a deep breath and without saying a word, helped him stand. Momo was wearing a ripped yellow night gown down to his thighs.

"Now, please hold me tight as we walk."

"Walk where?" Mehrik asked.

"To do something that I should've done a long, long time ago," he said grabbing Mehrik's arm with both hands. "One, two, three, four –"

"What are you counting?"

"Shush! Five, six, seven as in the Seven Warriors." He stopped in the kitchen, by the table. "For the life of me, I can't remember if it was north or south now."

Mehrik just looked at him without saying a word. He was

afraid the guards had damaged something else inside him in addition to his body.

"Oceano, oh Prince of the south, home of warriors and kings.

You bring rest to the restless and peace to the sea,

but in the north, lies dormant a monster that will release its offspring.

And when the terrible offspring will come, south of the south will be the key," Momo sang in a low voice, eyes shut, fingers tapping in the kitchen counter.

"What are you mumbling, Momo, did you make up that song?"

"Made it up, my boy? No, I wouldn't have been able to. It's an old one. Older than me, can you believe it?" Momo said with a chuckle. "It is from before my time, before my grandfather's time even. It's also not a song. It's foretelling. Let's see now, south, north, south, south. North is the one that's unique. Must be it. One, two, three, four, five, six, seven." He walked north and stopped not far from the front door. "Here!" He exclaimed in a triumphant tone.

"Here what?"

"Your heritage, I hope. It has been so long since I hid it. Grab your sword and something heavy. You'll need to break the floor just under my feet."

"Are you sure you feel well, Momo?"

"Do it, Mehrik, for me."

"I'll do it, for you. I'll be right back."

Mehrik walked to the kitchen and a moment later came back with a flat basalt rock. "This is the best I could find," he said unsheathing his sword and holding it in the spot that his grandfather had signaled. "I don't know who is crazier, Momo, you for making me do this or me for playing along."

"Maybe both. Maybe neither. We'll see soon enough," his grandfather said with a smile.

Three blows to the hilt were all it took to make it sink almost halfway, as if the ground underneath was made of wormflour. Four cracks branched out outwards from the blade. Mehrik shook the sword to expand the hole. The floor broke into pieces with a dry crack, exposing a pile of sand.

"That sand comes from your native land, my son," Momo said. "Go ahead, smell it, it'll take you there."

Mehrik took a handful of it and put it close to his nose. A salty and mineral scent filled his nostrils, transporting him to a place he had never seen. He imagined the sound of the waves crashing against the walls of Oceano, his homeland. His eyes let out tears of joy and sadness for a country and a life he only knew through his grandfather's stories.

"All is well dear. Let the emotions flow. The river you are feeling will turn into a sea soon enough. Dig some more, the truth awaits," Momo said with tears also rolling down his eyes.

Mehrik sunk his hands inside the hole and took out a small, round box made with a material he didn't recognize.

"It's called coral." Momo said. "Isn't it something? Came straight from the coast of Oceano. You should have seen it when I first hid it, all those seasons ago. It was red like fire and shiny like the reflection of the full moon at night. C'mon, open it."

The porous box was lighter than he thought. With extreme care, he placed it on the table and stared at it for a few moments.

"It's locked, but I don't see a keyhole," he said as he picked it up again and tried to force it open.

"Corals are zealous guards of the secrets of Oceano. They are not for everyone. Our people live by The Sea, why don't you try placing it in water."

Momo's words fueled his curiosity. Mehrik ran to the kitchen, took a container from the shelf, poured water in it, and placed the box inside. He kept it pressed against the bottom of the container to ensure every part got wet. The dry material softened up and expanded as it absorbed the liquid. A thin line became visible around the box. Not long after, a black oval started to take shape. Five paths grew from the black oval creating the arms of a sea star.

Mehrik looked mesmerized at the spectacle happening in front of his eyes.

A small triangular shape appeared on the center of the star, and little golden spheres crowned each one of the five arms.

"It's the same shape as my amulet!" Mehrik exclaimed grabbing his talisman and placing it in front of the coral box, "well, it is actually concave, the opposite."

"Will you look at that! What does it tell you?" Momo said with a wink.

"You can't mean –" Mehrik didn't finish the sentence. He took the box out of the water and fitted the talisman inside the star. Two clicks echoed in the hut as the internal mechanism was triggered. The top of the box sprang open. A pyramidal golden prism was the only thing inside it. It was about the same size as Mehrik's fist. He picked it up. It was softer, more polished than he expected, and so warm that he had to hold it through his shirt. "What is it?" He asked.

"The Core-Sole."

"The what?"

"The heart of the sun. The answer to the Hidden Chamber's secret."

"I don't understand."

"I know. Come, help me to the table and sit with me. It's time for a history lesson."

"Let me put this down first," Mehrik said bringing the prism to the table and then helping his grandfather to one of the chairs. He sat in another one and Lork perched in his shoulder.

"Where were you born, Mehrik?" Momo asked.

"In the Village of course."

"What if I told you a different story, one where you were born far from here, in Oceano. What if I told you that your father didn't die defending the Wall and your mother didn't die at birth," Momo said.

"I'd say you must be jesting. My only memories are from this place."

"We might be able to bring back older ones. What did you see when you held the amulet against your face?"

"I saw the waves of The Sea crashing against Oceano, but that is just because you've sang so many songs about it, Momo."

"You know there's more, Mehrik. You can feel it. Pay close attention, my dear, and open your heart to the truth. Your parents were the monarchs of Oceano. You are the heir to their throne. You're the rightful King of Oceano."

"Momo, that's nonsense," Mehrik said with concern in his voice, his grandfather didn't answer. He had a fit of cough so hard he almost fell from his chair. "Let me help you to your bed," Mehrik said standing up and grabbing him by the armpit.

"I'm well where I am, dear, thank you. Now sit down and listen to me," Momo said with the same gentle tone but with eyes that left no room for questions. "How many black seahawks have you seen other than Lork?"

"None," Mehrik said looking at his friend perching on the back of the pigskin sofa.

"That's because black seahawks are only for the Royal Family, your family," Momo said.

"That can't be true, Momo."

"But it is, and you are about to believe me. Are you sure you grabbed everything from the box?"

"I sure did. But I can look again." Mehrik said going back to the table and picking up the coral box. Inside, underneath a layer of pigskin to protect it from the Core-Sole, a small, flattened roll of parchment, roughly the same color as the coral, was almost perfectly concealed from peering eyes. Mehrik picked it up and opened it. It was a letter written in Oceanum, the language of his people. His grandfather taught it to him although he rarely spoke it anymore, not even with him. "I can't read this, Momo. It's in Oceanum. I haven't read it in so long."

"You want to learn what it says, believe me. And for that, you'll need to read it yourself."

"Can you read it for me?"

"No, I can't. You read in Oceanum to me for several seasons. It shares the same characters as Elgarian. This is something you need to do yourself."

Mehrik looked into his grandfather's eyes and knew he wouldn't budge. He has seen that determined gaze so many times before and on not one of those occasions he backtracked. "I know, I used to know this. I'll give it a try," Mehrik said looking at Lork. *He won't change his mind. I might as well do my best.*

"*Dearest son,*" Mehrik started and felt his essence shrank. He stopped for a few moments with his eyes fixed on those first two words. He didn't recall ever been called son. "*It's with my heart full of sorrow that I am writing you this letter,*" Mehrik looked up to his grandfather, searching for validation. "Does it really say 'son'", he asked.

"Yes, Mehrik, that's a letter from your mother, the queen." His grandfather said nodding his head.

Mehrik took a moment to process the information. He hadn't slept in a long time and had the sensation of being inside of a dream. The sound of his grandfather coughing brought him back to reality. Mehrik stood up and gently tapped his grandfather's back as he placed close to his mouth a napkin that was lying on the table. When Momo recovered, the piece of cloth was covered in red.

"This can wait, Momo, you need help."

"Nothing is more important than this, dear. I'm broken inside, there's not much that can be done to fix this old body of mine. This moment is the only thing I need. Please indulge me."

"I'll do it, but I don't like it," Mehrik said going back to his chair and taking the piece of parchment from the table. "*I see you in front of me, smiling in your cradle, with your tiny arms reaching out to me, and all I want to do is kiss you and hug you and never let you go. But I can't. I can't and it devastates my world. Thinking of all the love that will die ungiven tears my essence apart and fills me with anger and sadness. They are coming for me, for us. I can hear them in the halls, scratching the walls. I can hear them hurting and laughing and killing. I can hear my people, our people, scream. But they will not have you. Not you. You will survive and you will thrive, and you will, one cycle, become a king, the King of Oceano, but not this cycle, this cycle you become a refugee.*"

Mehrik stared at the parchment in silence. The stains his mother's tears had left in it were covered by his own. He was breathing faster, his hands, clenched into fists, were trembling. His grandfather was telling the truth. After a life of lies.

"Why?" he asked, looking at the person he loved the most in the world with eyes full of rage.

"She wanted it this way."

"I don't care!" Mehrik shouted. "She's dead, isn't she? You let me grow here. You gave me a story that wasn't mine. I could've gone back home and –"

"And you'd be dead, dear. And with you, the last hope of the Oceano throne would be gone forever. I'm sorry, my child, for having lied to you, for taking you away, and for having marked you unable to join the Skyroar army. There was no other way. You needed to grow here. Away from danger. Away from the outside world. Away from battle where the Oceano troops could recognize you or your seahawk. They have been looking for you from the moment we left. You must be strong. You must be ready. I did my best to give you a chance at survival. It's more than your life what's at stake here, Mehrik, I hope you realize that."

"How could you keep me away from my people and my dreams, Momo? I didn't ask to be protected! I just wanted to fight, to be a warrior, to help."

"It was not your decision to be made, it was mine, and it was my promise to your mother!" Momo exclaimed triggering yet another attack of cough, this one worse than the one before.

Mehrik patted his back as he gave him water.

"I'm sorry, Momo. It's just too much information, I feel like I'm waking up from a long dream."

"You are indeed. Now keep reading, please."

"There is nothing in the world I want more than to be your mother. To feel those tiny hands grow stronger, and witness how you'll become the great man I know you'll be. Because Mehrik, even now, I can see it in your eyes, you are your father's son. I'm the Queen of Oceano and I can't escape this fate, but you, my dear son, can. Marinius, my beloved aide, will take care of you. He'll sneak you out of Oceano and will find a safe place to raise you. I trust him with my treasure and have asked him to only tell you who he is, and who you are, when is time. Until then, he'll be your grandfather. He will only give you the core-sole, and this letter when you are ready. Please don't hate him for lying to you. He is just following my dying wish. Hate me instead if you must."

Mehrik fell silent. He wanted to explode, to yell, to denounce the lies, and condemn a deception of impossible dimensions. His own mother had left him in the hands of a stranger that kept his origin in the dark, blocked his dream to be a warrior, and claimed love on an invented blood tie.

He looked at this new person in front of him with eyes full of rage and trembling hands. Tears of impotence ran down his cheeks. Marinius looked back at him with a bruised face, missing teeth, dry blood in his hair, and a tenuous smile full of love. His eyes showed sadness and empathy, but not regret.

Mehrik got lost in those eyes and saw himself as a kid, learning to walk in that very home, listening to beautiful songs in that very bed, being hugged and kissed in every corner of their little hut, and drowning in love and warmth every moment he was with him.

"Marinius? You are my family, and I couldn't ask for a better one," Mehrik said, as he extended his hand and closed it around Momo's.

His grandfather's hand closed around his, as tightly as always, full of love.

"Thank you, Momo. Who knows what perils you went through, carrying a baby from the farthest land in the Known

Territories to Skyroar. You were not only a hero to my mother. You are also my hero."

"Dear Mehrik, believe me, every drop of perspiration was worthy to see who you have become and imagine who you will be one cycle. Now keep reading, please," Momo said with a weakened voice.

"*Mehrik, you have the Core-Sole in your hands. It means you have the opportunity to expunge the sins of your parents. The Core-Sole is the key to forever destroying the Passage to Hell but be warned, it can't fall on the wrong hands or... Oh no! They're here, my love. Be strong, be all you can be and more. Be better than us. Be Mehrik. I'll be always with you, in your essence. I love you.*"

"She was the strongest person I've ever met in my entire life, Mehrik. You'll need to be stronger. Come closer, dear, my voice fails me."

"I could never hate you. I'll never stop loving you. I apologize for what I said before, Momo, I lost control. Thank you for all you've done for me. Without you, the demonic hordes would have killed me as well."

"Demonic hordes? I'm sorry, Mehrik, sometimes I wish the demonic hordes was what killed your mother," his grandfather said with a breaking voice, even his coughing was weak now.

"What do you mean? Who murdered my mother?" Mehrik asked. Momo opened the mouth to respond but only whizzing, coughing and blood came out. "Never mind, Momo, I'll go get a healer, should have done it long ago."

"No need," Momo whispered as he closed his eyes. "Goodbye."

"Momo? Momo?" Mehrik said shaking his hand. "No! Wake up! Don't do this to me!" he said caressing his wrinkled, pale cheek.

But Momo didn't move. He was gone.

"Goodbye, grandfather," Mehrik said.

He cried until no more tears came out, until his essence was drained, and he couldn't feel anything other than a black hole within. Then he fell asleep. He was so very tired.

Chapter Fourteen

DEAD.

Belgoriel was dead. The executioner of his people. The destroyer of the City in the Sky. The bringer of doom had ceased to exist. The horrific memories of a myriad faces made from purulent skin and rotten flesh remained seeded deep inside him. They would haunt his dreams forevermore, of that much he was certain. There was no time to dwell on this, however. He had an invasion to stop.

I hope every single essence finds the peace and rest they deserve after all the pain and suffering they endured trapped inside Belgoriel. Without a leader, the demons will start an unpredictable killing spree and, undoubtedly, they'll try to reach the Hidden Chamber to open the Passage to Hell. Their efforts will be uncoordinated and clumsy with no commander. We need to use that. First things first, I must see if Tabatha and the Seven Warriors are still here, Shiroan thought.

He ran up the unstable wooden stairs dodging the lifeless bodies of Elgarians, Solis, and Oceaners, some of them naked, most of them wearing the Skyroar army uniform. With each step, his concern grew. He would never forgive himself if something happened to her.

"Tabatha!" He exclaimed as he rushed the last few steps to the battlement where he last saw his companions. All he could think about was how similar this situation was to the one where Pontos had died. "I should've never left Tabatha alone," Shiroan said as he checked every fallen body. His heart almost beat out of his chest when he saw Vespertian wings covered in blood. He approached the corpse and breathed easily when he confirmed that it wasn't Tabatha. "I'm sorry," he said to the stranger as an apology for both, his dead, and the relief he felt.

Not finding her amongst the fallen, he turned his head to the sky. Nothing.

Where could she be? Did she go back to the Sixth Seal? Is she chasing dragons? Shiroan thought as he descended the staircase to the ground.

The clinging of chainmail and the rubbing of boots against the floor caught his attention. The sound was coming from the armory, a hollow space carved inside the Wall.

Inside, a peculiar group of warriors regained their breath and their energy.

Goldenmane, the Lionkin, sat on a pile of bone helmets and licked his wounds with his long tongue. Tabatha, the Vespertian, stood guard by the small opening that overlooked the battlefield with her bow and arrow ready to defend Skyroar. Kishi, the Elgarian-Icedorfer hybrid, ate stale wormbread out of a bag leaving a trail of crumbs that journeyed down from his chin to the floor. Gregoria, the Solis, stayed away from everyone else in the far corner of the room; double-edged spear behind her neck and resting in her shoulder blades.

Dry blood and ooze covered their clothes and armor.

"I can't believe Belgoriel is dead," Kishi said.

"I can. But the real question is: did we make a mistake killing it and sending the demonic hordes into chaos?" Shiroan said walking through the door.

"Shiroan!" Tabatha shouted without hiding her excitement.

"I'm so happy you're well, Blue!" Kishi said with a mouth full of bread.

"You were down there, Shiroan, what's that black weapon that the Icedorfer used?" Gregoria asked. "And I'm also relieved to see you didn't kill yourself."

"You mean this?" Shiroan said showing the dagger-sized piece of demonium that Marko had given him.

"Does that crystal really kill them forever?" Goldenmane asked walking toward Shiroan to get a closer look.

"Indeed. Now we have the upper hand. All we need is a plan." Shiroan said.

"Well, hero, let's hope is better than the last one," Gregoria said.

"I never forced you to follow me, Gregoria. You're here because you chose to be here," said Shiroan letting out a grunt.

"Well, of course I did. It's not that you could force me to do something I don't want to. The point is that I trusted you and that trust had led us nowhere."

"Nowhere, really? Isn't Belgoriel dead?"

"Not by your hand and, as you just said, we don't know if that was a good thing. Without Belgoriel, the demonic hordes may turn even more vicious out of desperation and rage. I don't think that single shard of crystal will make much of a difference when fighting against thousands."

"Leave him alone. You can't do anything here but there is nothing you could do at the Seventh Seal either. Have you not seen the number of demons that are going that way?" Goldenmane said.

"Doesn't matter. We are the Seven Warriors, the protectors of the Hidden Chamber. If it falls and we're still alive is because we didn't do our job. More than that, we have friends in the Seventh Seal that can't prevail against the entirety of the demonic hordes. If we were with them, at least we'd die together, with honor, as warriors," Gregoria said.

"Enough!" Kishi exclaimed standing up. He let the silence reign for a moment before he continued. "Blue couldn't know. You're either with him or you're not, but the whining has got to stop."

"Gregoria, for what is worth, my opinion was not different than yours for the longest time. It was only recently that I understood that Shiroan's actions were always aimed to protect us all. I'm with you to the end, Shiroan, tell me what to do next," Tabatha said looking straight at him.

"What he did may have been reckless, but it was also brave. He didn't run away, he volunteered to die first. I followed him then, and I'll follow him now," Kishi said.

"Kishi is right, look outside, how many demons we killed? If you hadn't left the Seventh Seal, hundreds more would be travelling to the Hidden Chamber," Goldenmane said.

"It only takes one to obliterate any chance to see the Prophecy come true," Gregoria said.

"That's why we'll go back," Shiroan said. "To win this war."

"That's not a bad idea, but how do you plan to pass beyond Torok? He won't let you through and Kaina is nowhere to be found," Tabatha said.

"Kaina will be wherever the dragons are, dead or alive. Torok may be gone by the time we arrive at the Sixth Seal," Shiroan said with a somber tone.

"Then we're wasting our time talking, let's move," Tabatha

said walking to the door.

"You can't come with us," Gregoria said with a firm voice. "Only the Seven Warriors can enter the Seventh Seal."

"You can't be serious," Tabatha said. "Don't you think that we are past that? Look around you. The Skyroar Law doesn't matter anymore."

"It matters to me," Gregoria said.

"We still can go together, at least until we reach the Sixth Seal."

"So be it. Gather your things and eat and drink what you can find. We leave in half a period," Gregoria said.

"Tabatha, can I have a moment with you alone?" Shiroan said as she was attaching her chest plate.

"Shiroan, we don't have the time, we must go to the Seventh Seal," Gregoria said with a commanding voice.

"I realize that, but we have half a period, do we not?" Shiroan said as he grabbed Tabatha's hand and walked down the balcony to an empty guard post.

Tabatha's eyes emitted a dim green glow in the dark of the night. He wondered how come he had never noticed it before. Flickering torches could be seen in the distance, moving back and forth along the moraine separating the Fortress from the Village. They disappeared one by one as the guards that carried them were killed by demons. Gregoria was right. They didn't have much time.

"Mother used to say that as long there was light in the turrets of the Fortress, Skyroar will prevail," Tabatha said looking at the bright orange dots ahead of them.

"This night, I wouldn't be so sure," Shiroan said.

"And you've always been the confident one amongst us," Tabatha said forcing a smile.

"Or rather the idiot, Tabatha. But we can talk about it at a less pressing time. Gregoria is right. You can't come with us to the Seventh Seal. Only the Seven Warriors are allowed in."

"I know, Shiroan. I was born here, remember? It's just –"

"Just what?" He said getting so close that he could feel her breath in his chin.

"You're insufferable. Insufferable and frustrating. You're this endless labyrinth where I'm trapped looking for a way out. I can't understand you and it's physically painful, and dangerous, to make myself vulnerable to you because of that. The moment I think I figured you out, you do something unexpected that will destroy my world one moment and rebuild it better and brighter the next. My brother died under your command. He died!"

"I'm sorry Tabatha, no time will be enough to atone for –"

"Let me finish. But then it turns out that your actions not only secured the victory of the Sixth Seal troops. They saved Skyroar. They saved me. You jump to the void to fight an army of demons as if you were going to the square market and I hate you for it. I hate you because you're the hero I want to be, and because you'll be killed, hero and all, and I'll end up without you. That's why I want to go with you, because that's the only way I'll know you're still alive."

"I'm no hero, Tabatha, I'm arrogant, selfish, and proud. The tip of your wing is more noble than my entire essence. But that's not what I wanted to tell you. Tabatha, I almost died down there, and I know our biggest battle is yet to come. You are right, I might not survive in the Seventh Seal, and I don't want to regret dying before telling you how I feel. It's your presence in my life what makes it worth living. Your eyes, green like Icedorf emeralds, bring me peace. Your voice, like the wind in the woods, guides me. The touch of your wings, heal me. I died inside when I saw you walk away from the Seventh Seal entrance, and I was too coward to tell you then what I'm telling you now. I love you, Tabatha" Shiroan said enfolding Tabatha's hands in his hands.

"Oh, you idiot!" Tabatha exclaimed, hitting him in the chest before wrapping his arms around him and enveloping him with her wings. Their mouths melted in an embrace that tried desperately to make up for the time lost and speak louder than their words ever could.

"Will this take much longer? It sure looks more fun than chasing uglies but slightly less urgent, I'd say," Kishi commented with a smile. Shiroan and Tabatha jumped back as if pushed by a spring.

"No need for that, kids, I've had good times myself. Excellent times even. Like what I just saw."

"Save it, Kishi. We're going, we're going," Shiroan said walking to the ladder.

"Are you still traveling with us to the Sixth Seal?" Gregoria said to Tabatha.

"Thank you, but I think I'll stay behind. I can be more useful that way," Tabatha said looking at Shiroan rather than Gregoria. "I'm going to the Fortress. We don't know where the loyalty of most of the Conclave lies, Mortagong might have less allies than he realizes. He's trying to destroy Skyroar after all. Goldenmane, will you join me?"

"I will. I know the Fortress back and forth and we can check the dungeons, if there are rebels, they will be in the cells."

"It's settled, then. We go now," Gregoria said leaving the armory, Kishi and Shiroan followed.

"Tabatha," Shiroan said walking towards her. "Thank you for this decision you just made. Take the black crystal with you. You'll need it more than I do," Shiroan said handing it to her. "You don't have any other way to kill them dead."

"You're going to face the largest part of the hordes. I can't take this from you."

"You're not wrong, but Gregoria's double-edged spear can obliterate demonphantoms."

"Good for her. What about you?"

"It makes us all safe. C'mon, we don't have the time for this, take it."

"Fine. Give it to me."

Shiroan handed her the long sliver of black crystal, and she caressed his hand as she took it from him.

Tabatha walked to a basalt table in the corner, placed it on top and in one movement unsheathed her sword and cut it down the middle separating it in two thinner pieces. "Here, now we both can kill them dead and neither one of us needs to spend the rest of their cycles as a demon."

Shiroan took the shard and smiled. "Next time we see each other we'll never separate again, that's a promise," Shiroan said kissing Tabatha gently in the lips.

"I'll hold you to that, Shiroan. You can count on it," Tabatha said walking out.

Chapter Fifteen

Mehrik woke up to the warm embrace of the twin suns rays. For a moment, the events of the past cycles felt blurry and vague, almost impossible. Like waking up from a nightmare. He could nearly smell the hot wormbread and tea that Momo always made him for breakfast while humming old Oceano songs. Only the acute pain coming from deep within his essence could remind him that he hadn't dreamt it all. The world outside may look the same, but inside, where it really mattered, it had changed beyond measure. It was gloomier, lonelier, darker.

Momo was lying on his bed. He looked peaceful, serene, *dead*. Before leaving him, Momo had made the most outlandish revelation. He, the deliverer with the dream of becoming a warrior, was the heir to the Oceano crown. Moreover, he had produced a letter from his own mother to prove it. Mehrik wasn't sure what to do with that knowledge or with the odd artifact he had found inside the box, the Core-Sole. For the time being, it was stowed away in his rucksack. There were, after all, much more urgent matters to investigate.

"I love you Momo," Mehrik said kissing the cold, bruised forehead of his grandfather. Covering him with a yellow, dirty sheet, he took the Hellblood flask from his chest and left the room without looking back.

"I wish Hellblood was transferable, so at least one of my problems could be solved," he said. "Well, I'll just have to continue being extra careful, and if the worst comes to happen and a demonphantom enters my body, I still have the Lavaheart gifted to me in that Elgarian town."

Lork knows Mehrik sad. Lork sad too. Mehrik will be well, Mehrik no need Lavaheart. Mehrik needs Lork, the seahawk telepathized as he perched in his shoulder and rubbed his head against his cheek. Mehrik didn't need anything more… or less. He needed exactly that. He needed his best friend.

"I know, buddy, let's go out. We have a long cycle ahead of

us."

Mehrik Oceano throne? asked Lork.

"I don't think so, my friend. Regardless of the letter, I find it almost impossible to believe I am the heir to the throne. Even if I was, I'm sure Oceano has since found a path forward without me. No time for this nonsense anyway, we've got places to be," he said opening the door.

As he was stepping out, he hung Momo's Hellblood in the handle to signal the healers that somebody had died inside. They would see it during their round and take the body away.

It wasn't long before Audax and Ingens painted the horizon orange, and when they did, Mehrik instantaneously wished the darkness would have lasted longer. As the sunsrays illuminated the streets of the Village, Mehrik's expression changed to one of unadulterated horror. Dry blood tainted the basalt walls and wooden doors of the Village's Main Street. Corpses piled up on the cobblestone road, some of them naked, most of them clothed. Healers were tending to the wounded while deliverers carried the dead away.

"Was I asleep so profoundly that I didn't hear the battle unfolding so close to me?" Mehrik asked Lork, perching on his shoulder.

Mehrik sad. Mehrik needed rest. Lork protected Mehrik last night, Lork telepathized.

Thank you, buddy. I know you did.

"What happened here, milady?" Mehrik asked a healer as she sealed a bleeding wound with a red-hot rock.

"Where were you last night when the demons came, boy?" she asked from her crouching position without looking up.

Mortagong! It's got to be him, Mehrik thought. "I was delivering a package in the North Wall," he lied.

"Well, we lost the West Wall, the demonic hordes entered Skyroar, some of them took the time to pay us a visit before continuing their path to the Hidden Chamber. If they stayed longer, there wouldn't have been a Villager alive to tell the tale," the healer said.

"I'll come back later and see how I can help, now there's somebody I must see," Mehrik said without waiting for the healer to answer back.

Long gone were the demonic hordes that devastated the Village on its way to the Hidden Chamber. The Hundred Kingdoms army, however, was a different matter. Mehrik was convinced Mortagong would lead them inside very soon to finish the job. He needed to alert someone, and, unfortunately, there was only one option, if he could even get to him.

"We'll need to visit the mayor," he said.

Mayor not good.

"I know you don't like him. I don't either. He's sleazy and will most likely try to capture me on sight. But look around, my friend, this level of destruction is beyond anything we've seen before. If we are not prepared to fight against the Hundred Kingdoms, the Villagers are as good as dead. Don't worry, I'm pretty sure the mayor hates Mortagong as much as we do, if not more. I'll use that to get my way," Mehrik said.

Bad idea, Lork communicated.

"We'll see," Mehrik said as he walked in the direction of the Town Hall.

The gorgeous cloudless sky and the twin sunsrays shining over the Hishiro statue made the surrounding devastation look more surreal. Mehrik resisted the urge to vomit as his nostrils received the stench of demon secretions carried by the morning breeze. Not even the cloth he was holding against his mouth and nose was enough to stop it. The odor penetrated deep down his throat and burned through his lungs. Incapable to retain control over his insides, Mehrik crouched by the Hishiro statue and threw up with such force that his eyes filled with tears.

As he recovered, Mehrik looked at every detail of the sculpture showcasing the Elgarian hero. Hishiro's left foot was placed on top of a dead demon, while he stabbed another one in the neck with his sword. His other hand held a bony head with a lower jaw broken in half. He had seen it many times, but it was the first time that he wondered how Hishiro had resisted the stench of the battlefield.

"I hope your Prophecy is real, Hishiro," Mehrik said looking at the statue's lifeless eyes. "Because it doesn't really look like we're winning."

The Town Hall was at the other end of the square. It was made of basalt, like most other buildings in the Village, but that was where the similarities ended. The main structure was held by six circular granite columns, each one as wide as a regular home. Marble statues embellished the four corners of the construction and all the windows had iron bars crossing them. Mehrik went up the steps leading to the oversized red oak door and had to step on his toes to reach the knob.

"No guards around, Lork, all of them must've been called to the Fortress," Mehrik said.

Or dead, Lork sentenced. It was clear to Mehrik that his friend still thought this was a bad idea.

"I hope the mayor is in," he said opening the door.

It was a familiar sight. As a deliverer, he had visited the Town Hall many times. The interior was decorated with the same furniture and ornaments as the Conclave members quarters. This has not gone unnoticed in the Village, that frequently referred to the mayor as the Little Preceptor.

Mehrik walked straight to the main dormitory on the upper west side of the building and knocked on the door two times. Nothing. He knocked two more times. Nothing. He swung at the door with all his strength, almost hitting Praktish, the mayor's secretary, as he opened it.

"I'm here to see Mayor Vaneshk. It's a matter of the outmost importance," Mehrik said with a solemn tone. He had seen Praktish before and wasn't especially fond of him.

"It is I who will decide the importance of your matter," Praktish said. The white of his eyes was red and his hands were shaking. Mehrik could tell he hadn't slept in some time.

"I'm a deliverer. I need to see him. The Village, and most likely Skyroar, are in danger."

"For a deliverer you were not fast enough, my boy. The Village was attacked last night already, didn't you get here walking through the streets?"

"That's only the beginning," Mehrik said with a harsh tone that he regretted immediately. He couldn't lose sight of his goal, he needed to speak to the mayor.

"His Excellency is taking care of this crisis, he doesn't have the time to deal with whomever comes knocking at his door," Praktish said realigning his purple vest with his white shirt.

"I apologize for my tone, sir, I must talk to him. I have a message to deliver. Could you please help me?"

"No, I can't," Praktish said in an offended tone as he rolled his eyes and stepped back to close the door.

Mehrik squeezed his left leg in, then his shoulder. Praktish, a Vespertian, was taller than Mehrik, but didn't possess his determination.

"Guards!" Praktish called, turning his head inwards when it was clear that Mehrik would make his way in.

Two guards came from the room to his right. Mehrik squeezed through the door and ran up a set of stairs on his left. They were fast. Mehrik was faster. Three doors greeted him at the top of the steps, the one in the middle wore the coat of arms of Skyroar, a volcano surrounded by a white marble belt and with two crossed swords above it. He rushed inside and locked the door behind him.

"What's the meaning of this intrusion?" Vaneshk asked from his bed. "Guards!" He said standing up so clumsily that he fell to the floor.

"They can't come in, your Excellency. We must talk. It won't take long," Mehrik said with a shaky voice.

"Who are you?" The mayor said squinting his eyes. "You're the Oceaner! The deliverer! The traitor!" He exclaimed. "Guards!"

"Listen to me, please. I need your help. You must gather all the people in the Village and evacuate. Mortagong is planning to take over the city. He has allied himself with the Hundred Kingdoms, their army is ready to invade," Mehrik said as he heard the guards bumping against the wooden door. It wouldn't be long before they brought it down.

"Have you lost your mind? Why would he do that? He's the Great Preceptor."

"You don't understand, he plans to imprison or kill every Oceaner, Vespertian, Icedorfer, Solis or Lionkin and have the Elgarians rule undisputed over all the Known Territories."

"That's impossible. How would you have come across such information without me knowing it first? It's clear that you are just trying to make me betray the Great Preceptor. Well, I'm not falling for it. His Eminence will be happy, grateful even, when I deliver you to him, in person," Vaneshk said taking a vase from the bedside table and throwing it at Mehrik. He dodged it at the last moment but that was enough time for the mayor to get to the door and unlock it. Vaneshk was a lot faster than his incipient stomach and greying hair would lead to believe. "Take him!" He commanded.

Mehrik assessed his options. He didn't want to fight. He was outnumbered. Hurting any of the soldiers would only make it more difficult to find the help he sorely needed. Without thinking, he stood behind the mayor and pressed his dagger against his neck.

"Nobody moves or the mayor dies," he said.

Bad idea, Lork messaged from behind one of the barred windows.

"You'd never do it, deliverer, you're not built that way," Praktish said.

"Try me," Mehrik said putting just enough pressure against the mayor's neck to let one drop of blood appear.

"Stay there, he'll kill me!" Vaneshk said with a breaking voice.

"I'm doing this for all of us. You too, mayor. You might not believe me now, but you'll be a believer soon enough."

"Even if what you are claiming was true, which it isn't, I'm an Elgarian, more than that, I am the most important Elgarian of the Village. I have no reason to be afraid."

"Are you certain? That's not what I've heard," Mehrik asked with a smirk. "Rumor has it you're a hybrid and your mother was a Vespertian," Mehrik said.

"That's a lie! How dare you!" the mayor said trying to squeeze from his grip.

"Is it? Let's see!" Mehrik said as he pulled down the mayor's night gown to expose two atrophied stumps protruding from his shoulder blades. "Nice wings," Mehrik said before pushing him forward and jumping through the opened balcony door. Lork was waiting for him.

Demonphantoms, the seahawk telepathized.

"Demonphantoms?" Mehrik said looking up. "Are you sure, Lork? How far? How many?"

Here. Many, Lork telepathized.

"It must be because of the battle in the volcano, they're hunting new essences to possess. Let's go, without my Hellblood I'm an easy prey," Mehrik said.

A group of soldiers was running down Main Street in his direction. Not far from the Town Hall there was an old alleyway in ruins leading to the west end of the Village. He might be able to get there without being seen. Only one way to find out.

"For Hishiro!" he said, jumping to the street as the Town Hall guards stormed the balcony.

He landed on top of a statue of the mayor and from there made his way to the ground. The wide avenue was empty except for the guards and Louise, and old Solis woman that sold pigskin in the Hishiro Square market. It was odd to see her there. Odder to see how she swayed from side to side of the wide street. But the oddest was to see her without a smile on her face. Mehrik had met Louise many times before, she was always in a good mood, greeting everyone and talking to everybody. Always smiling.

She wasn't smiling now.

Louise stopped moving. Her bloodshot eyes were devoid of life. Her mouth opened in a silent scream as her right hand moved to her chest and closed around her Hellblood flask. Her skull cracked as her face changed. The white blouse she wore was ripped off her body as her shoulder blades extended, her arms morphed, and her torso doubled in size.

"She's becoming a demon. Did Mortagong taint the Hellblood of everyone in the Village already? If he did, this will be a massacre," Mehrik said. "But why? It doesn't make sense to multiply the demonic hordes and put the Hundred Kingdoms at risk, not after I saw him self-proclaiming their king. They might have Hellblood, but they still can be killed. But what else could it be?"

"Stop!" a guard yelled.

The scream brought him back and made him react.

I can't leave, Lork. Not after seeing this. We must do something to help, Mehrik communicated to Lork as he evaded the guards but, instead of going to the alleyway, as planned, he ran back to Hishiro Square. He needed a place where he could warn as many people as possible in the shortest amount of time. It wouldn't be long before he was captured, or worse.

We might be late, my friend. Look for help, Lork, we're going to need it, he telepathized when he spotted a group of guards battling two demons in the farthest corner of the square.

"Listen to me! Everyone, listen! We are in grave danger, demonphantoms are flying to the Village, you got to leave while you still can!" Mehrik exclaimed.

"Get out of there, kid!" an old Elgarian man yelled from a nearby clay container stand. "You'll hurt yourself. What do you think the Hellblood is for?" He said pulling the necklace from under his blouse.

"The Hellblood won't work, it has been replaced. We must seek refuge before the demonphantoms arrive!"

"Don't listen to him! He's Mehrik the traitor. Praktish, go get him!" Vaneshk screamed from one of the balconies of the Town Hall.

"You need to go, now! Under the suns' light, the demonphantoms will be invisible until is too late. Please trust me!" Mehrik said with an angst-filled voice.

"Don't worry about us, traitor. Worry about you," An Elgarian woman said approaching him.

Mehrik realized too late he was surrounded. Villagers were walking toward him from every angle. He had no escape route. Praktish and his guards weren't far.

"You must believe me! You can't stay in the Village! We have all been betrayed!" Mehrik yelled with such force that he hurt his throat.

The Villagers ignored his plea, their focus was on him.

Praktish was almost within reach when he fell as if he had hit an invisible obstacle. Once in the ground, his legs twitched, his torso trembled, and he started to drool white foam.

"He's changing!" Somebody yelled before all sound was muffled by a horrible squeal. Praktish had fallen to the ground a Vespertian but stood up as a dragon.

A single breath of green fire burned to death the group of Villagers in front of it.

"Thankfully he's leaving, Lork. Flying to the Hidden Chamber, no doubt. We're safe for now," Mehrik said.

"Look out!" Shouted one of the Town Hall guards as soon as Mehrik finished the sentence.

Two demons rose from the crowd.

"Follow me! Now!" Mehrik shouted as he jumped down the statue and into Main Street. "We need to get to the Fortress!"

An Elgarian ran after him asking for help. Mehrik reached out with his hand just to find that her hands had changed into demon claws. Mehrik avoided the unexpected attack by leaning backwards and sliding to the side. The Villagers in the square were no warriors. All around him people were dead or being killed. It was too late.

Mehrik searched the crowd until he saw the tall banners of the Mayor's Honor Guard. "Mayor!" He called, catching up to him.

Vaneshk's pale face was distorted with horror. He looked at Mehrik with eyes full of tears and desperation. He was hunched over, leaning on a cane, almost as if he could physically feel on his shoulders the sheer weight of the predicament they faced.

"Don't hurt me, please. Guards, protect me!" he said as Mehrik reached him.

"I don't want to hurt you. I want to help. We don't have much time. You need to take as many Villagers as you can to the Fortress."

"Why? We'll be killed in the open."

"We're being killed here. If we reach the Fortress, we'll be able to hide. The closer we are to the Conclave, the safer we'll be. I'll stay behind and try to keep the demons at bay. I need a sword," he said looking at the guards. One of them, a young Solis stepped forward and gave Mehrik hers.

"I'm better with my spear, anyway. Where do we start?" She asked.

"Thank you. You must go with the guards and protect the Villagers, I'll stay here," Mehrik said.

"There's no honor in a foolish sacrifice. You'll be lucky to earn us a quarter of a period before you're killed. The demons will catch up to us in no time. I'll stay, who stays with me?" she asked, turning her head to look at the other guards.

"Me," said a well fed Elgarian wearing a chest plate too small for his body.

"And me." Said a short guard standing by his side.

"Anybody else? Well, then, it's the three of us only, it seems. I'm Yesenia. These are Ox and Lard."

"Thank you, Yesenia. I won't forget this. Mayor! You need to go, now."

"People of Skyroar! To the Fortress, run to the Fortress and don't stop until you get there!" Mehrik exclaimed.

The Villagers looked at each other, frozen in place. They didn't have any reason to trust him, and he knew it.

"Listen to the Oceaner! To the Fortress! Guards, escort me!" Vaneshk commanded.

This time, the Villagers listened. Nobody said a word, but a few of them gave Mehrik a furtive look of gratitude before leaving.

Half a dozen demons looked at the escaping crowd. As if guided by an invisible force, the creatures rushed towards the mass of bodies at full speed.

"We are the only thing keeping those Villagers alive!" Mehrik said holding Yesenia's longsword with both hands. "We must stop them but can't kill them. It's impossible to know who amongst us is wearing poisoned Hellblood. We go for the ankles or knees. We want them to be crippled, not dead. Avoid their secretions, it'll burn your skin."

"Understood, chief. Crippled, not dead," Ox said blocking the path of the first demon. The tall and wide Elgarian was still shorter than the creature, but he was undoubtedly heavier.

"Yesenia! One is getting away!" Mehrik screamed as he was sliding under one of the demons while slicing its right ankle. The thing squealed and threw its arms at Mehrik, nearly clawing him.

Yesenia rushed after it. She was a fast runner. The demon was faster. The last line of Villagers was as close as a stone's throw. It leaned forward with open jaws. Without any effort, lifted an Elgarian off the ground and threw him against a boulder. Mehrik heard his back cracking. A mother had her back sliced open as she crouched to protect her babies. Yesenia stopped. Mehrik wondered why. She was still sixty steps away. She couldn't possibly dare to throw her spear to a target that needed to be crippled, not killed, and was surrounded by innocent people.

She dared.

The spear cut through the air faster than an arrow. The demon didn't see it coming. It cut through its knee, severing its leg from the rest of the body. By the time it hit the ground, Yesenia had taken the spear back and sliced through the other one.

"Take the babies! Now!" She commanded a Villager before crouching by their mother just to confirm what she feared. She was dead.

Yesenia yelled when the claws of the creature pierced her side. With a quick turn, she cut its hand clean off the wrist. It opened its jaw and, with the other arm, leaped to her throat. It never reached her. Lard's sword had sliced its neck.

"Let's go! Run!" Yesenia screamed bouncing up and taking her hand. "The demon is dead. We need to move!" They ran towards a large boulder and hid behind it. Mehrik and Ox caught up with them.

"Are you well?" Mehrik asked Lard, who breathed with difficulty and was sweating profusely.

Lard didn't answer, his eyes rolled up, his arms swollen, his mouth filled with foam. It was too late for him. Ox observed paralyzed the transformation. Yesenia reacted without hesitation.

"Let's go!" She said cutting both ankles of the creature that had been Lard.

"All of the demons are dealt with, for now. We don't know how many more may be coming." Mehrik said.

"Good, but we might have a bigger problem." Ox said pointing to the East Wall. The Hundred Kingdoms troops were pouring in.

"They've taken down the Wall!" Yesenia exclaimed. "How is that even possible?"

"It isn't. They didn't take it down," Mehrik said. "Mortagong let them in."

"But why?" Ox asked.

"To kill us all," Mehrik said clenching his fists.

"What do we do now? Should we go join the Wall guards?" Yesenia asked.

"No, we are too late to be of any help. Besides, you and I would just be made prisoners on sight," Mehrik said.

"Look, they are not even fighting," Ox said, pointing at the place where the Hundred Kingdoms troops met the Wall soldiers. "They are just talking to each other."

It wasn't long before they shook shields and made their way, without rushing but without pause, to a group of Oceaners and Vespertian deliverers. All of them were made prisoners.

"Why are they doing this?" Yesenia asked. "We are all citizens of Skyroar, they should defend us."

"Mortagong has entered their heads. He convinced them that being an Elgarian comes first. Most of Skyroar are Elgarians, we must think that most of them will be with Mortagong," Mehrik said.

"Not me," Ox said with pride. "I would never join him."

"I believe you. The Villagers are our priority, we need to get them to the Fortress. We can come up with a plan once we are inside. If the troops find us outside, we'll suffer the same fate as them," Mehrik said pointing at the Oceaners being forced to enter a pig cage.

It wasn't long before they caught up with the last line, a group of elderly villagers carrying pigskin bags.

"You must leave everything here and walk faster. The Hundred Kingdoms army has breached the Wall. They'll be here any moment," Yesenia said.

"The Wall guards will protect us, my dear, no need to worry," an old Vespertian said lifting his cane.

"No, they won't. Trust me. Please, you must hurry, all of you!" Ox said, putting all their bags on his back.

Mehrik rushed to the front line, looking for the mayor. He needed to let him know that the troops were coming and, more importantly, make sure he sent somebody first to the Fortress to announce their arrival.

"I was a fool sending everyone up the hill without checking with the Fortress first. The archers may very well be loyal to Mortagong. I may have led the Villagers to a trap, Lork," Mehrik said.

Fortress guards shooting arrows, Lork telepathized, confirming Mehrik's fear.

The Villagers were too tightly packed for him to be able to run up the path, so he decided to get off the cobblestone path and climb the moraine. The fastest he could go in the slippery terrain was still too slow.

"Mayor! Stop!" he yelled from afar. "The archers are shooting!"

Vaneshk turned his head while an arrow scratched his temple. The guards around him fell wounded to the ground. Mehrik looked to the nearest turrets. There were three archers per station. He had sent the Villagers to their deaths. "Everyone! Move back! Retreat!" Mehrik yelled off the top of his lungs. Going from side to side, he grabbed the Villagers he could reach and pulled them back, away from the unfolding carnage.

"Why are you attacking us? Don't you know who I am? I'll have you all sent to the dungeons!" the mayor shouted disgruntled.

Mehrik grabbed his arm and pulled him back. Two arrows bounce against the cobblestone where the mayor was standing just a moment before.

"Mortagong must've left them instructions. He doesn't care about us. You need to help me get everyone to a safe place," Mehrik said.

"What are you going to do?"

"Whatever I can," he said running back towards the Village. "Yesenia, Ox, we can't make it to the Fortress, the guards won't let us through."

"We can't go back." Yesenia said.

"Or stay here," Ox added pointing at the Hundred Kingdoms troops that were getting closer.

"We need to buy the Villagers a fighting chance. How long do you think we can we hold them?" Mehrik asked.

"As long as you need us to, Oceaner," said a voice behind him.

Chapter Sixteen

Tabatha's mind was elsewhere, froze in the memory of a fleeting kiss and a confession that had taken entirely too long. Walking behind Goldenmane's footsteps, she ignored for just a moment the tragedy they were living to allow herself the smallest of smiles.

Shiroan, wait for me. I'm coming back for you, she thought. *Not even the end of the world will stop me.*

There was no way into the Fortress from the West Wall, so they had been walking east for some time. Walking in the open would have been suicide, their plan was to go alongside the Wall until the Village, and then follow the path to the Fortress. That was the safest way, but several periods had passed, and Tabatha was starting to wonder if they had made the right choice.

"Watch out!" Goldenmane said hiding behind one of the Wall's wooden beams. "The East Gate is being lifted."

"But… that's impossible. The opening mechanism was removed a long time ago."

"Impossible or not, it's happening."

"The Hundred Kingdoms army will flood our streets, Mortagong can't possibly be that crazy," Tabatha said in a vain attempt to deny what she was witnessing with her very own eyes.

The last time the East Wall gate opened was to receive those escaping from the Hell outside, back when Skyroar still accepted them.

This was not that.

As guards placed left and right to the gates pushed bone wheels the size of a Village hut, Tabatha prepared her bow and took an arrow from her quiver. Each wheel required several people to operate. The gate moved as slowly as a snail climbing a rock, unfortunately, it was already halfway up. With uncanny precision, her arrows pierced the hands of the warriors pushing the wheels. She didn't have the heart to kill them. The soldiers let go of the handles, but it was too late. The path to Skyroar was already there. The Hundred Kingdoms army poured through. They, and someone else.

"Mortagong! I can't believe it!" Tabatha said when she saw the Great Preceptor passing through, riding a moose, leading the army, and wearing the Hundred Kingdoms crown. Behind him, the soldiers that Skyroar had fought for so many seasons entered the citadel unopposed, almost welcomed.

"What did you do, little Elgarian," Goldenmane said.

"He just condemned us all to Hell," Tabatha said.

"The Villagers! We must get to the Fortress and warn the Conclave, they must send troops here before they kill them all," Tabatha said.

"Bad idea. If the Wall soldiers are on Mortagong's side, I guarantee you he persuaded the Fortress guards a long time ago," Goldenmane said.

"What do you suggest we do then?" Tabatha said letting out a puff of air in frustration.

"We go to the dungeons. Mortagong is nothing but cunning. If he's down there, he already made sure that any potential threats are neutralized, but I don't believe he'd have had the support to kill every deserter," Goldenmane said.

"So, he must have sent them to the dungeon. We free them, they help us. That… is smart," Tabatha said surprised at the strategic thinking of Goldenmane. "You were certainly wasted at your old job, Goldenmane, what's the fastest way there?"

"Going through the Fortress is the quickest but is also the most dangerous. We won't exactly blend with the Fortress dwellers," Goldenmane said.

"We don't have a choice, do we? Every delay may condemn somebody to death. Our chosen path here took too long already. Mortagong, the demons, the Hundred Kingdoms army, there are too many fronts opened," Tabatha said.

"The shortest road it is, then." Goldenmane said unsheathing his battleax.

"Just one thing, Goldenmane, remember that the guards are not our enemies, they're following orders, no killing unless it is to save an innocent life," Tabatha said grabbing his wrist.

"I'll try, but I can't make any promises. Mortagong killed my sister, whoever is with him, is my enemy," Goldenmane said.

They walked on a diagonal line towards the Fortress' nearest entrance. The metal door in front of them, about half the width than the main east door, was rusty on the edges and smelled like urine.

Tabatha wondered if there was even a guard on the other side.

She lifted the metal knocker and dropped it two times. Nothing.

She knocked again, pulling the ring higher and throwing it against the door with passion.

"A think I hear steps," Goldenmane said moving his sensitive feline ears forward. "Be patient."

A narrow rectangular slit opened, revealing a set of brown eyes behind two crossed metal bars.

"Who's there?" asked the guard.

"Tabatha from Vespertia. Sixth Seal Warrior, Commander of the Winged Squadron under Admiral Torok," Tabatha answered while Goldenmane remained concealed, with his back against the Fortress wall.

The square window closed with a click. Voices could be heard inside. Goldenmane lifted his hand-paw and showed three fingers to Tabatha, indicating the number of distinct people he could hear.

The window opened again, and the same two eyes appeared. "What are you doing so far from your post?"

Tabatha's mind went blank for one moment. *What was I thinking? Of course he'd ask that! I should have had an answer ready for this.*

"Even a warrior can go for a drink at the Village from time to time. A drink and perhaps some herbaltum as well. Don't tell me you've never done it yourself?" She said with a complicit smile topped with the most charming of winks.

"How dare you suggesting such a thing!" The guard exclaimed with a tone of indignation. "That's preposterous!"

"I'm sorry, my good sir, I didn't mean to accuse you of anything," Tabatha said backtracking. She needed a change of strategy.

"You do understand that you're supposed to come in through the east gate, right?"

"I know, I may have drunk… a little bit… too much… to find it," She said slurring the words just enough to make up her point without raising suspicion. "If I don't get to the… to my post, my commander is going to kill me, mate!" she said missing the doorframe as she tried to lean on it, adding what she hoped was the right amount of clumsiness to the performance. "I don't want to do latrine duty... again... please, could you make an exception? I'm sure you've been in my place before."

"The rules are clear, I'm sorry. Nobody–" The guard interrupted his lecture mid-sentence and got away from the door leaving the small window open. A commotion of people running and yelling orders could be heard inside. The metallic sound of unsheathed swords mixed with the thumping of leather boots against the marble floor. Something unusual, and big, was happening. Tabatha approached the door and listened carefully for any signs of danger. The square window was too high for her, but a quick leap and a swift flap of her wings allowed her to peek inside. She caught a glimpse of the last few Fortress guards turning a corner and getting lost in the main hallway. Tabatha batted her wings a couple more times, gaining enough altitude to place her feet on the border of the window while grabbing the top part of the doorframe with her left hand to help her balance.

"What are you doing? Are you out of your mind?" Goldenmane said.

Tabatha took an arrow from her quiver with her right hand and put it through the opening.

"The guards are gone. Something's off," she said. Her whole arm was now inside the window as she rubbed the arrow against the door hoping its tip would hook onto the locking mechanism.

It did. With as much care as she could have given the circumstances, she pulled the lock up, which in turn released the metal bar that kept the door closed.

"Let's go!" Tabatha said.

"That was impressive, I must admit," Goldenmane said.

"Well, let's hope it also is worthy, judging by the screams coming from the main hallway, we might be already too late."

"Only one way to find out. Follow me," Goldenmane said.

Tabatha grabbed her bow and nocked an arrow as she advanced. Even if she wasn't a fugitive, she was certainly helping one, and an obvious one at that. There weren't many scarred, one eyed, Lionkins in Skyroar.

Tens of Fortress guards flanked them on both sides as they ran east.

Nobody gave them a second look.

"The demons must've entered the Fortress," Tabatha said. "That's the only possible explanation."

"Perhaps. In any case, the guards are going east, and we must go west," Goldenmane said.

"Why would we do that? This is an invasion. We should help. I need to go back to the Sixth Seal, to my duty," Tabatha replied.

"We'll be able to assist better once we have more information. You're letting your instincts take over. It might be the demons, or Mortagong, or the Hundred Kingdoms or a mutiny, or something else altogether. We agreed on a strategy, and I plan to stick to it. I'm going to the dungeons to talk to Mortagong's prisoners so I can be prepared for what's next. You can do what your essence dictates."

"I'll go, but let's make it quick," Tabatha said giving a last look at the troops running away. *Hang in there Torok, help is coming. I promise.*

After a labyrinthine race through alleys, paths and doors, the landscape changed from marble to basalt, and the air became heavier and harder to breathe.

"What is going on?" Tabatha asked as Goldenmane came to a sudden stop just before turning a corner.

"Silence," Goldenmane whispered. "There is a soldier standing guard at the end of the corridor. We'll be seen if we take one more step. You need to go first and find a way to disable the guard. The moment I show my face I'll be recognized immediately and may be forced to kill."

"I'll go, if only to spare the guard's life. I still think we might be better off fighting for Skyroar, I'm concerned that the Hidden Chamber won't hold for much longer, Goldenmane," Tabatha said.

"Trust me, this is the right path. It's not cowardice to act strategically, to seek allies, to find out who's on our side. I lived my life in anger, resenting my sister for doing what was best to save most people, to have a true chance to win the war. I confused bravado with bravery, and the Lionkin paid the price. It took seeing my sister being murdered to realize that. The Conclave members loyal to her must be in the dungeon by now. They're the way to claim this battle with as little bloodshed as possible," Goldenmane said placing his paw-like hand on her shoulder.

"My brother died in front of me. He fell on the sea of lava, possessed, half transformed into a demon," Tabatha said, her voice breaking. "I loved him more than I love myself. In a world where everything wants to kill us, anything we do can be a mistake. Your plan comes from a place of love and respect, that's more than I can say for mine. I'll stand behind it."

"Thank you. There'll be plenty of fight left for us, trust me. Besides, we've heard no squealing in the halls so far, although the Fortress may be haunted by monsters of a different kind."

"Wait here," Tabatha said taking off her chainmail, belt, quiver, bow, and helmet to avoid looking like a threat. When she turned the corner, she opened her mouth, raised her eyebrows, looked back often and, in general, tried her best to simulate a panic attack.

"Are you well, woman? Is someone chasing you?" The guard said without moving.

Hell, he's not coming to me. Well, this is it Tabatha, now or never, she thought before tripping with an invisible obstacle and falling to the ground.

"Haven't you heard? We're being invaded! The Fortress is being taken as we speak!" she shouted as she extended one of her arms towards the guard.

"Invaded? Are you sure?"

"More than certain. I'm myself escaping from the demons that are roaming in the Fortress. They'll kill us all!" She yelled even louder.

"Here, let me help you," the guard said walking to her and grabbing her hand. "You can stay here for a few moments but then you need to go. Here, take my dagger. It might not be much but is better than nothing," the guard said helping Tabatha stand up.

"Thank you. You are too kind," Tabatha meant it. She had to act quickly, otherwise she might just not be able to do what needed to be done.

"Just doing my part," the guard said as he turned his head enough to give Tabatha an entry. She hit the back of his head with the hilt of the dagger. The guard froze for a moment in place before falling to the ground unconscious.

"Goldenmane! It's done, let's go!" She exclaimed.

"Is he dead?" Goldenmane asked as he took the keys from the guard's belt.

"Of course not. And that's a good thing, this guard, I assure you, is not our enemy. Please keep that in mind," Tabatha said.

"Have it your way," Goldenmane said under his breath. "But if we leave him here, he'll give the alert when he comes to his senses. Take the keys and open the door," he said lifting the soldier over his shoulders without any noticeable effort.

"Oh, stop complaining and let's go," Tabatha said.

"It's easy to tell you're not the one carrying him around," Goldenmane said with a growl.

"Less whining, more walking," Tabatha said as she ran back to grab her gear.

Lit torches marked the way through the basalt, windowless, passage. Holding the guard firmly in his shoulders Goldenmane led the way to another metal door that looked no different from the one they left behind. Tabatha opened it and entered a square room with a wooden table and stools.

"Frothos?" Goldenmane called. "Frothos, are you here?"

"Boss?" The thin Vespertian opened the door of what had been Goldenmane's office. "You came back, I can't believe it!" Frothos said with what Tabatha thought was genuine joy.

"I did, but not for long. Listen to me. We need your help."

"You're a Vespertian," Frothos said looking at Tabatha. "Glurius tar flirium." He said wrapping his body in his good wing and what was left of the other and leaning forward.

"Glurius tar flirium," Repeated Tabatha also wrapping herself in her wings and bowing.

"Good, now that you are best friends; Frothos, did they bring anybody since I left?"

"Like you wouldn't believe, boss. I swear on the Prophecy that I never saw more prisoners than the ones we have today. They made me put four or five in each cell. We've got no space no more. Moreover, most of them are wearing black robes," Frothos said whispering the last statement, as if to keep it secret from prying ears.

"Is there a dungeon where we can put this one?" Goldenmane said, leaving the guard on top of the table.

"Not really no," Frothos answered.

"Well, we can always chain him to a wall," Goldenmane said entering his office and coming out with a set of shackles.

He lifted the guard again as if he was made of feathers and carried him to a metal ring coming out of one of the walls. Holding the unconscious body over his left shoulder, he passed the shackles through the ring and around the guard's wrists. He then gave them a good pull to make sure they were locked and secured.

"We're ready, Frothos, let's see what you've got in there," Goldenmane said.

The moment Frothos opened the door, a stench of urine and sweat hit Tabatha like an anvil. Goldenmane and Frothos seemed impervious to the smell, but she had to fight hard the urge to vomit before she could follow them inside. Goldenmane peeked through the small rectangular visor of the first cell to his left where sixteen inmates, nine wearing Conclave robes, were sitting on the floor with no space to move.

"Help us! Help us please!" the Conclave members said in unison.

A hand appeared at the edge of the window. It reached for Goldenmane's face. "How many Conclave members are here?" Goldenmane asked.

"Hundreds," one of them answered.

"Hundreds? How did you allow this to happen?" Tabatha asked Frothos.

"We pledged alliance to Skyroar, and our mandate is to obey the Great Preceptor, is it not? The Great Preceptor himself asked me in person to incarcerate them."

"The Great Preceptor is a traitor!" Tabatha exclaimed. "He's also a madman in need of being stopped. How could you not see that?"

"I... I didn't. I apologize but I was alone. I did my job," Frothos said.

"Let him be, Tabatha. Frothos is loyal to Skyroar and did what he had to do. He's also a friend. There is no malice in him. He couldn't suspect the Great Preceptor," Goldenmane said.

"It's time to teach him then. First things first, let's open all these cells." Tabatha said, taking the bone keys from Frothos' belt.

"All of them?" Frothos asked.

"All of them." Tabatha replied. "It feels good being a traitor, doesn't it?"

"Not really, no. But it feels good to be working for you again, sir," Frothos said looking at Goldenmane.

"I'm glad to see you, Frothos. Where are the spares? Can you bring them to us? It'd be faster," the Vespertian ran to the main room. An instant later, he came out with two additional sets of keys. Tabatha had already opened four cells.

"Close both hallway doors, Frothos. We don't want anyone leaving before they listen to what we have to say."

"You'll all pay for this outrage! You hear me, all of you!" Said a Conclave woman upon release, her face red with indignation. "You can't treat the Conclave of Skyroar as if we were petty criminals or common prisoners. This is –"

"Oh, cut it out lady!" Goldenmane exclaimed. "We're the rescue party, you can figure that one out because we're opening the cells. Tabatha, you want to say something, don't you?"

"Yes, I do," Tabatha said after a pause, amazed at the way in which Goldenmane had spoken to the Conclave member. "Your Excellencies: Skyroar is under attack. You already know Mortagong has betrayed us all. What you may not know is that he has allowed the demonic hordes and the Hundred Kingdoms army inside the Fortress."

"This can't be true, Mortagong may have wanted the power all to himself, but why would he want to bring down Skyroar? What would that accomplish?" A robust Conclave man asked.

"We don't know, yet, but we do know the Hidden Chamber is at risk. If the demonic hordes reach the Seventh Seal, the Passage to Hell will reopen," Goldenmane said.

"We need to stop them, what would you have us do?" a Solis Conclave woman said approaching Tabatha. Thin as a twig and almost as short as an Oceaner, her look didn't warn Tabatha of the thunderous sound of her voice.

"We've lost control of the Fortress. We'll have to regain it if we want to have any hope of organizing an attack. Who among you can tell us how many Conclave members are with Mortagong?"

"It's hard to tell, dear, hundreds, at the very least," an old Elgarian with a ripped robe and a receding forehead talked from the crowd that had formed in the hallway. "A few cycles ago, Mortagong held a secret meeting in the Conclave Hall. Only Elgarians Conclave members were invited. I participated in the gathering. He asked us to join him on his mission to conquer the Known Territories so the Elgarians could rule uncontested, and he could rule over the Elgarians.

"He promised that The Hundred Kingdoms army was on his

side. Then he mentioned he had enough Hellblood to equip their army. I thought he was lying, where could he possibly get enough Hellblood for that?"

"But much to my despair, that wasn't nearly the worst part. He talked with the eyes of a madman. It was the scariest thing I've ever seen. I think he plans to kill any non-Elgarian that dares to opposes him and enslave everyone else. Not even Belgoriel frightens me more, if you can believe it," another Conclave member said with watery eyes.

"Because he believes he's right," said the Solis Conclave woman.

"Almost casually, he proposed a vote to know who agreed with him. He asked us with a smile, as if he was asking us our opinion on building a new square. Some of us, me included, shouted insults and were ready to leave, but he somehow calmed us down, helped by Louriel, of all people. Since Louriel was so close to Galanta, we decided to go along with the farce and vote. I was sure he would lose by a large margin," the Elgarian Conclave member continued.

"Yes, I was also sure the charade would show how little support he had, so we indulged him," said a third Conclave member, a young Elgarian with a robe stiff with dry blood. "Instead of throwing this madman immediately in the dungeons and ending that aberration of a meeting, we voted. We allowed for hands to be counted as if this was about how many kiosks should be allowed in Hishiro Square. Unforgivable error. It was the action of voting that sealed our fate. The instant the hands of the opposition were raised, Mortagong asked the Conclave members in favor, a clear majority, to move to the side while Louriel opened the gates of the Conclave Hall letting in a small army of Fortress guards. Elgarian Fortress guards."

"The Fortress guards brought us all here, which was most likely Mortagong's plan all along. He knew he had the majority; he just needed an excuse to get rid of the minority."

"The defectors and us," said the thin Solis. "The impure ones. I was forcefully taken from my apartment. When I resisted, I was beaten. When I spoke, I was mocked. When I refused to move, they dragged me," she said lifting her robe and showing deep cuts through her back. "Mortagong needs to be stopped. By any means necessary."

"Agreed. The good news is that Belgoriel is no more. It died last cycle at the hands of Icedorfers and the last Cloudhunter. The bad news is that without Belgoriel the demonic hordes went into chaos. They are on their way to the Seventh Seal as we speak," Tabatha said.

"And Louriel, well she—"

"She hasn't been seen since a few cycles ago. We thought she might be here, but she isn't," Tabatha said giving Goldenmane an urgent look that she hoped he could decipher.

"What she said," Goldenmane said under his breath. He was visibly upset, but he complied.

Tabatha wanted to know more about who to trust before daring to reveal who had killed Galanta. "Not now. Later," she mouthed to Goldenmane as she grabbed his hand for just a moment.

"With Mortagong ready to attack, and Skyroar invaded by the demonic hordes, it looks like we don't have many options left. What can we even do?" said a bald Conclave member from the back.

"We fight back," the Solis Conclave member said looking at him.

"My thoughts exactly," Tabatha said with a smile.

CHAPTER SEVENTEEN

The Fifth Seal was a cemetery.

Located on a natural plateau on top of a massive basalt column, it was the largest of the Seals. And it was packed with burning corpses.

"Skyroar is running out of heroes, Blue," Kishi said with an unusual grim tone as he covered his mouth and nose with the palm of his hand, trying to filter out the smoke. The white of his eyes was dark red and streams of tears ran down his cheeks.

"We were too slow," Shiroan said. "We still are. Every seal we encounter is the same. We need to move faster."

"We're going as fast as we can, but we can't catch up with the demonic hordes, let alone the dragons. We can only hope that each dead warrior has killed at least one demon and has delayed the advance of a few more," Gregoria said.

"The Sixth Seal is next, Blue, these deaths are recent. Let's keep going and see if we still can make some good," Kishi said with a raspy voice before going into a coughing fit.

"That's good news. Kaina, Torok and Mardack can hold the demonic hordes back for a long time," Shiroan said.

"You think very highly of your friends, Shiroan. I'm sure somebody else had the same thoughts about the ones from the Fifth Seal," Gregoria said as she casually kicked a scorched skull off the edge of the plateau.

"You'll share my opinion after you fight with them, Gregoria. Let's go!" Shiroan said walking towards the bridge that connected to the Third Seal and from there to the path leading to the Sixth Seal.

They didn't have to walk long before finding trouble.

"Watch out," Gregoria whispered as they passed through a wall of smoke. Two demons were ripping bodies apart at the gates of a burning tent. Without hesitating, Shiroan held the black crystal with his right hand and attacked the closest creature.

As it lifted its bony head, Shiroan leaped forward, slicing its throat from left to right. The fetid, warm thing that filled its body splashed his face, making him gag. The demon bloated and contorted as countless blisters formed around the wound. Shiroan couldn't look away as the monster transformed into a deformed pile of rotten flesh.

"Behind you!" Gregoria yelled. The second one was already in the air with its claws ready to slash his chest open. Shiroan lacked the right angle to pull the demonium piece and didn't have the time to draw his sword. Fortunately, Kishi tackled it from the side, pinning it to the ground. Gregoria unsheathed Phantomslayer and cut its head clean. The creature changed into the Elgarian that had been before. The demonphantom emerged from the body and tried to escape, but Gregoria impaled it before it could fly away.

"Thank you," Shiroan said.

"Later," Gregoria said. "Seventh Seal first."

The group walked down the narrow bridge towards the side of the mountain. All the seals were built in a circle, with the Fifth Seal at the center.

Even though the sea of lava was so far below, Shiroan could feel it burning his skin. Its orange light covered everything around them like the dim glow of a dying sun.

"It's empty," Shiroan said looking around the considerably smaller Third Seal. I imagine everyone ran to defend the Fifth Seal and died there.

"I agree. No demons on sight either. Looking at the trail of ooze, it's clear that that they are on their way to the Hidden Chamber," Gregoria added.

"There's food. Over here!" Called Kishi from the rests of a bonfire. "And water!"

Gregoria and Shiroan didn't move.

"Oh, come on! We haven't eaten or slept in a long time. We won't be able to sleep just yet, but we can, no, must eat something. We won't be doing anyone any favors if we are too weak to fight."

"He's right, Gregoria, let's grab something to eat and drink and continue our path."

"Listen to Blue. He knows best. Also, be fast or I'll finish all the pig entrails by myself. The stomach is the best part!"

The three Seven Warriors ate for a few moments in silence before grabbing a few more pieces of food to go. The water was on a large communal barrel, so they drank what they could and left the rest there.

"Be careful on the path, it's full of demon ooze," Shiroan said as he entered the narrow mountainside edge that connected the third and sixth seals.

It wasn't long before they could hear the battle. Not much after that, they were able to see the Sixth Seal soldiers fighting the demonic hordes in the distance.

"We aren't too late, you were right, Blue," Kishi said. "It remains to be seen if that's a good thing."

"A battle is being fought. We are warriors. We fight. This is nothing but good news," Shiroan said.

"I agree with him. It means we still have a chance to save the Hidden Chamber," Gregoria said.

"Kishi, you and Gregoria work together. You kill the demon, Gregoria kills the demonphantom. I'll use the black crystal to open a path to the far end of the seal, that's where the heart of the battle will be. Torok would have sent the best troops to defend the pass to the Seventh Seal."

"How about the dragons?" Kishi said pointing to the numerous creatures spitting green fire over the tents.

"If Kaina is here, she'll be battling them as we speak. If there are duranese arrows left, we could take a good number of the dragons down. Otherwise, it'll be up to Mardack," Shiroan said.

"Mardack? That crazy Elgarian we met when we escaped? What could she possibly do?" Gregoria asked.

"Why don't you ask her yourself once she's a little less busy?" Shiroan said looking at a dragon contorting in the air as Mardack sunk a spear down its eye.

"Too much talking! Let's go kill some uglies!" Kishi said unsheathing his battleax and rushing forward.

It didn't take long for Shiroan to leave Kishi and Gregoria behind. *Kaina, where are you?* Shiroan thought looking up at the dragons circling the seal. He knew it was a matter of time before the dragons found their way to the Seventh Seal. Without Kaina, they wouldn't have a chance to stop them.

Shiroan felt a knot in his essence when he passed by Torok's tent and saw it enveloped in green flames. Fearing the worst, he rushed to the remains of the structure. There wasn't much left.

"Torok!" He called squinting his eyes to try to see through the fire and the smoke. "Are you there?"

"If I was, I'd be unable to provide you with a satisfactory answer, don't you think?" Torok's voice came from behind his tent. "Now, if you are so kind, your support over here would be greatly appreciated."

Shiroan followed his voice and found a few other warriors fighting scattered demons. Three of them attacked the commander of the Sixth Seal, who was holding a sword in each hand.

"It's great to see you, boy," Torok said. "Do you still have your Hellblood around your neck?"

"I sure do." Shiroan said.

"Great, you'll need it," he said thrusting his swords forward.

"Hold on! Don't kill them. I'll show you a new trick. You'll like it," Shiroan said sneaking through to get by his side.

"Hope it's good," he said cutting through the ankles of the first demon and bouncing to the second one.

"Oh, it is," Shiroan said piercing the demon's chest with the black crystal. It swelled, blistered, and transformed in a lifeless gelatinous mass. Like with all others, no demonphantom left its body.

"You were right. I like it," Torok said with a crooked smile. His thick, red moustache was dripping ooze.

Shiroan finished the other two within moments.

"Let's go, Shiroan, there are more of us that need help," Torok said. As they approached the path that led to the Seventh Seal, another cluster of demons became visible through the smoke. A handful of warriors were fighting them.

"In the name of Hishiro! Look who decided to show up to the party! No worries big guy, we've saved some for you."

"Mardack!" Shiroan said with a heartfelt voice. "Rashiro!" The Cloudhunter said as he stabbed and sliced every demon in his path. The warriors observed in awe how they were reduced to a gelatinous mass in front of their eyes.

"Impressive. You learned a few things while you were away playing hero, I see," Mardack said. "These were the last ones on this side, sir," Mardack said looking at Torok. Her flying contraption had one half-opened wing hanging down like a dead limb from the harness. The other one was completely gone.

"And the north end is also taken care of," Gregoria said joining the group. "No more enemies around."

"You have the appreciation of my command and mine as well," Torok said nodding his head to Gregoria as a sign of respect.

"Many demons made it through. Including several dragons, probably enough to bring down the Seventh Seal, I would say," Mardack said. "Kaina went after the dragons, I wish I could join her, but my wings broke in my last fight."

"Kaina!" Shiroan said. "You've done well, Mardack. You're a fine warrior that has killed more dragons than anyone I know." Turning to Torok, he said: "I must go to the Seventh Seal, Torok. Kaina will need all the support she can get to save the Hidden Chamber. I can't let her face the hordes alone."

"I recollect an exchange where I distinctly stated that, once you leave the seal, you lose the right to return. Didn't I —"

"Torok, I don't want to fight you, but I will if I have to," Shiroan said interrupting him.

"Let me finish," The muscular Elgarian said twisting his red moustache with his left hand. "I believe I said that before we were betrayed by the Conclave and forced to face an unprecedented demonic invasion. Additionally, after seeing your mastery over swords, axes, and bows, I wouldn't dream of trying to detain you considering how depleted my army is. It would be unreasonable to think that me and the remainder of my troops can successfully stop you and your comrades. We'll save this particular fight for later, now it's time to win this war. Go and make sure the Passage to Hell remains closed as tightly as it is today. We'll stay here and handle whatever else comes your way," Torok said placing his hand on his shoulder.

"Thank you, sir, you're a good friend. I'll avenge every one of your soldiers."

"That's too much talk already, Blue, let's go! We'll have time to hear your boring speeches later," Kishi said.

"What the big guy said," Mardack seconded. "And you better bring Kaina back."

"One more thing," Torok said. "What happened to Tabatha?"

"She's fighting her own battle, sir. And I would bet my good right arm that she's winning,"

"I bet she is, kid. Let Hishiro give you the might," Torok said.

"To send the demons back to Hell," Shiroan, Gregoria and Kishi replied with a common voice.

Shiroan led the way to the Seventh Seal. He ran down the narrow path at an impossible speed, sorting through cracks and edges, and dodging treacherous puddles of ooze. Gregoria followed as fast as she could but was slowly losing ground and Kishi hadn't even tried to keep up.

Wait for me Kaina, I'm coming, he thought. Shiroan was leaving his essence in that run. He felt physical pain just thinking of Kaina, fallen in battle, dying alone. If he had stayed in his position, he could have helped Kaina and, perhaps, saved the Hidden Chamber. If something irreversible happened in the Seventh Seal this cycle, it would be on him.

He crossed the full width of the infamous Death Trap with one jump, clinging to the edge on the other side with his fingertips and pulling himself back to the narrow path with a single formidable effort. A steady current of warm air hit his face when he entered the cavern leading to the Seventh Seal. That could only mean one thing: the demonic hordes had forced the secret door open and were already inside. And three of the Seven Warriors weren't there to protect it.

Shiroan ran down the cavern as if he wouldn't have been fighting, without pause and without rest, for well over a cycle. There were many concerns going through his head as he sped up down the cave, but sleeping was not one of them.

The exposed entrance to the Seventh Seal greeted Shiroan like the roaring mouth of a dying rock giant. The gate was nowhere to be found. It took his mind more than a few moments to accept the reality in front of his eyes.

He had arrived in Hell.

The Seventh Seal had been taken and, perhaps, also the Hidden Chamber. The demonic hordes bit, scratched, flew, jumped, and ran through what had been, until then, the most inexpugnable sanctuary of all Skyroar. In the middle of the plateau, the hordes covered the sphere. It shone purple instead of the usual green and buzzed as if housing thousands of wasps.

"Shiroan! Let's go, we must get there fast!" Gregoria exclaimed, grabbing his arm.

To the left of the Hidden Chamber, below a cloud of demonphantoms, the clashing of swords was dampened by the hellish squeals. "Look," Shiroan said, "That must be where the rest of the Seven Warriors are. We'll start there."

The words had barely left Shiroan's mouth when they were attacked. Gregoria used Phantomslayer to kill in two movements, the demon first, then the demonphantom. Shiroan's black crystal made his job easier. One swing was all it took. As he moved forward, he kept an eye in the sky, hoping to find Kaina. He finally saw her in the highest part of the seal, ferociously fighting three dragons. Red stripes of blood running down her white fur. Shiroan ached to go help her but there was nothing he could do, yet. The Seven warriors needed him, so he focused on that. With a few swift movements and the priceless assist of the black crystal shard, Shiroan opened a path for Gregoria to move forward. The squealing of the fallen creatures caught the attention of the hordes biting and scratching the Hidden Chamber.

Lifting their snouts, they sniffed the air as they searched. Once they found their target, two dozen demons left the floating sphere and pounced. A chaos of claws, jaws, and teeth fell on them.

"What do we do? There are too many, we'll be dead before we can go through even half of them," Gregoria said as she dodged and stabbed.

"We need to watch each other's backs and be quick. Forget about the demonphantom, we're all wearing Hellblood, just kill one and go to the next," Shiroan said.

"Agreed, but there're even more coming. We'll have to have eyes on our backs," Gregoria said.

"It's always the same I tell you," Kishi said taking his battleax off the abdomen of a demon and sinking it in the back of a second one. "You take a little break and when you come back from vacation everything has gone to Hell. Typical."

"You took your sweet time, didn't you, big guy? Can you help us create a path to the rest of the Seven, they're over there," Shiroan said pointing to the spot where he believed Rexora, Parktikos and Botharhi were.

"I can do this all cycle with a hand tied behind my back, Blue. Let's go," Kishi said.

"Very well then. Let's finish this," Shiroan said.

So many demons were around the inner edge of the plateau that more than a few of them were falling to the sea of magma below. By the time he reached it, he was bathed in ooze and rotten flesh.

Shiroan wanted to throw up but didn't have the time. As they got closer, he could hear the voice of Rexora giving instructions. Shiroan continued fighting his heart out, eventually making his way to the small clearing where the warriors were fighting for their lives.

"Need a hand?"

"Not sure if one as smelly as yours," Rexora answered.

"It's melted demon stench, long story. We're here to help,"

"I figured," Rexora said with a smile.

"Parktikos!" Gregoria exclaimed.

Two demons had Parktikos on his knees, an open wound on his left side bled through a ripped shirt. Shiroan leaped forward and killed them both with one swing of his crystal.

"Are you well? Can you still fight?" Shiroan asked.

"To the death," Parktikos said as he used his sword as a cane to stand up. He was bleeding badly.

"I'm glad to hear your voice, Shiroan," Rexora said. "Your weapon. It consumes the essence of the beasts, yes? It kills them. Permanently. I see the demonphantoms dissolving."

"That's correct. Kishi and Gregoria are also here, we'll win this fight, we'll send the demons back to Hell, forever," Shiroan said.

"What's happening?" Gregoria asked, looking around in awe.

"They are retreating! This was easier than I thought!" Shiroan said.

"Shush! Can you listen to what they are saying? I believe they're talking about us. About you, Shiroan. They are afraid of you," Rexora said.

"As they should be! But how can you hear them," Shiroan said.

"The advantage of being blind is that your other senses become more acute. My hearing is better than most," Rexora answered.

"Where is Botharhi?" Kishi asked as he looked at the mass of corpses and melted entrails that surrounded him.

"He... didn't make it. When the demons arrived, he was our first line of defense. Fought with the intensity of a true Seven Warrior, but even that wasn't enough against the demonic hordes," Parktikos said.

"He died a hero," Rexora added.

"Shiroan!" Gregoria exclaimed, pointing at the Hidden Chamber. It had changed colors yet again. This time from purple to red.

"Look at the runes, they are blending and changing, they seem to be moving towards the gate! We need to get them off the sphere! They are opening it!" Shiroan shouted.

"Stop, Shiroan! What is keeping them out is not in the Sphere but in the cave. It's Lethos, it's the Magia. The demons must have gotten to him, that's why the Magia is weakening. If he dies, everything will be lost," Rexora said.

"Parktikos, Kishi, try to keep them out of the Hidden Chamber. Gregoria, Rexora, come with me, let's go help Lethos," Shiroan said already slicing his way to Lethos' cave.

"We should have left somebody guarding Lethos, this is my fault," Rexora said.

"You're not the one that decided to leave, so don't blame yourself," said Shiroan.

"Save the drama for later, we're here to fight not to whine," Kishi said pushing Shiroan and Rexora away. "Also, Blue, perhaps you want to go kill some uglies in the water cave, you smell like dragon breath," Kishi said.

"You sure don't smell like roses, buddy," Shiroan said with a smile as he took down the demons that obstructed his view of the ledge where Lethos meditated.

Four creatures were on top of a semi-transparent, green bubble that protected Lethos from the attacks. Claws and teeth screeched against the shield, white cracks formed around it and small holes became bigger with every hit. It looked like the incantation was about to shatter into pieces at any moment.

"Morter lanius dirium. Cartinomicon tar marcaris glorium. Morter ramilium morter. Portilus lau portialis. Glomius!" The Vespertian chant was barely audible above the scratching, the biting, and the squealing.

"Go, Shiroan! There isn't time," Gregoria exclaimed. "There are holes in his Magia shield already!"

Shiroan climbed up a macabre ladder built out of stabbed demons that exploded as he left them behind. He jumped high in the air to position himself above Lethos. When he landed, the black crystal was sunk deep in the back of a demon. With two swift movements he stabbed the demons covering the green bubble and kicked them off the balcony. Lethos was bleeding from his chest and neck. Pieces of the shield were scattered around him, as if somebody had shattered a pile of green ice. His chanting was almost inaudible.

"You'll be fine, mate. We are here," Shiroan told him holding him in his arms.

"The Hidden Chamber!" Parktikos yelled entering the cave. "They're breaking through."

"Lethos' enchantment is too weak. We will lose it," Gregoria said.

"Like Hell!" Shiroan yelled. "Rexora, come and do what you can for Lethos. Gregoria, Parktikos, let's go save Skyroar, after all, we're heroes, aren't we?"

"We're behind you," Gregoria said.

The sphere shone with a red bright light. It was still floating at the center of the seal, but made sudden movements from time to time, as if invisible hands were pushing it in every direction. The basalt platform that led to the door was filled with demons, many of which fell to the sea of lava when trying to reach the moving target. He needed another way in.

Shiroan ran to the edge and jumped across the sea of lava, barely clearing the twenty steps gap to the Hidden Chamber. His fingers grabbed the rough edges of the runes but slipped on the ooze covered holds. He moved his feet searching for anything that could support his weight. The moment his left hand lost its grip, he found an edge wide enough for him to propel up to the top of the sphere. He landed on a demon, and as he did, he kicked it off the edge.

The rest of the hordes on top surrounded him but didn't attack.

They must know what the crystal is. They must know this is what killed Belgoriel, Shiroan thought.

The sphere shook and trembled with such force that its sides smashed against the seal's edges. The demons that got caught between the wall and the sphere were crushed to death, like apples being stepped on by a moose. Shiroan had to lay down and grab the tiny edges of the runes to avoid sliding off the Hidden Chamber. Helped by their sharp, long claws, the creatures slowly climbed closer to him. If he tried to grab the black crystal from his belt, he would lose his grip and fall to his death. When Shiroan felt the warm and heavy drool on his back, he realized he might not have a choice.

"Incoming!" Gregoria's shouted as she flew towards him

holding Phantomslayer with both hands. "You always need to do everything the hard way, don't you?" Gregoria said landing on top of him.

Using Gregoria's weight as an anchor, Shiroan pulled the black crystal and reached the ankles of the demons closest to him. The rest of the creatures stepped back tripping each other and sending several off the edge. The ones that stayed didn't last long.

"Let's go after them!" Shiroan shouted standing up, the sphere seemed to have stabilized, although it still shone red.

"Watch out!" Gregoria said grabbing Shiroan's shoulders and pushing him down.

The Cloudhunter felt a rush of air brushing his neck as a large white body flew past him, rubbing his skull and crashing in the Seventh Seal's floor.

"Kaina!" he yelled, crossing the entire distance to the plateau with a single, desperate, leap. The drakovore was bleeding from her snout, and forefront paws were broken. She stretched her neck and wagged her tail at the sight of her friend.

Shiroan hugged Kaina's wounded snout when a whooshing sound made him look up. The dragon that had been chasing her friend had completed a wide circle and was now plummeting towards them at full speed, to finish the job. Shiroan stood between Kaina and the dragon, black crystal held high. His chances to hit the eyes or the abdomen of the dragon were close to zero, but he was not budging. The dragon passed them by, quick like lightning, too fast for Shiroan to do anything when he realized its true target: the Hidden Chamber. The claws of the dragon closed around the edge of the half-unhinged door, and, with a mighty pull, it ripped it off and let it fall to the sea of magma below with a victorious Squeal.

"We're losing the Chamber!" Kishi exclaimed.

"Kaina," Shiroan whispered, foreign to what was happening around him. The drakovore, lying down flat on the basalt floor, was motionless. "How are you, girl?" He said lifting the eyelid covering blue eyes as big as his hand. The drakovore didn't react. "I can't feel her breath," he said placing his hand in front of the snout. "I can't feel her breath!" He exclaimed.

The demons were inundating the sphere, two of them already reaching for the door.

"Shiroan!" Gregoria shouted from the top of the Chamber.

"Let's give Blue a moment, he'll catch up," Kishi said.

"I don't need a moment!" Shiroan yelled. "Friends died. The seals are in ruins. The rest of Skyroar may be gone already. We must fight."

"And fight we will, but look at us, we're exhausted, and I can hear many more enemies coming. Probably more than we can handle. Without reinforcements, we will not prevail," Parktikos said.

"Let them come. I don't care. This isn't the cycle when Skyroar falls, this is the cycle when the Seven Warriors do the one thing we were chosen to do: succeed where everyone had failed, save the Known Territories, and send the demons back to Hell!" Shiroan said kissing Kaina's neck as he stood up and tightened his grip around the black
crystal.

"Whatever you plan to do, Shiroan, you better do it fast. The hordes coming our way aren't our main concern right now," Parktikos said pointing to the two dragons entering the Seventh Seal.

Chapter Eighteen

"Sehrsil!" Mehrik exclaimed. "Marko! How did you find us?"

"Ask your bird. He's the one that showed us the way," Sehrsil said pointing to the sky.

"But I thought you were in Icedorf? Where are Paumeron and Faranides?" Mehrik asked.

"Icedorf is no more. Paumeron and Faranides fell like warriors," Sehrsil said.

"I'm sorry. I hope their essence finds the essence of their ancestors. What happened?"

That's a conversation for another time, let's focus on what we can still save. What's the situation?" Sehrsil said.

"Mortagong. Mortagong is the situation. He killed the Great Preceptor and took her place. Not only did he betray us with Belgoriel, he is also leading the attack of the Hundred Kingdoms army on Skyroar. If we want to survive, we must find a way to enter the Fortress without being killed by its guards. And it needs to be quick, the Hundred Kingdom army is on our heels," said Mehrik.

"You can count on us, but we don't have the time or the people to take on an entire army. There are only five of us, it seems," Marko said.

"No. Not five. Six," said one soldier stepping forward.

"Seven."

"Eight."

Soon, a group of roughly fifty soldiers had stepped forward from the crowd, swords unsheathed, ready to battle.

"Our allegiance lies with Skyroar, not with Mortagong. We're afraid but we aren't cowards. We'll fight," said a stocky soldier with a battleax in each hand.

"Thank you," Mehrik said.

"What's the plan, Mehrik?" Sehrsil asked.

"I don't have one, yet. How long can you hold them?"

"Not long. They outnumber us by at least sixty to one and can send five times that many as reinforcements. This might very well be the prowess we can't achieve."

"No. We can't afford to lose," Mehrik said looking at the crowd caught between two fronts. "If we do, they die."

"I'll breathe my last breath here, but we'll save them," Sehrsil said. "That's the promise of the Queen of Icedorf. Go find a way in. We'll find you time one way or another."

"Thank you," Mehrik said with a half bow before rushing to the front of the line. The clashing of the swords reached his ears. He needed an idea, badly.

Lork, what shall I do? he telepathized.

Save them all, the seahawk messaged.

"Always the optimist, my friend."

He was close to the vanguard when he heard a scream louder than the rest.

"Mayor!" Mehrik ran to him as he fell to the ground contorting. Vaneshk pulled his Hellblood flask from his neck and threw it out.

"It doesn't work! The Hellblood doesn't work." He said with a red face and foam coming out of his mouth. "You were right. They only want the pure ones," he said before starting to grow and change. His screams transformed into squeals. The thing in front of him wasn't a person anymore. One after the other, more Villagers were possessed, Solis, Oceaners, anybody that wasn't Elgarian. Mehrik didn't have Hellblood to protect him. He didn't care.

He had a job to do.

"For the Prophecy!" Mehrik yelled, swords unsheathed, ready to die in the battlefield. Lork attacked first, Mehrik followed suit, the demons looked at them with disdain before running away.

Notwithstanding the arrows raining on them, the creatures reached the Fortress. When Mehrik saw them climbing the wall and heading to the crater, he understood what had happened.

"They don't care about us, Lork. They're trying to reach the Hidden Chamber! The demonphantoms fallen there are coming out here to possess another body and come back to the battle. Everyone! Listen up!" Mehrik said to the villagers. "You can't trust your Hellblood anymore, open your eyes for demonphantoms."

"What do you mean?" A Villager near him asked. "Are we at the mercy of the monsters?"

"We are, for now," Mehrik said looking up. "Lork, you must go in and find a way to unlock the door for us, you're my only plan, buddy, but then again, I've never needed another."

Yes, Lork telepathized as he flew to the turrets and searched for one that he could use to sneak in. It wasn't long before he found it.

"Hold this line! We need to stay here a bit longer," Mehrik said. "Lay close to the ground or hide behind boulders. We're mostly out of the archer's reach, but those arrows can travel the distance. I'll be back, wait for my signal."

Mehrik left the main path without waiting for an answer and ran to the moraine. Zigzagging up the hill, he used his speed and the large rocks around him to avoid the incoming attacks. The last stretch offered no protection. Two turrets, one on each side, had archers ready to bring him down. Seasons of deliverer work had made him fast, but he wasn't faster than an arrow.

He changed directions as often as he could manage, struggling to build momentum on the slippery terrain. Every time he turned, his boots slid on crushed stone and dirt. He was almost there when the first dart sank on his left thigh.

Mehrik's exposed skin peeled off as he rolled down the gravel. By sinking his nails on the ground, he stopped and got back on his feet.

I still can make it; he thought looking at the Fortress. With a pronounced limp, he moved up the hill. The safety of the oversized doorframe was a few strides away when the second arrow hit him in the side.

Mehrik crashed against the door. He was safe from the archers. Bringing both hands to his abdomen, he checked for a wound and couldn't believe his luck. The Core-Sole, which he carried alongside the Lavaheart in a pocket on his belt, had deflected the projectile. It still scratched his body, but it was a minor injury. He couldn't say the same of the one on his leg. The dented tip would tear apart his flesh if he tried to pull the arrow out, bleeding him to death. He had no choice but to sever the shaft as near to the skin as possible with his sword.

It wasn't a clean cut. Mehrik screamed in agony as the arrowhead slashed more of his muscles. On the verge of fainting, Mehrik finished the job with his teeth.

Lork, buddy, where are you? Mehrik said, leaning his back against the door as he held his thigh with both hands.

He fell all the way back when the metallic gate opened, and he lost its support. The strong arms of Goldenmane prevented him from hitting the floor.

"Are you well?" Goldenmane asked. Lork and Tabatha were with him.

"He's hurt, look at his leg," Tabatha said. "Bring him inside, Goldenmane. I believe he's bleeding out."

"They're coming!" Mehrik Exclaimed using Goldenmane forearms to stand up in one foot. "The Hundred Kingdoms Army will be here soon. We must gain control of the Fortress and bring the Villagers inside."

"We already did, Mehrik, for the most part the Fortress dwellers are with us," Tabatha said.

"Not all of them. The archers are keeping the Villagers away. They need to be stopped," Mehrik said.

"The turrets, of course! Mehrik is right, we haven't gotten there yet. The archers are still following Mortagong's orders! Take care of him, Tabatha. I'll take care of them," Goldenmane said.

"It shouldn't be long, Mehrik. Now, let me see that leg," Tabatha said.

"This can wait," Mehrik said leaning against the wall. Lork, follow Goldenmane and come back when the nearest turrets are secured," the seahawk didn't wait for Mehrik to finish his sentence before taking to the air. His thoughts were faster than his words. "Tabatha, Mortagong did something to the Villagers' Hellblood. It doesn't work anymore. The demonphantoms can possess them. Even if we bring them here, they'll be doomed unless we find a way to protect them."

"There's no other way, Mehrik, you know that. Without Hellblood, nowhere is safe. Their best chance will be to leave Skyroar," Tabatha said.

"We can't. The Hundred Kingdoms troops are waiting for us outside. It'll be a slaughter," Mehrik said.

"I might be able to help," a short, grey-haired, wrinkled Elgarian woman wearing a ripped Conclave member robe said. "I apologize, I couldn't avoid overhearing your conversation. But I agree with Mehrik, the first step is to bring the Villagers to the safety of the Fortress. I believe I can help with the Hellblood issue, as long as Mortagong left any supplies left we can use," she said.

"You're an Elgarian," Mehrik said. "You overthrew Galanta and put Mortagong in her place. How do we know we can trust you?"

"My name is Mariam, I was the Minister of Science for Galanta, and considered her both a friend and a hero. I quit my Ministry when Mortagong took power. I didn't raise my voice against him. I was a coward then. I'm here to change that. You don't have to trust me, but from where I stand, you don't seem to have a lot of options."

"You're correct," Mehrik said. "I don't trust you."

"And, as Mariam said, we don't have a choice, Mehrik. I'll stay close to her. I'll make sure that she delivers on her promises. We can't wait here. We won't survive," Tabatha said.

Mehrik nodded.

Lork came flying down the hall. *Archers stopped. No more arrows,* he telepathized.

"Thank you Lork," Mehrik said rushing back to the door. "Come on in! It's safe now!" he shouted, stepping out as he waved his arms.

At first, the Villagers moved cautiously forward, stopping every couple of steps to assess the situation. Once they were confident that the attack had ceased, the crowd almost trampled Mehrik in their anxious race to reach the safety of the Fortress.

"Lork, this will take a long time, you better go and check how Sehrsil is fairing," Mehrik said as he quickly jumped to the side. He let out a groan of pain when his injured leg touched the ground.

It was clear that, regardless of how fast the tide of people moved, they'd come to almost a complete halt when they reached the door. It didn't matter how much they pushed, only two could go through at a time.

Warriors fighting. Sehrsil losing. Little time, Lork communicated from the sky.

"You!" Mehrik said holding the shoulder of a Villager entering the Fortress, "Once you go in, look for Goldenmane and tell him that we need the archers to protect us against the Hundred Kingdoms' army."

"Goldenmane?" the Villager said letting out a pant, his round face, red from the effort, signaling confusion.

"A one-eyed Lionkin in a dungeon guard armor. You are bound to recognize him the moment he's in front of you. Can I count with you?"

"You're Mehrik, the Oceaner aren't you?"

"I am," Mehrik said fearing his answer would only make things worse.

"You can put your essence at ease. I'd never let down the warrior that unmasked Mortagong and brought us to safety," The Villager said drenching his sweat and entering the Fortress. His words stayed with Mehrik for some time, unable to decide if the Villager was being truthful or was mocking him. It didn't matter as long as he passed on the message. All their lives depended on it.

"Perhaps I should go myself, Lork. That's the only way to be sure," Mehrik said.

Marko in trouble. Goldenmane in battlement. Mehrik helps Marko, Lork telepathized.

Mehrik didn't hesitate. As fast as his wounded leg allowed him, he carved a path through the river of people and limped his way to the last line of defense, where a handful of heroes offered their lives to save others.

"Where?" Mehrik asked Lork. He could see Sehrsil, Ox, and Yesenia but he couldn't find Marko.

There, Lork messaged as he flew over the heads of a group of Hundred Kingdom's soldiers. In the middle, outnumbered and surrounded, Mehrik saw Marko. Or rather, Marko's bear-shaped helmet sprouting from the crowd like a white mushroom. As he rushed to help, he noticed the four children taking cover between his legs. Sword unsheathed, Mehrik targeted the mooseskin knee protector of the soldier closest to him, one of the soft spots of the armor, and sunk his blade deep, retrieving it as he entered the circle.

"I'm here to help," he said.

"I figured," Marko said with a smile.

Mehrik stood by Marko, leaving a space in the middle where the children could be safe from swords and daggers. Mehrik didn't have armor or a helmet. He had never been trained as a warrior. His leg was being ripped apart by the arrow tip at every move, but he fought alongside his friend. He swung his sword with more passion than skill, bringing down soldier after soldier. He knew that if he failed not only Marko, but also innocent children would fall.

Lork fought by his side, sinking his claws in ears and eyes, moving so fast that no blade could harm him, and no hand could hold him.

"More are coming, Mehrik, we must find a way out," Marko said bleeding from his neck.

Lork, you need to call Sehrsil's attention, Mehrik telepathized. A moment later, the seahawk was darting away from him at full speed.

Shortly thereafter, Sehrsil arrived, followed by Ox.

"Ox, take the children and carry Mehrik with you, he's in no shape to fight," Sehrsil said.

"I can fight," Mehrik protested.

"Yes, you can, but we need you for much more than this battle," Sehrsil said as Ox offered his arms. Mehrik, exhausted and on the verge of collapsing, grabbed them.

Then he heard the canyon rammers.

Six of the most vicious animals in all the known territories puffed and stomped their way to them. Their layered exoskeletons made them almost invulnerable, and the four long arched horns on their heads could pierce through armors as if they were made of wormbread. Despite being larger than a polar bear, and considerably heavier, canyon rammers could run as fast as moose. They had no choice but to fight them.

"Look, behind them," Marko shouted.

The beasts were leading the way to a fresh regiment of soldiers, too many to count. Even if they killed the canyon rammers, they would have to deal with them, and the rest of the demons.

"Shoot!" Sehrsil yelled at the archers. A rain of arrows bounced off the animals' hide as if they were apples falling from trees.

You're sick, Mortagong, so very sick, Mehrik thought as he watched them trampling everything on their path, the Hundred Kingdoms soldiers included.

"Ox, put me down and bring the kids to safety," Mehrik said. "You need to be as fast as a deliverer if we want to survive the canyon rammers."

"What about you? You've got to come with us," Ox said.

"Sehrsil, Marko! Turn around, come to us!" Yesenia screamed to Sehrsil as she pushed a group of Villagers to the Fortress.

"Stay there, go to the Fortress," Sehrsil yelled. "You too, Mehrik."

"They're unstoppable. They'll bring the door down, perhaps even the wall. Somebody needs to organize things inside," Marko said.

"Go, Mehrik. I promised I'd buy you some time and that's exactly what I'll do," Sehrsil added.

"At least in the Fortress, we'll have a better chance to survive," one soldier, pale with fear, rebuked. "I did my part, I'll see you inside, maybe. Who's with me?" he added as he left for the Fortress, half of them followed. Half of them stayed, including Yesenia and Ox.

"Go inside, Mehrik, you're in no condition to help. You've done more than enough for us. The people inside need you. You give us hope," Ox said running downhill.

Mehrik stood in place. His friends were ready to face unbeatable creatures. His leg hurt and pulsed whether he was moving or not. Had he helped bring hope to Skyroar? It didn't feel that way. Not at all. What was in front of them wasn't the face of hope, quite the contrary. It was the face of devastation.

"We're dead," said Yesenia as the canyon rammers made the ground tremble.

"Then we die with honor," Sehrsil said thrusting forward.

Chapter Nineteen

The origin of the Book of Hishiro was one of Skyroar's best kept secrets. More than a few believed, even to this cycle, that Hishiro himself wrote it. This was of course at odds with the sacred scripture itself, which described unequivocally how the greatest Elgarian hero of all time had sacrificed his life to close the Passage to Hell and save the Known Territories from certain doom.

It didn't really matter who authored it, how it came to be, or who found it. The Book of Hishiro simply was, and that was enough. Skyroar had been built around its words. The seals, the Fortress, and the Wall existed because of it and for it. The Prophecy commanded them to protect the Hidden Chamber at all costs. Sure enough, this instruction had been followed to its last consequences. Season after season, battle after battle, and corpse after corpse. Skyroar had but one purpose: to wage war against everything and everyone trying to prevent the fulfillment of the Prophecy.

For the longest time the Wall resisted, unmovable, unbreakable, unbeatable. A colossal warrior made of rock, wood, and metal. The Villagers were the blood running through Skyroar's veins. Many generations of children could only become soldiers, healers, or deliverers. All of them, like everyone else, living for words written by the dead: *I forfeit my life so Skyroar can live. Let the core of the mountain be the keeper of the Passage to Hell and let us all be the guardians of the mountain. And forget not that if we fail and Skyroar falls, Hell will rise, and we will be no more.*

Its message was clear, at least according to the Conclave. Skyroar needed to protect the Passage to Hell within the Hidden Chamber at all costs. If they failed, the rest of the demonic hordes would enter the Known Territories and kill or possess everyone. Skyroar citizens wholeheartedly believed on their mission. They all thought that when Belgoriel was killed and the demonic hordes were defeated, the Prophecy would be fulfilled and the gateway to Hell would cease to exist.

Just like everybody else in Skyroar, Shiroan knew the Prophecy by heart, having recited it more times than clouds are in the sky. He just never thought that it would be on him to save it. Belgoriel's death only succeeded in throwing the demonic hordes into chaos. Hell had risen all around them. The Hidden Chamber, cracked, broken, and violated, shone with the fiery red color of defeat.

He understood, entirely too late, the extent to which the Great Preceptor, the Seven Warriors, and even Tabatha, were correct. He left his post to go play hero one too many times. It was no different from the cycle when Ponthos died. He should have stayed then; and he should have stayed now. His pride and his stupidity had killed one of his good friends before. This time around, he might have doomed his very best friend, and perhaps everyone else.

Hiding his face in Kaina's blood-stained fur, Shiroan wept. For the first time since she had found him, cold and scared, in the corner of a broken, dying city, he felt hopeless.

"Shiroan!" Gregoria exclaimed. "Come! We need you here! Now!"

The Cloudhunter struggled to rise from the depths of his essence. He heard voices far away and had the vague recollection of being in the middle of a battle. The warrior in him shook him up and forced him back into reality. After giving Kaina a last kiss, he walked towards the Hidden Chamber, where Gregoria, brave and defiant, kept the demonic hordes at bay.

With the determined pace of he who walks to certain death, Shiroan traveled the narrow plank connecting the Seventh Seal to the sphere. Out of instinct, almost as an afterthought, he unsheathed the demonium crystal and sliced his way forward. Demons fell dead by his side as he advanced. Parktikos followed him, sword in hand, protecting his back. Gregoria, standing by the broken door, moved to the left to let him through. She didn't say a word. Shiroan placed both hands in the frame of the unhinged door and lowered his head to peek inside. Gasping, he pulled out his head so fast that Gregoria had to grab his arm, so he didn't fall to the lava.

"How? This isn't possible," he said even though he just saw it with his very own eyes.

"I've no idea what you're talking about, Shiroan, but you better enter and figure it out, we're pretty busy here. I'll cover your back," Gregoria said.

Shiroan nodded his head in agreement and entered the Hidden Chamber. He looked around the room, focusing on every small detail as he gathered the courage to focus on what he had seen. A soft green light illuminated the inside. The basalt walls were bare and rough, without runes or marks. Dark brown wooden panels had been used for the floor. Two rusty chains ending in iron shackles were nailed to the ceiling of the sphere. Restrained by them, arms extended upwards, and wrists covered with dry blood, was a person so thin it was almost possible to count all the bones on his body. His knees were so raw that muscle and tissue were visible. Clearly the result of being forced to a perennial kneeling pose on top of a carved basalt pedestal displaying runes and a spiral of grooves. He wore the remnants of a brown robe —probably white once— and a myriad of vaguely familiar symbols had been burned on his blue skin.

Shiroan was petrified. Of all the things he expected to find inside the sphere, a Cloudhunter, a Cloudhunter monk to be precise, wasn't even in the list.

The head of the monk hanged lifeless to the side. The symbols on his blue skin glowed with the faintest of greens. The monk looked beaten up, dirty, starved, and old. *He looks like he had been trapped here for hundreds of seasons, how is that even possible?* Shiroan thought.

His bald scalp, arms and legs were covered with a thin layer of cinders. The long, brownish nails of his hands and feet curled and twisted like snakes in a pond, almost as if they had never stopped growing.

The narrow grooves carved in the basalt pedestal below him meandered down to the ground before converging in a small hole at the bottom. The miniature network was painted in dry blood. Shiroan followed the path of the blood to the monk's left foot. He took a step back when he noticed the rusty metal nail inserted deep in his ankle. Its tip was crowned with a stone disc. And the disc was attached to what looked like a machine with several moving pieces that Shiroan hadn't seen before. Suddenly, a click loud enough for him to hear over the battle sounds outside, echoed in the room. As the cogs of the machine turned, the stone capping the nail was lifted, revealing a hollow interior. Shivers traveled down Shiroan's spine as a stream of fresh blood started to drip steadily from the nail, filling the grooves and, from there, slowly finding its way to the small hole in the chamber's floor.

What the Hell is a Cloudhunter monk doing inside the Hidden Chamber? And how can a dead man bleed? The Sacred Book doesn't mention anything about any of this, Shiroan thought, still wondering if his eyes were playing tricks on him.

It took him a few moments to regain the composure. When he did, Shiroan approached the monk and cleaned the dirt off his face with his sleeve. It was warm to the touch, almost as warm as his own.

"Could he still be alive?" Shiroan said moving the remains of his robe to the side so he could search for a heartbeat. He jumped back as he saw a black hole in the place where his chest should be.

"We won't be able to hold the demonic hordes much longer," Gregoria said gasping for air as she entered.

"I don't understand. What's all this?" Shiroan said slowly turning his head towards her.

Gregoria looked at the monk for a few moments.

"So that's where the Hellblood comes from," she said.

"What do you mean?"

"His blood is filling the bucket below the sphere. The one we send to the Fortress once is filled. That Cloudhunter has kept us alive."

"What about the black hole in his chest? What does it mean?"

"I don't know. But the one thing missing here is the Passage to Hell."

"The Passage to Hell! The monk somehow trapped it in his chest to keep it closed! That's who the demons are after! They want to kill the monk to open the gateway to Hell and destroy the source of Hellblood! That's what Hishiro's Prophecy was about!" Shiroan exclaimed.

"Hishiro didn't mention that we would be torturing mercilessly a Cloudhunter to keep the gateway to Hell closed," Gregoria said.

Out of nowhere, the monk started to shake and tremble. His convulsions became so severe that the shackles cut his wrists open, and his knees lifted from the pedestal.

"If you finished sightseeing, we could use some help, Lethos is in trouble," Kishi said from the entrance.

"We need to get him down first, before he bleeds to death," Shiroan said.

"And who is our new friend?" Kishi said as he approached to help.

"I'm not sure. Hang on, pal, we've got you," Shiroan said jumping on the platform and forcing the shackles open with this sword. Placing his arms around his neck, he helped him down.

"The shaking stopped but he is losing a lot of blood from the foot and wrists. He also lost the green glow he had when I found him," Shiroan said.

"The Magia was helping him before. If we assist Lethos, he can bring it back, I'm sure," Gregoria said.

"Let's cover his wounds first, then we can go," Shiroan said carefully removing the nail from his ankle and ripping his own shirt to improvise a bandage.

"I don't think we have the time, Shiroan, a new wave is here. We must go and fight outside. We can't win from here," Gregoria said.

"He's right. Sorry, Blue," Kishi said.

"If that black hole is really the Passage to Hell, and he's the only thing keeping us safe, I got to stay and protect him. If we all go, the demons will enter and finish the job," Shiroan said.

"As you wish. Good luck," Gregoria said stepping out.

"Well, it's just you and me against the hordes, buddy," Shiroan said patting the monk's shoulder and, in doing so, touching the border of the black hole.

Shiroan fell on his knees as he felt a crushing weight on his chest. It felt as if a moose had stepped on it. Breathing had become an almost impossible endeavor. He pulled both his arms towards him only to realize that one of his hands was trapped inside the black hole. Impotence overcame him as he realized that not even all his strength was enough to take it out, the more he pulled, the harder it was to breathe.

It wasn't long before he was unable to see or hear. Shiroan remained immobile as he was dragged to a bottomless abyss that froze his essence and blurred his mind. He searched for any familiar sight, a wall, even a demon, but everything around him was dark as the blackest night. He panicked when realized that he couldn't feel his arms, or his feet, or his body. The purest fear overtook him. He wanted to scream but had no mouth. He was nothing but darkness.

"…out! Shiroan!" The voice of Kishi, coming from nowhere and everywhere at the same time, surrounded him like a sheepskin blanket. He felt the large hands pulling back on his shoulders removing him away from the dark, returning him back to his body. He was once more in the Hidden Chamber, standing in front of Hishiro.

"What the Hell happened!" Shiroan said.

"No time, the uglies are here. Can you fight, Blue? I can use the help," Kishi said as the demons entered the room.

Shiroan didn't answer, but with one movement sliced two throats before leaping forward to stab a third one in the stomach.

"You can. I'll take care of the things outside, don't miss me too much," Kishi said as the fourth and fifth demons blistered and exploded behind him.

My best strategy is to receive them at the door and kill them one by one, Shiroan thought as he reached the circular doorframe. He could see Kishi already on the other, swinging his battleax to anything that moves.

Shiroan had killed at least twenty of them before the creatures slowed down. *Are they planning a different strategy?* He thought.

"Yes, indeed," he answered his own question as he saw all the demons standing at the bridge looking up.

"Hell! The demons are on the roof of the chamber!" he exclaimed as a multitude of claws descended from above and grabbed his wrists. As he was being lifted in the air, Shiroan twisted and kicked in an effort to break free.

The pestilent ooze emanating from their skin and his own sweat allowed him to escape, but the momentum could just be stopped by him hitting the ground. As he landed, his hand hit the sharp edge of the bridge so hard he dropped the demonium crystal to the sea of magma.

The demons didn't miss the fact that he had lost his extraordinary weapon. Every one of them ran towards him. Shiroan unsheathed his sword and swung it in circles, hoping to be able to keep them at bay until he came up with a better plan. His priority was protecting the entrance to the Hidden Chamber. The Prophecy wouldn't fall this cycle. Not because of him.

His blade sliced, stabbed, nailed, hit, smashed, and pierced. A continuous stream of demons fell to the lava, each one immediately replaced by another coming from the plateau or the top of the sphere. Rivers of viscose blood and ooze ran down his face and arms. Claw marks covered the metal plate of his armor and his half-helmet had been ripped off his head. But he didn't back down. If there was a boundary between bravery and stupidity, he was about to reach it. It didn't matter. All that mattered was to keep the Passage to Hell closed.

Shiroan was strong, stronger than most, but not even he could hold back that many demons. Like an arrow shot from a bow, Shiroan was thrown all the way to the back wall of the sphere, surpassed by the sheer quantity of his enemies.

I only have two advantages, my Hellblood and the size of the Hidden Chamber. I must kill the ones inside and come back to the door. I can't let them get to the monk, Shiroan thought.

In an almost maniacal spree, yelling and growling like an animal, Shiroan murdered his way to the door, gaining precious space with each step forward. When he cleared half the sphere, he gave the monk a side look and was relieved to find him in the same condition he had left him.

Once Shiroan was able to fight his way to his original position, a pile of dead Elgarians, and Solis covered the wooden floor behind him. Not a moment had passed before a pair of clawed, bony hands closed around his skull.

He pushed his sword through the demon's eye and threw it off the bridge, then he leaped away from the sphere entrance to avoid the attacks from the demons above him.

Well, I solved one problem by creating another, at least as bad, probably more, Shiroan thought. He struggled to keep his balance on the platform while fighting the hordes around him. His body was sticky with dry blood and his boots slippery with demon ooze. Eight arms squeezed him like a spider hunting a fly. Claws scratched every bit of unprotected skin and the pressure forced the air out of his lungs. He was running out of options.

He swung back with his sword with such force that it slipped from his hand and went down the precipice. Without skipping a beat, he drew his dagger out and continued battling the demons. He had lost reach and power, but he had gained velocity. Shiroan sliced throat after throat as he pushed them to the sea of lava. Just when he thought he was regaining control, he saw two demons getting inside the sphere. "Gregoria! Kishi! I need you! Now!" he shouted but the two warriors had problems of their own. They were covered by a mountain of demons. Shiroan could only see Phantomslayer appearing every now and then like a seahawk hunting on a sea of black clouds.

"Kishi!" Shiroan yelled as loud as his lungs would allow him. Demons flew in all directions as Kishi's smiling face raised above them all.

"What's wrong, Blue, did you run out of breath?" Kishi said.

"Come! Quick! I can't hold them anymore. They're entering the Hidden Chamber!" Shiroan yelled.

Kishi said something he couldn't hear to Gregoria before carving a path using his battleax and his fist. Shiroan did his best to hold his position, but armed only with his dagger, he was more a target than a threat. He switched to hand combat, hoping to use his superior balance and greater speed to maneuver in the narrow bridge. It worked.

For a few moments.

He punched a demon in the groin and pushed him to the edge as he back kicked another one attacking from behind. Without stopping, Shiroan charged against the next one, before facing a group of three.

"Now!" Shiroan heard Kishi yelling at Gregoria. Turning his head, he saw the Solis intertwining her arms with Kishi's and jumping in the air to land with her feet in the plank.

Shiroan didn't have the time to welcome the reinforcement. Another demon had reached the entrance of the Hidden Chamber. With a couple of quick movements, he dodged three of them and found his way to the door. Dagger in hand, arm extended forward, his only focus was to keep them from entering. Big mistake. Two more pounced at him from the top of the sphere, landing on his chest, and pinning his body to the bridge while holding his arms above his head. Dirty claws sunk deep in his wrists. Another one quickly came to help by standing on Shiroan's legs. He tried to slide free, but their weight kept him in place. Its fetid smell invaded his nostrils. Warm drool spilled on his face. He could even taste the revolting breath. In an impossible move, Shiroan was able to throw his dagger to the closest demon, sinking it into its eye. Squealing in agony, it let go of its grip, freeing his right arm. Shiroan claimed back his weapon and stabbed the demon in the groin. It growled, opened its jaw wide and thrusted his head forward. It was going for his throat.

"Get off him!" Gregoria yelled as Phantomslayer sliced its head off.

Shiroan, free from the waist up moved out of reach but having miscalculated the distance, found himself hanging heads down off the edge of the bridge, supported only by the demon that was standing on his legs.

"Gregoria!" he exclaimed, but the Solis, attacked from the front and the rear, was deeply engaged in battle.

The warmth, slightly sulfuric, smell of the lava hit his face at full force. Drops of blood dripped from his fingertips.

Looking down, the demon stepping on his legs realized the predicament Shiroan was in. So, it simply took a step to the side.

Shiroan tried to keep hanging on the platform, but the demon ooze had made the surface too slippery. His legs lost its grip and sent him plummeting to the sea of lava like a blue boulder. Gregoria extended her arm, offering Phantomslayer as a lifesaver, but a demon tackled her, throwing her to the other end of the plank. The look of sheer terror in Gregoria's face as she was pushed away sent Shiroan the clearest of signs. This was the end of the road. As he approached the melted rock, his mind seemed to capture, with pristine clarity, every detail of his surroundings: Kishi reaching out with his massive hands extended past the edge of the plank; three demons accompanying him on his fall, probably pushed by Gregoria; the Hidden Chamber, shining deep purple, battling to survive. The magma below burning his face and chest as he came closer.

It is over, he thought. *I failed. I failed them all. I'm dead.*

Chapter Twenty

A handful of battle-weary warriors separated six canyon rammers from thousands of innocent people. Taking down one charging canyon rammer was an almost unsurmountable task, six was just unthinkable, but these warriors were not in the habit of shying away from impossible odds. On the contrary, these were the type of warriors that laughed at those odds and bended the world to their will.

Sehrsil and Marko stood tall with their chests slightly forward. Their boots rested by their side. The fight in front of them required every single trick they had, including the razor-sharp claws at the end of their hairy toes. Their eyes were fixed on the advancing beasts. They held their swords with both hands, ready to strike. Mehrik could feel their determination. To stop the unstoppable, however, determination wasn't enough.

"I hope somebody else has a plan, because I'm out of ideas," Mehrik said.

"Why aren't you inside? Ox, didn't I ask you to bring him in?" Sehrsil said looking at the robust Elgarian guard.

"I tried, he's not easy to handle," Ox said.

"You don't know the half of it," Marko said.

"Well, the fact is that I'm here and we have only moments to act. What do we do?" Mehrik asked with a voice unable to hide his fear. He almost regretted having lost the chance to hide in the Fortress. Almost.

If Sehrsil and Marko, two Icedorfers without a reason to defend a city that had made their lives a living Hell, were prepared to die for Skyroar, he was ready to die with them.

"Don't go for the heads that's suicide. Don't go for the body either, that's where its hide is the thickest," Yesenia said.

"That doesn't leave us much of an option, does it," Marko said.

"There's only one way to slow down a rammer. You need to

break its throat. Push your blade in through the gap between the chest and neck bone plates, their only soft spot, and twist it."

"That's nonsense! Its throat is their best protected part. When they're charging, their heads are down," Marko complained.

"Exactly," said Yesenia.

"They're almost here!" Ox warned.

"Hishiro, help us," Mehrik said.

Then the vast cloud of seahawks fell from the sky like a hurricane of feathers and courage.

The birds attacked the canyon rammers from every direction. They scratched, clawed, and ripped their eyes and throats so fast that the beasts couldn't do anything other than disperse in a desperate attempt to escape. Three rammers fell to the ground, eyeless and with bleeding ears. Two rammers crashed against each other with such force that they lost conscience. One rammer, blind and mad, continued its charge to the Fortress.

Sehrsil reacted before anyone else. Moving forward, she stood in the rammer's way. As it approached, she let herself lie flat on the ground. The blind beast ran directly to her. Sehrsil moved just enough so the hooves wouldn't stomp her. With uncanny precision she lifted her sword at the perfect time. Her blade went deep inside the beast's throat. The rammer didn't stop. The momentum carried by the beast pulled Sehrsil with her. She let go of the hilt. The canyon rammer took a few more strides before falling to the ground. A cloud of dust surrounded its massive body as it slid to a complete halt. It was dead.

"This isn't over!" Ox yelled. "The Hundred Kingdoms army is still coming our way."

"What the Hell happened? Where did those birds come from?" asked Marko.

"They. The Army of Oceano happened. My people," Mehrik said with deep pride in his voice while pointing to their right.

The mountainside was, as far as his eyes could see, covered in red coral helmets and pearly armors. Hundreds of short, bronze-skinned soldiers led the way, followed by countless rows of knights riding sea lizards. Their swords and spears were pointing forward, and they kept the shields close to their chests.

Having completed their mission, the seahawks flew back to their masters. They covered the sky like rainclouds before a storm.

The Oceano flag – a black seahawk, wings wide open, carrying a snake in its claws against a blue-green ocean – waved at the end of a long pole carried by one of the soldiers.

Mehrik had only heard about the Oceano army through Momo's stories. Legendary quests of brave soldiers and fearless generals filled the uneasy nights of his childhood and shaped his dream of becoming a warrior. Momo was a vivid storyteller, but there wasn't an adjective, regardless of how superlative; or a narration, regardless of how embellished, that could have ever described the magnificent spectacle unfolding before his eyes. He had never been so proud of his heritage as he was right at that moment.

"Friends or foes?" Sehrsil asked.

"Foes," Yesenia answered. "Oceano has made many attempts to breach the Wall. They wanted to get to the Hidden Chamber and take its power, just like everyone else."

"Perhaps this time is different," Mehrik said.

"I realize they are your people," said Yesenia. "I've also fought Solis warriors when they've attacked the East Wall and know how it feels."

"It's more than that. The sheer size of the attack doesn't make sense. Oceano had always sent smaller tactical squadrons to the Wall, never something of this scale," Mehrik said.

"They're hitting us when we're down. I wouldn't be surprised if they were acting in agreement with Belgoriel, or even Mortagong," Ox said.

"That would make sense if Mortagong's plans didn't include conquering them. If they were supporting Mortagong, why would their first action be to defend us? No, there's something else. I'm sure," Mehrik said.

"That's true, but Oceano is far. To arrive at this precise time, they had to leave at least one cycle and a half ago. Let's not read too much out of a coincidence. They might not be here to help Mortagong, but it doesn't mean they're on our side, Mehrik," Marko said.

"People change. I have. More things have broken in the last few cycles than the Wall. As long as they want to end this war, I'm counting them as friends. To me the only battles ahead of us are against Hell and against Mortagong. This is our war. It must also be theirs. If it isn't now. It'll surely be when we talk to them."

"Nice speech, Mehrik, but the truth is you don't know what you don't know. Marko is right. We can't assume anything," Sehrsil said.

"Sirs and ladies, should we go inside and continue the conversation in a safe place? The Hundred Kingdoms' troops have stopped, but they could resume their attack at any moment," asked one of the soldiers as he shifted his weight from one foot to the other. Mehrik could see how the hand holding the sword was trembling.

"There isn't a safe place anymore. The Wall is down; no amount of strategy is going to prevent those armies to find a way in," Marko said.

"The Hundred Kingdoms troops stopped to assess Oceano's intentions. They're probably sending an emissary to talk to them as we speak. If the Oceano forces are looking to destroy the remnants of Skyroar, which, Mehrik, you must agree, is more than plausible, they'll likely join them in battle. We must regroup and come up with a plan," Sehrsil said.

"But what if they're willing to join us?" Mehrik asked.

"If the Oceano army is here to help us, they'll be briefed on the situation. The Hundred Kingdoms' troops are but a fraction of what they have beyond the East Wall. They may have sent for reinforcements already. If they want an easy win, they'll move fast," Sehrsil answered looking at the Oceano army stationed one thousand steps from them.

"In other words. We need to go talk to them. I'll do it. I'm one of them after all," Mehrik said as he limped forward.

"Don't be ridiculous, Mehrik," Sehrsil said. "You'll never make it alive."

"I'll send Lork ahead."

"Can he talk?"

"He can communicate with other seahawks, yes."

"But if they're hostile the bird won't have a chance. You saw how many seahawks they have," Yesenia said.

"You're right. Then we'll have to take the risk and get closer," Mehrik said.

"Enough talking and more doing. Let's go, Mehrik, hop on my back and hang on," Marko said.

"Are you sure, Marko, you don't have to do this," Sehrsil said.

"Yes, we do. Mehrik is right, understanding their intentions is a priority," Marko said.

"It's settled then. I'm going with you. The word of a queen still has value in the Known Territories," Sehrsil said. "The rest of you go inside and wait for a signal from us. If they're hostile, you'll need any able hand you can get."

As soon as the trio separated from the group, a small squadron of soldiers from the Hundred Kingdoms' army mobilized to intercept them.

The long stride of the Icedorfers gave them the edge, even with the added weight of Mehrik and through rough terrain. But the danger went beyond the soldiers chasing them. Arrows from the Hundred Kingdoms' archers landed too close for comfort and forced them to zigzag down the path.

"We got to move closer to the Oceano army. They won't risk accidentally starting a battle. It's our only chance," Marko said.

"Or our last mistake," Sehrsil said without stopping.

As Marko had predicted, the rain of arrows from the Hundred Kingdoms' soldiers came to a halt, and the troops pursuing them turned around. They were safe, for the few moments it took for the coral-tipped arrows of the Oceano army to start landing around them.

"What now?" Marko asked. "We can't get near them. We can't go back."

"If they wanted to hit us, we would be dead. It's an easy shot. This is a warning wave," Sehrsil said.

"Kill me and send me to Hell!" Marko exclaimed. "Look at the soldier in the front, the one on the sea lizard, and tell me I'm not imagining it."

"Guntharhi!" Sehrsil said.

"You really mean Guntharhi? It's hard for me to tell with the helmet. Lork, go check!" Mehrik said.

Guntharhi. Friend, Lork telepathized.

"It's him, indeed. How did you recognize him?" Mehrik asked.

"He's still wearing Icedorfer pants. He hasn't changed since the last time we saw him, that pig. And the scar from his chin to his cheek, that's not a common one," Sehrsil answered.

"Guntharhi! Guntharhi!" Marko yelled off the top of his lungs as he put Mehrik in the ground and waved his hands. "It's us!"

Mehrik hadn't seen the Oceaner that saved his life back in the dungeons since Sehrsil expelled him from Icedorf, all those cycles ago. He clearly had found his way back home. With him here, it should be all that much easier to convince his countrymen to help them.

Guntharhi took off his helmet, confirming beyond a doubt that it was their dear friend. He stood on the back of the sea lizard and used his hand to shade his gaze from the twin suns rays. Falling back on his saddle, he rode towards them. As he did, the Oceano archers assumed a resting position.

"It's really you! I can't believe it. What an odd place to find you, old friends!" Guntharhi said getting off and holding their hands. "What's going on here? No! Don't tell me yet. Let's go talk with General Pohlinaris."

The group walked with him closer to the mighty army of Oceano.

"Boy, get General Pohlinaris here immediately," Guntharhi ordered one of the foot soldiers.

"What happened with you, Guntharhi? You left Icedorf without saying goodbye," Sehrsil said.

"It's a long story, princess."

"It's queen now," Marko said before feeling Sehrsil's elbow hitting his ribs.

"It's Sehrsil, as always," she corrected both.

"Of course. I heard about what happened in the City of the Thousand Lights. I want to express my dearest sorrow for the unjust fate that fell upon your people. It was most definitely an undeserved tragedy that marked the Known Territories forever. Please rest assured we will do what we can to help you find the revenge you deserve."

"Thank you, Guntharhi. It wasn't easy for us, but it wasn't completely unjust either. Thousands died but hundreds survived. We're resilient people. We'll rebuild our numbers and our shelters. We're not seeking retaliation. Our quest is for justice and lasting peace. Mehrik helped me understand the errors in our ways. And we've made more than a few," Sehrsil said.

"That's more hope than what we can afford," Guntharhi said.

"Now, let's talk about you. How did you get back to Oceano?" Marko asked.

"General Pohlinaris is here," The foot soldier announced forcing a change of subject.

"General, sir," Guntharhi said grabbing his right shoulder with his left hand, the military salute in Oceano.

"Commander," he said dismounting from his emerald-green sea lizard. "Is this the traitor?" he said with his eyes fixed on Mehrik.

"What?" Mehrik said.

"Traitor?" Marko said.

"Guntharhi, what's going on?" Sehrsil said unsheathing her sword. As she did, a thousand infantry soldiers did the same. Marko followed suit. Mehrik, still trying to process what was happening, placed his hand around the hilt of his blade, but didn't draw it. Lork descended from the sky and landed on Mehrik's shoulder.

"Are you allies with Mortagong? I can't believe it. Mehrik is no traitor, you know that Guntharhi," Marko said.

"Mortagong is our enemy, just as it's yours. Mehrik's betrayals didn't start with you, or with Skyroar. For him, lying and fleeing is almost a family tradition," Guntharhi said.

"The black seahawk, I can't believe it. You were right, Guntharhi, this was a worthy journey," General Pohlinaris said.

"Sehrsil, let's be reasonable. Put the sword away. You and Marko are powerful warriors, but are you more powerful than two thousand soldiers?" Guntharhi said.

"I'll be reasonable when your mouth begins to spit more than nonsense, and even then, it'll depend on what you have to say," Sehrsil said keeping her sword in front of her, ready to strike.

"I don't have the time for this. Let's take the traitor and leave. Make sure he has the Core-Sole," the general said. "Kill the others if they interfere."

"No!" Guntharhi said. "They saved me and many of our soldiers from certain death, these two. I beg you the briefest of moments to negotiate."

"You have a tenth of a period," Pohlinaris said walking away.

"I need nothing more, general," Guntharhi said turning to Sehrsil and Marko. "Listen to me and, Sehrsil, reflect about what you would have done in our place. As your people, our people had our reasons to fight this war. Our reason isn't somewhere inside the volcano's heart. It is right in front of you, or half of it at least.

"Many seasons ago, a King of Oceano, whose name I shall not

mention, disregarded his royal duty to serve his people and turned against us. He betrayed our heritage and threatened with destroying our most powerful possession, one that belonged to us by right of conquest.

"A bloody battle ensued. Brother against brother. Sister against sister. Royalty against subjects. After heavy losses and irreparable damage was caused, our mighty army was able to overthrow our monarch. The royal family was captured. Everyone but the queen's aide and the baby prince were accounted for, and the object, the Core-Sole, was lost. The aide, Marinius, had fled with the baby and the Core-Sole.

"We searched everywhere throughout Oceano, the Hundred Kingdoms, Icedorf, even Tenebris and couldn't find them. We concluded they must be hiding in Skyroar, so we tried to enter the citadel by any means necessary, attacking the Wall was just one way, there were others. But when we got inside, we could never locate him. We heard the rumor of an Oceaner becoming a Seven Warrior and, naturally, we believed it had to be the son of the king. We lost all hope, it was impossible for us to reach the Seventh Seal.

"When our paths crossed with Mehrik and, by chance, I saw the Royal Talisman hanging from his chest back at the dungeons, I just couldn't believe it. After all, he had been captured fighting with us, or so he said. When I saw the black seahawk, I was sure it was the traitor. Since I thought he lived outside the citadel, I made sure he escaped with us, so he could take me to the Core-Sole. Back at Icedorf, when he confessed to being a Village-dweller, a sea of despair took over me. The Core-Sole was, after all, in Skyroar and I had just left it there.

"I came back to Oceano, and we planned a final assault. Entering the citadel, thanks to the Hundred Kingdoms, was much easier than expected, I must admit. And now that Mehrik walked to us willingly, taking him and the Core-Sole back to Oceano will be a breeze. Let us go, my queen, and you will find in Oceano a most loyal ally, I guarantee it. Try to stop us, and you'll only condemn your people to lose a queen on top of their king," Guntharhi said kneeling in front of Sehrsil.

"You sound a whole lot like Mortagong," Mehrik said. "Same goal, different methods."

"Shut up!" Guntharhi said. "I'm talking to the queen. You

deserve nothing but scorn. You know, I left my family, my home, to look for you. Like so many other Oceaner spies, I was tasked with the mission of travel the Known Territories searching for you. I had to let myself being caught as a prisoner of war to enter Skyroar and search the one place where a mistake would get me killed. I was tortured in your prisons. My body was broken, and my essence shattered. My cycles in Skyroar only augmented my contempt for you and my hate for the citadel. You can keep your speech to yourself. The only thing I want to hear from you is the location of the Core-Sole."

"I don't know what you're talking about," Mehrik lied.

"What will you do with him?" Sehrsil asked.

"First, he'll guide us to the Core-Sole. If he doesn't remember where it is, we know how to refresh his memory. Then, he'll have to respond for the sins of his parents, such is the fate of he who carries treacherous blood. The royal lineage must end with him and there is only one way to ensure that. You can leave and consider your life a gift from Oceano," Guntharhi said.

"Keep your gift. You're not taking him anywhere," Sehrsil said.

"He's coming with us. I don't want to harm you, but make no mistake, I will."

Lork, jump to the floor behind me and, very carefully, take the satchel from my belt pocket and go. They're so concentrated fighting that they won't notice. Do it now! Mehrik messaged while Guntharhi was focused in Sehrsil.

Lork helps. Lork hide bag, The seahawk telepathized as he hunted a small mouse from behind a rock. With astonishing dexterity, he took the pigskin satchel using the same claw where he was holding the mouse. When he took off, the bag was completely concealed from prying eyes.

"Last chance. Marko, talk to her. Help her understand you can't win, let us take the traitor and go. You still can survive this," Guntharhi said.

"It's a beautiful cycle to spill some Oceaner blood," Marko said looking at Sehrsil.

"Stop!" Mehrik exclaimed. "This isn't your fight. You've done enough for us already, for me. I'll go with them. Your people deserve a queen. Skyroar is still in danger. Wasting your lives here accomplishes nothing."

"I won't allow you to go with them. They'll kill you the

moment they find what they're looking for," Sehrsil said.

"My queen, I ask you as a friend, please go. You will not survive this fight, and I don't want to be responsible for your deaths. You belong with your people. You can help the Skyroar people escape. You can make a difference."

"We have a war bond, dying together is the greatest honor," Marko said. "But you are still the Queen of Icedorf, and your duty is above all else."

Sehrsil didn't answer. The hand holding her sword was trembling. Her fiery purple eyes were fixed in Guntharhi.

"My queen, this is my life and my decision. I expect you to respect it. You have trusted me before; I just ask you to trust me once more. I'll be taken to Oceano and there I'll talk to our king and will correct any misunderstandings. You, Marko, and Paumeron, have been more than friends, you're family. You've given me the greatest gift, the courage to be all that I can be. This is me using your gift. This is me taking control. Be well and be safe," Mehrik said with cloudy eyes.

"So be it," Sehrsil said sheathing her sword. "Our paths will cross again, Guntharhi, mark my words."

Lork, go with Sehrsil. I'll be gone for a long time to a place that's not safe. The leather satchel you grabbed has the Core-Sole. Protect it with your life and hide it in an unreachable place. When you are ready, come find me in Oceano. But be careful, please.

Lork loves Mehrik, the seahawk messaged as he flew like lightning to the Fortress with the satchel secured between his claws.

I love you too.

"I'm ready," Mehrik said stepping forward. "Let's go home."

Chapter Twenty-One

Tabatha was glued to a spyhole in the Healers Quarters' wall witnessing the events unfolding outside. She went from rage, to fear, to surprise as the small group of warriors defeated the canyon rammers, avoided the Hundred Kingdoms' arrows, and appeared to befriend the Oceano army.

"I hope you know what you're doing, little friend," she whispered. "You might be an Oceaner, but they aren't your people, we are. Even if their seahawks saved you, I still wouldn't trust them. Oceano has threatened Skyroar for many seasons. Be careful, please."

Tabatha forced herself to look away and focus on the task at hand. What was happening beyond the Fortress, however important, was not under her control. This was and, according to Mariam, it had the potential to save them all.

The Healers Quarters —a room almost as big as the Conclave Hall— was crowded with Villagers. The Minister of Science, and two seasoned healers were standing behind a basalt counter. They were sorting Hellblood vials on the shelves that covered the back wall of the room.

"This is all my fault! I should have been suspicious of Mortagong when he asked to experiment on how to soil Hellblood or, at least, enquired what his purpose was. I was such an arrogant fool! Every demonic possession of a Skyroar citizen rests upon my shoulders," Mariam said with teary eyes and a broken voice.

"Let's not dwell in the past. Now is our chance to save the future," Tabatha said in a neutral tone. She wasn't in the mood for sympathy, especially not for someone like Mariam, who had full control over the choice she made.

"Your words are wise. We have plenty to do in very little time. Next!" She exclaimed.

A shy Solis girl stepped forward, she had to be lifted by her mother to reach the top of the counter. Behind them, a long, sinuous queue of Villagers filled the room and extended beyond the quarter's entrance, all the way to the marble staircase that led to the main floor.

Mariam wiped out the tears and dirt from the face of the little girl with a wet cloth. Then she gave it to her mother so she could clean the scratches and dry blood from her legs.

"I need to see your Hellblood flask, can I?"

"Will the monsters get me if I give it to you?" the little girl asked.

"No, I promise," Mariam said.

"Then yes. I don't want more hurting," the girl said.

"Nobody does, my dear," Mariam said pulling the chain to lift the vial. A close examination in front of a torch was all she needed to reach a verdict.

"Is it tainted?" Tabatha asked.

"I'm afraid so," said Mariam.

"Am I sick?" The girl asked.

"No, you aren't, but your Hellblood is. We need to change it. I'll be quick, but I do have to prick your little finger," Mariam said taking a long and thin needle from a jar full of water.

"Mommy?" the girl called.

"It's all well, it'll keep the monsters away," she said.

"Do it!" the girl said, covering her face as she extended one hand to Mariam.

"All done, my dear," she said passing the needle with a fresh drop of blood to her assistant.

The Healer emptied the needle in a vial with Hellblood and crushed herbs and mixed it with enthusiasm. Once the liquid acquired a homogeneous aspect, she placed the cap and sealed it with paste made with pig fat and sand.

"No time for a nametag this time," the healer said tying the string around the girl's neck.

"I don't understand. Why did Mortagong have to infect the Hellblood if it only works when mixed with the blood of the person it protects? Wouldn't it have sufficed to change it?" Tabatha asked.

"My guess is that he didn't want to take any chances. Inactive Hellblood could still be used if recovered intact. The substance I developed renders it inert, whether mixed with our blood or not. Hellblood is also quite scarce, so ruining the one on our necks would save the rest to fulfill his plans, and would raise no uncomfortable suspicions," Mariam said.

"Hellblood was meant to increase and retain power for the Conclave, you included. No doubt about it," Tabatha said. "We could have saved thousands more; we could have earned the respect and help from those opposing us. The fate of Skyroar could have been so much different if the greed didn't cloud the judgement of those tasked with guiding us."

"Passion without knowledge is a dangerous combination, my child," Mariam said taking a Hellblood flask from the shelf and mounting it in a small base in the counter. "Hellblood is not some herbal infusion mixed with mystical herbs, as the common folk believes. It's quite literally blood from Hell. Or more accurately, blood from one that has been in Hell."

"What are you talking about? Is it demon blood?"

"No, it's something a great deal scarcer," Mariam said taking the index finger of the little girl's mother and pushing it against the thin needle. A few drops of blood fell into the vial and quickly dissolved with the rest of the contents. Mariam mixed it, sealed it, and gave it back. "Take good care of it."

"What do you mean scarcer?" Tabatha asked.

"I mean it's not an endless resource. It can be depleted if used in excess and, if that happens, then we would all be at the mercy of the demonic hordes. It means hard choices needed to be made and, as the Conclave, we made them. We took the burden it brought to our essences. Ruling not to share the Hellblood with our attackers was easy. Closing shut our doors to refugees and limiting the number of newborns in Skyroar wasn't, but we made them, nonetheless. Explaining them wouldn't have helped anyone, so we didn't."

"But Skyroar is only refugees. There isn't one person here that didn't come from somewhere else," Tabatha said.

"And that's why it was harder. Think back, when was the last time you saw new arrivals in the Village? How many seasons ago? You see, my dear, there is a limit to how generous we can be, and that limit is set by the Hellblood."

"Why help us now? You can let us die and go join Mortagong," Tabatha said.

"I'm here because I was wrong. Mortagong lied to us so much that I can't honestly say if he ever told us the truth. I killed many by omission. This is my time to save people by action. I'm not young anymore. I'm not afraid of death, but I'm afraid of dying without making amends. This is where I start, we'll see where I end," Mariam said.

"You have my trust. I hope you can also earn my respect," Tabatha said with a gentler tone than before.

With the queue organized and the plan settled, Tabatha went back to the spyhole to check on Mehrik. "Are the Oceaners leaving and taking Mehrik?" Tabatha exclaimed. "Mariam, we don't have much time. When the Oceano army is gone, we'll be at the mercy of the Hundred Kingdoms."

"We're working as fast as we can," one of the healers said.

"Work faster."

"We will, but that's not our biggest concern. We won't have enough Hellblood for everyone. It looks like a good amount has been taken from the shelves. We're running out," the healer said.

"Do your best. I'll buy you some time," Tabatha said taking a last peek through the spyhole.

"Probably not enough, I'm afraid. I'll do my best. Let Hishiro give you the might," Mariam said.

"To send the demons back to Hell," Tabatha answered placing her hand on Mariam's shoulder before addressing the Villagers: "If you have your Hellblood already, leave the room. If you are still waiting, you got to move in, break the line, squeeze in as tight as you can, fill every crack and corner!" she exclaimed as she walked to the door. All eyes were fixed on her but not many people reacted. "I meant now!" Tabatha shouted. "We'll be soon facing enemy troops in the Fortress; if you don't want to die, better start following my orders!" This time the message worked; the Villagers filled the room until their shoulders touched. "Whoever received new Hellblood and is able to fight, follow me!" Tabatha commanded. Over fifty Villagers had joined her by the time she got to the first floor.

"Tabatha! We are in trouble," Goldenmane said. "You've got to listen to what Sehrsil has to say."

"I know they took Mehrik. I saw it. The question is why?"

"It's a long story. In short: our humble deliverer is the heir to the Oceano Throne. Their people murdered his parents and have been hunting him since. He's being taken prisoner and could be executed once he reaches their city," Sehrsil said.

"What? Why did you let him go?" Tabatha asked.

"He asked me to and that's enough."

"You sent him to die!" Goldenmane roared.

"I allowed him to choose his fate, as a person of his character and stature should. I respect and trust Mehrik more than I do any of you. This vexes me greatly, but we can't concern ourselves with it. Mehrik's choice might have sentenced him, let's be sure to make good use of the time we have. The troops are coming. Do you have a plan?" Sehrsil said.

"There's only one thing to do, and even that may not be enough. We must make the Fortress as impregnable as the Wall," Goldenmane said.

"What do you mean?" Marko asked. "Is your proposal to stay here and die?"

"At least for now, yes, we must stay. The Villagers are still receiving their Hellblood in the Healer's Quarters. I would offer you and Sehrsil some, Marko, but I'm afraid there isn't enough for everyone," Tabatha said.

"Well, that's a surprise. Don't worry about the magic potion, we'll survive without it, as usual. But nobody will make it unless we can slow the Hundred Kingdoms troops down. The Hellblood won't help you against their swords," Sehrsil said.

"We will barricade every door, window, spyhole, and crack. But we must do it while keeping the army away or we won't have enough time to finish the job," Goldenmane said.

"That's impossible," Yesenia said.

"I've done impossible before. It looks like we are stuck here, so we need to make this happen," Sehrsil said.

"Hold on, Goldenmane, if you keep the Hundred Kingdoms army out, you are also sealing us in, we'll end up dead anyway, just more slowly," said Tabatha.

"That's not going to happen. I know a route through the crater," Goldenmane said.

"I'm in," Tabatha said with no hesitation. The crater was closer to the Hidden Chamber and therefore closer to Shiroan.

"From there, we can reach Arboris. I can guide us through the tunnels. There's water and we can find food there. Then, we can regroup and think about our next move," Goldenmane said.

"How do you know all this, Lionkin?" Marko asked.

"It's a matter of survival. You don't live for so many seasons in the most remote section of the Fortress without learning every one of its secrets." Goldenmane said.

"Let's do it." Sehrsil said. "We've got three or four periods of light left. We must be on our way by dusk, that's when we can expect the Hundred Kingdoms to launch a full force attack."

"Agreed. I suggest you and your companion lead our warriors in the turrets. We should have enough arrows to keep the bulk of the army away. Every available archer, I'll take care of the barricades. We'll regroup at sunsdown," Goldenmane said.

"I accept your suggestion," Sehrsil said.

"Not every archer. I'll stay in the ground and help Goldenmane. My bow might be useful when the Hundred Kingdoms finally go through the barricades, in case we are still here," Tabatha said.

"There might be a way to close the access through the hallway permanently," a Solis Conclave member said taking a step forward. "We just need to bring down the nearest support columns at each side and that section of the Fortress will collapse on itself."

"Those columns are massive. There's no way to take them down. Without mentioning that we might not be able to reach our escape passage," Tabatha said.

"We wouldn't be trapped; our exit will still be accessible. And I'd like to look at those columns, we have strength in our numbers," Goldenmane said.

Not for the first time, Tabatha was pleasantly surprised at Goldenmane's natural way of taking control. Whoever took the decision to waste his life in the dungeon clearly had made a big mistake.

"We have a plan then. Archers! Follow me!" Marko shouted as he and Sehrsil ran upstairs to the turrets.

"How much time do you think they can buy us?" Tabatha asked Goldenmane.

"It all depends on how many arrows they have. Are you giving them yours?"

"Not a chance. My quiver and I are inseparable. Also, I have a hunch we may need it where we are going. They'll have to make do with one less bow and a few less arrows," Tabatha didn't mention that she wanted to be prepared in case Shiroan needed her help after they escaped the Fortress. She couldn't even imagine what he was facing on the Seventh Seal amid the worst demonic attack of all time.

Resist, Shiroan, I'm coming, she thought.

"Fair enough. Everyone, listen to me!" Goldenmane talked to the crowd, raising his voice to a thundering roar. "The east entrance door must be sealed and the passage leading here barricaded. I'm asking for volunteers to carry any statue, bench, pedestal, rock, or pebble, and throw it in front of the door. Keep adding until the hallway is filled with debris!"

"You! Come with us," Goldenmane said pointing to a group of ten Villagers standing a few steps from him. "We got to bring the Fortress down."

"With our bare hands?" asked one Elgarian.

"That's a good point. We'll need tools," Tabatha said.

"There are maintenance sheds with hammers, ropes and other equipment concealed behind each fifth column. After we find the first one, the other ones will be easy to spot," Goldenmane said.

"Found it!" Said Tabatha waving from one of the tool sheds. "This one is filled with shovels, ropes and pickaxes."

"Well done. Let's start with the south columns, they're closer. Come, this way."

"Shouldn't you leave this here?" a soldier said as he attempted to take the quiver off Tabatha's back. Before he could start unbuckling it, Tabatha extended her wings and, with just one flap, sent the soldier to the ground.

"Keep your hands to yourself or I slice them off your wrists. My bow and my quiver stay with me. If you touch me again, I'll be carrying one less arrow," Tabatha said as she turned her head, sending the soldier a gaze that matched her words.

"Fine. I wish you don't come to regret this decision."

"I only regret the decisions others make for me," Tabatha said turning back to join the rest of her squad, which was frozen in the ground, with their eyes fixed on her.

"Are you done scaring the troops?" Goldenmane said with a smile.

"That'll depend on the troops," Tabatha answered.

"What's the plan if the army of the Hundred Kingdoms intercept us when we're in the crater, Goldenmane?" A Fortress soldier asked. "I'm not as familiar with those paths as I'm with these ones. And most of the people here are not fighters."

"Don't concern yourself with it. Even if they find out we

escaped. Why would they send their army down there? They don't know how many warriors are still standing or if demons are prowling the area. They'll need every one of their soldiers to win the war. Their battle is worthy as long as it's against defenseless Villagers. Why would they risk being slaughtered by dragons?"

"Why would we?" Retorted one of the guards.

"Because I know the exact way that'll take us in and out of there in one piece," said Goldenmane.

"That's good strategy for a dungeon master, Goldenmane," Tabatha said genuinely impressed.

"I wasn't always one," Goldenmane said.

"I can tell," she said.

"We've arrived. There and there are the columns the Conclave member asked us to take down. You!" Goldenmane said turning to a couple of men carrying pickaxes. "Start denting the column on your left. You two take the one on the right. Don't stop until they fall!"

"Let's tie the rope around them so we can pull them down once they're weakened," Tabatha said.

"What if there're people in the levels above?" Asked a Villager.

"The main armory is what's above us, all soldiers at this point have either joined us or joined Mortagong. It's bound to be empty. Let's do it, Tabatha. It's a good idea," Goldenmane said.

Tabatha untangled the yellowish ropes. Rigid and thick, with a myriad of sharp loose thread lacerating her fingers, the rope was harder to manipulate than she anticipated. At every loop or turn, the old, dry fibers complained with a soft cracking noise that cast suspicions over its true strength.

"Hold this for me, please," she said handing one of the Villagers one end of the rope as she extended her wings.

Tabatha flew to the upper edge of the cubic base where the circular column rested, looped the rope around the thick marble column three times before flying to the other one to do the same.

I hope this works, she thought as she came back to the ground and gave the other end of the rope to the Villager.

"Now what?" the Villager asked.

"Now we pull. We need a few helpers here!" Tabatha yelled to make herself heard over the noise of the pickaxes.

"You heard her," Goldenmane said with a roar. "What are you waiting for? This isn't a party!"

Five Villagers moved forward and grabbed the rope, three on one end, two on the other. Goldenmane joined them, grabbing both ends, one with each one of his large hand-paws. "Now, it's time to pull as hard as you can. The moment it cracks, everyone runs out of the way!" he commanded.

Tabatha squeezed behind Goldenmane while holding the left side of the rope, the one with two Villagers, to even it out. The Lionkin was so massive that all she could see in front of her was his majestic golden fur and the muscles at work underneath it.

"Now! Pull!" Tabatha commanded. "Harder!" she added. *I hope those pickaxes weakened the base enough for the column to break,* she thought as she pulled with all the strength she could muster. Splinters from the rope lacerated her hands and sent drips of blood to the marble floor. Her face went red. Her body leaned back. Her legs pushed forward. Her thighs felt as if they were ready to shatter.

She was about to give up when she heard Goldenmane's left shoulder pop, so invested was the Lionkin that he dislocated it in his effort to bring the column down.

He didn't say a word.

Goldenmane simply let one end of the rope go, coiled the other around his right arm, and continued pulling. Tabatha was holding the side of the rope Goldenmane had let go. His incredible strength was enough to start pulling Tabatha towards the column. Opening her wings, she flapped with all her strength to counterbalance the strength of the Lionkin. One of the Villagers fainted out of exhaustion.

C'mon Tabatha, you're a Sixth Seal Warrior, you've got this, she said lifting her feet from the ground and pulling with both arms as her wings swooshed back and forth.

"Almost there! Go! One last effort!" Goldenmane shouted. Tabatha exerted so much force that she felt she was going to explode.

A dry crack, so loud that could be heard over the pickaxes hitting the rock, resonated in the hall.

"Halt!" Goldenmane roared. "Silence!"

Everyone froze in place. As the echoes of the crack disappeared, a subtle rumble, reminiscent of the sound made by the bags of pebbles she used to play with as a child, filled the room. It grew in intensity, almost imperceptibly at first, then faster and faster, until her world filled with the boom of a thousand thunders.

"Now! Run!" She heard Goldenmane yell, as the columns fell in front of her.

The intense sensory overload kept her in place until the thick cloud of dust hit her in the face. She ran to safety.

"The Villager!" Tabatha shouted remembering the man that had blacked out in front of her.

She stopped on her tracks. Her heart sank when she turned around. A pile of rubble covered the hallway from bottom to top. She rushed there, ready to dig him out. Then Goldenmane appeared. He was carrying the Villager on his good shoulder.

"Thank you, Goldenmane," Tabatha said.

"Don't. Let's go. We still need to deal with the other side. Is there a healer amongst us?" Goldenmane asked looking at the group.

"I'm not a healer but a Village caretaker," answered an Elgarian man in the back still shaking from the collapse of the columns. "But I need a few moments to recover."

"That works. Stay with him until you're both ready to go back to the group. We are leaving in no more than three periods, with or without you."

"Yes, sir. Understood." The Elgarian said.

The group started to retrace their steps heading to their next objective. Tabatha took a last look at the ruins behind them. The dust had settled, exposing an unbreachable wall of marble and basalt where the majestic main hall of the Fortress once was.

"Couldn't the Hundred Kingdoms troops find another way to reach us now that the walls are down?" Tabatha asked.

"Not in a thousand seasons. The Fortress is built around the uneven side of a mountain. At some places, the builders had to carve through its slope to ensure a perfect round shape. This is one of those places. By bringing down the columns, we did more than collapsing the roof of the Fortress, we brought down a part of the volcano. That's why the Conclave member suggested this strategy. The Hundred Kingdoms will need ten cycles and several regiments of soldiers to clear a path. We're safe. At least on this side," Goldenmane said.

"You think that Skyroar will be around after this is over?" Tabatha asked.

"Skyroar will prevail as long as the Hidden Chamber stands.

That's what we believe in and live for, isn't it?" A Fortress guard answered.

"Not really," a Villager said from the back. She was a young Solis, no more than fifty seasons old. Almost as short as an Oceaner, barefoot, hands bleeding from pulling the rope, dressed in a ragged, brown shirt and pants that were torn at the knees. She didn't look like much, but her clear voice demanded attention and inspired respect. "Many of us don't care about the sacred books, the Prophecy, or the Hidden Chamber. We just have the time to survive. My ancestors came to Skyroar because the alternative was being possessed by a demon. I was born here because of them. It wasn't by choice, make no mistakes."

"You could have left anytime you wanted," the Fortress guard said.

"Clearly you haven't been outside the Fortress in a long time, or perhaps ever. Nobody can choose to leave Skyroar. Our hands, our bodies, and our blood are needed here. We're called to preserve the Prophecy and protect the Fortress. Our lives have no value beyond serving the greater good, and serving the greater good is almost undistinguishable from serving the Conclave," the young woman said with a strong voice. Her speech sounded almost rehearsed, as if she had practiced it in her head for a long time waiting for the right opportunity to deliver it. She had found it.

"You and I are not that different. In Skyroar, we all have a role to play but we're all equal," the guard said in a conciliatory tone. The red in her face denounced that the words from the Solis had stricken a nerve. It was unclear to Tabatha if that redness evidenced rage or embarrassment. Perhaps both.

"Are we, though? How am I equal to you? Where do you sleep at night? Are you awoken by the squeal of demons or the screams of the wounded? How many of your relatives have died at the hands of our enemies? How many children are you required to have? There's an abyss between us, you just can't see it because you are so high up that everything else looks hazy. We're all at war, but we're much closer to Hell than you'll ever be. I don't know what's worse, that you're too ashamed to admit it or that you have started to believe your own lies."

"How dare you doubt the ways of Skyroar? We exist to protect the Prophecy and to preserve Hishiro's legacy. We live selfless lives to give the Known Territories a chance of survival, living as one and striking as many!" The Fortress guard shouted while looking at the Solis with rageful eyes.

"Well thought words, you certainly make Mortagong proud," the Solis said knowing the exact impact of the phrase that had left her mouth.

The guard closed her fists so hard that her nails drew blood. Her arms were trembling, and her eyes looked at the Solis with unabridged fury. But she stayed silent. She looked around at faces that didn't provide the empathy she sought, or rather, the one she was used to receiving. Letting out a long sigh, she let her gaze soften, and her hands relax. Her face returned to its natural light almond tone. A poor attempt at a smile died at her lips as her eyes returned to the Solis.

"We'll have words, young one. I want to hear more from you. Your message, although hurtful, contains truths that we, I, have ignored," she said taking a deep bow.

"We're here," Goldenmane announced as he separated from the group and walked to a nearby statue.

"Well, did you do it? Did you bring it down? I imagine you did, judging by the sounds that reached us," an Oceaner woman said.

"We did," Tabatha said, "but that's only half the job. How's the situation outside?"

"The barricade is completed and holding, but a few of our archers have been wounded by enemy shots," a guard said pointing at a group of people laying down on the floor being tended by healers. "I'm joining the next wave of reinforcements, but we're running low on arrows. Once we're out, they'll have all the time in the world to bring down every obstacle we've placed on their way —" The soldier stopped talking and his face became pale as the snow when he heard Goldenmane's howl of pain.

Every gaze looked for him. The Lionkin was walking back from the statue as he rubbed the shoulder he had dislocated.

"Are you well?" Tabatha asked.

"Nothing that a firm blow against a hard surface couldn't fix," he said with a smile. "Now, to the matter at hand. Don't you worry about the Hundred Kingdoms army. Keep resisting, we'll be back soon. This battle is ours," Goldenmane said with a confident voice.

"How long before we reach the other columns?" Tabatha

asked as they left their improvised base.

"Half of a period at most."

"Good, let's make it a quarter," Tabatha said accelerating her stride as she gave Goldenmane another glance to ensure he was well. She still couldn't believe what he had just done. *Is there any limit to his physical prowess,* she thought.

"You! Take a few tools and every rope you can find from those sheds and catch up with us," Goldenmane asked two Villagers that were ahead of the group.

"Yes, sir," they said.

The hallway was deserted, nobody could be seen or heard. It was hard to believe that just the last cycle these corridors were filled with life. Marble busts for each Conclave member since the foundation of the city stood at both sides, looking at them with eyes that, Tabatha felt, were loaded with disappointment. They had failed them. The Wall had fallen. The Village was in ruins. The Fortress was becoming a death trap. Was it already too late to save the Hidden Chamber? Would they be responsible for the complete devastation of the Known Territories?

"We're here. That's the column we need to bring down."

The hallway widened in front of them, forming a circular courtyard with long marble benches at each side. A column as thick as twenty Vespertians rose from the ceiling to the roof, embedded in a shallow pool filled with small red and white fish, and algae. One look was all it took to bring despair into Tabatha's essence. The column of epic dimensions was the very definition of an unsurmountable task.

"You must be jesting," Tabatha said.

"I'm afraid he's not. The underground river that feeds this fountain is the same that provides water to Skyroar. The base of this one is at the bottom of that river, well below the Fortress floor. This is the strongest of our columns because it also supports the most weight in a truly unstable area. If we bring it down, the Fortress may be lost forever," a Conclave member said in an emotionless tone.

"We can praise the builders of Skyroar some other time. It's time to get to work. Everyone! Go grab a tool and start hitting the column as hard as you can!" Goldenmane commanded.

"The ropes won't be as useful as more pickaxes for this one. The column is wide enough for everyone to help chopping it down,"

Tabatha said as she took a swing at the colossus of marble with such force that it bounced back, making her fall in the water.

Ignoring the explosive pain in her arm, she stood up with a jump, grabbed the pickax, and hit the column again, and again, and again. Her furious blows reflected the anger of endless seasons fighting an inherited war against impossible odds.

Not very long ago, Tabatha still had hope. She even thought that she would live to see the cycle when the demonic forces were beaten and sent back to Hell. Only now she realized how much of a fool she had been. Every battle, every demon, every dragon she killed accomplished nothing more than strengthening the power of the real enemy, the one at home. A sense of inevitability took over her essence. A feeling of impotence, of being condemned to watch their fate unfold, unable to bend it. She wasn't but a guest contemplating the end of the world.

And that made her mad.

A cloud of dust painted her wings white. Fragments of marble, some as large as fists, were thrusted in all directions with each blow. Only one other person was making more progress than her, perhaps because he was more powerful, or because he was angrier. Probably both.

Every time Goldenmane hit the column, chunks the size of pig heads detached from it, making the fish in the water swim in every direction searching for cover. The outcome of all the other volunteers added together wasn't close to that of the mighty Lionkin.

"This is going to take forever!" Tabatha shouted over the deafening noise.

"That's not surprising, dear," a Conclave member said clearing his throat. "These columns were made to last an eternity. The builders of Skyroar planned for every scenario, including this one, I'm sure."

"Not for every scenario," Goldenmane said in between blows. "They didn't plan for me. This column is going down, you can be certain of it."

The Lionkin, having shaved off a large part of the column in front of him, looked briefly at the result and moved to the left to continue his work. The Elgarian that was by his side stepped back leaving his barely dented spot to him, wise decision.

"Look!" A Villager shouted pointing to the end of the long

hall. "Hundred Kingdoms soldiers!"

The incoming troops covered the wide avenue like a carpet of armor, swords, and spears. Their steps echoing in the walls were a prelude of what was coming. The soldiers didn't change their pace. Like a pack of wolves that cornered a wounded moose, they knew that the Skyroar rogues didn't have anywhere to hide.

"They must have entered through the southeast door. I imagine the guards had left the turrets and posts a long time ago," a Fortress guard said.

"How did they know where to look? That door is not easy to find," said another guard.

"Mortagong, clearly," Tabatha said.

"Shouldn't we escape while we have the chance?" A Conclave member asked.

"Escape where? While the column stands, there is no escaping, there is only delaying our demise. Goldenmane, it must go down, now. Can you make it happen?" Tabatha asked.

"I need more time. How long before they reach us?" Goldenmane, who hadn't even turned his head to look at the upcoming threat, asked.

"Not very long. They're close," Tabatha said.

"The Conclave member might be right, then. Go, gather everyone and leave. If we can't bring it down, it doesn't make sense for people to die here. We can put a better fight back in the east entrance, where there are more of us. With any luck, some of the Villagers will reach the crater."

"But we don't know where to go?" A Conclave member said.

"Frothos will be able to take you to the crater if I don't make it. He's the one that taught me the secret path," Goldenmane said.

"I won't leave you," Tabatha said.

"I'm not asking, soldier. We don't have the time to argue."

"I already have a commander and it isn't you. You can't do this alone. You need coverage. I'm that coverage," Tabatha said grabbing an arrow from her quiver.

"Fine, you want to die, be my guest," Goldenmane said between blows.

"I'll stay, we'll see about dying later," Tabatha said taking aim.

"You!" Goldenmane shouted at a Fortress soldier. "Collect everyone and leave. We'll meet back at the east door. If we are not there in half a period, leave without us."

"Yes, sir," the soldier said. "Listen! We must go. If we stay, we'll be killed!"

Nobody moved.

"Quick! They're shooting at us!" He lied, seeking a reaction.

It worked. The group dropped everything and ran down the hall.

"Go with them," Tabatha said to the Conclave member, who was frozen in the middle of the path, staring at the approaching army.

"I'm staying. I'm Gregorik, a Conclave Member of Skyroar and an Elgarian. If they reach us, I'll try to reason with them."

"You must be crazy. With all due respect, these are our enemies we are talking about, they won't listen to what you have to say," Tabatha said. "Under these circumstances, they don't care about how important you are, or who your people are. They just want you dead."

"We'll see about that," Gregorik said.

"The world where you lived doesn't exist anymore. You have no power here. You need to go. Now," Tabatha said to Gregorik as she let the first arrow go, as a warning. The troops were one thousand steps away.

"No!" Gregorik said, lowering her arm. "If you do this, there'll be no chance at my plan!"

"Your plan won't work. You'll kill us all."

Seven hundred steps.

"No, they'll listen to me. They'll respect my robe. I'll tell them that I'm ready to join them, I'm an Elgarian, after all," he said looking at Tabatha while grabbing the arm holding the bow with one hand and placing the other one in her shoulder. "All will be well."

"There's no version of this where we end up well. If you let go of my arm, we can at least have a fighting chance."

Six hundred steps.

Tabatha could see now see the silver details in their armors and the leather boots, tinted red with paint made with cayenne and berries.

"Mortagong and I worked together for a long time. He'll protect me."

"Do you see Mortagong anywhere?" Tabatha shouted, trying one last time to reason with him.

"You don't get to talk to me like that, child. I'm a powerful member of the Conclave. I'm –"

"Look out!" Tabatha yelled, opening her wings, and pushing the Conclave member to the side. She expected the worst. She was right. Three arrows had pierced his back, killing him instantly.

Four hundred steps.

Tabatha didn't have the time to feel sorry. Lying down in the fountain, arms placed on top of the marble edge, she shot arrow after arrow, targeting heads and chests with uncanny accuracy. Before the head of a wounded soldier touched the ground, another one was already falling. Ten warriors with ten bows wouldn't have done a better job than the brave Vespertian.

"What the Hell are you doing back there, Goldenmane?" Tabatha shouted.

"Whatever I can, how far are they?"

"Two hundred steps. They've slowed down, as they must now dodge the dead and the injured, but I'm running out of arrows."

"How many you have left."

"Not enough."

"I'll finish this now. You are not dying today," Goldenmane said dropping the pickaxe and taking a few steps back. He targeted the weak spot he had carved, much thinner than the rest of the column, but still a good two palms in diameter. Propelled by his powerful legs, he rammed against it, channeling all the energy he could muster through his good shoulder. Circular waves formed in the water of the fountain, the ground below Tabatha's body shook, and the column let out a thunderous roar that resonated with such force that the Hundred Kingdoms Army stopped on their tracks for a moment.

Then everything went quiet. The column was still standing. The Hundred Kingdoms Army resumed their attack.

"Last arrow," Tabatha announced.

"Go. I'll catch up."

"I'm not letting you here to die," Tabatha said drawing her sword.

"You stubborn winged creature. Just go!"

"Bring it down, then we can both go!" Tabatha shouted lifting her sword to deflect an incoming arrow. Her extraordinary green eyes, moving at the speed of thought, detected three more, that she dodged with flawless precision. Then ten more, she tried to avoid them all, but one scratched her left arm and another one pierced her right thigh. Tabatha fell to her knees.

The Hundred Kingdoms Army was almost there.

It was when she stood up that a third arrow lodged in her right calf.

"Now, Goldenmane. Do it now or we're dead!" she shouted.

Such was the raw force of Goldenmane's tackle that two of the marble benches split in half. A thunderous noise filled the hallway as the column gave way with the loudest of cracks, leaving her ears ringing. The cloud of dust that followed took her sight. Tabatha smelled the sweat of the soldiers and felt the vibration of their boots on the floor. *They're here,* she thought.

As she swung her sword forward in blind rage, she was lifted from the ground and taken to safety.

"Are you well?" Goldenmane asked.

"I've been better. I've also been worse," Tabatha said with half a smile.

"The column has fallen," Goldenmane said.

"I figured. What happened to the Hundred Kingdoms Army?"

"Only three of them made it through, I took care of them, the rest are trapped on the other side. We're safe."

"For now. Good job there, a tad tight, but you did it."

"Can you walk?" Goldenmane asked, leaving her in the ground.

"I can see and hear again. And I don't need to walk, I can fly," she said spreading her wings as she rubbed her eyes.

"Let's leave this death trap behind then. We took down the two main entryways, but there are others."

"Agreed. Let me ask you something, Goldenmane, why did you choose to be in the dungeons? You're clearly a skilled warrior and an experienced commander. Skyroar would have surely had a better use for your talents than watching over prisoners, wouldn't they?" Tabatha asked.

"I was as much of a prisoner as the people on those cells," Goldenmane said. "Skyroar and I had our differences a long time ago. I committed certain acts that were condemned by the Conclave and ended up being sentenced to a life in the dungeon, as its master."

"Couldn't your sister help you?" Tabatha asked.

"My sister was the one that sent me there."

"What happened?"

"Does it matter? Skyroar is falling. My sister is dead. The past is better left behind, we've had enough in our hands trying to secure our future."

"It matters," Tabatha said. "There are things that could consume you from inside unless you find a way to let them out."

"Maybe. But this is not the time for stories. We need to move faster," Goldenmane said.

The trip back to the group was quick thanks to Goldenmane's long strides and Tabatha's wings. The path to the entrance was now completely sealed and, even if thumping and clashing echoed from the outside, it was clear that making it through that barrier would take the Hundred Kingdoms army enough time to allow them to escape.

"For how long they have been trying to get here?" Goldenmane asked.

"At least for a period," a Fortress soldier said.

"How are the archers doing?" Tabatha asked.

"We ran out of arrows," Sehrsil said from the stairs. "It's time to leave. There are enough of them to bring down the Fortress wall ten times over."

"We can't go before the Hellblood replacement is completed," Tabatha said.

"No need to worry about that," Mariam said walking downstairs. "We ran out of Hellblood."

"How many villagers left?" Goldenmane asked.

"I'm not sure, didn't count them; enough to be worried," Mariam replied.

"Is there a way to obtain more Hellblood?"

"Not here. In the Hidden Chamber, perhaps."

"We'll have to make do. Anybody without Hellblood should travel in the middle. The Icedorfers will cover the back," Goldenmane said.

"Don't dare telling our queen what to do!" Marko said.

"All is well, Marko, we'll do it," Sehrsil said before turning to Goldenmane. "But once we are out, we'll have to go back to the North Wall, not to Arboris, we need to find our people."

"Fair enough. Tabatha and Frothos, you'll go in the vanguard with me," Goldenmane said.

Tabatha heard Goldenmane's voice from far away, as if he was talking behind a waterfall. Everything around her dissolved in front of her eyes leaving only blackness. When she recovered her sight, Tabatha wasn't in the Fortress anymore. She was in the same cave where she had the first vision cycles ago. This time, however, she was surrounded by demons and Lethos was sitting with his legs crossed on a ledge, bleeding badly.

Tabatha unsheathed her sword and swung at them just to realize that her sword went through them as if it was made of smoke. The demons weren't moving. They were like statues made of rotten flesh. She detailed the yellow claws, the tiny red eyes, the jaws overpopulated with twisted fangs, the drool frozen mid-way to the ground, the thin legs, and the round abdomen just below its protruding rib cages.

She gagged at the foul smell coming from their oozing skin and moving her head to the side in search of air, she saw two warriors, swords drawn, also frozen. One of them had his sword through a demon's throat. The other one, knee to the ground, had sliced a piece of ankle that floated motionless in the air surrounded by equally stationary little chunks of flesh and drops of black blood.

It was then that she noticed she was looking at the scene from above, as if flying. No, not flying, levitating. Her body, including her wings, shone with a green, ethereal aura.

"This is... unexpected. I have called for one that can receive my Magia and two have come," Lethos said. "My children, the Magia can't die with me, and I'm dying," he said as he breathed with difficulty.

Tabatha looked around her, searching for whomever else the old Vespertian was talking to, but couldn't see anyone, at least not anyone that was not frozen solid.

"Lethos, you are hurt, how can I help you?" Tabatha asked.

"You can't. Or if you can, it doesn't matter. It matters that you come. Come to me. Fast. Hell will break lose and I can't stop it... Perhaps one of you can... You must at least try," Lethos said in a whisper.

"This is crazy, can't be real. Just another dream."

"The Seventh Seal. Come to the Seventh Seal. Hurry... you... you need to get here before Shiroan falls," Lethos said between bursts of cough. Placing both hands in his abdomen he let out a cry of pain. "I need to go now... no... more... energy."

"Tabatha!" Goldenmane shouted in her ear, but she could barely hear him. "Are you listening to me!"

"Shiroan!" Tabatha said.

"What?"

"I need to go to the Seventh Seal, Goldenmane. I'm sorry. Can't explain, you'll need to trust me," Tabatha said.

"I must go too," Frothos said.

"Are you the other one the old man mentioned?" Tabatha said looking at Frothos.

"I saw the old Vespertian, but didn't see you," Frothos said scratching his head with his thin long fingers.

"I'm not surprised. Goldenmane, we need to go. I'll find you; I promise. What way to the Seal?" Tabatha said.

"You can't go by yourself, it's suicide," Goldenmane said.

"There's no choice, trust me," she said holding Goldenmane's hand.

"What did you see in your vision?"

"The Seventh Seal is falling. Lethos, the Seventh Warrior, is dying. Shiroan may die soon. Frothos and I can help," Tabatha said.

"Then go," Goldenmane said. "Frothos can take you to the secret passage. He knows where it is. We'll follow through with the plan. Do what you must. If you succeed, we'll meet in Arboris. If you don't, then we'll all meet in Hell."

"Thank you, Goldenmane. Skyroar is in good hands if it's in yours. Let Hishiro give you the might," Tabatha said.

"To send the demons back to Hell," Goldenmane recited.

"Thank you, for everything. You've made me better," Frothos said hugging Goldenmane even though his head only reached to the chest of the Lionkin.

"Let's go," Tabatha said. "It looks like stopping Hell will be on us."

Chapter Twenty-Two

From the moment that Kaina landed in Hishiro square all those seasons ago, Shiroan was convinced to be the last Cloudhunter. His belief was not only based on the stories from the Village's elderly, his broken memories, or the undisputable truth that he was the only one of his kind around. Those facts were nothing but confirmation of what he and Kaina saw with their very own eyes the cycle they flew to the City in the Sky.

Back then, he was still a guard in the West Wall. After an especially heinous attack, he needed more than his usual place to calm and energize. Once he directed Kaina to fly southwest, she understood where he wanted to go. A long howl full of angst and powerlessness signaled the arrival to the remains of his birthplace. The majestic towers, the hanging bridges, and the intricate gardens he had seen so many times in the canvas he kept at home were all gone. Only debris, ruins, dust, bones, rust, and charcoal could be seen in the vast plateau. Even the cover of clouds that once wrapped the city had disappeared, as if the pain of sharing space with such devastation was too much to bear.

Two entire cycles Shiroan explored every corner, cranny, pile of rubble, and fallen building. He didn't stop until utterly satisfied that no Cloudhunter and no drakovore had survived. Hopeless, horrified, and carrying more anger than he had brought with him, he flew back to Skyroar, leaving the City in the Sky behind, forever.

The moment he returned to his duty at the Wall, he accepted the burden of his heritage.

The moment he entered the Seventh Seal, he accepted his fate.

The moment he set foot in the Hidden Chamber; his beliefs shattered in as many pieces as stars are in the sky.

Shiroan wasn't, after all, the last Cloudhunter.

Falling to certain death, mere instants from being devoured by the sea of lava, none of that mattered. He did all he could and then some. With his eyes closed, serene but not defeated. He thought of

Tabatha. *I'll love you forever,* he thought, as the fumes of the magma burned the skin of his face.

As it turned out, the book of his fate hadn't yet turned its last page.

Shiroan opened his eyes and hugged Kaina's thick and furry neck as he struggled to find his balance.

"Kaina! You're alive!" He exclaimed.

The drakovore, no more than two palms from the lava, let out a growl as it rose towards the plateau.

Shiroan kept his arms tight around her neck and did his best not to spoil Kaina's rescue.

"I should've let your saddle on, Kaina. Not sure what I was thinking back there" Shiroan exclaimed as the drakovore emerged from the precipice.

She tripped on landing, rolled down the Seventh Seal floor, and sent Shiroan crashing against the basalt. As soon as he regained control, he stood up and rushed to her.

"You're still bleeding." He said kneeling by her side. "You shouldn't have done this, girl. You don't have the strength. You can't die because of me. You're the best one amongst us."

"Blue! Glad you're alive but we could use your help!" Kishi yelled from the Hidden Chamber.

Shiroan looked up. The demons were unleashing their unrestrained fury at a sphere that had lost any vestige of a green glow.

It bounced against the edge of the plateau without pause. Every time it hit the rock, it sunk in the hole a bit more. Whatever force that kept it floating for all these seasons was quickly fading.

"The monk!" Shiroan exclaimed. "He can't die! Be strong, Kaina, I'll be back. I promise. Wait for me," he said caressing her neck.

His hand closed around thin air when he attempted to unsheathe his sword. *Hell! I can't help without a weapon, what can... My longswords, of course! They are back in the barracks. Please resist just a little longer,* he thought.

When he came out of the cave holding his blades, five demons were waiting for him.

"I don't have time for this!" he exclaimed as he beheaded the closest demon. Its head fell to the ground, quickly followed by the rest of its body. Shiroan knew that he had just sent one more demonphantom to the Known Territories, but he had no choice. *Better one than thousands*, he thought. Dodging the claws of two others, he stabbed and sliced with unmatched skill. His torso bent at impossible angles as he deflected fangs and pierced their bony chests.

Three demons were down. The other two looked back, searching for reinforcements that didn't come. A few steps behind them, the orange light from the lava marked the edge of the precipice. With a smirk in his face, Shiroan leaped forward, feet first, pushing them to certain death.

The Hidden Chamber was taken. The monk couldn't be alive. It would be absurd to believe so. But Shiroan needed to see the corpse with his own eyes. Gregoria and Kishi were doing their best to protect the Hidden Chamber against the demonic tide. Tens of demons covered what was left of a bridge shattered by the chaotic movements of the falling sphere.

"You took your sweet time, didn't you, Blue?" Kishi said as he pushed a demon to the sea of magma.

"I can't force my way through, Kishi, there are too many claws, too many fangs, and too little bridge, I'll be killed before I can reach it," Shiroan said.

"Well, you'll have to think of something fast, otherwise, you'll have to go find the sphere at the bottom of the lava," Gregoria said.

"That may be the best outcome, to be frank," Kishi said.

"No, I have to get in there, the monk might still be alive."

"He must be dead, Blue. Look in front of you, the Hidden Chamber is filled with demons," Kishi said.

"It's true, as is also true that I must try. This is the only thing I ask, my friend: bring the rest of the bridge down," Shiroan said.

"I hope you know what you're doing," Kishi said walking towards the bridge.

"Me too," Shiroan said as he followed the erratic movements of the sphere, looking for a pattern where there was none. Taking a leap of faith, he guessed where the door would be and jumped into the void. He was right.

As he fell inside it, he heard the rumble of what was left of the bridge falling mixed with the squealing of all the demons that were piled on top.

The situation was as critical as he feared, if not more. The Hidden Chamber was filled with demons, all of them staring at the same spot. The place where the monk was.

"Perhaps this wasn't my best idea," he said to himself as he felt the bony, oily arm around his neck, pulling him back. Shiroan couldn't breathe, the demon arm, thin but powerful, compressed his neck with such force that his bones cracked. Swinging his arms back he attempted to get a hold of the slippery head of the creature, soon noticing how all the strength would abandon his body before he could get a firm grip. He changed tactics and decided to release the pressure to his throat by grabbing its arm and pushing it out. *I can't believe this worked!* Thought Shiroan as it let go of him and retreated. Turning his head while gasping for air, he smiled when he saw why. Kishi and Gregoria had killed it. They had found their way to him. Not everything was lost.

"Well, what are we waiting for?" Gregoria said stabbing the back of the nearest demon.

With precise blows, Shiroan finished the two next to him. All the others inside the Hidden Chamber attacked them in unison. Dodging claws and fangs as well as they could in the reduced space, the three warriors stabbed, sliced, and carved. Four creatures separated Shiroan from the monk.

"Hey, uglies, come get me!" Kishi yelled when he realized what Shiroan wanted to do. The demons leaped forward. Shiroan jumped to the top of the platform to gain reach. Holding the remaining longsword with both hands, he made a half turn, slicing clean the head of the fourth one.

"Wake up!" Shiroan said once he was in front of the monk. Then he let out a scream of pain. He turned around just in time to prevent the claws of a demon from reaching his neck. Without giving it a second chance, Shiroan sunk his blade in the creature's chest as he fell to his knees. Inspecting his side, he saw the four deep wounds its claws had left. Blood streamed down his hips and dripped to the floor. Kishi and Gregoria continued battling the never-ending supply of demons. *We'll lose if we keep this up,* Shiroan thought.

"Kishi, Gregoria, guard the door and don't let any others in. I'll take care of things here."

"The uglies are all yours," Kishi said going to the opening.

Shiroan charged at the nearest demon and sliced its chest with the swing of his sword. The last three pounced on him. He took a step back and tripped with one of the dead bodies that covered the floor of the Hidden Chamber. Before he could stand up, a demon put its foot against his neck. When he lifted his weapon, the other one hit his hand so hard that his sword slipped and crashed against the wall.

Lying on top of a dead, naked Elgarian, with foul drool dripping on his face, claws piercing his arms, and the weight of two creatures keeping him in place, Shiroan was running out of options. He tried to call for his friends but the pressure on his chest was so oppressive that he was unable to utter more than a wheezing sound.

The long demon heads, resembling a thinner moose skull, widened at the jaw where fangs protruded in all directions. Its faces were so emaciated that it looked as if they were made only of grey skin and bones. Purple veins pulsed through every part of their bodies. But it was inside their fiery red eyes, deep like bottomless pits, where Shiroan caught a glimpse of something he had never seen before. There was fury, rage, hatred, but there was something else: desperation, fear, sadness even, something that Shiroan couldn't explain. Or perhaps more than what he was willing to accept.

"Hell!" Shiroan shouted as he felt the fangs sinking on his shoulder. "Focus, you idiot!" he exclaimed as he twisted, kicked, and pushed in a desperate effort to break free, that brief distraction almost cost him his life.

His longsword was out of reach. The armor wouldn't withstand a second bite. The blood left his body in gushes. And he still had no plan.

The blade emerged through the demon's chest as it fell to the ground. A moment after, it had transmuted into an Oceaner.

Behind the demon, the monk stood tall, proud, and alive.

"Watch out!" Shiroan yelled extending his arm as the other demon attacked the monk, leaving a deep wound on his hip. Faster than a thought, Shiroan ripped the sword from the flesh of the dead Oceaner. The monk hit the ground as Shiroan sliced the demon's throat.

"You won't die this cycle," he said.

"Yes, I will, but that's not important. What truly matters is that you are here," the old man said.

"What does that mean? Who are you?" Shiroan asked.

"You might know me as Hishiro —" he started saying before he screamed in pain and brought both hands to his abdomen.

"You can't be Hishiro, Hishiro was Elgarian. And he is dead."

"Ah, the Prophecy, I almost had forgotten about the Prophecy," Hishiro said in a low, breaking voice. "Yes, the Prophecy is made up, and not by me. I never was much of a poet. And, as you can see, I'm also not much of an Elgarian."

"So, we have been keeping the Hidden Chamber safe for nothing? All this is a lie?"

"I wish I had the time to rest and talk, but I don't. And you don't either."

"You can't answer two questions?" Shiroan asked. He was nothing if not stubborn.

"I know very well you won't let this go. The Prophecy is loosely based on facts, I did forfeit my life to keep the Passage to Hell closed, even if I didn't die. The Conclave just rewrote history in whatever way they needed to gain and then retain control over Skyroar. It is also true that if the Hidden Chamber falls, all will be lost. And that's where you come in."

Shiroan was at a loss for words. Just by being there, the monk had changed his understanding of reality. Now, Shiroan felt as if Hishiro had taken a battleax and crushed to pieces every belief he had ever held.

"You'll have to work with me, Shiroan. I'm a Cloudhunter. I'm alive. Hell is inside me. The fact that I'm awake talking to you means that I failed. I'll be dead soon, without your help, the Known Territories are lost."

"That can't be true, the Prophecy —"

"Are you listening to me? There's no Prophecy! There are no heroes. There's only us, imperfect people doing the best we can and hoping it'll be enough. I need you to focus. I can't give you a history lesson right now. Look at me!" Hishiro said removing his robe. His blue skin was purple with the blood from the wounds of the demons. The black hole had expanded to cover his entire torso. "You are looking at the reason why Belgoriel made sure to kill the Cloudhunters first. Nobody else can do this. I'm wounded, old, and the Magia healing me and allowing me to keep the Passage to Hell closed for so many seasons left me. There is hope, but not for me."

"You might have never said a Prophecy. But you did save us all," Shiroan said looking at a body torn beyond what he even thought possible.

"I did my part and paid dearly for it. A price so colossal it has taken all my will not to beg you to run away. But I know you, Shiroan. You'll stay and you'll do your best. As painful as it is to me, I already know what your choice will be," Hishiro said, short of breath and trying to control a fit of cough.

"What do you mean?"

"It doesn't matter, there isn't time. This is what truly matters: cherish every moment with her as if it was the last one. There are not many more left," his words drown on the blood filling his mouth. Closing his eyes, he smiled and squeezed Shiroan's hand hard before letting go.

Hishiro was dead.

And with his death, all Hell broke loose.

CHAPTER TWENTY-THREE

Tabatha and Frothos had been walking in silence for two periods. Not long ago, they were transported in front of a Vespertian man glowing green. The man asked them to join him in the Seventh Seal before it was too late.

This is the second time this happened to me. Both times I dreamed with the same place and the same person. The first time I didn't give it a second thought, but this time Frothos saw the same thing, and Shiroan could be in danger. I always thought that the Magia was nothing more than children's stories, but this is something I can't really explain, at least not yet. I must find out more, Tabatha thought.

The Magia had always been a big part of her Vespertian heritage. She grew up with the stories of this ethereal and powerful energy unique to her people. Everyone else around her believed it was as real as the ground beneath their feet.

Tabatha always had the same question when asked about it: 'If the Magia is really that powerful, how come our people suffered the same terrible fate as everyone else?'

In her mind, if the Nexus —the guardian of the Magia— was real, its failure to protect them could only mean that it really wasn't that powerful, or that it really didn't care. Either way, winning the war was up to them and nobody else. And that, in her opinion, was not a bad thing.

"Have you experienced what we saw back in the Fortress ever before, Frothos?" Tabatha asked.

"I haven't, no, it was my first time. The first time that I felt the Magia," Frothos said with a tone full of hope, reminiscent of a child.

"Do you really believe that was Magia?"

"I do, what else could have been?"

"No idea. Not Magia."

"I know it was," Frothos said lowering his head and slurring his words.

"I hope you're ready to be disappointed," Tabatha said with a hint of arrogance she regretted instantly.

She was a cynic, but that didn't mean she had to confront Frothos' beliefs in such a direct way. Regardless of his job as a prison guard, his essence was gentle, and his demeanor sweet, almost delicate. Considering how he lowered his head, and started to drag his feet, it was clear she had upset him.

"I assume you wouldn't want to hear about the first time the old Vespertian pulled that trick on me?" Tabatha said with a smile that only made things worse. No response. Their conversation had ended.

They continued walking in silence. The only discernable sound was their wings rubbing against the narrow, rough walls of the passageway. The marble halls of the Fortress were but a memory as they struggled to fit through low-ceiling caverns and thin cracks that connected one road to the next.

Neither of them carried torches, but their extraordinary pupils were widened at their maximum diameter, absorbing the little light available and amplifying it enough to allow them to find a path. In those parts of the route where the darkness was complete, Frothos led the way, guided by the invisible map drawn in his mind.

Every now and then, they would pass through slim waterfalls filtering streams of water from the ceiling. Luminescent worms, translucent shrimps and milky white bugs filled these little sanctuaries, and crawled away when the echoes of their footsteps reached them. Tabatha had lost all sense of direction. She couldn't tell if they were going up, down, north, south, east, or west; not that it would have made a difference.

"What's the story of this place, anyway? How come you even know it?" Tabatha asked, not so much to quench her curiosity as to present a new peace offering to Frothos. She could tell he was still hurt by her careless words.

"People think my dungeons are the most isolated place in Skyroar. But people are wrong. Secrets usually live deep, whether they are inside our essence… or inside Skyroar's essence," Frothos said.

"What does that even mean?" Tabatha said with some unintended annoyance in her voice. All she wanted was to make small talk. She didn't really need more riddles. Lethos was cryptic enough without Frothos adding to the mix.

"We know Skyroar secrets, Goldenmane and I. That's why I'm not allowed to leave the dungeon. People above doesn't want me to share them."

"So, what's the secret of this place?"

"It was carved by demons."

"What?" Tabatha said. Now that she had gotten a straight answer, she wasn't sure she believed it.

"Do you see the scratches in the walls? Use your hands to feel them if you can't," Frothos said.

The green in Tabatha's eyes had disappeared, displaced by her completely dilated pupils, yet she couldn't see the cave with enough detail to perceive the marks. Extending her hand, she touched the wall from left to right on a wide arc.

"Claw marks!" Tabatha exclaimed.

"Yes. Demon claws, they carved it many seasons ago. As the ones in the front lines spent claws, fingers, and fangs, they were trampled and replaced, leaving dead bodies that became nourishment for the wildlife that can survive these deep down in the mountain."

"Why did they have to do this?" Tabatha asked.

"They were escaping."

"Escaping from what."

"Escaping from Hell."

"Look! There's something there!" Tabatha said pointing to a bright dot of orange light at the end of the corridor.

Tabatha felt an undeniable sense of relief at the sight of what could only be the exit. She refrained from the urge of running towards it, knowing how unforgiven the floor was in the wet patches. Using all the patience she could muster, she continued down the cave at the same pace, swallowing the frustration of seeing the tiny circle growing so slowly that it didn't seem to grow at all.

"The Second Seal!" Tabatha exclaimed standing on a ledge. Impressive. What the Hell?" she added with a grim voice.

Down below, the basalt terrace where the Second Seal stood was still burning. Tabatha took flight and made a wide circle, looking for demons or survivors, she only found devastation and death.

Frothos spiraled down to the ground, his good wing breaking the fall just enough to arrive at the seal unharmed.

"Is this the same path that Goldenmane is going to take?" Tabatha asked, landing by his side.

"It must be. There isn't any other," Frothos answered.

"In that case, we need to buy him time. It's clear they'll have to move as fast as they can," Tabatha said as she entered inside a large tent. She came out a moment later with a couple of ropes, a few bolts, and a pickaxe.

"What are you using that for?" Frothos asked.

"Goldenmane and the rest of the Villagers will have to find their way down the ledge somehow. We'll do the work for them. She said before flying back to the end of the hallway. She used a pickaxe to fixate two metal bolts to the ground, then she tied one rope to each bolt before flying back to the seal holding the other ends.

"Almost ready, Frothos," she said as she bolted them to the ground. "Hope this holds," she said pulling both ropes with all her strength. "Frothos? Where can he be?" She said, looking around. He wasn't in sight.

"Tabatha!" Frothos exclaimed.

His voice came from behind a tent. When she found him, Frothos was walking with an Elgarian woman dressed like a Conclave member. "I found this lady, she says her name is Louriel, she's a Conclave member."

Tabatha had heard that name before. She was one of Galanta's confidants, and her best friend. She had also pushed the dagger that killed her, according to Goldenmane.

I must be careful, Tabatha thought.

She also recognized her face from the time she was summoned to the Conclave to talk about Shiroan, although her red hair seemed to have many more white strands than she remembered. Her face also looked thinner and with more wrinkles, almost as if she aged twenty seasons since they last met.

"How did you get here, your Excellency?" She asked to make conversation while she thought of the best path forward.

"Please, call me Louriel, we're past titles at this point, aren't we?" Louriel said with a wide smile. "I frankly don't know. I don't remember a great deal of the past couple of cycles."

"Is that so?" Tabatha said.

Louriel's vague answer only increased her suspicions.

"Yes, I recall Mortagong betraying us, and then the rumors about the demonic invasion. The next thing I remember is waking up in a tent here."

"And where were you going?"

"I'm looking for a way to get back to the Fortress, find anyone that can help me remember, but all I see is desolation. I was half convinced to be the last survivor of Skyroar until I saw Frothos," Louriel said.

"You're not. But not many of us are left. We're here, and—" Frothos started saying.

"Hold on! Before talking further, I'd like to make sure we can trust you," Tabatha said, preventing Frothos from disclosing Goldenmane's plan. "With all due respect, under our present circumstances, you'll understand we need to be sure," she added, trying to cover her reaction. Louriel didn't know she knew about Galanta, and it was best to leave like that for now.

"And what circumstances are those?" Louriel asked.

"The end of the world," Tabatha answered.

"There's no reason for you to suspect me, Tabatha. I've talked on your behalf numerous times at the Conclave, setting you as an example. As somebody to include in the shortlist to become a Seven Warrior. I remember your courageous and fair words when Shiroan was nominated. I realize the dire situation we are facing merit some level of distrust, but I also believe I have shown you my loyalty, more than once," Louriel said with a smile that Tabatha couldn't resist.

"Thank you, your Excellency," Tabatha said in a softer tone. "You're one of the good Conclave members, it's just hard to tell who to trust anymore after all the events from the last cycles."

"You can always rely on me, Tabatha. I'm on your side. Come with me to the tent, there's something I want to show you."

"I'm convinced. There's no need," Tabatha said.

"Even so, c'mon, indulge me," Louriel said entering the large tent in front of them.

"Wait here. If I call you, draw your sword an come running," Tabatha whispered to Frothos before following Louriel's footsteps.

Inside, the large round table in the center of the tent was broken in half. Maps and diagrams had burned down to cinders. A smaller wooden table, with a matching pigskin stool was sitting in the corner. The bodies of three dead soldiers reminded Tabatha of the tragedy that was unfolding around them.

"I need to get going, your Excellency. What is it that you'd like to show me?" Tabatha said.

"See it for yourself," Louriel said pointing to a box made of interwoven bones pinned to the far edge of the broken table

"Hope this is worthy," Tabatha said, holding it with one hand as she opened the redwood lid with the other.

"I don't understand. What does this mean?" She asked as she looked confused at the box filled with arrowheads, some of them cracked and broken. When she realized that Louriel had moved out of sight, it was too late.

"It means you're not very smart, my dear," Louriel said grabbing her from behind so she couldn't extend her wings and placing a dagger against her throat. With a quick twist, Louriel snapped the Hellblood necklace that rolled on the table before falling off the edge on the other side.

"You better think through your plan carefully, Louriel, there aren't many ways for this to end up well for you!" She said with false bravado. The truth was that, where they stood, Tabatha couldn't do much to free herself.

"Oh, I have," Louriel said.

"Did you? I haven't seen any demonphantoms since we arrived, removing the Hellblood will accomplish nothing."

"We'll see about it. You'll serve me well, undoubtedly better than this weak body. I wouldn't even be able to win a fight against the idiot walking with you. You're strong and muscular and can fly. That's just what I need, I'm sure," Louriel whispered in her ear with the softest tone, with a rhythm that syphoned her will, with a secret voice behind the voice she heard.

"What are you talking about?" She whispered entranced.

"It doesn't matter, just relax, it'll be over soon," Louriel said. "Embrace me. Surrender to Melgorth."

A dark ethereal shadow rose to the top of the tent as Louriel fainted and fell to the ground.

Tabatha wanted to ask for help but couldn't speak. She wanted to run but her legs wouldn't move. Her eyes were fixed in the pattern the demonphantom created in the air. She had never seen something like that before. It was beautiful. She wished to see the waves and the turns and the dance forever.

Melgorth descended over Tabatha and then she drank it all, letting out a quiet moan as she was possessed. She attempted to resist but couldn't. She made a mighty effort to concentrate, to defend her mind from the darkness entering it, but every thought shattered and sank out of her grasp. She wanted to rip the creature off her essence, but she wasn't strong enough. There was no escape. She had been corrupted, her body usurped, her mind stolen, and all she could do was observe as it happened.

Tabatha's link with the outside world disappeared. She couldn't see, smell, touch or hear. All she could do was feel the creature draining her from all that was good, pushing her down a bottomless pit, imprisoning her in a cage made of impotence and desperation. She couldn't even cry. Her eyes had ceased to be her own. She wanted to scream but had no mouth to let the agony out. She hoped to die without realizing she was already dead.

You've met Lethos! The Hidden Chamber has fallen. The gateway is most likely opened! The voice echoed in the nothingness that surrounded her.

What's the origin of this thought, where does it come from? Tabatha's essence felt like a tangled bundle of yarn with no ends to hold. Her thoughts were closer to insanity than reason. She had lost her body, couldn't see, hear, or talk. She had been reduced to her essence, and her essence was trapped inside a monster.

At last, I'll be free! I must go back to the gateway!

It's got be him. Are you saying these things, Melgorth? Tabatha thought. Then her world went black with what could only be described as being lifted by a powerful current.

"Tabatha!" Frothos exclaimed as he shook her shoulders. "Tabatha, are you well?"

Tabatha opened her eyes and saw him looking at her from above. She was lying down on the ground with a stinging pain in the back of her head. Frothos helped her up. Turning her head to the right, she threw up a yellowish, viscose liquid that tasted like death. Bringing her hand to her chest, she was relieved to find the Hellblood flask around her neck. The thing inside her was gone.

"I am now, thank you, Frothos," she said. "What happened?"

"I put the Hellblood back where it belongs, and you fainted. I think I saw a Demonphantom leave your body," Frothos said.

"It was him," Louriel, who was standing behind Tabatha, said. "It was Melgorth."

"Yes," Tabatha murmured.

"I'm truly sorry for what happened. I… I just wasn't in

control."

"I understand. I felt it. I didn't know demonphantoms could take over people without changing them into monsters, or that we could survive them."

"This one can. He lived inside me for who knows how long. His essence and mine merged. I recall bits and pieces of the unspeakable things he made me do. I believe that I hurt Galanta in some way. I hope she is well," Louriel said.

"Oh, Louriel, I'm so sorry. Galanta is dead. Mortagong killed her," Tabatha said, unable to confess it had been hers the hand sinking the killer dagger in her best friend's body. This wasn't the time to do it and, if she died without that knowledge, all the better.

"Oh no!" Louriel said, placing her hands on the table to avoid falling. "This is all my fault."

"It isn't. It's Mortagong's. He's behind this and we will track him down once we deal with the demonic attack on the Seventh Seal," Tabatha said.

"From what I could gather while he lingered inside me, Mortagong and Melgorth had an agreement of sorts. But whatever it was, Melgorth always planned to use Mortagong and then discard him, just like the rest of us. I think he's the only one of his kind in the Known Territories."

"Melgorth said when he was inside of me that the Passage to Hell was open! He's going to the Seventh Seal as we speak. I don't know what his plan is but it's clear we must stop it," Tabatha said with urgency on her voice.

"This is bad," Frothos said.

"More than we can imagine. We need to go. Are you coming?" Tabatha asked Louriel.

"I'm afraid I would only be a liability. Not only I'm not a warrior, I also don't have a Hellblood flask anymore. I would just become another demon to fight. You were lucky that Frothos was here to give you back your Hellblood and expel Melgorth. In my case, it has been lost for many cycles now. The vial around my neck is from somebody else, a useless ornament to avoid raising suspicions," Louriel explained.

"I agree. You need to go straight to Arboris. If the Passage to Hell has already fallen, demonphantoms will be pouring in and you'll be helpless," Tabatha said.

"Why Arboris?" Louriel asked.

"That's where all the survivors from the Village and the Fortress are going. You're ahead of them but not by much, they'll catch up with you, at least the ones that can make it all the way."

"How can I ever repay you? You've been only too kind."

"Make sure to stay out of the reach of demons. That'll be enough for now."

"I'll do my best. I promise," Louriel said.

"Let Hishiro give you the might," Frothos said.

"To send the demons back to Hell," Louriel answered as she walked away.

"It's still you and me, Frothos. With the difference that we've lost time we didn't have. Can you fly?"

"I can't. Not all the way to the Seventh Seal. Not with this useless wing," Frothos said as he shook the remains of his right appendage.

"I know what we can do," Tabatha said with a smile. "We'll fly together."

"But I'm too heavy for you to carry me."

"I didn't say I'll carry you. I said we'll do it together," Tabatha said as she intertwined her left arm with Frothos' right arm and opened her right wing. "The key will be mastering this ahead of the lava passage that leads to the Seventh Seal. Even the smallest mistake there will mean certain death."

"I'm not sure how this'll work, but I trust you," Frothos said spreading his left wing.

"Now, start flapping!" Tabatha said as she batted her right wing back and forth. Keeping her left wing immobile required an effort larger than she anticipated. After ascending a couple of palms her left wing sprang open forcing them to separate. Frothos crashed against the basalt floor. Tabatha's landing wasn't much more gracious.

"Hold on," Tabatha said grabbing a pigskin belt from a robust dead guard. She used it to secure her left wing to her waist.

"Again," she said locking her arm to Frothos'.

They batted their wings but lacked coordination, as Tabatha's went up, Frothos went down. This time they couldn't even take off before rolling on the ground.

"Again," Tabatha said from the floor. "We have to

synchronize our timing better. Our wings are roughly the same span. This should work, must work! Now, go!"

They got off the ground. Frothos started just a tad too late, but Tabatha was able to correct the delay by adjusting her speed just before they hit the ground again.

The odd couple of Vespertians rose to the crater sky that Kaina and Shiroan had traveled so many times.

"I can't remember the last time I flew," Frothos said. "Thank you."

"We're going to the heart of this battle. We'll be surrounded by demons and will have to face whatever was lying inside the Hidden Chamber. Let's get there first, then you can decide if you still want to thank me."

"I spent so many sunless cycles in the dungeons, so many seasons, that I don't even know anymore how old I am. Being somewhere else, flying, even if it's within the crater, even if it's an instant and then I die, is enough for me to die happy."

"You're a good Vespertian, Frothos, your essence is purer than most," Tabatha said.

As they flew to the Seventh Seal, she scanned every crack and crevice in the road below. The Fifth Seal was as devoid of life as the second, regardless of where her eyes turned, she saw devastation, death, and desolation. The bodies piled up on the field and hung from the edges of the walkways, some of them naked, the ones that once hosted the demons, most of them wearing bloody armors and broken chainmail.

A wall of fire, fueled by tents, arrows, spears, clothes, and boots, could be seen at the far end of the seal. It blocked the view to the Hidden Chamber. As they approached it, Tabatha couldn't help but look away. Piles of naked, deformed, charred bodies covered the ground like a macabre carpet. Some of them, still alive, twirled and curled, possibly wondering why the sweet relief of death had forgotten them.

"That's horrible," Frothos said to Tabatha.

"Perhaps, but also heroic," she said. "By burning their weapons, their camps and even themselves, the soldiers sacrificed it all to give us a chance. The demonphantoms can't possess dead bodies, and that wall of fire must have stopped a big number of demons from crossing."

"We'll make them proud," Frothos said.

"We will indeed," Tabatha replied with her sight locked in the Sixth Seal and her thoughts focused on Torok, Mardack and Rashiro.

They flew over the sea of lava that separated the Fifth Seal from the Sixth. It was much shorter than following the path along the side of the crater. It was also much hotter.

"Hold on tight," Tabaha said. The heavy sweat running down their arms made it much harder to keep them interlocked.

"I'm slipping," Frothos said.

"Almost there," she said just before losing her grip. "Frothos!" She exclaimed as he spiraled down.

Getting all the momentum she could gather, she tackled Frothos and pushed him toward the Sixth Seal. They both crash-landed in the ground.

"Are you well?" Tabatha asked.

"Yes, I think I am."

"We need to find cloth to wrap around our arms, Frothos. We'll be much closer to the lava when we fly to the Seventh Seal."

"Couldn't we walk there?" Frothos asked.

"Even if the cave leading to the seal was still standing, it'd be too slow. We don't have the time."

Tabatha looked around and felt as if she had never left. The tents, ballistae, tables, and benches were unchanged. A smoking cauldron rested over a basalt base filled with red hot charcoal.

The only missing thing was people, death or alive.

She turned her head in every direction looking for survivors, searching for her friends, but she couldn't find them. Her essence begged her to go down and search for them, but she knew that she couldn't. Spending time at the Sixth Seal could mean arriving to the Hidden Chamber just a moment too late. Not seeing her friends' dead bodies gave her hope. If they were alive, they would have to fend for themselves just a little longer.

"The lava channel is down there," Tabatha said as she ripped the side of a tent with her sword. "Take this and wrap it around your arm. It'll absorb the humidity from our perspiration and allow us to keep the grip longer."

Frothos followed the instruction without saying anything. But Tabatha could see in his eyes that he was afraid. It was only logical. She was scared as well.

"I'm ready," Frothos said.

"The magma will burn the tip of our wings and the walls will be so close that the slightest change of course may bring us down. Are you sure you want to come with me? You can always find your way through the cavern and meet me there." Tabatha asked.

"We're on this together, I'm staying with you. You saved me once. You'll save me again," Frothos said.

"Well, I might but –" She stopped herself realizing that Frothos was just being nice and trying to find reassurance. "Thank you. I've got you."

"I know," he said with a smile. Tabatha found herself believing in his words. There was something about Frothos. Something genuinely kind.

Then she saw the cloud of demonphantoms passing through the walls in front of them.

"They're coming from the Seventh Seal," Frothos said.

"Indeed. I've never flown through a flock of them, and this isn't the best time to learn what it is like. Let's go down and into the passage and hope we make it through."

"No margin of error," Frothos said as they glided into the channel. The heat of the magma was almost too much to bear. Tabatha's skin felt on fire, her eyes burned, and her wings were about to melt. As she adjusted to the tough conditions, their pace misaligned, and Tabatha's wing rubbed against the wall. To regain balance, her boots touched the magma, immediately catching fire.

"Higher! Higher!" Tabatha yelled as she corrected the cadence of her wing and hoped that their speed was enough to put out the fire on her feet.

It was.

Tabatha had never flown through the lava channel before. Doing so was treason of the highest magnitude. She didn't care. There was too much at stake to abide by ancient rules. She was where she was meant to be. What she couldn't know, and wasn't expecting, was how narrow the passage became at the end. So narrow that there was no way for them to fit in with their wings extended.

"Oh, Hell! This one is going to be a tight one," she said to Frothos.

"More than tight. Impossible."

"We left impossible behind a few periods ago, my friend. Go

faster! As fast as you can!"

The Vespertians flew at incredible speed to an unavoidable crash. Tabatha didn't care. "Faster!" she shouted. Her wing felt ready to rip off her back. Her left wing was barely contained by the belt around her waist. Her dorsal muscles were about to explode. Their arms were losing their grip. "Faster! Closer to the ceiling!" she yelled twenty steps from the narrowest part of the passage. Her wings hit the top of the cave with each flap.

"Close your wing. Now!" she commanded as she hugged him, hoping to have gained enough momentum to go through the narrow opening without falling into the lava.

An eternity passed. Tabatha's eyes fixed at the edge of the passage, just a few steps away. The heat of the lava burning her face, warming up her chainmail, threatening to keep her away from the Hidden Chamber, from Shiroan, forever.

"Now! Fly!" she yelled the moment her shoulders passed the edge of the cave. The hot, sulfuric smell hit her nostrils, burning her lungs, and threatening to shut down her brain. A large bubble of lava inflated in front of them. She flapped hard and fast, hoping that Frothos did too. The tip of her wing sunk on the molten rock sending waves of pain down her spine.

She didn't care. They were gaining altitude. In front of her, the Seventh Seal. They had made it. At least for now.

CHAPTER TWENTY-FOUR

"Let's go! You'll die if you stay here," a voice in the distance said.

She struggled to open her eyes.

"We don't have much time," the voice repeated with a sense of urgency. "Conclave member! Wake up!"

Louriel opened her eyes. She felt as if she had slept for seasons. Her eyelids felt so heavy that she could barely keep them up.

She was still in the Second Seal, exactly where Tabatha had left her.

"Goldenmane?" she said with clothes drenched in perspiration. "I must have fallen asleep after Tabatha left."

"Did you see Tabatha? If you tried to hurt her—"

"I did see her and Frothos," Louriel answered interrupting him. "They are both going to the Seventh Seal. May Hishiro protect their journey. Why would I hurt them? I apologize if my behavior is off. I just had the most vivid of nightmares, or rather, I dreamt of a nightmare I lived a long time ago. I need a moment to recover," she said with a shaky voice.

"Don't expect any favors from me, Louriel. Not after what you did to my sister. You should be grateful I don't kill you on the spot," Goldenmane said.

"Please accept my condolences. Tabatha told me what happened. I wish I could have stopped Mortagong in time to save her life. I was not myself," Louriel said standing up and extending her hand.

"What do you mean Mortagong? You know very well it was you who killed my sister! If you have forgotten, your dagger might help you remember. I still smell her blood on it," Goldenmane said pulling it from inside her robe.

"I... I have no words. She was my best friend," Louriel said with eyes full of tears as she saw the bloody weapon. "Goldenmane, I don't expect you to believe me, but I was possessed until Tabatha found me. There is a demon, Melgorth, that can enter and leave bodies and at will. Those bodies preserve their shape, but their essences are imprisoned. Galanta was killed by its hand, not mine. It was my body, but it wasn't me."

"Possessed? Please give me some credit. You aren't dead and haven't turned into a demon. Don't take me for a fool. This is just a story you made up to justify what you did to her," Goldenmane said.

"Look at me, Goldenmane. At my face. At my wrinkles. At my white hair. How many seasons have I aged since you last saw me. I might not have changed into a demon, but you can tell that something unnatural has happened to me, can't you?" Louriel said with eyes devoid of emotion.

My hands killed my best friend. How come I didn't resist? How come I let that creature inside me do such a horrible crime? Louriel thought. She was already struggling to cope with her reality, realizing that it was her hand the one that pushed the dagger inside Galanta, might just throw her over the edge.

"How do I know you are not possessed right now then?" Goldenmane asked.

"Because Tabatha and Frothos saved me. You can ask them the next time you see them. Melgorth even tried to possess Tabatha before escaping."

"Tried?" Goldenmane asked with genuine concern.

"Yes, Tried. Frothos the Vespertian with a single wing, saved her. She's well now."

"Good Frothos. Look, I don't know what to think and don't have the time to sort it out. You'll have to join us. I don't believe you and prefer to keep you close. We can talk more when we're safe," Goldenmane said.

"Join who?" Louriel asked.

Goldenmane walked her out of the tent and showed her the lines of refugees occupying the seal, large groups were still coming down the secret passage using the ropes that Tabatha had prepared.

"Who are these people?" She asked, looking at the large gathering.

"They are the refugees from Skyroar. Villagers, Fortress guards, Conclave members. Skyroar has fallen, Mortagong opened the East Wall doors, the Hundred Kingdoms army took over the Village and the Fortress, and the demons are probably in the Hidden

Chamber as we speak. We are all that's left of the citadel. Us and the Seven Warriors. Can you walk?"

"Better than most. But something to eat and drink would help," Louriel said joining the group.

"Traitor!" A Conclave member yelled from a distance. "That Elgarian is a traitor! She's on Mortagong's side. Goldenmane! Detain her!"

"Conclave member Henrick is right," Louriel said in a strong commanding voice. "I betrayed the confidence of the city, but I wasn't myself doing it. I was possessed."

"If you were possessed, you'd be a demon!" Somebody else yelled. Slowly, an angry mob formed around her.

"There's this demon, Melgorth, who can possess bodies without changing them. It can also leave them when it chooses so," Louriel repeated knowing that her story would have the same impact with the survivors as with Goldenmane.

"I don't know if Conclave member Louriel is telling the truth," Goldenmane said stepping closer to Louriel. "But I'm not certain she is lying either. She's under my protection, for now."

"How do we know that she isn't possessed now!" Another person yelled from the crowd.

"You'll have to trust me," Louriel said looking at her detractors.

"It's too dangerous." Somebody shouted.

"Leave her here!" exclaimed another.

Goldenmane roared so majestically that everyone went silent. "I said she's under my protection. I saw her kill my sister and I know she would have given her life for Galanta. You don't trust her, I don't trust her either, not yet. But she's coming with us to Arboris and that's the end of the discussion, unless somebody feels like challenging me," Goldenmane said retreating his lips to show four menacing canines the size of a hand.

Nobody talked.

"Very well, then. Let's walk. Arboris is still a long way from here. She needs water and a ration of wormbread. See to it that she receives it," Goldenmane said to nobody in particular, although a few people ran to fulfill his request. "Louriel, stay with me. I'll keep your dagger. I'm sure you'll understand."

Louriel nodded in agreement. As they walked, she thought

about the reaction of the crowd. What was really concerning wasn't that they wanted to lynch her but rather that she couldn't feel anything as they insulted her. She wondered if the beast had taken something with it when it left. Even the world around her looked different, more distant, darker, than what it had been before. She may have survived the attack of the demon, but at what cost?

"How did you get here?" Goldenmane asked.

"I remember only bits and pieces. The final strong memory I have is from many cycles ago. I was preparing to go to bed in my apartment and suddenly I felt an intense pain in my chest, almost as if I had been hit with a hammer or a rock. Then I started to lose control over my senses, one by one. The sight was the first one to go. The smell was the last one. My essence was trapped inside my body. I tried to scream but my voice had deserted me. Then I became aware of Melgorth. He was there, with me, using my body as his own. I attempted to resist but he's too strong. Who knows what else he made me do. The few things I recall are already such a heavy burden to bear –"

"If what you're saying is true, and I'm starting to believe you, his actions are his and his alone. You won't be judged for them."

"Are you sure? Look around you, the judgment has already been passed. How much time before we arrive to Arboris?"

"I don't know, it'll be a long journey since we can't go through the Fortress and we have children, and elderly and wounded people among us. If we all work together, it should take less than a cycle," Goldenmane answered.

"I hope that's enough to get there safely," Louriel said with concern in her face.

"It must be," Goldenmane said looking back at the large group behind him. The line extended as far as he could see. "Failing would mean the end of the Known Territories, I am sure."

"You're right, and to succeed, we may have to face hard choices. I just hope we don't get to that," Louriel said.

"The hard choices already happened, milady. We are refugees hiding inside a volcano being flanked by enemies and demons. We could have stopped this. You could have stopped this."

Louriel didn't reply. She knew Goldenmane was correct. The Conclave allowed this to happen. Thanks to them looking the other way for so many seasons, they were journeying to a place that might very well turn out to be a death trap. But difficult as it was to accept it, that death trap had become the best option they had to survive.

Chapter Twenty-Five

Tabatha and Frothos crashed on the Seventh Seal plateau.

"I see no dragons, good news," she said looking up.

"But there are demons everywhere!" Frothos said with fear in his voice.

"Especially around that floating sphere," Tabatha said unfazed. *Shiroan, please tell me that's not where you are,* she thought, although she knew in her heart that's exactly where he'll be.

"What do we do?" Frothos asked.

It was then when Tabatha realized that Frothos didn't have real combat experience. He spent most of his life at the Village and the Fortress. He had never been in a battle. Bringing him to the Seventh Seal might have been a mistake.

"Frothos, listen to me, you need to avoid fighting as much as possible, if attacked, aim your sword at the ankles. That's the safest way to bring a demon down. If we are to believe our vision, that cave over there is Lethos' hideaway. I'll fly ahead of you to clear a path. Follow me as soon as you can."

"I'll be there," Frothos said closing both hands around the thinnest sword Tabatha had ever seen.

"I know," Tabatha said.

Shiroan, wait for me, I'm coming, she thought as she took off.

She shot arrow after arrow, all of them hitting their targets. Her accuracy was uncanny, even for a Vespertian. As she landed in the cave, she put away her bow and grabbed the black crystal. Every demon she wounded swelled before exploding, leaving nothing but a puddle of flesh and entrails.

The cave is full of them, Lethos, please don't be dead, she thought as she danced her way forward, skillfully avoiding jaws, claws, and paws. She couldn't see Lethos, but she did hear the unmistakable sound of a sword slicing demonic flesh. She followed it to a terrace so filled with demons that she couldn't find a place to land. At the center of the horde, a solitary, courageous warrior kept the demons at bay and protected Lethos who, legs crossed, and eyes shut tight, chanted in an almost inaudible voice surrounded by a transparent green shield full of holes.

The snarls of the creatures echoed in the cave. The screeching of their claws against the rock made Tabatha's teeth hurt. She still couldn't believe one Elgarian woman was able to hold a cavern full of demons back, even if that Elgarian was a Seven Warrior.

"I'm here to help." Tabatha said finally finding a spot to land. "I'm Tabatha, I come from the Sixth Seal."

"Good, start helping, then." The Elgarian woman said without turning her head. "I'm Rexora."

A demon pounced from the right and targeted its extended claws at Rexora's throat. She didn't seem to be aware of the imminent danger. When the creature was only a step away, Tabatha used Rexora's shoulder as leverage and took it out.

"Are you blind?" She asked. "How did you survive this long?"

"By being alert." She answered. A creature snarled on Tabatha's left ear as it fell dead to the ground. Rexora had finished it even though she never saw her move.

"I am, by the way," she said.

"You're what?"

"Blind."

"So, how did you know?"

"I can see the demonphantoms," was her simple answer.

Tabatha and Rexora swung and shot until no more creatures were in sight. The floor of the cave was covered with the people that they had possessed, and the gelatinous remains of the demons that Tabatha had killed with the black crystal.

"Every other demon is going to that sphere in the middle of the Seal," Frothos said from the cave's floor. The ooze dripping from his sword surprised Tabatha. She didn't think he had it in him.

"The Hidden Chamber!" Rexora exclaimed. You need to go there and help. I'll protect Lethos."

"No," Lethos said with a broken voice. "Tabatha, you're here because I won't be," The old Vespertian said extending a trembling, thin arm towards her. She grabbed his hand. "I'm the guardian of the Hidden Chamber. I keep the Magia alive. The Magia keeps the essence healthy. Before I die, the Magia needs to find a new Nexus, a Vespertian, true and pure, able to hold it in and use it to restore the balance to our world. Just as I have done, and as many have done before me. You're the new Nexus, Tabatha, but first, you need to be willing to accept your role."

Tabatha's mouth was open, but no words came out. The Magia was real. In all honesty, she should have believed in it long ago. After all, she had seen dragons and felt its green fire breath burning her skin, and her essence had been summoned in front of Lethos not once, but twice before. She had been taught as a child about fantastic feats that the Nexus had done throughout Vespertian history. Moreover, in the coldest and darkest nights, she had heard the elderly whisper about the unstoppable monster that could be born if the Nexus was ever possessed.

Instead, she managed to convince herself the dragons were just flying demons and her encounters with Lethos unusual dreams. Growing up without ever meeting the Nexus, it wasn't hard to dismiss the tales of the mythical protector as a myth created to appease children living in constant fear in a world at war. The option would have been accepting the Nexus had abandoned them, allowing her people to be slaughtered and possessed. She had chosen to believe the Magia didn't exist because it was easier than believing it just didn't care.

Now, looking at the Magia face to face, she realized how wrong she was. The Nexus had never deserted them. He had saved them. He used his power to keep the Hidden Chamber sealed and the Passage to Hell shut. He was a true hero. And he was dying.

Is this what I am meant to be? Am I the next Nexus? Do I even want this? Do I deserve it? Tabatha thought with doubts that wrinkled her forehead and forced her to look away.

"Be quick, my child, the Magia needs a channel, and the Known Territories need the Magia," Lethos said.

"Are you the one maintaining the Passage to Hell closed?" Frothos asked from the bottom of the ledge, as if he was unaware of the crucial event that was unfolding.

"No, not me. I'm not strong enough. I am the one that helps the one who does. Tabatha, what's your answer?" Lethos said coughing blood and leaning forward with a moan.

"I need a moment," Tabatha said almost whispering.

"Do what your essence dictates," Rexora said putting her hand on her shoulder. "You are strong and noble. Your decision will be the correct one."

"I'm given no choice here, my friend," Tabatha said looking at the Hidden Chamber. "The survival of our world is the only reason I fight. We are bound to do what it takes to save it. I'm ready," Tabatha said. *Shiroan, be safe,* she thought feeling in her essence that taking this mantle would separate her from everyone else, including him.

Lethos strengthened his hold of Tabatha's hand. Tears of frustration, fear, joy, and sadness, all at once, populated her eyes and streamed down her dirty olive cheeks. She didn't back down. She had never shied away from duty and wasn't about to start now.

"Martirius longui Magia. Largorius martiri Magia. Vidi lanius dirium. Esencialis ramilium Magia. Glomius infini!" Lethos chanted holding her hand. Tabatha didn't feel any different. She looked at the old Vespertian searching for answers.

"Martirius longui Magic. Largorius martiri Magia. Vidi lanius dirium. Esencialis ramilium Magia. Glomius infini!" He repeated as his eyes glowed green, and a green aura surrounded his body. Tabatha closed her eyes and took a deep breath. She internalized every single word from the enchantment and let herself go. Then she opened her eyes.

"Odd. I didn't feel a thing. Is this it?" she asked.

"I'm afraid not, my child. I can't understand what happened. Too much Magia already leaked from my body, I'm afraid. We might be too late."

"Or you may've been looking in all the wrong places," Tabatha said staring at Frothos and the intense green glow that enveloped him like an armor. His eyes, wide open, shone with an even brighter shade of green and his whole body was floating in the air.

"Who are you?" Lethos whispered.

"He's Frothos, the other Vespertian you talked to," Tabatha said.

"I didn't contact any others, only you," Lethos said.

"Well, he had the same vision I had. He saw you as well. And he heard the call," Tabatha said.

"But I chose you."

"And the Magia chose him," Rexora said. "I can see it inside his essence. He's the one, old friend. You are wise, but the power within you is wiser."

"Bring him to me. Quick," Lethos asked.

Tabatha flew to Frothos and pulled him to the ledge. He was almost too hot to carry.

The old Vespertian took his hand. "Listen to me, my son: the burden on my shoulders has been lifted. My responsibility is now yours —" a fit of cough interrupted him. He spat blood as he leaned back and forth. "Save the Hidden Chamber. Help the Cloudhunter. Use the Magia, my child. Look for the words in your essence. Look for the secret in... in... you," Lethos said before closing his eyes and falling to his side. Tabatha grabbed his head and back and helped him to lie down in the ground.

"He's dead. His essence is gone. Frothos, I hope you are a fast learner," Rexora said pointing outside.

Only the very top of the Hidden Chamber was visible now. A crack loud like thunder echoed in the cave. It came from the interior of the sphere.

"What are the demons doing?" Frothos asked.

"I'm not sure, they seem to be congregated around the sphere. That's surely where Shiroan is, that's why Lethos told you to help the Cloudhunter. You must help Shiroan," Tabatha said.

A soft sound, like the buzz inside a hornet's nest, increased in intensity as it mutated to a low howl, reminiscent to the wind running through the Village streets on stormy nights.

Then the black river of ethereal shapes emerged from the Hidden Chamber.

"The Passage to Hell opened wide with Lethos' death. Let's go there, we must rescue anyone still there and then push it to the lava," Tabatha said.

"That won't work," Rexora said. "It has been tried before, the Passage to Hell will rise from the lava. All we can do is fight until Frothos finds the way to close it."

"I don't know what to do," Frothos said.

"The only one that did is dead, my friend. But if we don't figure it out, this war is as good as lost," Tabatha said.

"There are hundreds of demonphantoms out already," Rexora said.

"We can't waste more time. I'll go to the Hidden Chamber and help the rest of the Seven Warriors," Tabatha said as she tried to look through the black river of demonphantoms and the greyish mass of demons.

"If they're alive, they must be near the sphere, where most demons are gathered."

"I'll be back!" Tabatha exclaimed as she flew out of the cave. Kishi and Gregoria were fighting more demons than she could count on the inner edge of the plateau.

"Tabatha!" Kishi called. "Blue is inside! We can't get there fast enough, go!"

Tabatha descended and felt a blast of despair enter her body. The Hidden Chamber was invaded by a swarm from Hell. Even with the black crystal shard, there was almost no room to dodge every claw, and avoid every bite. Recovering instantly, she dove inside brandishing the demonium.

Be alive, Shiroan, please be alive, she thought as she sliced her way through the entrance. What she found was beyond anything she could have imagined.

A dark black circle floated in the center of the room, as if a piece of the night sky had fallen and stationed there. The edges of the black hole were blurry, uneven, and created ripples in the air like the ones a rock would create in a quiet lake. The opening spat a myriad of little shadowy drops that made a popping, wet sound as they entered, as if they were bursting a membrane. Each drop grew and transformed in a demonphantom before her eyes.

It was then that she realized she was staring at the Passage to Hell.

The first demon inside the Hidden Chamber pounced at her from the side. With reflexes honed by hundreds of battles and movements ingrained deep in her subconscious, Tabatha dodged and charged before her conscious mind had even registered the threat. The other three —crouched in a corner— snarled at her. Two of the creatures leaped forward. The third one stayed put. Behind it, Shiroan was unconscious in the ground.

"Shiroan!" she exclaimed slicing the throats of the first two without even looking at them. The last one had its claws around Shiroan's Hellblood. It was ripping it off his chest.

"Let him alone!" she yelled as the sharp piece of crystal sunk in the demon's back. The creature turned its head with red eyes full of rage, and a twisted jaw that Tabatha could have sworn was trying to smile. Pushing it away, she threw herself at Shiroan and opened his shirt. The Hellblood was gone.

The vial had rolled out of reach as the sphere shook from side to side. She rushed after it. Tabatha froze with terror as she turned towards Shiroan and caught a glimpse of the tail end of a demonphantom entering his body.

"No!" Tabatha shouted as she chased the Hellblood bouncing on the floor like a grasshopper. When the pedestal at the center of the room blocked its path, Tabatha jumped over it, grabbed it, and hurried back to Shiroan.

The demonphantom was nowhere to be seen. It was latching onto his essence.

"Fight it, Shiroan! Wake up! Fight it!" She shouted. A sudden movement from the sphere sent her flying to the opposite wall.

Tabatha gasped when he looked at her with empty red eyes. "It's me, my love. I'm coming!" Tabatha exclaimed.

Tears of blood ran down Shiroan's eyes. For the briefest of moments, he seemed to recognize her.

Shiroan Opened his mouth wider than what it looked possible. She was almost there. He let out a soundless scream as the demonphantom that tried to steal his essence was expelled from his body. Tabatha took the Hellblood vial and pressed it against his body. She had the perception that the demonphantom had left his body before she could touch his chest with it, but she could very well be mistaken.

It didn't matter. He was alive.

Sitting down, Shiroan coughed up black blood. Tabatha sat down by his side and hugged him tighter than she had ever hugged anyone before.

"All is well, Shiroan. I'm here," she said.

"Tabatha? How did you find me?" Shiroan said with a mix of confusion and relief.

"It doesn't matter. What matters now is to reseal the Passage to Hell and leave the Hidden Chamber. We still can win this fight outside. You and I, together," Tabatha said holding his hands.

"It's not that simple, Tabatha. I must stay inside," Shiroan said pulling her to his chest and covering her with his arms.

"Like Hell you are!" She exclaimed. "There's nothing you can do here. This happened because of Lethos' death, because the Magia was weakened," Tabatha said.

"Lethos is dead? That complicates things."

"Maybe not. Frothos is here, the Magia lives within him now. This can be fixed. He just needs some time to figure out how."

"That's not how it works, Tabatha. Lethos kept the Hidden Chamber sealed and protected, but he wasn't the one sealing the Passage to Hell."

"If not him, then who?" Tabatha said.

"Hishiro," Shiroan said.

"Hishiro? That's impossible. Hishiro died hundreds of seasons ago. You know the sacred scriptures as well as I do," Tabatha said with concern in her voice, thinking that the demonphantom may have blurred his mind.

"The books are mistaken. Intentionally, I suspect," Shiroan said pointing to Hishiro's dead body.

"A Cloudhunter? I thought you were the last one. But he can't be Hishiro, the Sacred Book says—"

"That he was Elgarian. I know. It was a lie, a falsehood just like the Prophecy."

"You're not making sense, Shiroan, you're the strongest warrior I know, but even you can be hurt. Your judgement may be clouded by your health."

"I'm sane and well and what I'm telling you is what I saw. What Hishiro himself told me before he died because Lethos couldn't heal his body any longer. The Prophecy was wrong, his death was never meant to seal the Passage to Hell, it was meant to open it."

"So, what do we do now, how can we close it again?"

"You can't. Only a Cloudhunter can close it," Shiroan said holding her face between his palms. Tabatha knew, just by looking at him, the implication of his words. "Our essence is unique. It can merge with the Passage to Hell and keep it inside. It's a colossal effort that will drain our essence quickly, but with the help of the Magia, we can keep it close for a long time, perhaps forever."

"And nobody else can do it, because you're the last Cloudhunter," Tabatha said taking a step back.

Shiroan took a stride forward, but she took yet another one back. He extended his arm, but she rejected it. Shiroan tried to hug her, but she blocked him with her wings.

"If I don't do this, our world will die. You'll die. I can't allow that. I just can't," Shiroan said.

"I know. And I hate you for that," Tabatha said.

"Hate yourself, Tabatha, you're the one that made me better. I'm selfish and arrogant and an idiot, but I also want to be more like the person you deserve. I do this because this is what you would have done in my place," Shiroan said wiping the tears from her face.

"I always knew you were a hero, Shiroan, but I never wanted a hero. I wanted you!" Tabatha said jumping to his arms and kissing his lips as if it was the last time.

Because it was.

"Go! Close the gateway and save us all."

But please come back to me, she thought.

"I love you, Tabatha," Shiroan said, giving her his vial of Hellblood as he walked towards the black hole, still vomiting demonphantoms.

"Have you lost your mind? You'll be possessed!" Tabatha said with eyes wide open.

"Oh, you have no idea," Shiroan said with a crooked smile.

"Do it then! Let's finish things here so we can go home," she said with no hope.

Shiroan didn't answer but the eternal sadness in the eyes that looked back at her didn't leave room for misunderstandings.

He stretched his arms and closed his fingers over the edges of the Passage to Hell. Tiny electric storms exploded around his hands, while flashes of lightning traveled up his arms, drawing long dark blue lines on his skin, all the way to his neck.

"Shiroan!" Tabatha yelled but didn't dare to approach him. She had to believe that he knew what he was doing. She had to.

The demonphantoms stopped leaving the Hidden Chamber in their endless stream. One after another, they entered Shiroan's body and stayed there, but Shiroan didn't give any signs of transmuting into a demon. His arms continued pushing the Passage to Hell inside his chest. As he did, it shrank. It was half its size already. Most of his light blue skin was crossed with lightning-shape scars and his hands were white hot. Drops of blood fell from his nose and ears.

When the Passage to Hell was the size of a moose head, Shiroan pressed it against his chest, letting out a scream filled with such pain that it sucked the strength from Tabatha's legs. He pushed it further. As it reached the size of a sheep's head, the black hole disappeared inside his body.

His eyes turned red, and tears of blood joined the streams that were already covering his face. His body convulsed with violence, bringing him to his knees.

"It burns! It burns like Hell!" Shiroan shouted off the top of his lungs as he vomited a black, foul-smelling, viscose substance that Tabatha had never seen before.

"I've had enough," Tabatha said walking to him. Shiroan's eyes returned to their clear blue-grey color for an instant as his hand signaled her to stay away.

"I've got this," he said with a deep, rough voice that she felt was coming from far away.

"I trust you, Shiroan," Tabatha said standing in place. "You're the strongest person I've ever met. If there is somebody that can save us all, it's you. I know you can. This is what you were born to do."

Shiroan's muscles, tense as the string of a bow, tensed even more. His body went from convulsing to shaking, then back to convulsing. She could hear his bones cracking. Nobody knew Shiroan as she did and, for better or worse, she knew that he would succeed or die trying.

A dark red halo surrounded his body. The ethereal shapes of demonphantoms showed through his skin just to be pulled inside before they could break free. Blisters appeared all over him. His body was swelling up. A crackling sound came from somewhere within him.

Tabatha was about to look away when she saw the subtle blue glow. It started as a faint spark in his chest, growing in intensity and brightness until all she could see was that light. It inundated the Hidden Chamber, passed through her body, and exploded so brightly that she couldn't keep her eyes open. It warmed her skin without burning it, embraced her without touching her, comforted her without uttering words.

When she opened her eyes, Shiroan was sitting on the pedestal, legs crossed, and eyes shut. The Passage to Hell was closed.

"You did it, my love," Tabatha murmured. "Now let's go home."

He was breathing, although at such a slow rate, that it was almost imperceptible. His body was straight, and his elbows touched his knees. Tabatha caressed his cheeks before shaking his shoulders with care.

"Shiroan! Shiroan, wake up, you did it! you destroyed the Passage to Hell!" The Cloudhunter didn't move. She tried to uncross his legs but couldn't. They weren't stiff, they were tightly locked in place.

"Tabatha! Help!" Kishi called from the outside.

Turning her head, she saw through what was left of the Hidden Chamber's entrance countless demons attacking Kishi, Gregoria and Rexora.

They won't last long, but I can't leave Shiroan here, Tabatha thought.

"Come back to me!" She shouted, hitting Shiroan in the chest. A sudden explosion sent her flying to the other side of the room.

She ran back to him, took out his armor and opened his shirt. There, in the middle of his chest, the Passage to Hell.

"You didn't destroy it! You are just keeping it inside you. You are keeping it closed," Tabatha said as her heart sank in despair.

Shiroan didn't react.

Tabatha looked outside again. The attack was only increasing in intensity. She scanned the room looking for her black crystal. It was lodged in a small crevice at the other end of the room.

As she went to pick it up, the walls started to shine green. The symbols in the pedestal and the wall filled with the Magia that Lethos had passed onto Frothos. Tabatha lost her balance as the Hidden Chamber, resting sideways against the edge of the Seal, straightened, and floated to the center, where it belonged.

"Tabatha!" Rexora shouted.

Tabatha! She heard Frothos calling her inside her head. *Help!*

The world was ending.

"I can't stay with you, but you know that. You acted like the hero you are, now it's my turn."

The Hidden Chamber had stopped shaking. It was now completely stable.

"I love you. I'll always will. Wherever I am. Whenever I live. Wait for me, my love," Tabatha said as she left the Hidden Chamber.

The sphere floated serenely in the center of the empty space, shining with such intensity that she had to squint her eyes. The Magia filled the space where the gate had been and started to rebuild it, stone by stone. "No! Don't close it!" Tabatha yelled as she rushed back to the sphere.

She tried to pull the gate open with all the strength she could muster. All her might wasn't enough. She was trapped outside.

Tabatha! Frothos' scream exploded inside her head, shocking every fiber of her being, and bringing her back. At the same time, the green light enveloping the Hidden Chamber dimmed and flicked as it started to descend to the sea of magma below.

"I'm coming, Frothos," Tabatha said as she flew as fast as she could manage to the cave where she had left him. He was enveloped in a cocoon of green light, completely covered with demons. His chest was bleeding, there where claws and fangs had been able to pierce through the green armor of Magia.

Holding the Black Crystal with both hands, she sliced through the demons in the ledge, carving her way to Frothos.

"Frothos, are you well?" Tabatha asked.

"I'll survive," Frothos answered covering his wound with his good wing.

"The Hidden Chamber is falling to the sea of lava!" Gregoria yelled storming in the cave.

"Can you stop it? Can you lift it back?" Tabatha asked. "Better yet, can you open it? Shiroan is trapped inside."

"I can bring it back, but I can't open it," Frothos said. "It matters not. Shiroan is not with us anymore."

"What do you mean? Is he dead?"

"His essence is gone," Frothos replied. "I'm sorry."

"No!" Tabatha yelled. "You can't know that! Bring him back. Open it!"

"He can't do it," Kishi said climbing to the ledge and hugging Tabatha. "He can't open the Hidden Chamber without unleashing Hell upon us. You just witnessed that."

"I don't care. I need to be with him. I love him. This —"

Tabatha was interrupted by a loud rumble followed by a seism that increased in intensity.

"It's an earthquake!" Gregoria yelled. "We got to go."

"It's worse than an earthquake, I'm afraid. It's an eruption," said Rexora.

"What? That's impossible. Skyroar has been dormant for hundreds of seasons," Gregoria said.

"It's the Magia. My power is still far from that of Lethos. The energy unleashed when Lethos died made the volcano angry. I used the little power I had to save the Hidden Chamber, but I couldn't save the Seventh Seal. We must leave."

"Where is Parktikos?" Kishi said looking around. Outside, huge boulders were falling from the sky. The roof of the crater was shattering. The ground behind Tabatha's feet vibrated with such force that the basalt cracked like an eggshell.

"He redeemed himself. He gave his life so Lethos could do what needed to be done to preserve the Hidden Chamber," Rexora said.

"If we make it out. We won't talk about his treason. Ever. To anybody. He was a Seven Warrior, a hero amongst heroes," Kishi said.

"Agreed," said Rexora.

"I don't like it, but I'll comply," Gregoria said.

"What will happen to the Hidden Chamber?" Tabatha asked.

"It is safe. The Magia will protect it. It'll survive."

"As long as you don't die," Gregoria added.

"I'll come back for you, Shiroan," Tabatha said.

The round path of the Seventh Seal was crumbling down like dry wormbread. Tabatha saw the group zigzagging, dodging rubble and crevices and trying to keep their balance. No demons were around. They were either dead or gone.

"Run to the outer cavern!" Kishi's yell was so potent that Tabatha heard it above the noise of the mountain's roar. "It's the only way out!"

The moment he finished his words, a boulder the size of a Village hut blocked the entrance as a second rock destroyed the bridge uniting it with the Seal. No Seven Warrior was allowed to ever leave according to Skyroar sacred books, and the volcano seemed determined to ensure that the scriptures were respected.

"Is there any other way out?" Tabatha asked landing by the small group.

"I don't think so. We're trapped. Tabatha, how many can you carry?" Kishi asked.

"One, with Frothos' help, two," Tabatha said.

"Frothos is in no shape for flying, even if he had both wings. He's bleeding badly. The effort required to transport us will prove fatal, I assure you. He's the only one of us that must make it out of here. Once he's safe, you can come back for us," Gregoria said.

"You know there won't be time for that. The lava will consume you much before I can make it back. I won't leave you to die. I won't leave Shiroan."

"You don't have a choice, kid," Kishi said. "Living to see another cycle is sometimes the greatest sacrifice of all. The easy way out is to stay here and meet our fate. Anybody can do that. It takes a hero to live with the decision you're about to make. Now go save us all."

Tabatha didn't move. She looked at the Hidden Chamber. She looked at Frothos, the last hope of Skyroar, dying. She looked at the heroes in front of her, wounded, beaten up, but not defeated. Never defeated.

The world was falling apart around the Seven Warriors. They didn't care. They were still trying to help those that had done nothing for them, other than condemning them to a life inside Hell. They were the real heroes, not her. She was there because Lethos had made a mistake. It didn't matter. She would make them proud. She would do what needed to be done so everyone else could live. That's what Shiroan would have done.

"I'll carry you to safety, my friend, you've done well, more than well, but you can't afford to fly. Put your arms around me," Tabatha said approaching Frothos.

Kishi nodded at her as a sign of respect. Tabatha nodded back.

Frothos closed his arms around her neck and let out a scream of pain. The lacerations on his chest were worse than she had thought. Kishi ripped the shirt from below his chainmail and used it to clean and cover his wounds.

"Let Hishiro give you the might," Kishi told Tabatha.

"It's a little late for that, isn't it? The Prophecy didn't seem to care for us as much as we cared for it," Tabatha said in a harsh tone before taking off with Frothos. It was unfair to spill her anger on Kishi, but fairness didn't seem to matter in the Known Territories anymore.

Boulders of all sizes approached her from every direction. Through subtle movements of her leathery wings, Tabatha was able to dodge the largest ones. With the little will she had left; she resisted the urge to go back and check on the Hidden Chamber.

Frothos must survive, he's my mission now, she thought. Her swift maneuvering kept the smaller rocks from hitting Frothos, but her wings were still plagued by pebbles and debris. She could only hope that no stone big or sharp enough to make a sizeable hole in them reached her.

The top of the crater was not too far. The shy rays of the twin suns pierced the cloud of dust and cinder like spears of light, marking the spot. She just hoped that the ongoing eruption had carved an opening wide enough for them to go through.

"Almost there, Frothos, be strong," she said. Frothos didn't answer, he was mumbling Vespertian words. *That's good, my friend, keep the Magia flowing, keep Shiroan protected, I'll get you out of here,* she thought.

The edge of the crater was within her reach when the boulder hit her left shoulder, blinding her with pain. She was pushed back as if she was nothing but an annoying gnat. Frothos slipped from one of her hands and pulled her further down. In a quick maneuver, she closed her wings so she could catch up with Frothos and get a good hold of him. Ignoring the sting from her palpitating wound, she recovered the lost ground. The size and frequency of the falling rocks increased with every passing moment.

We need to leave before the layer of rocks covering the crater collapses on us, Tabatha thought, as she collected scratches on her face, arms, and body. Taking a deep breath, she let the rage that consumed her essence be her fuel and, batting her wings with strength she didn't have, pushed forward.

The warm rays of the twin suns and a pristine blue sky bathed her face as she erupted from the volcano and flew through the incipient cover of dust. The serene scene brought her peace. For the slightest of moments, she believed that she was awakening from a horrible dream. A quick look down was enough to bring her back. Frothos was bleeding to death, and she didn't really know how to help him. The cinder elevated to the skies like a dark mantle. Below it, the deafening rumbling of Skyroar announced the arrival of a thousand hells to the Known Territories.

Tabatha searched for Arboris, still a long way from her. Bringing Frothos to the forest and coming back would take too much of the little precious time she had, leaving him anywhere else was too dangerous. Her potent gaze scoured the area seeking a sign of hope, which she found in the unmistakable shape of Torok. He was walking down the mountain, followed by Mardack and a few others. A big smile crossed her face. Not only because they were alive, but also because she may still have time to save what was left of the Seven Warriors.

The smile was replaced with concern as a large, incandescent, basalt rock zoomed by her side.

"Are the rocks raining upwards now? You've got to be jesting me," she said looking down. A dense plume of smoke was coming out of the crater, engulfing everything on its path. Boulders of all sizes were expelled at full velocity from the inside of the dark cloud. Tabatha had never witnessed a volcano erupting; she didn't have to in order to predict that the magma couldn't be too far behind.

She plummeted towards the small group of Sixth Seal warriors, hoping that Frothos would resist the sudden acceleration.

"Torok!" She shouted as she landed. "Sir," she corrected herself.

"Tabatha? Is that you? Praise the Prophecy! I'm cheerful to see you're still amongst the living. Judging by the appearance of your fellow Vespertian, I won't make the same statement about him."

"Sir, I need to ask you to trust me as I beg for a favor. His name is Frothos, he's the key to keeping the Passage to Hell closed. You must keep him safe and alive, sir."

"Frothos? Is this the Frothos that works as a dungeon keeper? How is he the key to the Passage to Hell? Is it related to the green glow surrounding him?"

"He is. I can't stay to explain. Take him with you and go to Arboris. You'll find friends there," Tabatha said helping Frothos to pass his arm around Torok's waist.

"You've earned my trust and my respect, Tabatha. I will give you the vote of confidence you ask. We'll do as much as we can to keep Frothos safe."

"Thank you, sir, I'm forever grateful."

"You do as your essence dictates, green eyes, but be careful, you're strong and brave, but you're not made of duranese," Mardack said giving her a big hug. "Now go makes us proud!"

Ashes and dust storming down tainted her head and shoulders as the sky turned from blue to the darkest shade of grey. The smell of sulfur took residence on Tabatha's nostrils and the explosion of a thousand thunders resonating inside the crater pushed everyone into action.

"Soldiers! We need to continue North. We're going to

Arboris!" Torok commanded with his raucous voice. "You two, take diligent care of the Vespertian and keep the pace. Carry him if necessary."

"Thank you, Torok," Tabatha said already on the air. "Our fate is now in your hands."

Chapter Twenty-Six

Her mouth was protected by a piece of cloth ripped off her shirt. Her eyes didn't have that luxury. A river of tears battled the hot ashes attacking them. Each breath she took burned her throat and filled her lungs with asphyxiating smoke. Her wings, covered in cinders, felt heavy and slow, almost as if she was flying through water.

The volcano vomited rocks of all sizes into the dark sky. Pebbles came from every direction, brushing against her wings, scratching her skin, and bruising her body. Skyroar's wrath was beyond powerful, it was unstoppable. The Prophecy, Tabatha thought, had finally befallen.

As she went deeper inside the ocean of smoke, her field of vision narrowed down to the point that she could only see what was right in front of her. That's how she missed the moose-sized boulder coming at her from the left.

Once Tabatha saw it, it was too late. She could only curl into a ball and close her wings around her body. The boulder burned her as it passed her by. She entered the crater at full speed. Her wings were still folded around her. As she uncurled herself and opened her eyes, she thought she had gone blind. The darkness was near absolute inside the volcano. Blurry shapes surrounded by a ghostly orange glow was all the evidence she had that she could still see. The ashes of pulverized rock felt hotter as she descended. Her skin was as dry as a piece of old wormbread, and her lungs hurt as if stung by an army of wasps. There was no pause between the explosions now, just a continuous rumble amplified by the acoustics of the mountain.

Tabatha wouldn't be able to resist for long. Her senses were overwhelmed by the chaos surrounding her. Her perception of the world was distorted. Gasping for the little breathable air available, feeling lightheaded and dizzy, she couldn't differentiate left from right or up from down. Fainting and falling to the sea of magma was just a matter of time.

This is useless! I'm lost! Tabatha thought just before noticing a brush of green on the orange canvas below. *The Hidden Chamber!*

The light was dim but enough to serve as a beacon. She locked her eyes on the small ray of hope shining through the smoke and invested all her remaining energy to get to it. The Seven Warriors couldn't be far.

"Kishi!" she yelled with a raspy voice. "Rexora!"

The landscape had changed beyond recognition. She couldn't find any familiar milestones. The sea of magma had risen, covering every plateau, every ledge, every hope.

There is no way the Seven Warriors survived this. I wish I could get to the Hidden Chamber, but the lava is approaching too fast. If I'm dead won't be able to help anyone. I must go, Tabatha thought.

Tabatha felt the heat cooking her alive. The phantasmagoric orange glow transformed into a light brighter than the twin suns. And considerable hotter.

Tabatha turned around in mid-air. With the assistance of the pressure released by the volcano, she quickly gained altitude. The magma was still getting closer. Her shoulders and back hurt, her wings cut through volcanic shards, each flap filled her with pain. The proximity of the lava filled her palms with blisters. An explosion so loud that left her ears ringing echoed in the crater. The mountain was dying, and she was dying with it.

There was nothing she could do to dodge the large boulder that hit her from behind. Once the initial shock passed, she realized that being pushed by the rock was actually faster than flying, so she folded her wings and rode with it. It was almost too hot to withstand, but the magma about to swallow her was a whole lot hotter. She breathed with relief as the boulder rushed her out of the crater, away from the lava. *I'm sorry, my friends,* she thought as the rock lost momentum and fell.

Tabatha opened her wings as her improvised transport crashed against the side of the mountain. A second boulder hit her in the shoulder, breaking her clavicle and pushing her to the crater. An audible crack when she landed preceded intense pain on her left foot. Her ankle was broken.

"Hell!" she exclaimed as she strived to take off. Her broken clavicle had rendered her right wing useless. Unable to put any weight on her injured foot, Tabatha used her sword as a cane and took two steps before rolling down the moraine.

A sizzling sound made her look up. It was the magma coming down the mountain, devouring everything on its path, including her if she didn't move fast. Opening her wings once more, she tried to fly. The pain was indescribable, almost unbearable, but she took off. It was hard to compensate for the weaker wing, but she stayed in the air, on an erratic path, just a few palms above the ground, but in the air.

Tabatha landed on one of the Battlements of the Fortress. She couldn't advance any further. The crippling agony was so severe she threw up on the floor. She hoped the magma wouldn't reach her there, but there wasn't any way to be sure. It didn't matter, she was too exhausted to move.

Lying down at the top of what once had been the proud seat of Skyroar's power, her strength drained by the futile effort of trying to rescue her friends, Tabatha cried dried tears of frustration and shouted so loud that she lost her voice. She had done precisely one good thing: deliver Frothos to Torok. Only one. She couldn't save the Seven Warriors. She couldn't save Shiroan. She couldn't save herself.

For as long as she could remember, Tabatha had been taught that Skyroar was the protector of the Known Territories. Her essence was filled with rage and fear, with stories of war, death, and devastation. Her mind was burdened with a responsibility she didn't quite understand but never doubted. This cycle, she had failed her sacred duty. The Hidden Chamber had been violated. Skyroar had fallen. The Seven Warriors were dead. Frothos and Torok, even Goldenmane and the refugees, couldn't have had enough time to get to Arboris and, even if they did, the lava would consume the forest and everything inside it. If this was Mortagong's plan all along, Tabatha had to recognize his intelligence and keen vision. He had wiped out from the Known Territories the whole citadel while unleashing Hell on the rest of his enemies. Impressive.

A blinding wave of pain went through her body when she sat down. The lava was almost at the Fortress, judging by its mass, and the state of the structure, she would soon be one more casualty of a war that never seemed more pointless. She was ready. Her only regret was dying away from Shiroan. If, like so many in the Known Territories believed, the essence survived beyond death, perhaps they'd meet again, in a different place, under different circumstances.

As the magma consumed the marble and the smell of sulfur filled her nostrils, Tabatha considered jumping to a swift end, but she just lacked the energy to move. Closing her eyes, she found inside the peace that the outside world denied her.

"Ponthos, Shiroan, wait for me, I'm coming," she murmured as she fell asleep with the wide smile and light blue eyes of Shiroan carved in her essence.

Chapter Twenty-Seven

He carried three children on his back. Six little hands wrapped tightly around his neck and shoulders. Battleax held high, ready to react at the first sign of trouble. Goldenmane was the unlikely guardian of the Skyroar refugees. He had lost his eyepatch periods ago in the Fortress, somewhere in the crater. It didn't matter anymore. At first, the deep scars running through the place where his eye once was frightened the kids, but their natural curiosity prevailed, and his face ended up being a source of discovery and entertainment. He couldn't say the same of the adults, who looked at him with fear and mistrust. That wasn't because of the lost eyepatch. They had looked at him with disdain since the first day he stepped in Skyroar. Even after leading them away from certain death. Even after fighting their fight. He was still treated with contempt. His past was the only cargo he had brought from the citadel. Ironically, it was also the only one he wanted to leave behind.

"They're hungry and thirsty, confused and lost, and, more than anything else, they're afraid. Don't take it personally. For what is worth, I trust you at the same level I trusted your sister. The courage you've shown in the past cycle doesn't come as a surprise, not to me."

Goldenmane had recognized Larin since he first saw her. Short white hair, skin a tad lighter than most Elgarians, the athletic frame of someone much younger. Her appearance was unmistakable even without noticing her wooden leg.

"You walk fast for an old lady that's missing a leg," Goldenmane said changing the subject. He had received so few compliments in his life that he didn't know how to react to them.

"Perhaps it's not a matter of me being fast but of you being slow, my friend," she said with a wink. "What's your plan when we get to Arboris?"

"I'm still thinking about it. I could use your help. You're remembered as one of the cleverest generals of Skyroar. All I know is that Arboris can only be seen as temporary shelter, nothing more," Goldenmane said.

"I fully agree, and because of it, we need to come up with a plan, quickly. The demonic hordes may not be able to possess most of us, now that we have changed our Hellblood vials, but still can kill us. The Hundred Kingdoms won't take too long to track us down and, without weapons and only a handful of warriors amongst us, we'll be at the mercy of their swords," Larin said.

"You're right, of course. It's clear that you've thought about this with a lot more detail than I have. You remind me of my sister, she was the one with the brains."

"I'm sorry about Galanta, Goldenmane. I can only imagine how hard it was for you to lose her," Larin said placing her open hand on his chest as a sign of condolence.

"Thank —" Goldenmane didn't finish the sentence. Even if he did, nobody would have heard him, so loud was the roar of the volcano.

"Look!" Larin said pointing to the top of the crater, a massive plume of smoke and ash was invading the blue sky.

"It's happening. Skyroar is erupting," Goldenmane said.

"May the Prophecy save us all," Larin said.

"The words of an old book won't serve us here, Larin. We depend on ourselves. Yesenia!" He called.

"Yes, sir," Yesenia answered, she was walking with Ox a few steps from him.

"Make your way to the front of the group, as you do, ask people to move quicker. We must get to Arboris. Now," Goldenmane commanded.

"What about those that can't go any faster?" Yesenia asked.

"Find help to carry them. We don't leave anyone behind, got it?" Goldenmane said.

"Yes, sir. Ox, let's go," Yesenia said disappearing amongst rows of refugees.

Goldenmane was at the end of the gathering. He considered going to the forefront but decided against it. There, he wouldn't be able to ensure that everyone stayed safe and close together.

Galanta might be dead, but what they lived together all those seasons ago in the Sandlands was still fresh in his memory. Back then, Galanta, as the first-born female, was the heir to the throne.

She was to become the Empress of the Sandlands and he the Commander of the Lionkin Army. Galanta always behaved as a true empress. Even at Skyroar, as much as it hurt him to admit it, she was an example of generosity and sacrifice that amplified his own selfishness. Goldenmane had decided to let his rage take over his essence. He isolated from a world he blamed for stealing everything from him, without realizing he was only punishing himself. Galanta, on the other hand, rose above the anger and devoted her life to making things better, and to do whatever good she could from the privileged position she earned. She was a true hero. He was just following on her footsteps and, if the darkening sky was any indication, he was about to fail Skyroar the same way he failed the Sandlands all those seasons ago.

"Faster!" Goldenmane shouted. "Move faster!"

"Hold on! let us catch up first, Goldie," said a voice. Turning his head, he saw an Elgarian woman with messy, long grey hair, a dirty pigskin overall, and carrying a strange concoction on her back. Behind her, Frothos was on the shoulders of a very tall Elgarian man with a bushy red moustache.

"Frothos!" he exclaimed, with excitement that quickly turned to concern. "Are you well? Where is Tabatha?" Frothos' skin, usually olive, was pale as an Icedorfer, his hands, covered with blood, were placed on his abdomen.

Frothos didn't answer, he was murmuring words he couldn't understand, his eyes were looking past him.

"He's been like this since Tabatha dropped him with us. I'm Torok, Commander of the Sixth Seal. I take it this is all that's left of Skyroar?"

"Give or take, yes. You said that Tabatha dropped him with you and left? Did she say where?" Goldenmane said.

"No, she didn't, judging by what's happening inside the mountain, I'd say she's acting as the warrior she is," Torok said.

"And what happened to you, my friend?" Goldenmane said inspecting Frothos' wounds. "It doesn't look good. We're heading to Arboris, the Hundred Kingdoms army and the demonic hordes are after us, are you able to carry him that far?"

"If you can haul all those children, my good sir, don't doubt for a moment that I can transport one Vespertian for as far as it's needed," Torok said.

"Good, let's go then, we are being left behind," Goldenmane said.

"Are you still ignoring me, Torok. After all these seasons, I'd have expected that the past was truly behind us," Larin said catching up with Torok.

"Larin! I'm very pleased to see you well. Of course, I'll speak to you. I will always speak to you, even after what unfolded amongst us. I care for you," Torok said.

"Quit the drama, Torok, it's been such a long time. And I also care for you," Larin said passing her arm around his waist.

Goldenmane was about to interrupt the reencounter with a grouchy comment when he heard the scream a few steps ahead of him. Letting the kids in the ground, he rushed forward to find a Solis compressed under a boulder.

"It fell from the sky! Rocks are raining from the sky!" an Elgarian man yelled.

"We need to keep moving," he said looking up.

Rocks of all sizes flew through the immense cloud of smoke covering most of the sky. "There's nothing we can do for her now. We're risking our lives by staying here."

Goldenmane sniffed the air. The smell of sulfur was so potent he felt he had returned to the dungeons. He observed the crown of the crater and fixed his eye on an orange bright dot that quickly enlarged, engulfing the top of the mountain before spilling out to the sides.

"Kids, hop on!" Goldenmane asked the children. "Arboris is close, let's go." *I just hope that we won't be running to our deaths,* he thought.

As they ran down the moraine Goldenmane was trying to figure out a plan, Arboris was inside a secondary chimney, even if the whole forest didn't explode with an internal eruption, the lava could easily climb up the crater and kill them all. And he hadn't yet figured out how they'll enter once they got there. *Oh, sister, how do I miss you,* he thought looking back at the sea of magma rushing their way.

Off the corner of his eye, he caught a glimpse of a different boulder coming out of the ashes. Light grey and with what looked like wings moving at each side. *A drakovore!* He thought.

"Kaina!" Mardack exclaimed.

"Shiroan?" Torok said, turning his head.

As Kaina got closer they saw she was carrying three people on her saddle and one between her jaws.

"Give her some space!" Goldenmane said as Kaina landed.

"We've lost the Hidden Chamber. Where is Frothos?" Gregoria said jumping off the saddle.

"He's here," Torok answered.

"Is he alive? Is he chanting?"

"Yes, barely."

"Then we've got a fighting chance," she said approaching Frothos.

"We're what's left of the Seven Warriors. I'm Kishi, this is Rexora and down there with Frothos is Gregoria," Kishi said as he dismounted. Little clouds of ashes formed around Kaina as he rubbed off Kaina's fur.

"Tabatha!" Goldenmane and Torok said in unison as Kaina, with outmost care, opened her jaw and let the Vespertian in the ground.

"She's not a Seven Warrior, but sure battled like one. We retrieved her from a battlement at the Fortress. She's the one that saved Frothos and, in doing so, she saved us all. We'd all be dead if not for this dirty hairball," Kishi said patting Kaina on the neck.

"Where's Shiroan?" asked Torok.

"Inside the Hidden Chamber. We believe that as long as Frothos keeps chanting, Shiroan will continue to be alive. The Gateway to Hell is closed thanks to him," Rexora said.

"I'm not surprised, although you might have to explain to me how," said Torok.

"No time. We must keep going. Help me get Tabatha on the saddle, I'll fly with her and Kaina ahead and look for any sign of trouble," Gregoria said.

"Agreed. The lava won't stop for us," Goldenmane said.

Once they reached the edge of the Arboris crater the lava was halfway down the mountain. It wouldn't be long before it caught up to them. The faster among them were already climbing the rock wall to the forest, Kaina was flying in circles, probably looking for the best way to enter.

"You haven't asked, Goldenmane, but I'll tell you anyway that there's a path to the forest. It was used to pull wood out. It's a tunnel on the east side, unless you have a better plan, I suggest we look for it," Larin said.

"You should have told me this earlier! People are already up the crater. We wasted precious time!" Goldenmane roared, letting out the frustration of seeing Frothos in agony and the impotence of being unable to save him or, for that matter, anyone else. For the second time in his life, he would be responsible of the downfall of the survivors of a dying city.

The eyes that looked back at him were perhaps the most powerful he had ever seen. He felt Larin's gaze pierce through his skin and wrap around his essence like a Sandlands serpent. Her voice, however, was full of genuine understanding when she said: "I know how hard it's for you, my friend, but you're not alone. I thought you had a plan and didn't want to interfere. If you want our assistance, we're here. I'm old and Torok is older," she said with a wink while looking at the red-haired Elgarian. "We have the experience and knowledge to sort this out."

"Thank you, Larin, I apologize. Yes, please, I need your help," Goldenmane said. He had forgotten the last time he had apologized… or asked for support.

"Torok, you know where the tunnel is, don't you? Go to the front and direct everyone there. Goldenmane, we must find something to seal the entrance. Once we are inside, it'll keep the lava and our enemies out. Can you manage that? Mardack, search for Gregoria, when you see her, ask her to locate the position of the Hundred Kingdoms army and the demon hordes. Then report them back to me. For all we know, they could be preparing an ambush," Larin said with a firm voice, somehow looking taller than she did just a few instants ago.

"Talked like a true general, Larin, I missed that," Torok said.

"Retired. Retired general," Larin said. "Now go, every moment counts."

"At your service," Torok said running towards the front.

Goldenmane followed him feeling that a heavy burden was lifted off his shoulders. After all, they may have a chance to survive.

"What's happening?"

"Are we going to die?"

"Help us, Goldenmane!"

Questions and supplications filled Goldenmane's ears as he ran through the crowd. He ignored them all and continued his path. He found Ox at the feet of the Arboris crater.

"Where's Yesenia?" he asked.

"She's up there, looking for a way to the forest," Ox said pointing to the top of the crater.

"I was wrong, that's not the way in. Everyone should come back. The entrance to Arboris is through a tunnel on the east side. Torok is leading the way," Goldenmane said.

"I'll go and let her know," Ox said.

"No, I need you here. We have another mission. Send someone else, then follow me," Goldenmane asked.

Torok was already at the forefront of the group. Goldenmane walked with the crowd while observing the terrain, looking for anything that could be used to seal the tunnel, but every rock he saw was either too big, or too small, or too far.

"I'm here sir, what are your orders?" Ox said.

"We got to come up with a way to close the cave once everyone goes through," Goldenmane said turning his head at the volcano. The lava had engulfed the Fortress, and it was spilling down its walls. The smell of sulfur combined with that of burning wood, pigskin, sheepskin, and dead bodies. "And it's got to be now."

Yesenia was shepherding down the mountain the few people that had climbed it. Half the Villagers were already lost inside the passage to Arboris. Everybody had done their part. He wouldn't be, couldn't be, the one responsible of the destruction of what was left of Skyroar.

"I don't see anything, sir, if only we could rip a boulder from the crater," Ox said.

"That's it!" said Goldenmane. Look, directly above the cave, there is a narrow ledge that we may be able to separate from the mountain with the right pressure. Take your battleax and come with me!"

"Where are you going?" Larin asked. "The lava is almost here."

"I know. Keep going, I'll go last," Goldenmane said going up the crater.

Ox and Goldenmane stood on both sides of the ledge as the people found their way to the tunnel. The streams of lava, after being slowed down by the Fortress' walls, had regained momentum.

"Hit it in the fissure, as hard as you can, as many times as possible. Be careful not to lose your balance," Goldenmane said as he unleashed his fury against the large piece of rock.

Ox was a strong Elgarian man, one of the strongest Goldenmane had seen, but still wasn't a match for his might. Sparks and pebbles flew in all directions with each blow. Some larger pieces made Goldenmane hesitate for a moment. He couldn't afford for the boulder to break in two. He needed it in one piece.

"Goldenmane! You must go. The lava is almost here!" Tabatha shouted from Kaina's saddle. Goldenmane smiled, happy to see her awake. But he didn't budge.

"Ox, go to Arboris, I'll catch up with you," he said.

"I'm not leaving you here, sir," Ox said.

"It's not a request, it's an order," Goldenmane said.

"I'll go, but I don't want to."

Goldenmane jumped to the side that Ox had been hammering and swung his battleax hard, harder, the hardest. The ledge was loosening up. The upper part had been detached but the crack hadn't opened all the way. The lava was getting closer. Goldenmane hunched between the narrow ledge and the roof that covered it and pushed outwards. Then hit it, and pushed it, and hit it again and again.

The lava had reached Arboris. It wouldn't be long before it entered the tunnel. Goldenmane roared and as he tried to break the mountain. The boulder gave up and slid down. He was falling with it.

The giant piece of rock covered the entrance of the cave as if it had been carved with the sole purpose of shutting it down. Goldenmane was outside. The lava was twenty steps away. He wasn't worried, even before looking up, he raised his arms and, as he knew she would, Kaina flew close enough for him to grab her paws. *Thank you, Tabatha,* he thought.

The lava surrounded the crater and threatened to take over Arboris as well. It didn't. Their plan had worked. As they flew to the forest, Goldenmane looked at the grey, black, and orange layer that had once been the citadel of Skyroar. All that was left of the guardians of the Prophecy was now in Arboris. Beyond its walls, the demonic hordes and the Hundred Kingdoms army were looking for them, and there was no doubt in his mind they would find them.

Perhaps all their efforts had been in vain but now, with the twin suns hiding behind the horizon, having survived the unleashed wrath of the heart of the Skyroar Volcano, he didn't want to believe it. He wanted to believe they would find a way to prevail. He wanted to think that, this time around, surrounded by new friends, he would find the way to save his people. And he would make his sister proud, wherever her essence was.

EPILOGUE

The light from the dawning suns shone through the holes of the rough black fabric that covered the cage where he was trapped. Audax and Ingens were still out when he was placed in the cart pulled by four sea lizards. The army hadn't stopped once. Not even to eat.

He understood most of what the voices outside said but not everything. As a child, Momo spoke Oceaner to him, but he always answered in Elgarian. His time trying to pass as a war prisoner in front of Guntharhi had been the only time, perhaps ever, that he had chained more than a few words in his mother tongue. Judging by the result, he hadn't done the best job at it.

His buttocks hurt from sitting down on the rough, wooden floor of the cart. His ribs were bruised from crashing against the metal bars every time the wheels hit a rock or passed over a hole. He hadn't eaten, or slept since he was captured, but he didn't feel hungry, thirsty, or tired. He felt at peace.

At peace because he had followed his essence, even when it seemed the wrong thing to do, even if his choices led to prison or torture.

At peace because he realized he didn't want to be a warrior after all. He just wanted to be Mehrik.

Locked in a cage, isolated from the rest of the world, taken to a fate as dark as uncertain, he smiled, then he laughed as he hadn't laughed in a long time because, regardless of what the future held, he was exactly that. Just Mehrik. Just himself.

"What are you laughing about, Mehrik?" said a voice from the outside.

"Nothing," Mehrik said.

"Is that right?" said the voice opening the curtain.

"Guntharhi?" Mehrik said with a serious face.

"Oh, but don't stop for me, go ahead, laugh all you can now. I assure that you won't be laughing anymore once we arrive to Oceano," Guntharhi said letting out a sinister cackle that almost threw him off the sea lizard he was riding.

"I once considered you a friend Guntharhi. I may one cycle

consider you a friend again," Mehrik said.

"That's so noble, I'm sure Guntharhi would cry if he could hear you. Me, I'm just keen to be left alone with you. Oh! How will I enjoy myself once you're thrown in the dungeon. You don't know how many headaches you've caused me, Mehrik. As insignificant as you are, since Kishi gave you the bottle of Hellblood for the Conclave, you've been nothing but an annoyance. Now you've become an annoyance I can't tolerate any longer," Guntharhi said leaning forward to look at Mehrik in the eye.

"How do you know about Kishi and the Hellblood?" Mehrik asked.

"Oh, because I was there," Guntharhi said with a smirk and a wink.

"Melgorth," Mehrik murmured. "Melgorth!" He yelled. "Somebody, anybody, listen to me!"

"Yell all you want; nobody is close enough to hear you. And even if they were, nobody is going to believe a traitor. Now sit down and relax, it's a long journey to Oceano and you want to make sure to enjoy every moment of it," Melgorth said using Guntharhi's mouth.

"I'll unmask you the moment we get to Oceano," Mehrik said.

"You can try. Worst case scenario, they'll Guntharhi and I'll just possess somebody else, and then somebody else. But don't worry, I haven't forgotten you, I'll get to you. First, I'll break you, then I'll eat your essence, then I'll kill you from the inside," Melgorth said.

"I'll be waiting for you," Mehrik said.

"You won't have to wait long," Melgorth hissed pushing Guntharhi's face against the metal bars.

"I know, and I'll be ready for you," Mehrik said.

"I'm sure you will. in the meantime, be quiet, I need to think," Melgorth said hitting Mehrik's head with the hilt of his sword so hard that he felt as though his skull had cracked.

Then everything went black.

THE SKYROAR TRILOGY
BY BALTHAZAR DUSK

Book I: Hellblood
Book II: The Hidden Chamber
Book III: The Passage to Hell

<u>Published by</u>: Frogasus Press, LLC.

Please subscribe to the Frogasus Press email at: **http://www.frogasus.com** to receive updates about our future releases.

Thank you for being a reader. Thank you for choosing this book among many.

FROGASUS PRESS

Made in the USA
Coppell, TX
23 March 2024